Simon L

Song In The Wrong Key

First published in Great Britain in 2012 by Lane & Hart Ltd

Copyright © Simon Lipson 2012

The right of Simon Lipson to be identified as the Author of the
Work has been asserted in accordance with the Copyright, Designs and
Patents Act 1988

All rights reserved. No part of this publication may be reproduced, stored in
a retrieval system or transmitted, in any form or by any means without the
prior written permission of the publisher, nor be otherwise circulated in any
form of binding or cover other than that in which it is published and
without a similar condition being imposed on the subsequent purchaser.

All characters in this publication are fictitious and any resemblance to real
persons, living or dead, is purely coincidental.

A CIP catalogue record for this title is available from the British Library.

Trade Paperback
ISBN 978-0-9570987-0-1

Typeset in Garamond MT by Hope Services Ltd
Printed and bound by Lightning Source Ltd
Lane & Hart Ltd, 128 Cheapside, London EC2V 6BT

Simon Lipson is a former solicitor and businessman who now works as a stand-up comedian, impressionist, writer and voiceover artiste. He has appeared on numerous TV and radio shows including *Loose Ends* and *Weekending* on BBC Radio 4, *Interesting...Very Interesting* on Radio 5, *The Stand Up Show* on BBC1 and, God help him, *Celebrity Squares* on ITV (that was a long time ago when he didn't know any better). He also co-wrote and performed his own series, *Fordham & Lipson*, on Radio 4. Simon lives in London with his wife and two teenage daughters.

Praise for *Song In The Wrong Key*

'Simon Lipson is a brilliant writer. He has an easy, readable style, and can make you laugh out loud or battle back the tears. The characters are rounded, the dialogue's natural, the ending...well, I won't give too much away...I thoroughly recommend it and will be buying everything else this author writes.'

Steph Daggs, Author

'It is as good as *One Day*; not as poignant, but more amusing. Consistently laugh-out-loud funny, occasionally sad, always plausible. Rounded, believable characters, brilliant dialogue and a thoroughly satisfying ending. The pleasure bargain of the year.'

H & H, Amazon Kindle Reader

'This would make one of those classic and humorous movies about modern life in England in the genre of say, Four Weddings & A Funeral. Loved this book. It's very funny throughout but that doesn't stop you from investing in the characters and their lives. It gives you everything in its truthful and self-deprecating portrayal of parenthood, friendship, relationships, marriage breakdown and career dilemmas. It also offers brilliant and hilarious insights into sudden fame – very relevant in this X Factor age – and the tackiness of Eurovision. Highly recommended.'

Weekender, Amazon Kindle Reader

'It has so many sharp, splutteringly funny lines, but never at the expense of character and story. Poignant, warm and true.'

Ivor Baddiel, Author

CHAPTER 1

I'M A LITTLE bit suspicious of people who smile on the Tube; specifically, commuters who smile *to themselves*. I have no problem with foreigners in fluorescent cagoules, laden with maps and sheaves of leaflets espousing the many joys of anybody's-guess waxworks and open-top bus rides in the rain. They're abroad and don't know any better. Smile away. And gabbling, reeking lunatics holding onto empty liquor bottles for dear life are often very cheerful and capable of creating their own blissful space in otherwise sardine-packed carriages, like penicillin in a Petri dish. They can smile all they want to, though preferably nowhere near me. But that bloke in a suit who, without any obvious visual or aural stimulation, is just bloody smiling – well, he bothers me. What I want to know is – what's so funny, Smiley? What entitles you to be light of mood when all about you, whey-faced drones with their shark-dead eyes are drowning in quotidian gloom? Worse, The Smiler, snubbing his nose at propriety, is invariably keen to broadcast his anarchic streak. So he'll catch your eye to rub it in. He wants you to know there's a party in his head and you're not invited. And that's when I get to thinking – and I'm sure he knows this – have I done something to amuse him, something I ought to be embarrassed about? Has he spotted a matted glob of blood on my collar, unwitting evidence of a careless shave? Or do I have a hole in my crotch revealing my 'Oh crap, it's Monday' pants (they were a birthday present, by the way, which I wear on Tuesdays pursuant to my own anarchic streak, thank you). And anyway, why's that funny? A bloody collar, an unstitched seam, a witty pant? Ok, maybe I'm being a bit over-sensitive, maybe it's not me at all or, indeed, anyone else in the carriage. Maybe something funny's just occurred to him.

I don't care. I don't like it.

That's the thing about the London Underground. People forget who they are; that they got on the train with distinct and, in many

1

cases, complex personalities. Yet once ensconced within the sterile anonymity of the seething warren, arcane rules of non-engagement kick in. The haughty, physical defence of personal space; the flickering, fascinated eyes watching stations hove into and out of view, stations they've flickered at a thousand times before; the intense 'I'm reading, don't disturb me' po-face. Woe betide anyone making eye contact. That's why The Smiler stands out. He's not to be trusted.

But, you see, that morning, it was me who broke ranks. I'm normally a pack-dog, an automaton, a leave-me-alone merchant, someone whose mind is ostentatiously elsewhere. But I was smiling – yes, *to myself* – a smile interlaced with the odd gentle convulsion. Maybe, hopefully, it was me pissing everyone else off for a change as I ran a mental video of the night before. Me, in the kitchen, clattering about, hopeless-dad-fashion, trying to conjure a meal for Millie and Katia under cover of the laboured comedy routine of which they'd long since tired. Undeterred by their indifference, I ploughed on. Where was the pasta? What the hell's *spelt* when it's at home? Which one's the special pasta saucepan? How long do you boil it for – or do you fry it? Do you need to add meat to Ragu or merely slop it on cold from the jar? In truth, I didn't know the answer to too many of these questions. Millie wore the weary look she'd inherited, gene-for-gene, from her mother, eyelids fluttering, barely tolerating my ineptitude and ham-fisted witlessness, while Katia smiled wryly as she chewed on a waxy rod of cheese of indeterminate colour whilst skim-reading a Jacqueline Wilson book I'd have found too racy and sophisticated at eighteen, much less eight.

Sunday evening meals were invariably my domain and I took the responsibility extremely semi-seriously despite my absence of domestic skills. Lisa always seemed to be on top of it when she was in charge, not militarily, but with that languid efficiency that mums do so well. But she'd gone out to her book club meeting to discuss some impenetrable Nabokov treatise – which she'd actually packed in after thirteen pages (as it turned out, she'd got further than most) – so I couldn't refer to her higher authority. Soldiering on, I finally got the water to boil, chucked in the penne with a flourish – a steaming splash burnt my hand (important lesson there) – and stuck the Ragu jar in the microwave. Yes I took the lid off, come on. As I collected the requisite plates, cutlery and glasses, I began to sing '*Home*,' the all-time Michael Bublé classic. In my book anyway. The kids pointedly ignored me, embarrassed for and by me, so I waltzed closer to them, knives and forks for dancing partners, forcing the poor things to cower at the table. Katia pulled her book around her face in an attempt to insulate herself from the crooning nutter, while Millie stifled a smile as she coloured in a pencil-drawn map of Ireland, Peru or possibly Jupiter in her exercise book. I leaned down, singing first into Katia's, then Millie's ear. They cringed theatrically.

'Come on,' I pleaded, 'you always used to love it when Daddy sang to you.'

'That was when we were young,' said Millie, now seven.

I smiled and picked up the song where I'd left off, upping the volume extravagantly and losing a little tonal accuracy in the process. Millie looked up dolefully, half covering her ears, wincing. 'The thing is, Dad, your singing...' she said. I nodded, awaiting her sweet little put-down, '...it's shit.'

Shit? I blame the mother. I never say 'shit' in front of the kids. Ok, I might occasionally slip it in if it's contextually appropriate, like 'what's this shit you're watching kids?' Otherwise? Never. But, even allowing for Millie's little cuss – in fact largely because of it – I was The Smiler on the train that morning, a contented man breezing along, not a care in the world.

Funny how your life can change in an instant.

I battled my way up the escalators at Holborn station, slipped, Astaire-like, through the snapping jaws of the automatic barrier and skipped up the final set of stairs into the hazy sunlight. The cold morning air was thick with fumes, the traffic jammed and furious, but I didn't care. I was awash in smugness, still congratulating myself on those brilliant kids of mine, my wonderful, tolerant, capable wife, my overall domestic bliss. I observed the poor bastards whose lives couldn't possibly be as rich as mine, trudging to wherever they were doomed to spend yet another pointless day.

I floated east along High Holborn, all but whistling a happy tune, arriving outside my office building within a couple of joyous minutes. I spun through the revolving door, nodded at the security guy – who, as ever, looked down at his desk gravely as though he had several pressing security issues on the go and couldn't possibly allow himself to be distracted – and, eschewing the lift, hopped up the three flights of stairs to my floor. I bundled through the double doors and strode sunnily into the open plan office area where half the staff were cranking up for the day. The other half, like me, were late. I nodded with what I hope could never be interpreted as condescension at the handful of underlings lining the path to my executive office tucked away in the far left hand corner. A couple of yards from my door, I was intercepted by Pete Moore, my immediate superior. Of course, he was only superior in terms of job title, salary and perks – and, ok, he lived with a young Spanish model in a Docklands penthouse, had a first class Oxford degree in some social science or other and drove something silver and supercharged – but that's not how you judge a man, is it? Pete and I went way back. In fact, I started at Edmonds & White IT Systems a month before him and was, briefly, his boss. But Pete was all thrusting ambition, a ruthless operator who lived to work – when he wasn't spending his vastly inflated salary on exotic holidays and expensive women. His greatest skills were licking the right arses and looking ferociously busy even when he wasn't, a deadly combination with which I could never compete. Good luck to him. The poor guy had no family to coddle him in their warm, loving embrace after a hard day's work. I wouldn't have swapped anything I had for anything of his. Ok, that's not strictly accurate, but I don't want to split hairs over anything as vacuous as money, status, property or stunning señoritas.

Pete placed his hand gently on my elbow and guided me away from my office and towards his. 'A word?' was his sole, solemn remark.

Pete's cavernous suite was cold, not because of the surfeit of smoked glass, the soulless décor or the absence of family photos, but because of his face, his manner. You always know, don't you?

'Got a problem, mate,' he said, his voice flat, foreboding.

4

'Don't tell me. Those morons at Delta-D complaining about the network again?' I could already feel myself drowning, but didn't yet know which ocean was sucking me down.

'No. They're fine.'

'Yeah,' I scoffed without conviction, 'had to work my butt off to get them onside. Bunch of complete…'

'We're letting you go.'

'…wankers.'

'Mike? We're letting you go.'

'Ok mate. Let's do lunch later, yeah?'

'Mike. I'm not pissing around. This isn't coming from me.'

'Look, I've got stuff piled up on my desk, so…'

'They thought it'd be better if I told you.'

'Ok. Now, I may look cheerful enough, but I'm actually beginning to get a bit worried, Pete. I thought,' I chuckled pitifully, my heart thudding, lungs barely able to replenish the oxygen they were hyperexhaling, '…I thought I heard you say you were letting me go, but obviously…'

'Elliott and Barry hauled me in last thing Friday. They're making you redundant. No other way to say it.'

I let that one sink in as I struggled to breathe. 'They can't do that.'

'They can. They have. I'm really sorry, mate. You think this is easy for me?'

'Oh poor you,' I said with desperate sarcasm, 'you'd better sit down.'

'My hands are tied, Mike.'

'Why me? What about…what about Arnie? He's useless. Or Christine?' I was pleading now, pathetic, emasculated. This was as good a point as any to slump into the über-modern, supremely uncomfortable leather armchair reserved only for the best clients. Pete stifled a wince.

'She's on half what you're on…and, you know…'

'Big tits,' I mumbled in a sad echo of the mock-laddish banter Pete and I occasionally engaged in before his accession to executioner-in-chief. And Christine did, indeed, have a sizeable bust, which didn't

5

excuse it, I know, but we're men and we can't help ourselves sometimes. But right now it wasn't remotely funny, even if everyone tacitly acknowledged that Christine's rise was largely due to the tongues-out enthusiasm generated by her most prominent physical feature.

'She's pulling in the business, Mike; making the boys upstairs happy.'

'Big tits do that,' I said, shaking my head like a defeated schoolboy, 'I'm at a massive disadvantage.'

Pete rolled his eyes as though this sexist nonsense was, belatedly, beneath him. He'd invented it, the bastard. 'What can I say?'

'I've been here longer than Arnie.'

'But Arnie's just nailed that Freestone contract,' said Pete, hammering home another irrefutable nail in my coffin, 'otherwise he'd probably have been the one to go. You know business is bloody tough. Someone had to take the bullet.'

'Someone?' I knew all of this, of course, but you never quite see it coming. 'Didn't you argue on my behalf? Didn't you tell them how unlucky I've been? I mean, if I'd pulled off that deal with Virgin, Elliott and Barry could've fucking retired.'

'But you didn't.'

I pinched my thumb and forefinger to within a centimetre of each other. 'I was this close.' I wasn't even in the neighbouring solar system.

'They think you fucked it up. And right now, it's costing us to keep you on. You're not bringing in the fees. You're not even paying for yourself.'

'Costing us?' I whined. 'Us?'

'Them. I mean them, the company,' Pete said in a hollow display of personal loyalty of which he then thought better. 'Well no, I don't. It is us, isn't it? We all have to make our contribution. I'm part of the family here. We're all in this together.'

'Are we?'

Pete sighed. I wish I could say this was hurting him, but the guy was a consummate actor whose prime concern was covering his own backside.

'And, Mike. How long have we known each other? Of course I pleaded with them on your behalf,' he lied. 'Come on.'

'I was top fee earner…'

'In 1998, Mike.'

The internal phone buzzed and Pete held up an apologetic finger as he rounded his desk to take the call. He spoke sotto voce, but I cupped my ear. 'Yes. Yes,' he whispered, 'won't be long. I'll pop up in a minute. Ha, ha. Coffee'd be great. Any croissants? Mmm. Ok.' He put the phone down, turned to face me and quickly readjusted his features until they settled on the sympathetic mien he'd probably practised in the executive washroom mirror.

'Is that how you pleaded for me? Over a nice plate of flaky pastry?'

'Stop it Mike.'

'But I've got kids and a wife and a mortgage…all that shit. What am I going to do? I'm forty-two.' It was lame, after the event. It wasn't going to help.

'We've put together a really good package. Six months' salary. And you can keep the gym membership until the end of the year. Uh?'

'Great. I'll *jog* to the bankruptcy court. My God, Pete. Six months' money? After all these years?'

'And…you can keep the car.'

He'd obviously kept that up his sleeve in case I had the temerity to whinge. Hardly a clincher. 'Oh, magnificent. Can't afford to fill it up, but maybe I can fold the seats down and move in when the Nationwide forecloses on my fucking mortgage.'

'You'll find something in no time. You're a good man.'

'Look, fuck the package. Why not reduce my basic, load it in favour of commission? It'll motivate me. Maybe that's what I've been missing.'

'My hands are tied Mike.'

My mouth opened but nothing came out. I was all done begging. I gulped in some air and whimpered, 'But I'm forty-two.'

'What about Lisa? She's earning good money, isn't she? You're not going to starve.'

Which was true, of course. My financial protestations were born of shock, indignation, humiliation, not the facts. Lisa comfortably out-earned me; had done for years. Maybe that made me easier to get rid of. But I still needed a reason to get up in the morning. And I was only forty-two. Did I mention that?

'That's it for me. Who wants someone of my age in this game?'

'The references will be great and…'.

'Yeah? Michael Kenton worked for this company for 17 years. He is reliable, capable, trustworthy and diligent. That's why we got rid of him.'

'No-one's going to take that inference. People in the business know it's tough. The competition's horrendous. There are new companies sprouting up as we speak, ready to undercut us.'

'I know,' I muttered, 'I know.'

'Hey, and…tell you what, I'll see if I can have a word with David Lewis at Crack-IT. I heard he was after someone experienced on the technical side.'

'Yeah, right,' I sulked.

'That'd be perfect for you. Maybe sales isn't your thing any more. You were always a techie at heart.'

'Yeah.' I squeaked up off the armchair and gestured at the door. 'I might as well…'

Pete laced a smile with his best approximation of tragic empathy and put his arm around me, but felt immediately uncomfortable and turned it into a stilted pat on the shoulder.

I trudged out and slunk along the corridor, dead man walking, until I reached my office. It already looked deserted. There was no point sitting down, no point settling into my comfortable little kingdom; better to clear it out and clear off. I rifled through my desk drawers, finding all sorts of items I'd forgotten I had – a liveried letter opener, my Top Fee Earner plaque from 1998, a useless, frayed felt tip pen given to me by Millie who insisted I use it at work. I removed the family photos from my desk – the gap-toothed ones of the kids in their prim, ill-fitting school uniforms, the one of my parents when they still had a future, the yellowing shot of me and Lisa looking lean and shiny-faced, toasting the camera in a long-forgotten restaurant in Mykonos. I dithered over the pens, the calculator, the plastic ruler, the stapler, all of which were company property, then decided to take the lot. Screw you, Pete, screw all of you. I win!

I piled my sad little bounty into a couple of the Tesco bags I kept in my bottom drawer. It was pathetic. I was pathetic. Two plastic bags full of useless crap. Was that all the last 17 years had amounted to? I stood by the door, bags hanging limply from one hand, empty briefcase from the other, and looked around the room one last time. I almost bade it farewell, then realised it was only a bloody room, one in which I was no longer welcome.

What was I going to tell Lisa?

CHAPTER 2

Kɪᴅꜱ ʟɪꜰᴛ ʏᴏᴜʀ spirits, don't they? No matter how low your ebb, the sound of your own child's sweet, innocent voice will always drag you up like ballast from the deepest grunge-filled pit.

'Hi Dad. You look really shit,' chirped Millie as I sloped through the front door and into the kitchen.

It was midday. I'd spent an hour or two sitting catatonically in Starbucks in Kingsway before dragging myself down into the crater of Holborn station to begin the slow trudge home. The Tube is a very different animal mid-morning. Half-empty, eerily quiet, infrequent as hell, catering only to tourists and flotsam and jetsam with nothing much else to do. And now me.

'Thanks. And stop saying shit.'

'You do. All the time.'

'I'm forty-two. I'm allowed.'

'I'm seven, I'm…'

'You're not.'

'I hate you Dad,' barked Katia as she entered the kitchen holding an open paint pot at a precarious angle. Like Millie, she seemed blissfully unfazed by my premature return. 'You said you were going to take us skating on Saturday but, like, I just spoke to Mum and she says you were, like, lying? Because you're going to football?'

'What football?'

'You're going to watch that rubbish team you support. Mummy says.'

'Lying? She actually said lying?'

'Lying.'

'That's not a lie, is it? I must have just forgotten.'

Bea pottered into the kitchen. A 'student' studying something that didn't actually require her to attend a formal educational establishment, Bea looked after the kids during holidays and after school. She was twenty-two going on a very prissy eleven. 'Hello Mr Kenton.'

'Bea. Everything all right?'

'Millie's been a bit difficult this morning, haven't you Millie?'

Millie snarled under her breath as she wrestled with a doll. I'm sure the word 'shit' was in there somewhere.

'You're early, Mr Kenton.'

'Bea, come on, call me Mike, please.'

'I can't.'

'Michael, at least.'

'It's not appropriate,' she frumped as she tucked her too-tight blue jumper into her even tighter, violently clashing blue corduroy trousers which were a good four inches too short in the leg. 'Should I go?'

'No. No, of course not. I didn't expect…I finished early. I'm sure you've got a whole programme of exciting things lined up to do with the kids today.'

Bea shrugged her meaty shoulders. 'We got a DVD from Blockbusters. Shrek 2. You can watch it with us if you like.'

Millie screwed her face into tight knot and was only just polite enough not to voice her objection. How could she tease and torture Bea if I was sitting there?

'Er, no, thanks. I need to do some things upstairs so…I'll leave you kids to it.'

Another shrug. 'Ok, Mr Kenton.'

I heaved myself up the stairs as though my pockets were weighted with breeze-blocks and shuffled into the bedroom, closing the door behind me. I ripped off my tie, threw my jacket on the floor and slumped onto the bed face down.

And then I cried into the pillow.

'Pete? How could he, the bastard?' growled Lisa.

'Ach, don't shoot the messenger.'

'All those years. For what?'

'I know. Great start to the New Year.'

'Doesn't get better than this.'

Lisa was prowling around me like a furious cat as I lay prostrate atop the duvet in my faded blue towelling robe and M & S moccasins.

11

I'd hardly moved all afternoon, emerging from the bedroom only briefly for a quick shower which, rather than refresh me, had dampened my spirits still further. If Norman Bates had pitched up in Chiswick for some reason and found his way into the bathroom with his stiletto, I'd have let him get on with it.

'Didn't you tell him we're going to struggle financially?' said Lisa.

'He knows that's not true.'

'So?'

'They're not running a charity, are they? What do they care?'

'Well what the hell are you going to do?'

Lisa was already thinking beyond the emotional impact. Ever the practical one. 'I don't know. I'll have to find something.'

'I mean, seriously, we can't afford to be smug about it. It's all very well saying we're ok, but when you add up the school fees and the mortgage and the council tax and…all the other stuff we have to pay for…'

She was right. My salary tipped us into the warmer climes of *comfortable*; without it, there would have to be sacrifices. Maybe the exquisitely tailored Jaeger suit Lisa was wearing would have to last her a while longer. Just as well there were another twelve in the wardrobe.

'Why you?' she said.

'I don't know. I keep asking myself the same question.' Even though I knew the answer.

Lisa smiled, her features softening at last, along with her tone. 'I kept telling you, though, didn't I? You were always vulnerable. You're not a salesman, Mikey.' Her first response was always that of a street fighter in the face of adversity, but she knew when to don the kid gloves. She draped her jacket neatly over the chair in the corner and sat in it, crossing her slim, shiny legs with a swish. She wasn't quite ready to offer a consoling cuddle.

'Why didn't they fire Arnie? He's useless.'

I shrugged, but he was making the company some money, useless or otherwise. What did that make me? 'I thought I was doing ok. I nearly got Virgin.'

'But…you said they blew you out of the water after the first submission.'

Oh yeah, of course I did. That's not what I told Pete, mind. Sometimes it's difficult to keep track of which fib you've spun to whom. 'Yeah. Ok, they did. But if I'd got in to see Branson…'

I'd have had more chance of running Branson down on my bike in a Wolverhampton cul-de-sac.

'Don't want to be…I mean, I did tell you to go back to hands-on IT maintenance, didn't I?' said Lisa. 'You're a geek.'

'That's a compliment, right?

Lisa arched her perfectly plucked eyebrows with mild amusement. 'So, have you been in touch with any recruitment agencies or looked on the internet…or have you just been lying there feeling sorry for yourself all afternoon?'

'Lying here feeling sorry for myself. Ok? Leese, I've just lost my job after 17 years. My career's in tatters. I have no income. And I'm forty-two, which makes me…unemployable. Probably need a day to absorb that little feast of good news?'

Lisa rose regally from the chair, her lustrous, mid-length black hair swaying like liquid silk around her chiselled face. She floated to the bed and smiled, then deposited a tender kiss on my glowing cheek. 'Tomorrow, then,' she said.

And then we had sex. Now I recognise that any neutral observer would identify this as the most blatant pity-fuck in history. But it wasn't. Honestly. Lisa occasionally came home from work bristling, hackles proud and prickly, raw edges sticking out at awkward angles, and the only way to file them down into soft little bumps was a bout of fierce intercourse. Great marital sex is usually the first thing sacrificed at the altar of children, mortgages, pensions, work…life. Or so I'm told. Well not in our house. Everything else might have been up in the air, my career down the pan, our relationship on the brink of flat-lining, but sex, when it happened, was always electric.

We lay there afterwards, Lisa caressing my chest with her efficient, warm hand while I stroked her damp neck with the back of a finger. It was perfect but transient, the nagging ulcer of our new predicament hanging over us like a pall. Downstairs, shirty little voices were beginning to rise, the familiar genesis of a major row over nothing.

Time to get up and referee. I disentangled myself from Lisa's luxury limbs and swivelled, ready to stand. Lisa placed her hand on my back and whispered, 'I still love you Mike. Don't worry, you'll muddle through.'

Still? It wasn't the most ringing endorsement. I stood up with a grunt and started to put on my towelling robe, but a fierce bang foreshadowed the arrival of the puce-faced Katia who barrelled through the bedroom door yelling, 'Mum, she just took all my yellow paint and chucked it in the sink…'

Millie clattered in behind her. 'No I didn't. I was painting and she just…'

Both of them stopped in their febrile tracks, eyes wide, horror-stricken, as I hurriedly covered my crotch with the robe. But the damage had been done, prompting a sudden volte-face. They fled, a fiery ball of revulsion, their exaggerated screams turning, eventually, to mirthful mockery and cries of, 'Yeugh, gross! Oh. My. God!'

Sadly, it wasn't the first time my genitals had engendered ridicule.

How do you tell your kids, who love you unreservedly and think you're invincible, that you've got no job, no income, no prospects and your pride has been blown out of the water? Answer. You don't. They don't care. They care about kids' stuff like what's for supper, where's the remote and why do you always blame me when she did it? So I told them I was taking a break from crappy old work and, while I bet all their friends' dads would be mightily jealous of me lounging about at home all day, I'd rather you didn't mention it to them thank you. Although I was trying to act as if everything was normal, we did order pizza, on a Monday night, so they must have sensed that something was up, although their faces were buried too deep in pepperoni to care. They'd already had their supper, but Bea's cooking was a shade uninspired, even for the relatively unsophisticated palates of kids aged seven and eight, so they were only too delighted to tuck in.

I was dreading their going to bed, taking with them their animated chatter and bubbly innocence, leaving Lisa and me alone with only a chilly silence to fill but, as if I hadn't suffered enough bad karma for one day, Shrek 2, a horrifying glimpse of my tackle and a surfeit of pizza dough had knocked the stuffing out of them. For possibly the only time in living memory, they volunteered to turn in without being asked. I followed them up, helped them with their teeth and pyjamas and tucked them in. I've always loved that last cuddle of the day; Millie, with her sweet, chocolatey breath who always turns to soft, wet sand in my arms; Katia, bouncy, giggly, ticklish, inviting a tussle. Lisa always complained that I got her too excited, but our little routine invariably drained the last vestige of energy from her tiny body; fizzy to spark out in seconds.

I shouldn't have felt less like a man for being jobless, not in this day and age, but I'm old fashioned about things like that. I couldn't look Lisa in the eye when I came back down and entered the silent vacuum of grim reality. Lisa made no attempt to rekindle the what-do-we-do-now? conversation. It could wait. There were no pat answers. Maybe she was being sensitive to my predicament, but I sensed something else in her demeanour.

I had done this *to her*.

I need to be honest here, so bear with me. Our marriage had been uncomfortable for a while. No, 'a while' doesn't quite do it. I'm talking years. Lisa's burgeoning career as Assistant Creative Director of the up-market *Marc Rouillard* fine art gallery in Mayfair was her raison d'être. Aside from her general duties, which made full use of her agile, organised, creative mind, she mixed daily with artists, showbiz types, minor royalty and people famous for being famous – or twats – before coming home to solid old me. She was a good mother, strong, loving, solicitous, and always made a point of doing interesting things with the girls on the weekends when she wasn't working. But I was still, and always would be, Mike, the humble plodder, employed by a dreary company struggling to compete with slicker, smarter outfits. And now I couldn't even boast that withered feather in my cap.

Ours was the classic mis-match. She got an upper second class degree in Fine Art from Cambridge while mine was a dodgy 2.2 in Computer Studies awarded by the revered academic hothouse that is

Brunel University. Her parents lived in a large Tudor house with grounds (a 'hice with grinds' as her father, an old school investment banker, would have it) in rural Somerset, while mine were of solid, stolid Stoke Newington stock, an area which had become gentrified in spite of them. We'd met nearly eighteen years earlier – I was a struggling IT contractor in what was a relatively underdeveloped industry – singing for pennies in a faux French brasserie in Crouch End. I'd harboured dreams of pop stardom for too long and was finally coming to terms with the fact that my core audience had settled at around nine die hard devotees. On a good night. Including my parents. I'd found my level; a garlic-soaked greasehole where, every Thursday, I arrived straight from work in my grey C & A pinstripe, having humped my guitar case to the office and thence out to north London on a succession of over-crowded trains. They gave me my own stool, of course, on which I would perch whilst singing standards for an hour. *Easy Like Sunday Morning, Broken Wings, Careless Whisper,* MOR crap, really, but easy, accessible crap.

One rainy February night, Lisa arrived with a bunch of posh girls on an initially genteel but increasingly raucous hen night. And she'd got drunk and fallen for the singer in the corner. It started as a joke – landed gentry bonks bit of semi-rough – but, unbidden, our relationship acquired a momentum neither of us had anticipated. It was love, fiery, molten, inexorable.

How do you explain chemistry? Trick question. You can't. That's the whole point. It's ephemeral, beyond reason. Objectively, there was nothing to bind us. Our backgrounds, education and interests were so radically different, we often wondered, with the smug assurance of people secure in the knowledge that it didn't matter, what it was that kept us together. But we made each other laugh, enjoyed each other's company, had an uncanny meeting of minds on political and social issues – I'd come in a shade from the left, she a long way from the right – and we rarely argued. Somehow it worked. More than worked.

We married a year later and bought a compact but pretty little garden flat in Chiswick. By then I was a junior systems technician with Edmonds and White earning sufficient money to eke a mortgage out of the Abbey. I was happy to support us while Lisa worked her way up from PA to Assistant Creative Director in record time. Ever the flyer. It was idyllic, two young newlyweds with a bit of money, boundless ambition, terrific prospects – hers, increasingly, more exciting than mine – and very little responsibility.

We talked about children, often, but entered our thirties still feeling too young, too immature, too burdened by the need to lay foundations to take such a life-changing step. But, in hindsight, maybe we were already thinking it might not be forever and that kids would only complicate things down the line. Then along came Katia. She was unplanned, of course, but the news that she was germinating inside Lisa hit me like a wrecking ball. I remember crying with joy, then bewilderment, then abject inadequacy. How could an idiot like me possibly be a father? What did it entail? How the hell would I cope? But nature kicked in and I embraced it with an élan I didn't know I possessed. We both did.

We gave Katia every bit of ourselves, but when Millie arrived 16 months later, she proved that you always have more in the tank. Love doubles rather than halves. But so do fear, desperation and the pressure to earn more just to stand still.

The kids, like giant Hoovers, consumed so much of our time and energy that our relationship slipped onto the back burner. There was no time for introspection. Parenthood acted like a pause button, leaving those nagging questions about 'us' in abeyance as we struggled to cope with its demands.

It's difficult to pinpoint any derailing incident or chain of events. I just know I felt a sea change a couple of years before Katia was born, a time when the electricity was fading and we were rolling gently downhill. We had no obvious problems, nothing you could put your finger on. We still went out, saw films, sat and read the papers together on Sunday mornings. We got along. Maybe that was the problem. What incentive was there to confront the underlying apathy, to fight? Perhaps a little friction would have stirred something up, a little nit-picking, but that wasn't in our DNA.

Maybe chemistry has a shelf life. You stick two compounds together in a test tube and they fizz, over-excitedly at first, then settle down with a few bubbles nestling at the top. Eventually, the mixture becomes cloudy and inert. That was us, and getting inerter by the minute. We were just a couple sharing common causes now, getting by, doing ok, bringing up the kids, retiring, dying. If we got that far together.

Thing is, in spite of everything, I still loved Lisa. I always loved her, couldn't imagine being without her. I think she loved me too. Maybe like a brother, or like the father of her children. And that can sometimes be enough.

I'm just not sure she respected me any more.

We sat watching the news for a while, exchanging the odd monosyllable whilst staring resolutely at the screen as though God himself had stepped in for Huw Edwards. Around ten thirty, I got up to make some tea and Lisa followed me into the kitchen. She sat at the table as I pottered about and, perhaps uncomfortable with the idea of going to bed with so much left unsaid, we finally got around to talking. I started it, uttering some platitude about it being for the best, how it was a dead-end job with no prospects, a welcome and necessary kick up the arse for me. Tomorrow was another day, she chimed, the slate was clean, it was an opportunity not a disaster. But when Lisa, cradling her empty mug, yawned ostentatiously during one of our growing silences, I smiled and told her to go up.

I was relieved to find myself alone with only Paxman for company. Not many people would admit to that. He was needlessly haranguing a water company executive who was clearly unsuited to public flagellation. It wasn't his fault it didn't rain last summer. Or maybe it was. Did I give a fuck? But I needed some background noise to drown out the voices in my head. Never mind the positive words, the cautious optimism, I knew I was finished, at least as any kind of player in the IT world. I'd peaked, barely halfway up the ladder. It was over. I was forty-two, which I may have mentioned.

I flicked off the TV and lights and trooped disconsolately up the stairs, my legs leaden, my head just opening the door to a vicious, jagged headache. I crept into Millie's room and sat on her bed watching her breathe as she lay cocooned inside her duvet. I stroked the peach-fuzz skin on her forehead, pecked her on the cheek and left. Katia, as usual, was all arms and legs, duvet everywhere but over her body, eyes half open on the lookout for anything suspicious. I rearranged the duvet around her, but she was already kicking it into a crumpled heap as I closed her door.

I hesitated outside our bedroom door. A light was on but I knew Lisa would be asleep with a book open across her breast. I couldn't face going in there. Even asleep, I feared her opprobrium seeping across the mattress and drowning me. So I headed for the spare room which doubled as my study. I hadn't been in there for months. At one time, it was a haven, a personal space where I would pick up my acoustic guitar and sing a few songs. I might even record something on the PC. But I'd lost all inspiration a long time ago; couldn't see the point of it any more. No-one was listening, not even me. I closed the door softly behind me and nestled into the spongy sofa-bed which sat tight against the back wall. My guitar lay slumped at a sad angle on its stand and seemed to be pleading with me to pick it up and give it some TLC. I couldn't let it down.

I started strumming and was surprised to hear that only a couple of strings were out of tune. I fiddled with the peghead until every note was where it was supposed to be. E-A-D-G-B-E. Ready. Now, a song. What song? I'd written at least a hundred as a young man but couldn't think of a single one, maybe because ninety-four of them were shit and had been auto-deleted. I dabbled with a couple of simple riffs, delighting in the pain in the tips of my now softened fingers as I pressed out the chords. I'd always loved that sound as it swilled around the wooden hollows of the body before spilling out; like a wine taster, I savoured every musical flavour, every nuance, before proclaiming it suitable for aural consumption. My hands, working together, were creating something harmonious in my now discordant life. A song started to form as I played – *In Love We Trust* – something I'd written for a girl called Faye but never had the balls to play to her. She'd been a fellow student at Brunel, a girl whose heart I was forever trying to

19

capture but who resolutely overlooked me in favour of safer bets. I pictured the eternally pretty nineteen year old Faye as I sang, dousing myself in the memory of her sparkly green eyes, olive complexion, curlicued lips and throaty laugh. Truth was, I often thought about Faye, my one remaining fantasy of perfection in an increasingly imperfect life. Where was she now?

In Love We Trust was a mid-tempo number which I sang, initially, in a half-whisper, not wanting to wake the kids or, God help me, Lisa. But soon I was lost in the sheer joy of the music, the release. The lyrics were second nature, the chord pattern innate. I strummed and sang with increasing gusto, tension lifting, cutting through the misery. The door creaked and I stopped, mid-falsetto, tailing off like a dying cat. It was Lisa, sinewy, naked, bleary-eyed. Was that a hint of a smile playing about her lips?

'Can you shut the fuck up. I've got work in the morning.'

CHAPTER 3

Squash. Now there's a stupid game. Two frenzied frogs trapped in an airless, minute space defined by four very hard, very unforgiving walls, vying to smash a lump of spherical rubber into one or other of them. Rackets swish and flail as rancid sweat renders the floor oil-slick-slippery. A slithering, bone-snapping collision is just as likely to bring proceedings to a premature end as a coronary. But worse than all that; it stinks. You stink. The court stinks. A zillion foetid microbes fester in the wooden floor and absorbent plasterwork, un-bleachable, immoveable, yet somehow sufficiently nimble to leap, flea-like, into clothing and hair where they live on and prosper. It's a smell to which you never become inured and which never quite leaves your nasal lining between matches.

Still, it gets me out of the house and gives me a chance to let off steam, feel virtuous and have a leisurely beer or four – with a side of chips – afterwards, so I shouldn't knock it. I've played more or less every week for eight years, but only against the one opponent: Chaz Lucerno. Don't be fooled. He sounds like a comic-book hero or a dangerously attractive Anglo/Italian footballer but is, in fact, five foot three, bald, pale and skinnier than cheap twine. And an accountant. Ouch. I play Chaz because he can't beat me. Never has, never will. He fizzes around the back court, gnat-like, grunting with the effort of retrieving my cunningly angled shots, while his desperate scoops float benignly up in the air for me to swat away at will. Not that I do, not all the time. Got to make a game of it, haven't you? I'm a big fish in a little puddle. That's my kind of sporting contest.

Notwithstanding, Chaz and I have been best friends, off and on, since we were eleven. Then, as next door neighbours, we were inseparable, and we remained close throughout our teens and early twenties, even as our paths forked at right-angles. Me scraping two A Levels, him acing four. Me, marooned in metropolitan Uxbridge studying something woolly and useless, him at trendy, cosmopolitan LSE getting a first. But we always got together when we could and never spoke about the yawning academic gap. After he qualified as an ACA, Chaz went off to work in Australia for a couple of years while I blazed my inexorable trail through the world of IT. We kept in touch for a while, but blokes don't do that sort of thing very well and our initial bout of enthusiastic letter writing soon diminished until all we could manage was the odd postcard. Unimaginably, there was no email back then and phone calls cost more than a house. A quick-fire chat at Christmas at a pound a word was as good as it got. Inevitably, we lost touch altogether until, nine years ago, we both pitched up at the same ante-natal class. He was, by then, living in gated splendour in Richmond and married to Denise, a strapping Australian girl who was his first and, I'm pretty sure, only conquest. I suspect he was hers too. Sadly, Denise miscarried, but Chaz and I seized the opportunity to revive a friendship which, if anything, was stronger for the break.

I think most friendships thrive on imbalance. I was always better looking (it wasn't difficult – big fish, *microscopic* puddle), wittier (same) and more confident in company. Poor Chaz was losing his hair at eighteen while I was experimenting with Duran Duran dye-jobs and Spandau Ballet fop cuts. I always had a reasonable looking girlfriend in tow and I'd sometimes invite Chaz to tag along on dates, not to rub it in, just to give him a night out. I felt for him but, on reflection, it probably only made things worse. I tried to set him up with girls – friends-of on double dates – but it never worked out. Youngsters can be so cruel, especially those of the female variety. One look at Chaz was usually enough to make them fancy me.

But he had brainpower, lots of it, allied to serious focus. He committed to his career in a way I never could, rising to junior partner in a top West End firm before I got my own office. Soon, he became Managing Partner and started ploughing his massive profit share into an impressively diverse private property portfolio. Meanwhile, I fumbled along the horizontal ladder at Edmonds & White, ploughing my salary into the weekly shop at Tesco and bemoaning the price of everything. My areas of superiority mattered more at eighteen but were almost irrelevant at forty-two. I'm sure he'd still swap a couple of my non-balding genes for a couple of his million quid, but while he's waiting for the staggeringly expensive cure – which he'll cover with the loose change in his track suit pockets – he'll just have to make do with living like a king.

Chiswick Health Club was the preserve of the wealthy and the connected. I fell into the latter category thanks to Chaz who was, of course, a Gold Member. As was our tragic wont, we sat there, post-match in the glittering bar, phwoaring impotently at the myriad toned-looking women as they flounced past our table. Yes of course it was self-mocking. What do you take us for, sad, middle-aged husbands? Truth is, lengthy marriages can do that to a man. As can short marriages. As can any bloody relationship or lack thereof. We're men. I've told you, we can't help it. And, as a paid-up member of the weaker sex, confessing my sudden career hiatus to another man did not come naturally. We don't do that sort of thing. We front up. But if not Chaz, who else was I going to tell?

'Fuck,' was his pithy rejoinder.

'Yeah, I know.'

'Why?'

'You know why? Because I'm a dinosaur. My technical skills are out of date and I couldn't sell a dummy to Bobby Moore. And he's dead.'

'What a player, though. The man could read a pass…'

'Sticking with me.'

'Sorry. Go on. Dinosaur.'

'Yeah, T Rex. *Past it*,' I whined, miming speech marks, 'in my game, anyway. I should've seen it coming. Idiot. I was completely vulnerable there but I just closed my eyes hoping it would go away. And now… I'm basically…useless.'

'But apart from that, how's everything?'

I laughed, but it hurt, saying it all out loud like that. 'Don't know what I'm going to do.'

'What did they give you?'

'Six months' salary. After seventeen years. No clock, no cake, no farewell party.'

'Mate, listen. And don't be embarrassed or too bloody proud, ok? I know what you're like.'

Oh no. He was going to offer me money. 'It's all right, Chaz,' I said, feigning stoicism, 'I'll survive. Lisa's doing ok and…'

'We need a driver…for the partners. Just to tide you over.'

In all honesty, I'd have swallowed my pride and accepted a few grand, but – and I'm not a snob; there's nothing wrong with driving for a living – I couldn't see myself ferrying smug, overfed accountants around London, doffing my cap and polishing the bumper while waiting for them to finish their Michelin-starred lunches. And anyway, you can't do that job properly without a licence. I'd amassed a few too many points and still had a month to go before getting it back. I know, I know – shouldn't have got caught.

'I'll be fine,' I said. 'Probably have two or three interviews in the bag this time next week.' Which was bollocks, of course.

'How's Lisa?'

'Who? Oh her. Pleased as punch. As you would expect.'

'It's not going to be easy for her.'

Chaz knew all about Lisa's predilection for the expensive wine over the house red, the way she eschewed the identical but cheaper item off the internet in favour of the one from the dinky, wood-panelled shop in Harrogate. It was in her genes. 'She'll have to cope, won't she? We're not going to starve.'

Chaz nodded and consulted his phone. 'Hey, listen. Why don't you two come over this Saturday? How long is it since we've done that, eh?'

It was eleven months. I could wait another eleven years. There's no reason why best friends' spouses should get on but, fuck me, ours were like Israel and Hamas. Denise was earthy, tough and bloody-minded while Lisa was sophisticated, tough and bloody-minded. They shared not a single view on the state of the planet, politics, religion, Kylie's hair – you get the idea. It must have been fun to watch, unless you were me. 'I don't know, Chaz.'

'Saturday after then.'

It felt odd walking the kids to the school bus stop in my track suit and trainers. For the last three years I'd carried out this pleasant task dressed in one of my mid-to-upper-range M & S suits – we're talking three figures – pinchy leather shoes and, in winter, the fleece-lined mac Dad left me in his will. Today, the chill biting through my insubstantial layers, I kissed their cool, ruddy cheeks and waved them off wondering whether the other parents were watching. From the window of the bus, Millie held up a fluffy brown teddy bear and motioned for me to wave it goodbye, same as she did every day. I waved. It never felt ridiculous.

I turned and headed, unconsciously, towards the station, then stopped and turned again hoping that this somehow looked like part of the plan. How I yearned to be opposite The Smiler on the tube this morning; I'd have forgiven him everything. I trudged back towards home where I knew Lisa would be painting the finishing touches onto a face which required no make-up. We'd barely grunted at each other over breakfast, but that wasn't unusual. It was the first day of a new term, a school day, and was typically tense and chaotic. We'd been like ships colliding noisily in the morning and getting quite pissed off about it. Lisa helped the girls with their uniforms and bags while I buttered toast, slopped juice into plastic cups and made grim packed lunches. I'm sure, when I was seven or eight, I just got myself up, made breakfast and made my way to school without troubling my parents, so either we were less mollycoddled in those days or they didn't give a toss. Given my mother used to leave me out in the garden in my pram in all weathers ('we all did it'), I'm plumping for the latter. Maybe that's why I'm so hard?

I stopped off at the newsagent to buy The Times. Was the rest of the world in as much shit as me? As I emerged into the piercing January sun, I realised I couldn't face Lisa, so I doubled back and headed for The Hungry Horse, a local workmen's café I used to pass on the way to the station, occasionally stopping to peer through the condensation to salivate at the wall-to-wall eggs, bacon and heart-disease sausages served up by a strangely slender Italian woman in an apron. I ordered a bacon sarnie and a cup of tea of so solid a brew, I could have turned it out and eaten it like blancmange. The sandwich, loosely contained within two breeze block bread walls buttered with great flat slabs of yellow grease, was succulent, overfilled and spectacularly calorific. Throwing caution and a probable cholesterol overdose to the wind, I ordered another. I scanned The Times, conscious of the fact that it wasn't the newspaper du jour in The Hungry Horse, earning several suspicious glances, not least from a couple of heavily-set blokes in paint-spattered sweat pants on the next table. But it was nothing I couldn't handle. I'm pretty tough with glances. It occurred to me that I was one of them now, a guy in a track suit who didn't go into an office in a fancy suit, a guy who drank bitter tea in a greasy spoon and scoffed animal fat. Except, of course, they had jobs to go to. And were a bit rough.

Lisa had gone by the time I dawdled home, burping and deep-breathing all the way as I did battle with a bout of coruscating heartburn. The house was deafeningly quiet. Only the pulse beating in my ears and the faint, occasional swish of traffic outside broke the silence. I flicked the TV on for company and watched a nauseating confessional show while I ate a slice of toast to combat the instant boredom. If nothing else, it forced the acid back into my stomach, delaying a no doubt fiercer assault later on. Sensibly, I took a couple of pre-emptive Gaviscons and washed them down with a cup of tea and a Tracker.

There was no point getting dressed. Dressed for what? I was already wearing my new uniform, something entirely appropriate to my working day. I brushed my teeth, then went back downstairs to make another tea. I read The Times in a little more detail, then tidied the kitchen in the wake of the morning whirlwind. Outside, the garden lawn looked a little long. Maybe it would do me good to get some fresh air and important exercise before I got down to a hard day at the PC. Those hover mowers don't push themselves, do they? But wasn't that rain pattering against the window? Perhaps I should wait for it to stop and let the grass dry. I could sit and watch it dry. I'd never done that before, actually watched something go from wet…to dry, so maybe it would help me unravel the mysteries of that particular evaporative phenomenon.

All the while, in the spare room, sat the computer with its speedy connection to the outside world, a world into which I would, eventually, have to dip my toe.

Guitar, computer. Computer, guitar. The ghost of Tommy Cooper floated through the room. I made a deal with myself. Five minutes on the guitar while the computer booted up, then I'd get right down to it. Right down to it! Recruitment web sites first, picking out appropriately senior vacancies, then a trawl through companies I'd like to work for, noting key names, telephone numbers and addresses. Then, draft up a cutting edge CV, start thrashing it out and begin the whole process again to make sure I missed nothing. Look out, world, here I come! It was going to be exciting, a new start, a chance for *me* to decide what *I* wanted to do, with whom and where.

Thirty-six minutes later, I was still drowning out the gentle hum of the computer with a pleasing sequence of rhythmic, chunky chords, bellowing out songs I thought I'd forgotten. It was good to have the house to myself and really let rip after the misery of the last twenty-four hours. I needed to let it out and I wasn't going to apologise to anyone for these few moments of catharsis before I got down to the real business of the day. I finished the last song in my limited repertoire before starting again with a more confident rendition of the first one. Followed by the second. I was beginning to flow. But, whoa, hang on, it was nearly eleven and I really had to get cracking. So I went down and made myself a cup of tea on the strict and inviolable understanding that I would sit at the desk as soon as I went back upstairs and go online. As the kettle boiled, I made a mental list of the sites I intended to visit. There was so much fertile cyberland to cover. I was feeling good about things, positive. Cup of tea, computer, all systems go.

But would you credit it? The grass was now dry, or very nearly dry, so I thought it prudent to take my chance with the mower in case it rained again later. Life's all about grabbing opportunities while you can. There was plenty of time for my assault on the IT sector and, anyway, people were always more approachable after the morning rush. No point calling or sending them stuff too early in the day.

It took a while to extricate the mower from the sundry garden tools and cobwebbed paraphernalia scattered around the little wooden shed at the back of the garden. To be honest, I'd never much liked going in that shed – too many little black things with legs and/or wings ready to pounce; so much so, in fact, that I'd only ever got as far as poking my terrified head through the door. As I lugged the mower towards the house, I realised I'd never used it before. It appeared to have only one lever, which I assumed was the thing that made it work. Simple? For someone with strong technical credentials, I'm a bit shit with household appliances. I unravelled the extension lead and plugged it into the nearest socket in the house, leaving the French doors open and flapping in the wind. I pressed the lever into the handle and was shaken by the sheer ferocity of the shiny orange beast before me. I could see why grass was no match for it.

Ten minutes! Ten lousy minutes. That's all it took. I continued to go over and over the grass long after the law of diminishing marginal returns had become the law of utter bloody pointlessness. Belatedly, I endeavoured to carve out the kind of striped pattern you see on the better football pitches, but failed through lack of technique and available grass. I was in danger of burning out the motor by now. Defeated, I unplugged the cord and wound it fastidiously around a flat orange plastic coiler, much more neatly than I'd found it. It's as well to take your time with something like coiling. I heaved the mower back into the shed and took a moment to tidy the place up – as well as I was able given my craven reluctance to go inside for longer than a few seconds at a time lest the bugs mounted a concerted attack. I even put up a couple of hooks to hang things on. I'd find stuff to hang another day. All in all, it looked pretty bloody good when I'd finished.

I ambled back to the house, slapping my dirty hands together job-done-fashion, and pulled at the French doors which had, by now, slammed shut. Irrevocably. Which idiot installed a latch and then forgot to provide working handles on the outside? Was that supposed to be some sort of security measure? Futile, surely. Any decent burglar would just break a window. They're not stupid, burglars. There was a distinct lack of thought in evidence here. I sat on the step in front of the doors wearing a wry, just-my-bloody-luck smile, seasoned with a hint of triumphalism which should have shamed me. How was I going to get on with anything constructive now?

After pondering that conundrum for a few long minutes, I heaved myself to my feet and made my way around the side of the house wondering if I had enough cash on me to keep me going in the local Starbucks for the next six hours. Which was when I spotted the wide open kitchen window, the consequence of an earlier toast-burning incident which had necessitated the disarming of a hair-trigger smoke alarm by creating a draught. Dammit. I managed to crawl through the gap at the bottom of the sash, though not without incident. A bucket had given me the necessary elevation, but I kicked it backwards as I thrust myself forward thus removing all support and sending me crashing down, groin first, into the kitchen taps. I screamed, ejecting oxygen at a molecular level, my paralysed lungs incapable of replenishing the lost elixir. Was this where my story would end, impaled by the balls on domestic sanitaryware dressed in my JD Sports track suit?

I needed a reviving cup of tea after that.

The problem with the internet is there's just too much stuff on it. I know that's a good thing in many ways, but it's also an unemployed, aimless, lazy man's worst enemy. It's extraordinary how one link leads to another and, before you know it, you've gone from the Sainsbury home delivery service to *AnalAccess.com*. I've never bought porn, not even as an acned schoolboy with raging hormones, but you can't help but be curious. There's tons of it, not all of it stimulating. Which means that quite a lot of it is. I defy any man whose imagination has been sexually piqued to simply let the moment pass and it's nigh on impossible when he's alone and the alternative is reading the report and accounts of some dull IT company in Willesden. Wearing a loose fitting pair of sweat pants with an elasticated waist doesn't help matters much either. Accessibility, you see. Too easy, too convenient; you don't even have to take anything off.

Now, we all know that any man who says he doesn't masturbate is either a liar or doesn't have a penis. But it was something I'd largely abandoned over the years. I suppose I'd drifted into a state of sexual ossification. Our marital bed had seen some regular action, but that was a long time ago in a place far, far away. The current and long standing apathy, characterised by resolutely going to bed at different times and rising early at the weekends, ostensibly to tend to the kids – who were, of course, much happier left alone in front of the box – was only occasionally leavened by the odd bout of furious sex. This was sex with a purpose – Lisa's – and I was merely there to provide a service when she came home frazzled. It was great, no question, perhaps all the greater for being so infrequent. Quality, not quantity. I'd settled into this lifestyle. All good things come to those too set in their ways to do anything but wait. I never instigated, having suffered too many headaches and bored rebuffs, so I'd learned to ramp up the hormones on an on-demand basis.

But now I was all alone in the house and somehow working to different rules. No rules, in fact. Lisa didn't factor into this new equation. I had no focus and allowed myself to be sucked into the seedy underbelly of internet porn; I'm sorry, but it seemed to me that I had to release this particular pressure valve before I could concentrate on the serious work of the morning…er, afternoon. It wasn't about pleasure or self-gratification, just a means to an end. It's quite important to stress that I didn't linger on the *AnalAccess* site in order to undertake the task. I'm from a nice family.

Ultimately, the whole operation was ill-advised given I'd been skewered by the kitchen taps not an hour before. As a younger man, I would occasionally essay a sexual position that bent bones and twisted ligaments, or required me to lift or manoeuvre my partner acrobatically. Fuelled by youthful adrenaline, I was as strong and invulnerable as Superman. Only afterwards would I be aware of my screaming muscles and creaking joints as the sexual novocaine leaked away into the sheets. It was as well not to get stranded in one of those heroic but ill-advised standing-up and carrying positions when my moment had passed. It would then be an agonising race against time to drop my partner on the bed before she hit the floor. Well, masturbating with bruised testicles is not dissimilar. Early on, the pain seemed counter-productive, but I pressed on and was soon into the realms of reckless disregard as I headed for my Pyrrhic victory. I sat and throbbed for twenty minutes afterwards, cursing the people responsible for *www. penishole.com.*

Ok, lunch, a quick stroll to walk it off, and then I was going to really get my head down.

'Dad!?' Millie's shrill voice woke me. It was 4.15. In fact, I was sufficiently startled to fall backwards off my chair, which is what happens when you fall asleep with your legs up on a desk, balancing only on the two back legs. I'd been unconscious since around 2.30 when, following my amble through suburban Chiswick after an over-lardy lunch – Hungry Horse again: chips, omelette (ham and mushroom, so quite healthy), chips, beans and chips – I'd come back and shut my eyes for ten minutes. Millie, following the noise, found me on my back, one leg still propped up on the desk, the other with my stricken guitar lying across it. 'Hiya,' I said with as much insouciance as circumstances allowed.

'What you doing Dad?'

'Me? Not much. Just, you know, resting.'

'You don't look very comfortable.'

'I'm not, actually,' I said, hauling myself upright. 'Just testing out one of those Yoga positions.'

'You don't do Yoga.'

'Not after that.'

'You making us supper?'

'Er, isn't Bea here? I thought she collected you and did supper and everything.'

'Yeah, but her cooking's shi…'

'Millie!'

'Well she's rubbish. It's either, like, frozen pizza or really naff, soggy pasta. Or spaghetti carborara.'

'Sorry, darling, but I'm working.'

'Yeah, right,' she sneered, having gone from innocent child to scornful adult in a millisecond.

'Anyway, I'm a rubbish cook, as you well know.'

'But not as crap as her.'

It was nearly half past four and I'd yet to register my name with any of the myriad recruitment agencies who were going to tell me that I was a bit senior for most of their vacancies, but that they'd keep my CV on file and let me know as soon as anything came up. But I had to do something. I dredged up a CV I'd drafted when I applied for some out-of-my-league job six years earlier. Tragically, it required virtually no updating. Six years of standing still. I fired it off and received a handful of impersonal, auto-reply acknowledgements. I then applied for various, mostly inappropriate direct vacancies, adding, where noteworthy skills and achievements were specifically asked for, a glowing, self-congratulatory paragraph making particular reference to the excellent rapport I'd established with Virgin. Others required little more than a one-liner, and I composed a simple paragraph which I encapsulated my story: *I have most recently been a Senior Systems Manager and Sales Executive with Edmonds & White.* I hoped the Proliferation of Upper Case Letters Would Obscure the Fact That I Was No Longer With Them For Some Reason.

The entire process took a little over an hour but, by God, did I feel virtuous afterwards. I pushed my chair back from the desk, took a deep breath, nodded my head in acknowledgement of a complex job well done, and picked up my guitar. I'd earned a break. I launched into a medley of my greatest hits, singing loud and proud, releasing the pent up tension of a long, tough day at the coalface. Katia and Millie popped their heads round the door, hands clamped theatrically to their ears, but I didn't let that deter me.

Sadly, basic intelligence deserts me when I'm lost in music. There was a time to stop, a time to be staring conscientiously at my computer screen, fingers on the keyboard rather than the fretboard. That time was two minutes past seven when Lisa walked in. I could have stopped singing at five to or even one past, assumed the requisite pose and been safe. When Lisa said she'd be home 'on time', there was no need to check your watch. 7.02 on the nose, timed perfectly so that she arrived just as Bea was leaving to ensure their paths crossed only fleetingly at the door. Bea's tedious, minute by minute recap of her child-minding day was most easily avoided by cutting into her own time.

'Busy day?' smirked Lisa just as I was launching into a chorus of *Hazel Green,* a cheesy song I wrote when I was fourteen. Hazel Green – geddit? That was the fictional girl's name and the colour of her eyes. I know! Breathtakingly shit, even for a clueless teenager. What was I thinking when I first scribbled these lyrics down? And how did I ever sing them with a straight face?

> *I caught her eye, it looked like hazel green*
> *From where I stood it could have been*
> *But anyway it gleamed*
> *I stared ahead, she did not see my face*
> *That's good for her in any case*
> *For I am not her ace*
> *She never looks at me*

And can you blame her?

'Ok, Miss,' I said, schoolboy-to-teacher fashion. Would that work? 'I've been at it all day. Just taking a break. Honest.'

She wasn't amused. Would you be? 'And?'

'I've made a shitload of applications, spoken to God knows how many agencies, et cetera et cetera. Broken the ice, ball rolling et cetera et cetera. It's not going to happen overnight.'

'Who have you applied to?'

This was getting forensic. 'I don't know…loads of them. They're all much of a muchness, aren't they? It's IT. Just got to sit tight and wait for something to come back. Throw enough mud, et cetera et cetera.'

The et ceteras were working, throwing her off. 'Mmm,' she mmm-ed, 'ok, I stink. I need a shower. Coming in?'

Another tough day, obviously. But twice in two nights? Thing is, I was feeling a bit spent and sore after my brief liaison with Andrea at *penishole.com* and my earlier ball-crushing exploits. In days gone by, the prospect of performing twice in a day wouldn't have fazed me but at forty-two, and after a day like I'd had, it was daunting. 'I've got to do some more work here. Better stick at it.' The very fact I'd used the word 'work' gave it the requisite sheen of gravity.

Lisa raised her artfully-arched eyebrows and flounced out. 'Sod you, then,' she said, which put me in mind of my earlier passing flirtation with Mia at *asspussy.net*.

CHAPTER 4

YOU'D HAVE THOUGHT that, after two weeks of battering away, someone, somewhere would have come back wanting to interview me, but you'd be wrong. I'd followed up my initial half-hearted foray into the IT jobs market with a more concerted blitz the next day, and an even wider, more indiscriminate shit-shovel the day after that. Now I was applying for vacancies whose job *titles* I didn't understand, much less their specifications. I even applied for vacancies in Watford and Hemel Fucking Hempstead, for God's sake, all to no avail.

All the while, I was waiting for Pete to deliver on his promise to give my name to David Lewis at Crack-IT, a niche company with whom Edmonds & White had occasionally ventured jointly. Was it just an empty promise thrown into the muck, flailing words of comfort to make himself feel a little less guilty? The shit, sitting there eating croissants while I was no longer even a thought in his mental out tray. All those years. For what? My anger and sense of rejection instilled a certain bullishness in me that usually only raised its ugly head when shouting at old ladies for going too slowly in their Austin Allegros or at unshaven, hefty yobs in baseball caps driving white vans, with whom I was often violently verbally aggressive, provided our respective windows were closed and they couldn't see me. I had nothing to lose but my pride which had long since sailed.

'Great to hear from you,' said Pete in a tone that suggested quite the opposite.

'How's business?'

'Ahh, well, actually…'

'It's all right, I don't give a fuck,' I said jovially. And I didn't.

'No, fair enough.'

'Listen, Pete, I won't detain you – you've got Christine's tits to ogle, haven't you? – so the thing is, remember you were going to have a word with David Lewis about me?'

'Er, yeah. Course,' he said, memory jolted.

'What did he say?'

I was interested in the precise nature of Pete's ensuing lie. 'David? He's been away. On biz, I think. Left him a message, so…'

I think I'd have been happier with *'he's not interested'* or, *'they're fully staffed right now and don't need any losers'* or better still *'sorry, I'm a complete prick – forgot to call him because you're lower on my list of priorities than trimming my nasal hair.'*

'Ahh. Right,' I said.

'No luck with the job hunt?'

'I'm forty-two.'

'Oh look, come on mate, that's not relevant. You're a good guy. Loads of outfits out there are looking for dudes like you.'

Guy? Dude? If I didn't need the bro' so badly, I'd have told him to fuck off. 'Well why not email me a list of them and hopefully none of the 796 companies I've approached so far will be on it.'

'That bad?'

'You know it's that bad!' I snarled, instantly regretful.

'I'm sorry mate.'

Mate, now? A knob like him doesn't have mates, and if he did, I wouldn't be among them. 'Fuck off with your sorry,' I snarled again with less regret. 'Be sincere for five minutes, will you? You didn't even call him, did you?'

But I was spitting vitriol at the wrong person. It wasn't Pete's fault, it was mine. I'd spent the last five years achieving very little, on the warped understanding that I was indispensable. And now I was paying the price.

'I'll call him…again. Ok?'

'Yeah, call him!' I snapped, still high on indignation. I needed to negotiate a quick route from there to grateful before his guilt turned sour. 'Sorry Pete. It's…just a bit difficult at the moment.'

'Leave it with me, yeah?'

I think Pete was probably a decent man, deep down…just an inveterate prick.

Stranger things…er…can't remember the rest of that saying, or if I've ever known it. Happen at sea? Happen at sea! No. Can't be right, can it? What the fuck does that mean anyway? You probably get the gist. David Lewis, of all people, called me the very next day, just as Winona of *Slappers.co.uk* and I were making acquaintance. Actually, it was David Lewis's office, but that was just as good in my book. A lady called Fearne asked me to tell her if I had any time available the following week for a meeting. It was a toughie. I shuffled The Times which was open on my desk on a sports page, as though rifling through my diary to find a slot in my heavy schedule, little thinking that any IT man worth his salt would have been making little clicking noises on his Blackberry. 'Can't do Monday,' I said, 'meetings all day…er…got a window on Tuesday morning, then it's Friday after that.'

'David was hoping you could come in on Monday at twelve.'

'I'll move some things around.'

It felt weird being in a suit and tie and those slick, shiny shoes again, weird to be up in town for a meeting in a big glassy building, like I'd been given a temporary pass back into the human race. For some small part of that day, I wasn't going to be Mr Track Suit breakfasting on grease with nowhere else to go but a small room dominated by an evil computer with nothing useful to say for itself.

David Lewis, it turned out, had had things moved around on him. He wasn't there when I arrived at twelve sharp on Monday and wasn't going to be back until three. Did I want to wait? What, with so many pressing appointments in the diary? Lisa's words were still ringing in my ears as I settled into a small, magazine-free, halogen-lit box inside another larger one. 'Look the part, be confident not cocky, ask questions, show interest in the company.' Or something like that. I hadn't been able to take it all in, not whilst brushing my teeth with my bruised balls hanging loose, but I'd interviewed enough hopefuls over the years to know that first impressions are the most important. And my first impression of David Lewis was that he was an arrogant, discourteous motherfucker. He had my number, so why didn't he or 'his office' call to rearrange? Fearne, a stout blonde in a suit that probably fitted her before Christmas, was apologetic and, after a ring round, managed to find someone else to see me. Someone else. That should have been my cue to leave, but I had time to waste.

Phil Watson was a senior underling in David Lewis's department. Phil was very wide across the face, the shoulders, the hips; the widest man I'd ever met, in fact. His face was pock-marked, squared off, all cheekbones and jawline and he was probably considered ruggedly handsome in some quarters. Combed-back, thinning hair, held needlessly in place with lashings of gel, exposed a widescreen forehead which balanced the open, gleaming smile he flashed briefly as we shook hands. Poor Phil. I'd been 'Phil' myself, often, when Pete couldn't be arsed to see a candidate. And there it was, in Phil's eyes, unmistakeably, the desperate look of a man asking himself *fuck's sake, why me?*

Phil led me widely into his office and parked himself in his wide chair like some very wide thing. We exchanged pleasantries, battled gamely through a difficult silence, chuckled a bit then got down to business. Such as it was. So, who was I exactly? I explained the Pete/David Lewis connection, which did little to alleviate Phil's confusion. He knew of Edmonds & White, of course, but didn't know Pete. Frankly, it sounded like he hardly knew David Lewis. I gave him a breakdown of my dazzling career without mentioning the word 'redundancy' preferring to make the whole thing sound voluntary, like I'd taken time out to seek a new challenge. After a minute or two of this tortuous fibbing, he asked in his estuary accent, 'So you're looking to come and join *us*.' Yes, Wide Phil! Spot on! This was incredibly upbeat and promising. I nodded enthusiastically.

All hope withered in an instant.

'Trouble is, we haven't got any openings – none that I know of, anyway. If anything, we're streamlining. One of our clients just went under…' Phil made a sad, wide face, '…took a bloody big contract with them. So, really, until we've generated some new business, we need to watch our numbers.'

'Aha,' I said thoughtfully.

'So – sorry, confused – what is it you actually do? Are you a sales guy?'

'I have been working on the sales side, yes.' I don't know why that sounded so vacuous.

'Hmm. Well, actually, that *might* be of interest.'

Hope rose a notch but ebbed instantly because I knew what was coming. Phil leaned forward, planting his meaty forearms on the desk, blocking out the light from the window as he loomed, wider than ever. 'So have you nailed down any decent contracts recently?'

Was 1998 recent or would that be stretching it? Most of my other triumphs in-between had nestled somewhere between insignificant and loss-making (or loss-leading, as I preferred to characterise them). I had no option; the old ones are the best: 'I was *this* close to landing a monster deal with Virgin. Monster. Fell down at the last hurdle because we couldn't fulfil one tiny little requirement. Bloody heart breaker.'

'Virgin? Wow.'

Yes, it was impressive, wasn't it? Wait until I told him about the Microsoft and Shell contracts I didn't get. 'But, you know, that's business, isn't it?' I said, waxing sage.

Phil nodded sympathetically. 'And…apart from Virgin…?'

'Oh, there've been some pretty chunky ones,' I said. Had Phil's training covered bluster-spotting? 'Er, Gamma Communications? Know them?'

Phil shook his head. Was I really going to elaborate upon the contract I'd secured to maintain three PCs and a server? It wouldn't have paid my train fare. 'But, it *is* tough out there, as we all know.' Which said it all. I had no more to add to that insightful dazzler.

Phil recognised the floundering idiot facing him for what he was, a floundering idiot, with nothing to offer a company which wasn't buying anyway. 'Well, I'll tell you what. I'll have a chat with David and he or I will get back to you. That sound reasonable?'

Never mind reasonable. Downright unbelievable. We shook hands and I sloped away accompanied by the glassily smiling Fearne who guided me downstairs and out the front door. Back amongst the shattering decibels of New Oxford Street, I stood for a moment, loosened my tie and headed for the nearest Starbucks. I placed my empty briefcase on a table and drank a skinny latte, notwithstanding that I hated coffee, even one diluted in sweet, sickly milk. I thought the caffeine might buck me up. It didn't.

So Pete's gesture had been empty, a sop, a guilt-assuager. He must have known there was nothing for me at Crack-IT. I could've been sitting at home idly strumming my guitar, or getting acquainted with Yazzmyn (sic) at *Hairymuff.com* rather than traipsing into town getting my hopes up. Net loss: £5.90 train fare; £3.70 latte and little cake; priceless self-respect, such as it was. I removed my suit, my still crisp white shirt and sensible tie and pulled on an old track suit. It was beginning to fray a bit at the cuffs and ankles but felt worryingly like something I was supposed to wear on a weekday. I made myself a ham sandwich and sat staring at the garden without registering, much less savouring a single mouthful. It was after two and a long, empty afternoon stretched ahead, followed by an even longer, emptier evening. Whither the next 25 years? I could have done without Lisa's triumphant beaming smile as she barrelled through the door at 6.45. Bea was still there with fifteen minutes left on the clock. What the hell was going on in our universe? Lisa was fit to burst. She cornered Bea in the kitchen for a moment, dispensed some instructions, then led me into the back lounge, leaving the kids to chomp on some fruit cubes whilst transfixed by a staggeringly unfunny American teenage sitcom on Nickelodeon.

'I've got it!' she trilled.

'Got what?'

'I'm going to be the new Creative Director.'

'Wow, great,' I acted. 'Fantastic.'

'And I told Rupert, there's no point paying me all that money if I don't have complete autonomy.'

'So…?'

Pause. Gush! 'I've got complete autonomy.'

'Brilliant.' I gave her a little hug, but she felt like a coiled spring and was way too wired to care. 'I'm thrilled for you, I really am.' And I was. I think.

She wriggled free. 'So I say whose work we display, I deal with the artists, I'm in charge of layout…that place is going to be sooo different this time next year.'

'How much?'

'Very different. By miles.'

'No. How much money?'

'Oh. Almost half as much again. Believe that?!'

Bloody hell. This *was* a bonus, given our circumstances. Financially, we'd be back to where we were before I lost my job. But this agreeable news was tempered by the dawning, unavoidable reality; she was soaring off into the professional stratosphere, a dot on the horizon I could barely see from my ever-deepening trench. Lisa flung her tailored jacket onto the sofa and started unbuttoning her silk blouse. She had that look in her eyes, hungry, needy, determined to blow off the steam generated by all this excitement. But hang on, we were in the lounge with the kids in the next room. What if they were to wander in to ask for a Cheese String only to find their parents sweating, grunting, connected at the groin? Or worse, Bea, though I imagine she wouldn't have recognised human sexual activity if she was taking part.

'It's not official yet, so don't tell anyone, ok? It's going to put a few noses out of joint so, you know, a bit of diplomacy's required before it's announced.'

'Who am I going to tell?'

'No-one. I'm just saying.'

'But who would I tell? Seriously. I don't know anyone,' I said, unnecessarily tetchily

'All right, all right.'

'Sorry. No need for that.'

'Come on,' she said, cajoling me like an errant puppy, 'let's celebrate.' Lisa marched out determined not to be brought down by my spikiness, and started heading upstairs as she continued to strip. We were, at least, going somewhere with a lock.

'Oh, I dunno,' I demurred, trailing behind her like a sullen child. 'Not particularly in the mood right now – really exhausted…'

'No, you twerp,' she said, swivelling at the top of the stairs to deliver a condescending chuckle. I'd forgotten that Lisa's sex drive was principally tension-led. When she was happy (or, as in this case, delirious) she was already fulfilled. 'Let's go out. I've offered Bea time and a half.'

She was already splashing the cash. 'Out?'

'It's on me.' Hmm. Hadn't we had a joint account for the last sixteen years? Admittedly my current contribution was somewhere between negligible and non-existent, but surely I merited credit for past performance. Perhaps not. Yet another sad step on the road to total emasculation. She barged through the bedroom door, cheeks blooming as she charged around on jet fuel. She was down to her pristine bra and panties now, her lithe, satin-skinned body shimmering in the half-light of a bedside lamp. I stood there with my green, 95% nylon track suit hanging off me like a sack and I'm pretty sure I'd never looked sexier. She grabbed her towelling robe and spun out of the bedroom towards the bathroom. 'Ten minutes and I'm ready. Get something decent on.'

'What's wrong with this?'

'Don't be an idiot,' she said, unamused, before gliding out on a carpet of air.

People change – and just because it's a tired cliché, doesn't make it any less true. Lisa was now so far removed from the girl I married, I barely recognised her sometimes. I'm not talking about her staggering physicality which still had the power to shock, nor her ineffable smartness. She'd always been a polymath who could throw all the balls – plus a few sharp knives – into the air and keep them floating serenely above her head until she was ready to pluck out the things that mattered. And she remained the ideal partner, a solicitous, kind and loyal friend and confidante who stuck by me even when I dipped below acceptable standards, even as our relationship faltered. But Lisa's life had been spiralling away from mine for a while. She now operated in a world I didn't understand and in which I had no interest. I couldn't blame her for being seduced by her glamorous work environment. It must have been jarring to return, night after night, to the mundane plod of suburban Chiswick, kids, obstreperous nannies, prosaic domesticity, financial realities…me. I'd changed too, of course, a bit better here, a bit worse there but, in essence, I was always a little bit average. Here's the list, for what it's worth: I'm not stupid most of the time, I'm reasonable looking, I can be amusing when I'm in the mood, I'm reliable and I'm a pretty good dad. An honest working man (was), a family man, never strayed. All very worthy, but I'm struggling to find anything there that sets me apart from any other ordinary Joe. I was beginning to think that Lisa felt she merited something more than that. And she probably did.

I don't like nouvelle cuisine. There's a reason. It's shit. Not the most layered critique, but there you are. I thought it had had its day, that restaurants had recognised that diners want something wholesome and tasty to eat as opposed to an aesthetically interesting arrangement of lonely scraps. I'd only just about bothered to make myself a soulless tuna sandwich for lunch, another symptom of the insidious apathy which was threatening to consume me. It had left me feeling empty but not especially hungry. But now we were here, in an actual eating establishment, I fancied something to eat. A decent steak, a few veg, some chips, maybe a slab of Banoffi Pie to finish, something real, chunky, Proletarian. But as I studied the menu at St Aubin, an achingly minimalist restaurant in the Fulham Road, I struggled to find something worth making the effort to chew much less swallow. Anything vaguely edible – a bit of lamb, for example – came served on a bed of braised stinging nettles with a shingle and cognac sauce and buffoon-udder terrine. Well you get the idea. I settled on *'veal tenderloin medallions wrapped in San Daniele Prosciutto, creamy pumpkin polenta with Brussels sprouts chiffonade and a wild foraged mushroom jus,'* although my barren plate suggested that the kitchen had pretty much run out of all of the above.

Lisa looked ravishing in a slinky, low cut silk dress whose provenance was a mystery. I'd certainly never seen it before. From her ears dangled earrings that looked suspiciously like genuine precious metal embedded with gemstones rather than the silvery, fake-pearl-type thing I tended to plump for when her birthday came around. A present from an admirer, or was she already spending her pay rise? I didn't want to know either way. She was effervescent, bursting with fresh initiatives for the gallery. I spent the evening nodding, congratulating, smiling and offering the odd observation of my own which she acknowledged sweetly but mentally dismissed before the words had left my lips. It was her night and I was genuinely delighted for her. She'd worked hard for this accolade, maybe too hard, and I didn't doubt that she'd tackle the role with commitment and innovative brilliance.

Later, as the waiter disappeared with my empty dessert plate – which was more or less how it had arrived – she kissed me quite unexpectedly on the cheek as though her surfeit of bliss needed some form of physical expression and I happened to be the nearest thing to her. I guess it was not unlike the joyous hug I gave a bloated, reeking oaf sitting next to me when Chelsea scored in the Cup Final. Couldn't get his stink off me for a fortnight.

It started to rain soon after we left St Aubin and we cowered in the doorway of a furniture shop so trendy it appeared to stock only a single steel chair. It wasn't going to stop any time soon and Bea would be getting itchy, so I dashed off – gallantly, I thought – to get the car which was parked at least a quarter of a mile away. In perfect synch, the rain began pelting harder until it formed a single massive raindrop. I got to the car, patted my waterlogged jacket pockets, shouted, 'Fuck!' into the sky and ran back to Lisa who was dangling the key from her little finger. She studied my sodden hair, laughing with, not at me I like to think, then leaned into my chest, heedless of the monsoon soaked into my jacket. Then she kissed me full on the lips, her warm, slick tongue probing my mouth, droplets of rain diluting her saliva. I hardened instantly, something I'd considered physically impossible a couple of hours earlier. It was the first time we'd kissed in a street... probably ever. She drew back, her eyes wide and fiery, and thrust the key into my hand. 'Quick,' she said, 'we need to get home right now! Fucking run!'

I was breathless *before* I scurried away again, adrenaline propelling me towards the car in something approaching a world speed record for a man of my age, height and weight with an erection jutting into his flies. I needed to look that one up. I squelched into the driver's seat breathing hard, switched on the engine and sped past 30 in first gear. I was there in seconds. Lisa ran towards the car through the downpour, her already snug dress now a saturated second skin. Once inside, she immediately sunk her hand into my groin and began kneading me, her head nestled into my shoulder, panting like a small dog. Softly, she said, 'Darling. I was waiting there for you and I realised I've spent all evening talking about me. I'm really sorry.'

'S'all right,' I gasped magnanimously, foot to the floor. I didn't honestly give a fuck. Not then.

'No, but it's not.'

'You've had a good day. A great day. You're entitled.'

'I feel terrible. Selfish bitch.'

'Don't be silly.'

'So come on, tell me about your day. All the details. Everything.'

This time I did break the world speed record – for penile detumescence – by miles.

CHAPTER 5

THE SEX WAS perfunctory. Lisa was all nervous tension, her head exploding with ideas for the overhaul of the gallery; she needed to open the safety valve. Dispensing with the niceties, she grabbed my vaguely resuscitating penis like a relay baton before I'd properly undone my flies, and rammed it home as soon as it sprang free. She was done and dusted in a couple of minutes and just about had sufficient patience to let me finish up. She was asleep seconds later, like a…like a man. I lay there with her sweaty head on my chest, her left leg wrapped around my thighs, her breathing deep, contented. My thudding, troubled heart, beating so close to her ear would never stir her. I'd somehow managed to rekindle a small fire, but mine had been a soft, straining erection that had only just held its own. All men understand the occasional necessity of heading off imminent orgasm with a mental image of licking some stinking bloke's rancid armpit or eating a maggot and snot sandwich but tonight I'd been on the other side of that fence, battling to overcome the disappointment I knew Lisa felt, and had tried so hard to hide, as I related the miserable tale of my abortive interview with Wide Phil. The conversation in the car had then turned to my continuing lack of success in securing a job or even an interview and, inevitably, my growing defeatism and disillusionment. She didn't want to hear all that, though, did she? Not today. Not any day. Yes she did her best to proffer support and encouragement, but it was a bit like finding out you've passed an exam whilst standing next to your best friend who's fucked it up. You want to dance down the street punching the air, but instead have to suppress that instinct and offer commiserations without sounding smug (like I'd know how *that* felt). So while none of my tribulations had quite doused her fire, the sex, which earlier had had all the makings of an impromptu expression of joy, ended up feeling like a consolation prize, the cuddly toy rather than the washing machine.

A proper pity-fuck.

The following morning, we were back to our usual mute selves, steering politely around each other in expansive detours. If anything, the atmosphere had taken a distinct turn for the worse. The stark reality of our vastly differing fortunes had, I think, hit home in the post-coital light of day and Lisa clearly wasn't handling it. I felt I'd dipped another notch in her estimation and was now slipping, spluttering for air, below the water line. Lisa left earlier than usual while I walked the kids to the bus, came home and fell asleep on the sofa. Another long, empty day lay ahead and I had to get some rest in to face it.

At midday, I was woken by the telephone. It was Chaz, sounding way too chirpy. Didn't he know what time it was? 'Anything?' he said, our habitual greeting down the years.

'Nothing,' came my stock reply, except this time I meant it.

'Keep at it, mate. Something will come up.'

'Yeah, course it will,' I mumbled, studying a line of grime beneath a fingernail.

'So how about you and Lisa this Saturday? I'm gonna stop asking you in a year or five. Then you'll be sorry.'

Wrong. I'd managed to fend him off for the last few weeks but knew I'd have to yield eventually. 'I'll ask the boss. She's super-busy, though. I'll probably need to make an appointment.'

'Yeah, well, these high flyers…'

'Tell me about it.'

For want of anything else to do, I called Lisa who, of course, was too busy to come to the phone. She eventually returned my call a couple of hours later. Is four a couple? 'Oh God,' she snapped, 'bloody Denise.'

'I know, but I can't keep putting him off. I'm beginning to feel a bit guilty.'

A female voice trilled in the background. Lisa covered the phone and entered into a lengthy conversation with whoever the hell it was. 'Sorry. What?'

'I was saying we've got to set something up…'

Her mobile rang and she was gone again, lost in cheery discourse with someone about something incredibly arty and amusing. 'Sorry. It's gone mad here. What were we saying?' she said, her voice flat, officious, disinterested, the tone she reserved for telephone conversations with me.

'Let's talk about it later.'

'No, no, no. Sorry. Chaz and Denise. You want to make a date with them.'

'No, not particularly,' I snipped, 'I'm just saying it's getting a bit embarrassing...look, shall I just tell him we're busy until 2037? He'll get the message eventually.'

'No! That's just rude. You know I like Chaz. Just have to tolerate that Antipodean shrew for an evening. Maybe I'll get pissed first, or something.'

'Why don't we all see a film together? Then it's just hi, eat your Maltesers, bye.'

'Not fair on Chaz. He likes to talk.'

'Well what shall I say?'

Lisa emitted a weary sigh. 'Say we'll go. We can always concoct a lie to get out of there if it's going pear-shaped.'

I smiled. 'Nice. I can see why they've made you the boss...'

'Gotta go.'

I have an aversion to dinner parties. There's always a bit of competitive tension lurking beneath the surface. Who's doing well, who's about to go tits-up; whose marriage is solid, who's sleeping around; whose kids are genii and whose delinquents. You start out with good intentions, of course, plenty of optimistic bonhomie, superficial chatter, forced laughter, but you know it's going to turn at some point, usually when some cretin says something like, 'We could do with another Maggie Thatcher to run this bloody country,' or 'I've got nothing against blacks but...' It's downhill fast from there. The shit spills out and you're confined for the evening with smug, smiling monsters who only *look* human.

I'd been dreading this one more than most but, fortunately, Chaz's other invitees, a surgeon and his third, scandalously younger wife, had cried off at the last minute thus significantly reducing the odds of a truly appalling evening. But we were still left to negotiate a difficult few hours with Chaz and Denise. We'd known these people as a couple for years, but only Chaz and I shared any chemistry. Everything else was frozen tundra. Lisa's failsafe was in place, provided Bea remembered to call us at 9.30 citing a mystery illness. She'd been prissily reluctant to collude in this subterfuge – faking sickness in children was somehow tempting fate – but Lisa offered her an extra fiver and money talks.

Denise was a no-nonsense, no-frills kind of cook. She bucked the trend; in my experience, dinner party hosts labour under the wretched misapprehension that ownership of a Gordon Ramsay cookbook automatically confers culinary expertise, when microwaving a Cup-a-Soup is beyond their normal capabilities. But there was nothing Gordon Ramsay about Denise's presentation or ambition. Her plates were artless; no interesting sauces, no sprigs of green stuff, no attempt at decoration and, if her food gave the appearance of grim edibility, its terrifying secret was revealed as soon as it hit the palate. Perhaps this was part of her plot to poison Lisa and I was collateral damage. What the hell did she add to the lamb chops to make them so bitter (battery acid?), or to the vegetables that made them so slimy (WD40?). But we knew what to expect and had more or less mastered the art of swallowing without chewing to minimise the horror. No wonder Chaz had never filled out, the poor bastard.

Lisa and Denise seemed to be maintaining an uneasy truce. The occasional cringe or jaw-clench as one said something perceived to be offensive would have been visible only to the initiated. Meanwhile Chaz and I breezed through our usual diet of trivia – football, people we used to know, Flake v Ripple – checking on our wives from time to time to ensure their eyes were still in their sockets rather than under the other's fingernails.

Chaz and Denise's massive modern mansion was host to a self-indulgent medley of chintz – brocaded sofas, mini-chandeliers, gleaming gold door furniture, Regency wallpaper, dark tables with curved legs and carved feet. Dizzying in its garishness, it was a veritable assault on the senses. Lisa, the doyenne of all things stylish, blamed Denise for this crude mockery of taste, but I knew Chaz was at least partly responsible. His parents specialised in tacky mock-grandeur and Chaz always talked about emulating their style when he made it big. Only a few years old but fitted out like a 1970s throwback, the house was one of six within a gated development in central Richmond. Chaz *had* made it big and kept his tragic promise.

Conspicuously lacking, though, was the sound of children wreaking havoc through all this bogus splendour. The place could have done with a few chips and scuffs, though only a wrecking ball could even begin to redeem it. They'd been trying for years and eventually given up when Chaz was found to have a non-existent sperm count. 'You'd think being bald, I'd at least have the compensation of a decent ejaculate,' he once said rather too loudly in a West End Tapas bar. Denise affected a so-what approach – she could take kids or leave them – but I suspect it was only to make Chaz feel better about his perceived inadequacy.

My battle with Denise's dessert, a solid block of bitter-chocolate-flavoured cement, commenced around 9.35. Bea was late. I was going to break a tooth in a minute. Although there had been no flashpoints between Lisa and Denise, why risk it? We could leave now, no questions asked. I couldn't push this hardened turd around the plate any longer. We'd primed ourselves for an early exit and were now awaiting liberation. Lisa's left leg jolted in furious spasm under the table, her eyes urgent, pleading. Things could erupt at any minute if her irritation found verbal expression.

Denise went into the kitchen to make the coffee. The rest of us sat back, no longer under scrutiny, to allow the gruesome, leaden slop to start sowing its devilish seeds of near-fatal indigestion. Oh for that phone to ring. Fuck's sake, Bea! Denise returned with a loaded tray and started doling out cups of her legendarily turgid coffee and the grizzly biscuits she'd baked with her own dead hand. Time to take decisive action. I excused myself and headed for the downstairs toilet. Inside, I fumbled for the lock, but the key was missing. No matter; no time to lose. I dialled Lisa on my mobile and heard it trilling in her handbag in the dining room. My name would appear on her screen and I prayed she'd act unsurprised. 'Hello.'

'Hi. S'me.'

'Oh, hi.'

'I can't eat any more of that shit…'

'Kattie? Oh. What's the matter with her?'

Thank God! She was immediately onside, probably affecting a look of grave concern, accompanied, perhaps, by a fretful hand to the brow.

'She's put an axe through her head,' I said.

'Oh no.'

'She wants mummy to come home right now and pull it out.'

'Yes, of course, Bea. We'll leave right away.'

Lisa hung up, but I continued. 'And that way, you won't have to eat those hockey pucks or drink that sewage, so I might actually have saved your life…'

Which was when the toilet door opened.

'Hi.' I said through a lame smile.

'If you wanted to go, why didn't you just go?' said Chaz, horribly wounded.

'Sorry mate. Really. It's just…Lisa wanted to get away because she's got an early start tomorrow, like six o'clock, or something and…'

'Six o'clock? On a Sunday?'

'Yeah. She's working on a new exhibition or something…'

'Really,' he said in an even, disbelieving tone.

'So we didn't want to offend you and everything…so…' *And everything?* Jesus Christ. I can lie with the best of them, but not to Chaz. And he knew it.

'Ok, Mike. Don't worry. It's been nice.' He made no effort to hide his disappointment in me. Why should he?

Chaz helped Lisa into her coat as she carried on with the pretence, unaware that I'd been rumbled. I could only assume Chaz was going to mention all this to Denise later, so I don't know why one of us didn't come clean. I guess, having committed to the fiction so wholeheartedly, he wanted to preserve Lisa's dignity. He mightn't have spared me if I'd been on my own.

'Which one's not well? Kattie?' he said, a malevolent twinkle in his eye for my benefit only.

'Er, Millie…no, yes, Katia,' said Lisa, unusually flustered, trapped in the lie. 'They've *both* been ill in fact. Temperatures, wheezing, coughing, the usual. They catch stuff from each other like wild fire. Colds, flu, lice…' Shut up. Please shut up. 'Kattie's just got herself into a bit of a state, that's all. Feeling sorry for herself, little love. She'll be fine in the morning.' If only she'd quit while she was marginally ahead. 'Kids, you know what they're like.'

Oh shit.

'Not really,' said Denise bitterly. Thank God we were standing by an open door, coats on, with our car five yards away. If only I could have started the engine remotely for an even swifter getaway.

'Well done again on the new job,' said Chaz, sidestepping the rising tension. He kissed Lisa on the cheek. 'At least one of you's bringing home the bacon. You're making it too easy for this slob.'

'Cheers mate,' I said, but I wasn't offended. Chaz and I had been trading insults forever. 'Isn't it time for your annual hair wash,' I riposted, patting his barren pate. 'That lonely little fella on top looks a bit grubby.'

'Go on, fuck off home,' he said, and we both laughed a mirthless laugh.

'He knows our game,' I said as we sped away. 'Chaz. He caught me in the toilet on the phone to you.'

Lisa took a deep breath – this could go either way – then laughed her beautiful head off. 'He caught you! Jesus! And there was me prattling on about Millie's temperature – or was it Katia's? – and he said nothing. What a sweet man.'

'He's a lot of things. Sweet?'

'He didn't want to embarrass me. Bless.'

'Yeah.' I echoed, 'bless.'

It went quiet for a moment 'So? Enjoy it?'

'Not the word I'd use. She's so bloody contrary sometimes.' Lisa chuckled. 'Credit to her, though. She held that sickly grin all night. She'll have a big Aussie face-ache in the morning.'

'It's only you. She's a kitten with everyone else.'

''Cos everyone else avoids her.'

My mobile trilled. It was Bea in a panic. The idiot had fallen asleep watching Holby City, which I suppose was a viable and wholly understandable excuse. I told her not to worry, that we were on our way, and hung up.

'By the way,' I said, 'I thought no-one was supposed to know about your new job.'

'That's right. No-one knows.'

'Except Chaz.'

'What you talking about?'

'He congratulated you on the new job.'

'Did he? Oh, yeah, right. I did say something to him. In the kitchen. Yeah. He asked me about work and I think I said I was in line for CD or something. No big deal. Who's Chaz going to tell?'

'Yeah,' I muttered, having drifted off halfway through Lisa's explanation. I was already thinking about Monday and the chasm that lay before me.

I didn't like Mondays. Actually, every day was a bastard.

CHAPTER 6

BEA JOINED US when Millie and Katia were four and five respectively, and I would contend that she's made a pretty decent job of caring for them. Yes, she's a bit of a bumptious squirt who isn't over-burdened with intellect and, yes, she can be rather prim and socially awkward. And, I'll grant you, she's not a middle-aged man's fantasy – frankly anyone stumbling across Bea in a fantasy has taken a catastrophically wrong turn. I mean, you've got a clear run at it in your fantasies, haven't you? and while unwelcome images can sometimes appear unbidden, bumping into that little goblin has got to be fatal to the whole enterprise. But the kids were fond of her and she always turned up (and left) on time. No major complaints. Solid, stolid, always there. So I didn't expect her to pop her officious little head around my study door while the overcooked pasta shells were flying downstairs, to formally tender her resignation *in writing*. I pleaded with her, trying hard not to sound pathetic, but she'd made up her mind. Why? You want to know why? Me. She felt 'inhibited and undermined' when I was around. Inhibited from doing what? Grilling fish fingers and wiping the table? Getting the girls into their pyjamas? Reading them stories while they listened to Eminem through their headphones? I'd never got in her way. I was rarely even downstairs when she and the kids were clattering about in their post-school frenzy. But apparently I'd been getting involved in issues she'd have preferred to handle without interference. Example: she plonked the girls in front of a puerile cartoon one afternoon and I, apparently, suggested they watch something a bit more challenging like Countdown. Not a capital offence. And it was the only incident she could cite in her defence. I promised I'd step back and give her free rein, but her mind was made up. She agreed to see out her two week notice period – was that in writing somewhere? – to give us time to find a new nanny to whom she would happily pass on her accumulated wisdom, guile and expertise. Alternatively, she suggested with customary pomposity, it would give me the time to re-jig my own work schedule so I could do the job myself. Anyone else referring to my 'work schedule' would have done so with a degree of irony. Not Bea. Irony was not represented amongst the many colour (sic) of her personality.

Lisa sneaked in as Bea was leaving. Bea squeezed out a tight smile, said nothing and scuttled off. Lisa appeared upbeat, another fulfilling workday at the gallery under her belt, but she could tell from my face that I had had no ordinary lousy, unproductive, pointless day at home and quickly adjusted her mood to match mine. I led her into the lounge and conveyed the news about Bea, foolishly leaving nothing out, not even that my criminal meddling in her unique child-minding operation had been at the root of her discontent. As Lisa's face tensed, her succulent lips thinning like spaghetti, I started waffling, thinking out loud, alleging that Bea had ulterior motives. But Bea didn't do ulterior motives – I knew it was stupid as soon as I said it – and Lisa offered up a stern, bang-to-rights smirk. I'd fucked up again, hadn't I? We could hear Millie and Katia at each other's throats in the kitchen and more food was about to fly. In a rare show of restraint, Lisa merely huffed and shot me that arch look of hers, the 'oh, what a surprise' one, and marched out with a self-righteous gait to sort them out. It was all down to her yet again, wasn't it? I couldn't be trusted with the simplest of tasks.

Lisa had cautioned me about the impossibility of finding a decent nanny to replace Bea. But she was wrong. We couldn't even find a crap nanny. We registered with several agencies and even took to scouring newsagents' windows, but all to no avail. The more we interviewed, the more Bea acquired God-like status in contrast. Some had no people or communication skills, the rest weren't that capable. As far as I could tell, none of them liked children. I could see where this was heading. That Lisa didn't actually say 'you've got nothing else to do' was but a minor detail. It hung in the air ever more heavily and the decision was taken wordlessly.

The truth is, the kids didn't want me to look after them. Bea was easy to handle, malleable, easily manipulated, undemanding. But I was Dad, and dads like me aren't any of those things. This was a new regime, austere, strict, educational. I insisted they do their homework as soon as they got in; if they didn't have homework, they had to read a book until dinner was ready; I made them eat semi-healthy food (grilled chicken fillets with low fat oven chips qualifies); I only let them watch Newsround instead of lame cartoons, to open their minds to what was going on in the world; and when Newsround was over, they had to bathe, get into their pyjamas and read again. It wasn't intended to be an intellectual hothouse, but I was in charge now and certain standards had to be met. Finally I had a bit of focus. Instead of sitting around surfing the internet and playing my guitar all day, perhaps dropping in on Lucinda at *muffs.net* if she wasn't too busy, I had to get them ready in the morning and down tools – ahem – at 3 to go and pick them up ahead of the evening schedule. I'd occasionally stop even sooner and nip round to Sainsburys to buy them their dinner. It took planning, organisation, attention to detail; nice to be employing some of the skills I'd acquired back when I was a man with a life.

It wasn't too long before the kids started hating me.

Just because I now had something to do, didn't mean I was happy or fulfilled, not even after my duties expanded beyond child-minding to encompass full-on house-husbandry. Lisa was right – what else did I have to do? Looking after the house and the kids is not a woman's role nor a man's. It's simply a role. Never mind all that ironic tits-talk. Yes, ironic. I'm PC to my boots, thank you. But it wasn't for me. I started yearning for the endless, mindless hours in front of the computer, the fruitless conversations with slack-jawed, disinterested recruitment agents and human resources managers, the pleasant, post-masturbatory naps. Most of all, I missed my guitar. Serious strumming and singing time was being ceded to dusting the blinds and sorting out the recycling bin. With so little time to myself now, I actually used the moments between chores to focus on my search for a new job, rather than pissing the whole day away following links to their inevitable conclusion or singing Lionel Ritchie standards. The need to find something to escape the misery was becoming increasingly urgent, so leisure time was at a premium.

I rustled up a couple of interviews for wildly inappropriate jobs which naturally came to nothing, but at least made me feel like I wasn't a complete pariah. I'd allowed my technical skills to stagnate so I started researching courses to bring me up to speed. Against my essentially un-gregarious nature, I even began networking at the club before and after my weekly slaughtering of Chaz. It all counted, didn't it? You never knew who might be interested. If nothing else, I felt like I was in the game.

Yet the more I tried, the less I achieved. Being out there and testing the water only highlighted the paucity of options available. My rising enthusiasm was met by ever-higher hurdles for me to jump. At home, the strain was getting to all of us. Millie and Katia started avoided me lest I suggested they start exploring Kafka. Lisa was coming home later and later, consumed by her new role, her interest in my plight decreasing reciprocally. Conversation between us descended to the basic functional courtesies, sufficient to see us through to the end of the evening without a row. Lisa took to showering, nibbling some food and going to bed, citing fatigue, leaving me to clear up and veg out in front of the TV. At weekends, when she wasn't working, Lisa arranged outings with the kids to which I was invited but not particularly welcome. Katia and Millie had had enough of me by Friday and just wanted some fun time with Mum.

I wanted to try and find a way beyond this stodgy impasse, but didn't sense much willingness on Lisa's part to discuss anything. Whenever I raised the subject of finding a job, she threw in a few words of encouragement, a condescending tip or two, but not much else. Our relationship was trailing in a very poor third to her career and the kids. In that order. This wasn't living, simply existing. Why didn't she want to talk any more? She couldn't have been content with the way things were.

How do you rekindle the easy familiarity which was once second nature? Our marriage had become polite, practical, all warmth having hissed out between the cracks like tired air through a London Underground grille. Where once I'd have sworn at her jocularly or given her a playful shove, now I was choosing my words carefully and genuflecting every time she accorded me even the mildest hint of affection. Pitiful. We were existing along parallel planes. If we didn't talk it out soon, it would fester towards its inevitable conclusion and I for one wasn't prepared to let that happen.

Time for a plan. It wasn't that inspired, to be honest, but I had to start somewhere. A Saturday night film, then a bite at Chez Malcolm (I know), a local eaterie where we'd shared many a pleasant evening in the past. Lisa hadn't been overly keen on my proposal but, to her credit, forced a taut smile and agreed. But even with relative goodwill abounding, it was hard to inject warmth into the sturdy igloo which was now our emotional home. We held hands like nervous first-daters as we walked round to the cinema – had hers always been so cold? – and later discussed the film with a reasonable level of animation. As usual, we agreed on just about everything, but there was a kind of nodding courtesy in the air which stood in for spousal intimacy. We *got along,* no more. At dinner we chatted about the kids, people we knew, sport (she humoured me), anything benign, but ever-longer silences punctuated the conversation as we sought to avoid the hotter issues of the day. Then, after she returned from her second visit to the toilet, everything went mute and we couldn't find a way back. It fell to me to utterly dismantle what was left of the evening.

'Lisa. Love. Listen,' I alliterated, taking her chilly hand. 'I don't think I can go on with things the way they are.'

'What's that mean? Us?'

'No.' But I did. Instead, I bottled it and went off on one. 'No. This. The whole…me being at home…'

'You can't get a job…'

'I'm trying! What do you think I do all day?'

'I really don't know.'

'I'm looking after the bloody house, aren't I? I actually know what all the dishwasher settings do; I can iron skirts to within an inch of their lives; I've started making my own pizza base. And when I'm not doing all that, I'm on the phone and scouring the internet and traipsing into town to meet 21 year old recruitment consultants who have to stifle their adolescent fucking sniggers behind their hands when I walk in. There's nothing for me. What do you want me to do?'

'*I* don't want you to do anything.'

'Well that's bloody great. Thanks. Very constructive.'

'I mean, it's not about what I want. What do *you* want?'

A job? Bea? Anything. Not this.

Lisa shifted her chair closer to mine and rested her hand on my shoulder. 'Don't get all agitated, ok? but I'm going to say this. You have to get out of the house or you'll go insane. We both know that. So…we'll just have to find someone to look after the kids, ok? and you…maybe you've got to think about something away from IT.'

'A new career at forty-two? Give me a break…ow!' I'd just bitten into a lump of gristle and the upper molar responsible for the electric jolt was now throbbing. It had been aching for a while but I'd convinced myself it was just a sore gum. Pain isn't always the body's way of telling you something's wrong…was the erroneous, self-defeating maxim I lived by, particularly in the dental department.

'You all right?' said Lisa as I extricated the diamond-hard slug from my mouth.

'Tooth. It's been a bit touchy.'

'Get it seen to. Don't mess about. Gary will probably fit you in tomorrow if you call him first thing.'

'I will,' I lied. 'Definitely.' And again.

Chez Malcolm had seduced us when it opened for business, our first three or four meals there distinguished by good food and excellent service. And the thing about a favourite restaurant, particularly a local one, is that you're much more forgiving when it turns to shit. The last couple of visits had been dire, the new management having engaged a chef whose capabilities didn't stretch to a mushroom omelette, much less any of the items on the worryingly lengthy menu. Lugubrious, tardy service, a dubious wine list and new wooden chairs with no cushions only exacerbated the misery. And this place was supposed to relight our fire? What was I thinking? And now gristle.

'Sorry. Go on. You were saying…' I said, the throbbing finally beginning to subside.

'Can't remember.'

'You were talking about a career away from IT.'

'Was I? Yeah. Sorry. No, not necessarily a *career*. Just something that earns you some money and gives you back some pride. I mean look at you. You're pathetic at the moment.'

'Well thank you.'

'I just mean in the way you've allowed it to beat you down.'

'So go on, genius, what am I going to do?'

'Well – and look, don't take this the wrong way – but, you've got your licence back, so you could take up Chaz's offer to drive for his firm, or maybe go mini-cabbing…'

'Are you out of your fucking mind? Me? Is that my path to redemption, then? A fucking mini-cab? Shit.' Lisa's perfect face looked perfectly shocked. 'And can you really see me chauffeuring Chaz around for a living? He's smug enough.' I was lashing out a bit, confusing rich with smug.

Lisa shifted back in her uncomfortable chair to avoid the spittle. 'Jesus, Mike. I'm not saying for a living. Just for now, to get you up and running again. It won't stop you looking for something better or training up in something new. You could do evening classes or…I dunno…something.'

'What are you going to tell your fart-arse chums at the gallery, eh? Oh, Mike? Yah, he's working in, like, executive transport? Er, no, not luxury private jets exactly. No not yachts either. Actually, more like late night, vomit-filled mini-cabs.'

'Stop it.'

'You stop it,' I retorted, a child now.

'Ok, fine, be a househusband the rest of your life.'

The image of me in an apron for the next fifteen years was grim enough, but it was the thought of being alone in the house, hairline gone, eyes wrinkled, stomach hanging over my trousers, waiting for the dreaded moment when Lisa walked in from work, another brilliant day in her stellar career under her belt, and completely forgot who I was and why I was there. I could no longer bear the silence. I was being cut adrift from life itself and, increasingly, Lisa. The longer this professional hiatus continued, the harder it would be to build the bridge back to sanity and self-respect. But driving a cab was not a means to an end, it was the bitter end. What would constitute career progression? A bigger car? Leopard skin seat covers? A new air freshener? Forty-two (remember?), a single area of expertise that nobody wanted and a single former employer who didn't think much of me. Not promising as CVs go. Maybe all I was good for was donning a paper hat and working in a burger bar, or manning a call centre in India or even, God help me, driving a cab? I wasn't listening to Lisa, though, was I? The nature of the job mattered less than getting back in the game. There had to be something out there for me, a first step, and I needed to find it. That or die.

On the way home, Lisa stopped and took my hand and I felt a lump begin to lodge in my throat. She was slipping away, even as she stood, apparently steadfast, in my corner. She looked into my moistening eyes and stroked my hair. 'I do love you,' she said.

'Why?'

She didn't reply.

I'm not a social animal. That is, I'm not anti-social, I don't actively repel people – not intentionally, anyway – I'm just not very good in rooms full of people I don't know and/or like. We're talking most rooms. I don't possess the internal mechanisms that generate and respond to small talk. I'm not overly interested in strangers' lives – why invest time in people you'll never see again? – and always end up talking about myself because it's easier. And probably very dull. I'm shy and slightly awkward and at most parties I go one of two ways: I either sulk in the corner sparrow-sipping a single glass of wine all night or say 'fuck it,' get horribly drunk and start being obnoxious. Occasionally this will spill over into making a full-blown arse of myself. Lisa, of course, was purpose-designed for gatherings. Even if gregariousness was not already a professional requirement, her natural empathy, megawatt smile, touchy-feely body language and apparent fascination with whatever drivel is being thrown at her make her a social star. She knows exactly how to flatter, to amuse, to gently provoke; the same words coming from my mouth would simply sound sarcastic.

Like a recalcitrant horse refusing to enter its stall, I railed against Lisa's pleas to accompany her to the party being thrown to celebrate her accession to God Almighty. The new Creative Director was ready to re-launch the gallery in her sparkling image. But my stubborn protests were for show. I knew I'd have to go.

In a few short days, Lisa had transformed the interior from a stark maroon cell into a dazzling, halogen-lit, geometrically flawless white space, re-branded *Marc Rouillard* as a fiercely hip contemporary art gallery and drawn up a whole new A-list. The man behind the woman behind all this magnificence couldn't stay at home watching Dr Who in his pants, could he? What kind of message would that send out? She was not only brilliant at her job, but had also created domestic perfection – doting husband, kids, the works. She had it all. She only wanted me to put in an appearance for a couple of hours, dress smartly, do my best to be civil and disappear after the gushing speeches which were integral to these affairs. No-one would notice or care by then. She'd get a cab home later. It was a reasonable deal except for the having to go in the first place bit.

Lisa spent the morning at the gallery, came home for a shower and a ten minute power nap and set off again at three leaving me to entertain the kids for a few hours. We took a stroll round to the pottery café where they spent nearly two minutes slopping paint onto a couple of plates, for which privilege I shelled out twenty-six quid.

At around seven fifteen, the new babysitter, Sophie, arrived and I familiarised her with the finer points of sitting on a sofa watching TV for £9 an hour. Sophie was sixteen going on twenty-four. In her tight pedal pusher jeans and clingy t-shirt – which must have belonged to her four year old sister given that it ended just below her ample bosom, leaving a gaping expanse of pierced flesh below – she looked startlingly mature. She'd only have to tolerate the kids for half an hour and then make sure they were in bed by eight, duties she acknowledged with a grunt.

A stab of pain in my jaw reminded me to take the antibiotics the dentist had prescribed for me the previous day. The pain had risen to epic a couple of nights earlier and only an overdose of Ibuprofen had got me through till morning. Even then I dithered, but finally conceded that visiting the dentist was going to be less painful than anything my tooth was throwing at me. It was, as I'd suspected, a putative abscess for which he'd put me on Metronidazole and Amoxicillin in an effort to quell the infection. I needed root canal treatment in the long run but the pills would delay that particular joy for a while longer. My face had yet to develop any tell-tale Quasimodo lumps, so I'd at least look fairly normal as I cowered in the corner of the gallery nursing a drink. I downed the pills with half an eye on the gormless Sophie who lay draped across the sofa watching *Celebrity Bloopers*, then trudged upstairs to change into my suit. I realised I was feeling a little buzzy about Sophie and her tight t-shirt. It was wrong, I know, you don't have to tell me, but I had to wait a moment before zipping up my trousers, which would have been absurdly tight *without* the tumescence in my pants. I hadn't worn the black Hugo Boss – my only concession to half-decent tailoring – in a year or more, and it had clearly shrunk in the meantime. My best white shirt was snug around the collar and the buttons battled to hang onto their holes around the midriff. All that nibbling on junk – the half pack of biscuits with my tea, the peanuts, the marshmallows (fat-free, sugar-solid) – was taking its toll and not even my vigorous dusting technique could keep the chubbiness at bay. In truth, I'd become increasingly slovenly over recent weeks, leaving some of the chores for another day or just plain leaving them. Playing squash with Chaz once a week was never going to offset such a mammoth onslaught of calories. I slipped the jacket on and felt it strain around the chest and shoulders. I'd spent so long in elasticated outerwear, I'd kind of lost track of fitted garments. I rifled through my other suits for a looser alternative but everything screamed 'Oxfam-ready.'

I tip-toed downstairs mindful of the straining zips and buttons and popped my head around the door to the kitchen where the kids were munching on chocolate biscuits whilst watching *America's Next Top Model*; things were slipping on both nutritional and cultural fronts. They didn't look up as I gave them the usual lecture about behaving themselves with the babysitter. I waddled through to the back lounge to let Sophie know I was leaving and found her lying on the sofa chatting in a strange, ersatz Jamaican patois on her mobile phone. She looked up as I waved. All I could see were her outstanding breasts and firm, pubescent body. She waved listlessly back at the fat old lech gone to seed.

I parked up nearly half a mile from the gallery – it was as close as I could get – and walked the rest of the way. It was cold but I was, nevertheless, overheating in my snug attire. Sweat slalomed down my forehead, snaked between my buttocks, soaked into the abrasive cotton/Polyester mix material under my armpits, the perspiration of an unfit, overweight man about to confront his worst nightmare.

I arrived feeling dishevelled and in need of a shower. From a doorway across the street, I gazed through the floor-to-ceiling plate glass frontage, brilliantly illuminated by Lisa's state-of-the-art lighting rig. Inside, the gallery was swarming with fashionistas, mega-famous actors and celebrities, arty men with long, swept back hair wearing achingly trendy glasses and classy women poured into slinky designer dresses. My woeful inadequacy drove me back into a doorway to consider my options. Lisa wanted me there but I wanted to turn and run. Would she really notice if I didn't turn up? Stupid question. Maybe I could get away with catching her eye from the window, thus registering my presence. She was at the very epicentre of the social maelstrom, distracted by admirers and sycophants. I could leave in minutes, duty done, and later complain that she didn't have time for me, *her own husband*. The moral high ground! Ha! Would that work? No, idiot. This was Lisa. She missed nothing. So what if she didn't particularly want to talk to me and was too embarrassed to introduce the lustreless, unemployed IT nobody to anyone of note? That wouldn't get me off the hook. My presence was required for show, the supportive, loyal husband, and Lisa evidently considered me sufficiently presentable to point at from a distance, my job spec merely requiring me to throw out a responsive wave at whichever wanker was by her side. The wanker would then observe social etiquette by waving back, before forgetting I ever existed.

I was still outside, but short of getting back in the car and driving into a wall at high speed – which, even then, might not excuse me unless a doctor formally declared me dead – I was out of options. I emerged from my hidey-hole and walked funereally across the road. I was met at the door by a handsome middle-aged woman in a sharp, tailored suit holding a clipboard. I mumbled my name. Very quietly. She scanned the list. It wasn't on there. Really? Oh dear. She was most apologetic. 'Well don't worry,' I said, 'I'll just, you know, go. Lists are there for a reason.'

'You can let him in Angelina,' said Lisa, standing behind her.

I smiled. 'Hey.'

Lisa planted a showy kiss on my cheek, then whispered, 'The fuck were you doing hiding over the road?'

Told you. Misses nothing. 'Just composing myself. Like taking a penalty in a shoot-out, you need to…'

'You're sweating. Ugh.'

'Well spotted you. Can't park around here, can you? I've walked miles.'

'Miles,' she said, taking a step back, eyebrows arched, disbelieving the silly boy.

'Half a mile, whatever. It's a long way in these shoes.'

Lisa looked me up and down to check that I passed muster. 'Come in and get yourself a drink, then. I've got to do the rounds. Catch up with you in a bit.'

'Dahling, that's wonderful. Can't wait. Toodle-oo.' My sarcasm cut her to the quick. Or would have if she'd still been standing there.

I squeezed through several tight bunches of arty guests chatting artily in a variety of exotic, arty accents, until I reached an opulent looking bar at the back. Sweating profusely, I asked the barman, a tall young man with a shaven head, for a glass of white wine. He looked amused and started describing the several expensive vintages on offer but I cut him short and pointed randomly at the nearest bottle. I took my glass and slunk behind a large sculpture of a phallus doing a handstand on a blancmange. I think. The wine was dry, super-dry, turning my tongue to sandpaper. Behind me, a group of wankers was engaged in high-brow repartee, culminating in a joke, the set-up of which I found impenetrable, much less the tag. Something to do with Matisse? They exchanged wry anecdotes and bitchy inside info, slinging barbs and witticisms of such erudition, they might as well have been in Swahili. Nobody looked at me and I was happy to leave it at that. I'd shown my face, notched up some Brownie points, job done.

Half an hour and three glasses of wine later, I was beginning to feel a little queasy. Maybe this was special wine, too rich and expensive for my Plebeian digestive system. My vision was becoming a little blurry, though I couldn't mistake the ephemeral beauty of Lisa as she shimmered past a gaggle of neighing arty-farts just in front of me. She anointed them with a witty word or two in passing, their faces suggesting they'd been touched by an angel. I'd never felt less attached to Lisa than I did at that moment. Who the hell was this woman? She sidled up to me beaming a magnificent smile, a smile for everyone else's benefit, not mine. 'You ok?' she said, knowing I wasn't.

'Ish.'

'Want to meet some people?'

'Nope. I'm fine. Really.'

'Ok.'

She didn't push that very hard. Probably only had the bar staff in mind anyway. I became aware of a tall, handsome and very familiar looking man approaching us. A halo of iridescent light glowed around his form, or was that the drink getting to me? His improbably green eyes locked onto Lisa's and she conferred upon him her broadest, toothiest smile. 'The dazzling Ms Cheynie,' he smarmed, swilling his dark chocolate voice around his palate before wrapping it smoothly around Lisa's maiden name. He took her hand, leaned down from somewhere near the ceiling and kissed her cheek. His lips were a bit too damn close to hers for my liking. It was then that I realised that

Don Ellwood, actor, auteur and all-round smarty-pants, had granted us an audience. Us? I was invisible.

'Don! You old dog, you made it!'

Don raised a coy, beneficent eyebrow.

Please don't introduce me. I'm begging you. Let me just slip away.

'Oh. Sorry. Don, this is my husband...Michael?' Wasn't she sure? It was a polite introduction, no fanfare, one made of necessity because I happened to be standing there.

Don's eyes examined me with lazy disinterest. Ahh, the husband. She could do better than that, surely. A clerical error on her part, no doubt. 'Hi,' I said. 'Call me Mike.'

He had no intention of calling me anything. 'Nice to meet you,' he said with rapier disingenuousness, his eyes already straying towards Lisa's cleavage. He'd covered the whole husband thing. They launched into animated conversation, all winks and esoteric asides, his fingertips occasionally stroking her upper arm for emphasis. They leaned into each other, laughing, glorying in their cosy chemistry. She made no attempt to move out of range. *I'm standing here! I'm right fucking here! The husband!* As yet another private witticism flew above my spinning head, Don delivered an unctuous wink which said: 'I think it's time for me to take her off your hands old son.' I wasn't sure whether it was this obnoxious flirting that was making me feel so giddy, but as Don swayed in front of me, I delivered a shitload of projectile vomit all over his dandy waistcoat and bespoke silk shirt. There'd been no obvious warning it was on its way. Don stood there and took it, too shocked to take evasive action. Lisa jumped back, gasping out a muted, horrified scream. The room fell silent. I vomited again, this time on the floor, retching uncontrollably until it was all out. As I spat and coughed, a ring of disgust formed, at a safe distance, around me. People were checking their expensive shoes for splashes, tut-tutting, oh-Godding. The next few seconds were a blur as Lisa grabbed my arm and wrenched me through the appalled throng which parted like the Red Sea to allow us access to the front door. She shoved me into the street and would have been happy to abandon me right there or, better, shove me under a bus to put us all out of our misery. Her first thought, I'm sure, was to run back inside to salvage the situation, but a niggling vestige of spousal duty appeared to hold her back. Or was it was just for show? We did have quite an audience out there. She tugged me around the corner, out of sight, and unleashed the rage which, hitherto, had been kept in check. 'What the fuck?' she blurted. 'You fucking…what the fuck was that?'

I was still wobbly, knees kitten-weak, the bile rising, readying itself again. 'Shit. Ugh. Dunno. I feel awful.'

'Are you bloody pissed? Fuck. How much have you had?'

'Two…three glasses,' I said. 'That's all.'

'Jesus Christ! You've made me look like a complete…'.

'Oh…no…wait. Wait! It's the pills.'

'What?'

'For my tooth. Antibiotics. You're not supposed to drink alcohol… oh shit!'

'And you did. You absolute fucking idiot.'

Another wave of nausea threatened then passed. 'I forgot. Sorry.'

'Sorry. Is that it?'

'What else can I say?'

'I've got to go back in there.'

'Sorry.'

'I can't look anyone in the eye.'

'Tell them…tell them…I've got cancer, tell them it's the chemo.'

'Fuck it.'

'Tell them I'm dying.'

'I wish you would,' she spat, marching away.

I stood there for a moment, trembling as the wind inveigled my aching, enfeebled joints, then set off on rubber legs back towards the car. I staggered past the gallery like a vagrant who'd mislaid his trolley, and saw Lisa inside floating from group to group, a desperate smile painted on her lovely face. A few of the guests spotted me and congregated by the window. I couldn't bear to disappoint them and chucked up another load on the pavement.

I took a cab home, the only thing I did right all night.

I lay in bed in the dark waiting for the front door to open. The house finally shook at around 3am. I listened out for Lisa's footsteps on the stairs, my heart beating noisily inside my aching rib cage, but the next sound I heard was her opening the study door, then closing it. There was a struggle as she battled to open the rusting sofabed, grunting, swearing under her breath until it was done. She walked out onto the landing to gather up some sheets and pillows from the airing cupboard, returned to the study and slammed the door shut.

CHAPTER 7

AT LAST! AN interview for a job I could actually do. I'd spotted a small ad posted on an obscure web site and followed it up with my customary ho-hum lack of optimism, but they'd responded inside a week. A tiny IT support company in Crouch End was looking for someone just like me, though probably not me, and it had to be worth a punt. 'Experienced' the ad said. In the IT world, that means twenty-four. They obviously hadn't read my CV properly and were in for a shock.

A week had passed since depositing half my innards over Don and Lisa hadn't uttered a single word to me that wasn't purely functional. I couldn't blame her. In that mood, there was no point even trying to mollify her. I'd just have to let the ire subside in its own good time. I'd probably be counting liver spots by then. But maybe…maybe if I got the job, we'd have the makings of a bridge.

I donned a safe pair of M & S jeans, trainers and a nicely ironed t-shirt. The interview was with a 'young, vibrant company' after all, so 'cool' was my watchword even if 'cool' and I were barely on nodding terms. The night before, I'd locked myself in the bathroom with a bottle of light brown hair dye in an attempt to hide the grey flecks which had started to cluster around my temples. If I say so myself, I did a pretty decent job of colouring my hair, as well as my scalp, ears, a little patch of forehead, the floor and several wall tiles.

I had to get across to north London for nine, so gave myself plenty of time. Taking the car would have meant stewing in a fuggy metal box for two hours and parking closer to home than Crouch End, so public transport was my only option. I'd asked Lisa to walk the girls to the bus, her grunt signifying agreement. As I left the house, she checked me over, starting low with my too-white Dunlop Green Flash, and finishing – via my baggy-at-the-crotch jeans and yellow Fruit of the Loom tee shirt (six for £10) – at my blocky, mauve hair. I thought I detected a smile – pitying? mocking? – but maybe she would only give it full expression later when she returned to her new base in the study. She turned away, got on her haunches and started fussing around the girls. Over her shoulder, Millie shook her head wearily as she surveyed my failed attempt at 'cool'. She was thinking I looked shit.

Crouch End is a bastard to get to from anywhere – even Crouch End – much less west London. It has no station at its centre and no buses arriving from anywhere useful. West to north entails an initial journey east or south, unless I've totally misunderstood the railway map. I'd left stupidly early but arrived in N8 with only couple of minutes to spare and was still sprinting up and down Crouch End Broadway looking for Flowerpot Mews fifteen minutes after my appointment should have started. *First impressions.* Didn't *anyone* know where it was? Flustered and angry, I finally stumbled across an alleyway between a record shop and a bakery and scurried down it. No flowerpots, just a motley selection of buildings and lock-ups either converted to commercial use or simply abandoned. At the end was a battered blue door with a sign bearing the exotic legend: 'PC Repair (Crouch End) Ltd.' I pushed a button and was buzzed in, then walked up a steep, narrow staircase covered in a threadbare carpet and piled high with old phone books and unopened post. The woodchip-covered walls either side were gouged and scuff marked. I arrived at a small landing at the top and made for a wooden door partially off its hinges. I knocked gingerly and heard a male voice beckon me inside. Wading through dead motherboards, circuits, keyboards and monitors, I entered a tiny, cluttered room at the rear. A chubby young man rose to his feet and extended a hand for me to shake. It looked clammy and yellowed from cigarette smoke.

'Yoh,' said Marcus Dale without quite making eye contact. Marcus was a squat twenty-three year old man-boy with scratchy, compensatory fuzz surrounded his cherubic face. He was prematurely receding and had formed his hair into a long, straggly wattle to disguise the fact. His Goth-logo'd black tee shirt strained to contain a belly which overhung soiled khaki shorts and workmen's boots. I was massively over-dressed.

'Soooo,' he said as if scanning my CV for the first time. 'You're over-qualified, aren't you.' It was a statement.

'I don't know. Am I?'

'Well, like, basically we fix PCs for small businesses, shops, a few home users that kinda…and we also look after small networks, do a bit of anti-virus stuff, et cetera et cetera. It's mainly getting people up and running and saving on the downtime. No rocket science. Yet. But, like, you've got to start somewhere, you know? We're a young business but, you know, we're getting a foothold, looking to build.'

'Yes, absolutely,' I over-enthused as though he'd just announced his company's imminent takeover of Apple. 'Sounds like a happening business.'

A happening business? I heard it but surely I couldn't have said it.

Marcus ploughed on apparently unfazed. 'What happened at your last place, then? Says here you were working on a contract for Virgin?' He pointed at the specific fabrication on my CV which I'd typed in bold to ram it home. 'Sounds a bit high-flying for us.'

'No. Not really. Lots of us were pitching for it. It was pretty tough for us guys fighting it out for the big ticket contracts. I mean, I probably could've swung it with Richard but…I just got a bit tired of the whole rat race thing. Decided to have a little bit of (I couldn't believe I was going to say this) me-time.' Shit, I did. Dress that man in Green Flash and he turns into a twat. 'I mean, basically, I needed to re-charge my batteries. I'd been thinking about going back in at grass roots level and getting that buzz again, so…I'm a techie at heart. I like getting my hands dirty.'

'Right.' Marcus mulled that load of cobblers over as he scratched at a livid spot on his forehead. He finally looked me in the eyes for a brief moment. 'I can't say there's much buzz here, really. It's just going out and fixing stuff.'

'But that's what I mean. You know, getting someone back up and running when they've crashed – it's a good feeling.' No it wasn't. What the hell was I talking about?

'So you weren't fired.'

'Fired?' I scoffed. 'God, no way. It was just a mutual parting of the ways. I'd had enough.' I ascribe my own meaning to 'mutual' which I know not everyone shares, but I was confident in my loose interpretation because I knew Pete would back me up if it came to it.

'Ok. Well, look, I need to speak to my partner Alex?' Not a statement, this time; a question. 'He's over the road at the butcher's sorting out their cash till. Trotter got stuck in the drawer. It's not really what we do, but why not? It's all about goodwill. But we've got more work than we can handle which is why…'

'…you need an extra dude to help out. Yep. Got it. Well, I'm up for it if you are.'

'Er, well, I…ok,' he stuttered at The Dude, 'I'll call you?'

Crouch End is not short of coffee bars. I'd estimate that it has one for every three local residents, serving up coffee in variations undreamed of when the first bean was ground. With so many hip and cosy-looking places to choose from, I stumbled into a dingy hole called Arabica and ordered a skinny latte, hold the flavour. I was on a diet, which had got off to a flying start that night at the gallery.

I sat reading The Times for a while, feeling disinclined to go home any time soon. It was warm and fuggy in there and, with a soothing jazz CD playing over the speakers, I soon drifted off, waking fifteen minutes later with the kind of embarrassing start I saved for public places. I wiped the drool from the corner of my mouth and squinted into the sunlight beyond the window. It was then that I spotted a familiar-looking frontage across the Broadway, though couldn't quite think why. It took a minute. Of course! It was the grungy brasserie where my musical gifts had finally found their natural habitat. And where Lisa and I had first met.

It was still a restaurant, though now called *Jaques* rather than *Debussy's Dilemma*, an eighties name that had survived into the nineties. It hadn't even crossed my mind until now that Crouch End, and specifically that restaurant, was where I'd spent so many middling-to-pleasant evenings crooning to a near-empty room. I had to go and check it out…sorry, have a look; the interview was over. Maybe I could relate this nostalgic moment to Lisa tonight and…then I pictured her flinty eyes and thought maybe not. I dodged across the Broadway and peered through the window. It was gloomy inside, the chairs piled upside down on tables, the décor apparently unaltered since my heyday. In the window, a sign read: 'Live Music Every Thursday. This week, Gunther Hrübisch sings with his synth.' It didn't hold obvious allure, but I suddenly felt envious of Gunther, with or without his synth. He was going to be singing in here, tonight, with a captive audience of, I dunno, maybe as many as twelve, just like I used to, and a squirt of the old performing juices shot through me. Then, through the gloom, a dark haired man of medium build entered the restaurant from a door to the rear. He spotted my nose pressed to the glass and headed towards me. I waved an apologetic hand and started to leave, but he unlocked the door and popped his head round the jamb.

'Mr French?'

'No. I'm just…having a look.'

'Oh, sorry. I'm waiting for…'

'Mr. French. Yeah (comic pause) Il n'est pas arrivé pourtant.'

Have you ever said something so ineffably stupid, so utterly, painfully banal that you wished you could cut your own tongue off with a chainsaw, stick it on a skewer and barbecue it?

'What?'

'French?…joke…bad joke.' He was too distracted by Mr French's imminent arrival to be properly appalled by my cretinous remark.

'Oh. Ok.'

'Are you the owner?'

'Yeah. Kevin Ingle,' he said extending a wet hand which he dried on his apron before shaking mine. He scanned the street either side of me. Mr French was clearly spooking him out.

'Mike Kenton. I was just reminiscing. I used to play here about fifteen, twenty years ago. Guitar, vocals that sort of thing. Standards. A few originals.'

'Really.' He couldn't have sounded more disinterested.

'Yeah. Good to see you're still doing live music here. So important to keep it real,' *Oh for fuck's sake, stop it.*

'Mmm.' Kevin seemed a little nonplussed. 'It's always had a music night so I didn't want to mess with tradition when I bought it.'

'Oh, right. That's great. Excellent.'

'Yeah.' He was aching for Mr French to come and bale him out.

'I still play a bit,' I ventured.

'Oh. Good. That's good.'

I was going to have to work a bit harder here. 'Well, I dabble really. You know, kids, wife, mortgage,' I said with the dull predictability of another ageing never-was.

'Shame.'

There was a moment here. Should I seize it? 'Yeah...although... I have been thinking about getting back into gigging.'

'Yeah?' said Kevin, finally making eye contact. 'Well good luck with that. I've got to, er...you know.'

Not quite the response I was after. 'Sure. No problem. Mr French.'

'Yeah, Mr French.'

Kevin nodded, then turned to go back inside.

Come on, you oaf, say something. 'Kevin? Mr Ingle. Er...just thinking, do you...have you...?'

He turned again. 'Sorry?'

'Ok, this'll sound a bit...look...you think I could, maybe, play here one night?'

'Ooh,' inhaled Kevin like a builder about to deliver a massive estimate. 'You're a bit...you know...'

Old? Staid? As unhip as a very unhip person? 'Oh, no, I mean, I can play anything. I'm pretty capable.' Meaning what? *Ladies and gentlemen, Mike Kenton will now sing to you pretty capably.*

'Capable?'

'I had a record contract once, way back, so, you know...' This was right up there with Virgin.

'Oh yeah? Who with?'

'Small label, gone out of business now. Not because of me, I hasten to...ha ha...hasten to add...ha ha.' Was he buying this shit?

'Tell you what. Come back tonight at, say, six, and do a little audition for me. Before it gets hectic. Can't hurt can it?'

'Great!' I over-enthused. 'I'll bring down the guitar and drum machine, do a few songs from my…'.

Kevin's eyes were now elsewhere. Mr French introduced himself. He looked pretty harmless to me. Apart from the gun. Ha. They shook hands and went inside.

'So…six then?' I said, pretty capably, to the closing door.

By the time I'd completed the return trek to Chiswick on a succession of lethargic trains and buses, I only had a couple of hours left to rehearse my audition set. I tried to picture the restaurant, the kind of diner it attracted, get a feel for what would and wouldn't work there. I decided to start with *Easy Like Sunday Morning* to show off my solid MOR credentials, then bash out *Babylon* a la David Gray. Assuming, after those two, Kevin didn't eject me to finish my set for the benefit only of the toothless Big Issue guy on the Broadway, I was going to hazard one of my own compositions, *Someone Like You,* a sweet ditty with a tortured lyric, written after a teenage girlfriend dumped me for a friend of mine, though not Chaz, of course. Imagine! I didn't just want him to take me on to sing standards. I had my artistic integrity to think about.

Things weren't going well. Co-ordinating strumming and vocals ought to have been a cinch for someone with my aspirations – same as a chef needs to be able to turn the oven on and stick a chicken in – but there's a world of difference between playing for fun and being performance-tight. I needed more time, but I had to collect my mother from her house in Twickenham to come and babysit the children who were under instructions to tell Mummy, if she bothered to ask, that Daddy had a late interview. Millie, perceptively I thought, asked why I needed my guitar for an interview, but I could handle a seven year old. I was just putting it in the car to take it to the repair shop on the way, wasn't I? Millie smiled and shrugged. 'Yeah, right,' she said. I think she bought it.

I dropped my mother off outside the house, almost killing her as I sped away before she'd quite got out of the car. There goes the other hip, I thought, though, in fairness, she only limped for a couple of strides. No time to waste on that. Shepherd's Bush was my destination, barely two miles away, but the car was screaming for a change up into second gear by the time I crawled into a car park behind the decaying shopping centre on Shepherds Bush Green, long since eclipsed by the sparkling monstrosity that is the Westfield. I found a spot inside twenty minutes and ran for the station, my guitar case clattering into a couple of traffic-mired cars, various knee joints, a small, angry dog (deliberate, that) and finally the railway turnstile which clamped shut around it forcing me to yank it free with adrenaline-fuelled desperation. All in vain, of course; I arrived on the platform just in time to wave farewell to my train as it disappeared into the tunnel. I waited seventeen minutes for the next one, a train so packed, the passengers had started to melt and homogenise. I squeezed in, my guitar case quickly becoming the focus of the many commuters into whose buttocks, hips and legs it now jutted. I changed onto another train at Oxford Circus which was solid with stinking humanity by the time we arrived at Finsbury Park. Nowhere near the door, I barged my way out, colliding with a huge, shaven-headed man who muttered, 'Fucking arsehole' through a half-set of teeth. Working on the theory that he was probably carrying a weapon, I jogged towards the stairs, but could feel him looming up behind me. He accelerated and crashed into my back, forcing me to touch down on the stairs. He carried on past me, spitting, 'Look where you're going, wanker,' words which echoed off the tiled walls. I wasn't going to let that pass without comment and unleashed a stream of fierce invective as soon as he was out of earshot.

I caught the boiling W7 bus which lurched like a wounded rhino all the way to Crouch End Broadway. I jumped off and started to run, sweat stinging my eyes. It was already 6.25, so reliability was now likely to be as much of an issue as my ability to sing in tune. I slowed as I neared *Jaques* and wondered, for no good reason, whether that was Kevin's middle name. It seemed unlikely. Ten yards beyond, an oddly familiar figure lumbered out of a pub. We each caught the other's eye but I was in too much of a fluster to register this shambolic man. That was until I caught sight of his bare, chill-reddened knees and bulging

Goth tee-shirt and realised it was my inquisitor, Marcus, holding a tool bag, looking gormless.

'Hi…Marcus,' I stuttered as I moved towards him.

'Yoh, Mike. You still here?'

I assumed he meant Crouch End. 'Couldn't bear to leave. Such a happening vibe here.' Oh God. Stop it.

We fell silent, the effort of finding another strand of conversation seemingly beyond us. Until he spotted my guitar. 'You a singer then?' he said, unfurling a sly, yellow smile, as though the very idea was preposterous. This was indeed a dilemma. The truth might confer cred and clinch me that job. Or he might think I had bigger fish to fry than fixing the knackered old Amstrad in the bicycle shop.

'I…yeah, I do a bit of singing.' I went the cred route. 'Used to be in a band, actually, did quite well, had a record contract at one time. Before you were born, probably,' I added with instant regret. *I'm not only old but I'm condescending.* Here's a tip – if you're going to lie, at least ensure that some benefit accrues to you.

'Wow,' he said, happily missing the nuances. But I knew what was coming. Doctors always get asked for impromptu diagnoses at dinner parties, don't they? 'Give us a song, then.'

'What…here, in the street?'

'Yeah.'

'But, I mean, I can't really, I've got…'

'Ahh! Only kidding, mate,' he said, giving me an insight into the sparkling world wherein lay his razor-sharp sense of humour. 'Maybe in the office one day, yeah?'

'Er, yeah,' I said, genuinely surprised.

'Lucky we bumped into each other actually. Saved me a phone call. Had a natter with Alex and we'd like you on board. If you're up for it.'

What, no other applicants? 'Oh. Yeah! Definitely,' I said, inexplicably excited.

'Give me a bell tomorrow and we'll talk terms and stuff. Ideally like to get you started in a couple of days 'cos we're swamped right now. Punters will start trying to fix their own computers if we don't get to them in time, and you know where that could lead.'

'Boom, meltdown, man.' Shoot me.

He looked at me as if I was insane. And suddenly unemployable. 'Er…yeah.'

'Ok, so…I'll call you tomorrow?' I said, holding my hand to my ear in the shape of a phone in case I wasn't making myself clear.

We shook hands and Marcus wobbled away like a new-born walrus. I stood motionless for a couple of seconds, smiling inanely, then realised that another five minutes had ebbed away. 'Shit!' I muttered as I ran back towards *Jaques* and crashed through the door in a panic. The lights were on and a slim, attractive, olive-skinned waitress was pottering about preparing tables. The restaurant was now open for business. 'Hi,' I said to the girl in her regulation all black outfit. 'Is Kevin about?'

'Back there,' she said with a dismissive nod of the head.

I approached a door with a small porthole window at the top. Kevin was inside lugging a plastic tray over to a dishwasher while a man in dirty white coveralls listlessly chopped root vegetables at a metal table. I went inside and waited for Kevin to catch my eye, but he was consumed with loading crockery into the tray. 'Kevin?'

He carried on loading. 'Yeah?'

'Mike? For the audition?'

'What?' he said.

'I was here this morning. You said come along at six.'

'It's half past.'

'Yeah, I know. Terrible journey…trains. You know. Really sorry.'

'Well I haven't got time now,' he said. 'That's why I said six.'

'Couldn't you just give me five minutes?'

'Too busy. Sorry,' he said unapologetically. I blamed Mr French for all this. Kevin had been perfectly pleasant before he showed up.

He finally emptied the tray and carried it across to the other side of the kitchen where he crashed it down onto a stainless steel counter. The prospect of my new, albeit mediocre job after so long in the doldrums ought to have imbued me with sufficient pride to walk away. But I'd come here to sing. So, slipping pride into a back pocket, I unpacked my guitar and hung it around my neck. I didn't have time to fiddle about tuning up, so launched straight into *Easy Like Sunday Morning*. My throat, still cold and dry from the icy February air, rendered my voice pleasantly husky.

'*I know it sounds funny but I just can't stand the pain…*'

Kevin and the hitherto catatonic chopper looked round. The port-holed door swung violently in and cracked my shoulder, sending me shooting forward as the waitress entered behind me. My left foot squelched into a plastic container full of animal fat and my leg threatened to get away from me. I just about hauled it back and regained my balance. A little thing like an involuntary splits manoeuvre wasn't going to stop me.

'*Girl I'm leaving you tomorrow…*'

The D string was a bit out, but I was in full flow now and I had an audience listening with, I sensed, grudging admiration.

'*Seems to me girl you know I've done all I can…*'

I ploughed on, got through to the chorus, belted it out, and stopped. I'd laid myself bare and could do no more. There was pin-drop silence, genuine stupefaction painted on their faces. I waited for the applause. The waitress was the first to speak: 'Kev, can you chuck me over that J Cloth? Table seven's fucking filthy.'

Kevin did as he was bid. Chopper resumed his indolent chopping; he'd moved onto turnips. Kevin crossed to a battered fridge and took out a huge lump of cheese wrapped in Clingfilm. I eased my foot out of the fat, shook it a couple of times and started to pack up my guitar without bitterness. All performers find themselves playing to unappreciative audiences at some time or other. It happens. 'Ok, well, thanks for listening,' I said over my shoulder as I pushed through the kitchen door. I trooped through the restaurant leaving a one-footed trail of grease in my wake. The waitress, who was now scrubbing the mucky wooden surface of table seven, watched me leave, realising I'd left her another vile mess to clean up. 'See ya,' I said.

Out on Crouch End Broadway, the frigid wind was a shock to my system and I pulled my coat high around my neck and shoulders. I walked slowly away from *Jaques* towards the bus stop feeling more dejected than I'd anticipated. It was going to be a long trek home. I replayed the sorry scene in my head, but felt I'd done myself justice in pretty difficult circumstances. And stepping in the fat – I mean, come on, it *was* bloody hilarious. Maybe they had a comedy night. Then, behind me, a voice pierced the traffic as it thundered up and down the Broadway. I turned to see Kevin standing outside *Jaques*, beckoning me towards him. This was my moment to show my distaste, to demonstrate that I was the bigger man, that I didn't need him or fucking *Jaques*.

I trotted towards him like a puppy chasing a stick.

'That was actually pretty good,' he said. 'Sorry, I was…I've had a shit day…'

'Don't worry, 'I said, 'me too.' Not entirely true, but it seemed the appropriate thing to say.

'Look, tell you what. Next Thursday, come and do twenty minutes for me. I've got a headliner on but he doesn't get here till nine so I could use a support act.'

'Seriously?' Kevin nodded. 'Sure. That'll be great. That guy's going to have a tough act to follow, though.' Ha ha. How droll.

'What, Eric Trevillion?' said Kevin reverentially, as though Mr Trevillion would be deigning to pop in on his way home from supporting the Stones at Wembley. 'Don't think so.'

Nice to think that even the great Eric Trevillion was happy to play to a single figure crowd in a grotty Crouch End eaterie for twenty quid and a pudding.

'Can't pay you or anything, but I can probably rustle you up a burger or something.'

'Yeah, sure.'

'On stage at eight thirty…prompt.' Kevin launched a hitherto dormant smile.

'Eight thirty. Got it.'

My first week at PC Repair (Crouch End) Ltd was notable only for the fact that, on my second morning, I reconnected a wireless network at a local travel agency by plugging in the router. Someone had probably kicked the plug out on their way through to the grubby kitchenette, but I wasn't there to point fingers. I was hailed as a genius and lauded by every member of staff as though I had saved lives, delivered babies and solved world hunger. I adhered to the core principles of the Techies' Manual – car mechanics swear by them too – by suggesting that although I'd had to push beyond all known technological boundaries to effect the repair, it was all in a day's work. Other jobs might be more glamorous (any jobs, I would contend), but this little scenario did make my lie about deriving pleasure from getting people up and running again feel a shade less deceitful. It really was quite rewarding in a sad, parochial way, and highlighted the pathetic dependency of the western world (including Crouch End) on those bloody machines and the people who service them.

I'd managed to push Marcus up way beyond his intended salary cap, so that I was now earning nearly a quarter of my previous salary. Still, it was considerably more than I'd been on for the past few weeks. And there were significant benefits on top like doughnuts on Fridays (if Marcus left any), a coffee machine which dispensed an odious but free brew and the use of the female toilet on our floor (no females in the building; they had more sense). Lisa was fairly sanguine about my professional resurrection, but at least we were talking again, if stiltedly, self-respect having been partially restored. She even re-inhabited her side of the marital bed, although the merest accidental physical contact sent her shuffling to its outer edge. I would, of course, need to ensure that she never got to within a hundred miles of the shithole where I spent most of my working day if I wanted to avoid sabotaging all my good work.

Lisa had persuaded Bea to return to the fold now that I was out of the way, and she graciously reprised her role as tormentee-in-chief. Like Lisa, I started to time my re-entry to the house just as Bea was ready to leave. I didn't want any more trouble. I even bumped into Lisa one evening as she cowered behind her favourite tree waiting for the clock to tick round to 6.59, something which prompted an unguarded spurt of laughter until Lisa stamped it out like a lit fag.

Marcus was proving to be an undemanding boss. I think he was slightly in awe of me, his inner geek – he had 'geek' running through him like lead through a pencil – tragically impressed by my knowledge of the workings of various prehistoric machines. He would sit, mouth agape, caster sugar glistening in his beard, as I related stories of cacophonous dot matrix printers and Atari consoles as though I was the Darwin of the personal computer. I never saw Alex. He apparently worked from his van, dealing with some of the more complex computer architecture within the N8 postal district, while Marcus and I serviced the prosaic and the mundane. I'm not convinced Alex actually existed. Perhaps he was a figment of Marcus's comic-boy imagination, invented to give the impression that the company handled more glamorous work than the crud he and I were lumbered with. I was busy but not overwhelmed and as I passed *Jaques* on my way to and from various site visits, I became increasingly consumed with my impending comeback.

On the Thursday of the gig, I awoke in a sweat at four thirty. I'd been having that dream again, the one where I'm alone on stage at a packed venue, guitar over my shoulder, but without a single lyric in my head, much less a chord. As I try to ad lib, the crowd grow restless and start spitting and hurling bottles at me. It was ducking into one and cracking my skull on the headboard that woke me so irretrievably. I slipped on my dressing gown and shambled into the freezing study where I flicked on the fan heater. I sat on the sofabed and directed the hot gust between my legs, making my shins hot and itchy. My guitar sat forlornly in the corner begging for attention. I knew I ought to rehearse, but feared that doing so would only highlight my ineptitude. I'd been working on my set for days, but was still fluffing chords and forgetting the words. I could pull out, of course, citing any number of ailments, but I knew that would mean never playing to an audience again. While this may have been a relief to audiences everywhere, I couldn't let this last chance slip. I'd never forgive myself.

I hooked the guitar around my neck, shuddering as the cold, smooth wood made contact with my bare thigh. I waited for it to warm up, then began strumming, my frigid fingertips smarting as they pressed into the cold metal strings. I sang in a mousey whisper, but punctuated and syncopated as though in full performance mode. I had ten songs in my repertoire but would probably only need six which I'd select as I went along depending upon the response – if any. I began to gain a little confidence as the songs took shape, imagining myself now on the makeshift stage with the audience glancing up at me between forkfuls of faux French food. And it felt good, inspiring, terrifying. I was determined to make myself indispensable to Kevin and maybe, in time, establish myself as the go-to music guy for every third division eaterie from Hornsey to Stroud Green. Then the floodgates would surely open; I might eventually scale the heights hitherto dominated by His Eminence Eric Trevillion himself and conquer Ally Pally and Wood Green as well. Something to aspire to, no? It wasn't a career move – even I wasn't that deluded – albeit twenty-five pounds a night, once a week, represented a decent Saturday night out with the kids at Pizza Hut, to include the main course salad bar. This was about doing something for myself, rediscovering that beautiful, cherished part of my life which I had allowed to die after I met Lisa.

Not that I'm blaming her, you understand.

I'd told Marcus I'd be a bit late – it wasn't like he was keeping records – to give myself time to walk the kids to the bus, get home, have a little practise and pack up my stuff. Lisa would be long gone by then and I'd be free to leave without sneaking out, guitar case in one hand, a little holdall containing jeans, a fresh shirt and a few Boots Essentials in the other. I couldn't tell her what I was up to. We were only just re-laying the marital bricks and mortar and any inkling of this middle-aged regression to the fripperies of my musical youth would only strip away the fragile patina of recovery.

I arrived at the 'office' – if that's not too highfalutin' a term for the cluttered hovel at the top of the stairs where I wiled away the hours between thrilling call-outs – and knew I'd have to assuage Marcus's curiosity when he stopped gorging on his all day breakfast and spotted the guitar case. Fibbing was pointless, although usually my first resort. I felt reasonably secure in the notion that I'd become a key member of the company – if that's not too highfalutin' a term for the motley founder, his ephemeral partner and the crummy, Conference League business that was PC Repair (Crouch End) Ltd – so didn't feel I'd jeopardise anything by inviting Marcus along to the gig. What was the worst that could happen? He'd laugh all through *Three Times A Lady*, have a drink and spend the next couple of days with his head buried in Danish pastries trying not to catch my eye. But when I extended the invitation, he started making dithering excuses about a pre-existing social arrangement, so I knew he was lying. Marcus didn't do 'social arrangements' and if he did, I wouldn't want to meet his crew. Even the mention of the great man, Eric Trevillion, couldn't sway him. What was the world coming to?

I couldn't concentrate, of course, my head spinning with lyrics and guitar riffs. Pressure. What if I forgot a key phrase or chord progression? Or what if it was all going too perfectly? I'd only spoil it by worrying about making a catastrophic mistake and then make one, the classic self-fulfilling prophecy. And what about my inter-song patter, my hair, that old D string which might ping at any moment, the sheer folly of putting myself through this in the first place? Fortunately, concentration was not the most crucial requirement for the tasks of changing a plug fuse (the scented candle shop), wiping the dust from a monitor which had 'gone a bit dull' (Saxon Menswear) and replacing a sound card (the music shop, where I spent an extra forty-five minutes messing about with the guitars to the obvious irritation of the lank-haired staff).

I called Lisa at two and told her I'd forgotten that it was my turn to be 'on call' tonight – a novel concept I'd invented, after much deliberation, on the train that morning. Did that make me sound indispensable or tragic? A grown man who, in a former life was of respectable middle management stock, required to wait around for calls from minor local businesses in case anyone stupid enough to be working after six actually needed a computer repair which couldn't wait until morning. It was all a bit unlikely, but she didn't seem over-concerned. She, too, was on call in her own way – a pseudo-art loving American internet billionaire had flown in unexpectedly and absolutely insisted on taking her to The Royal Opera House (his own box, naturally) followed by dinner at a restaurant which charged the same for a bottle of sparkling water as the four course special at *Jaques* plus wine. Lisa left it to me to ask Bea if she wouldn't mind staying on to look after the kids, which would involve her sitting, Sphinx-like, as they commandeered the remote control and went to bed wired and much too late. Amazingly, unlike Marcus, she had no wild social arrangements lined up. Bea never went out, we were reliably informed (by Bea), as she had to study so hard. There was just no time otherwise, doubtless, she'd be out there razzle-dazzling with the other crazy nannies. It occurred to me that Bea was someone who needed a good screwing to save her from early-onset-spinsterism, but the only likely suitor would be a male version of herself. Frankly, I didn't like where this ugly thought process was leading. Anyway, time and a half was ultimately persuasive and meant I didn't have to drag my (always-available, rather offended-when-not-asked-actually) mother into the fray again.

Marcus heaved his lumpen frame off the premises at seven, leaving me alone for an hour or so nestled amongst the detritus of dismantled computer hardware, techie magazines and several days' worth of his leftovers, sweet wrappers and too-late-the-damage-is-done diet drink cans piled high on the floor and every available surface. Understandably so; the wire bin beside his desk was already solid with the previous two weeks' compacted shit. I removed my guitar from its case and ran through my song list, forgetting every third word and botching alternate chords. It augured well. In a few short minutes, I'd be standing in front of an expectant audience battling to escape this funk of incompetence and turn in a performance which might ensure their food went down their gullets rather than tossed in the direction of the hapless singer. I clanged out another hopeless riff and started visualising myself on the next bus out of Crouch End, racked with regret but utterly relieved, a warm, safe option and so much better than the prospect of the twenty minutes of humiliation which lay ahead if I went through with the gig. Eight thirty was closing in on me like a thick smog now. I could only fuck this up.

I emerged onto Crouch End Broadway, my breath clouding in front of me as it spurted from my constricted lungs. The bus stop was off to my left, *Jaques* to my right. I stood there for five minutes, occasionally lurching a step or two in one direction or the other before returning to my position in the centre of the nightmare. It was cold, yes, but I was trembling like a drowning man in an Arctic ice pool on a particularly bitter day. 'Come on. Make up your fucking mind.'

But I knew I had to face it. So I was terrible; so the audience hated me; so I'd never sing again. So what? Embarrassment, ignominy, humiliation, failure? All relative concepts. Tonight's audience would comprise only strangers and I would survive the transient hot flush of shame. They wouldn't remember me in the morning anyway; they'd be too high on Eric Trevillion. What did I have to lose?

So, bolstered by quack psychology, I marched towards *Jaques* to meet my fate.

CHAPTER 8

I LOVE FACEBOOK. There, I've said it. I'm only a recent convert, but I'd recommend it to anyone. There's nothing like finding out that the class genius ended up as a probation officer in Slough, or that the little kid you suspected of being gay is married with seven children and works in air/sea rescue. I can't get enough of the appalling grammar, the big-upping, the profiles that hint at something mysterious like a job in Bangkok with an unnamed employer. And I particularly admire those middle-aged folk foolish enough to upload current head shots. A few betray wry self-awareness with an accompanying 'what-can-you-do-we-all-get-old?' caption, but most of these pictorial treats are offered up by the nerds and no-marks, the ones who were always going to be gargoyles. They look exactly the same, only older and gargoylier, but secretly hope someone will comment on how much they've changed for the better. But – and this is where it really takes flight – it's the ones who think they look pretty darn good now, who imagine their photos are eliciting envious coos, who really make a trawl so rewarding. Like the guy who's hung onto his hair and now wears it swept back in a greased-up fuck-you-Jack quiff just to make you feel inadequate. Never mind that beneath the splendid pompadour resides a ruddy face bloated by the years, the once sharp features now pudgy and ill-defined. Personally, I'd like to see more girls (women?) offering up some present day photographic evidence, but they're usually a little too coy and clever for that. So perhaps that's why finding an obviously current photo of Faye Lester on her profile was so surprising. I remembered Faye as down to earth, humble, someone who was virtually unaware of the mesmerising effect she had on everyone who entered her orbit, so I knew she hadn't put it there to show off her still radiant beauty. Quite the opposite; she probably thought she needed to jog a few memories in case no-one could quite remember who she was. But I never forgot her, and not just because of her looks. Thoughtful, funny, bright and generous, she never fudged, never said anything that wasn't true, never left anything hanging in the air. Maybe that's why she made sure her profile was complete, photo and all. Faye knew that she was considered attractive – even if she couldn't understand what all the fuss was about – without ever abusing her gifts; she had no side, no conceit. And that was the Faye I chose to believe I was looking at now, the Faye I last saw at Brunel University twenty-one years earlier.

I know I've mentioned this before – old people repeat themselves – but I always liked Faye. No, I mean I *really* liked Faye. What I actually mean is…ok, what the hell? I *loved her.* I wrote a song for her, didn't I? And it wasn't just hopeless adolescent infatuation but proper, right where it hurts in the pit of the stomach-type love. The sort of love you never quite get over, not least because it was unrequited.

Even at eighteen, she was completely together, the antithesis of the dissolute drunkards who posed as young adults on a quest for knowledge. She seemed older and more sensible than the rest of us, without forgoing her girlishness when occasion demanded. You could have a proper chat with Faye, and a proper laugh. Of course, I mainly wanted a proper fuck with Faye – as a precursor to a serious relationship, you understand – but I wasn't alone in that ambition. To the massive disappointment of all the straight (and, I daresay, half the gay) guys at college, she settled into a relationship with an unremarkable engineering student called Ray for a couple of years, which effectively stymied every attempt I made to make her see the light. She probably knew how I felt from the start although, if she didn't, I'm pretty sure the night when, through an alcoholic haze I said, 'I really love you, Faye. And I want to stroke your breasts,' she got the message. I continued to flirt clumsily with her for all I was worth, but she batted me away with affectionate, sisterly charm. We were close, but not nearly close enough for my liking. We lost touch in the third year as our respective courses diverged and I found myself in a non-exclusive, predominantly sexual relationship with a rake-thin posh girl called Rula (which, for me, remained resolutely exclusive, albeit not for the want of trying). But at a final party to celebrate our graduation, a party at which Ray was not present and Rula was non-exclusively surgically exploring some bloke's windpipe with her tongue, I had one last go at making something happen. Uncharacteristically, Faye was drunk as opposed to her usual in-command-tipsy and, bolstered by Blue Nun courage, I extended an arm in a mock-gallant gesture and swept her onto the sticky carpet as Kool and The Gang's *Too Hot* blared from an overworked ghetto-blaster. I swirled her around in something I imagined to be ballroom fashion, then reeled her in, pressing myself into her luscious body. I was immediately betrayed by an erection which took the edge off my ham-fisted little show and forced me to move off to the side, left thigh against left thigh, so she wouldn't notice. 'Have you got a stiffy, Mikey?' she slurred. She'd rumbled me, but I took it as a one time only invitation to kiss her, so I did. And she kissed me back, her sweet alcohol breath and busy, moist tongue sending me to the very limits of consciousness. Pushing my luck and misreading the signals, I suggested we go somewhere quiet. Turned out it was a surrogate fuck, a pity-kiss. She stroked my hair, smiled and said, 'Have a great life, Mike.'

And that was the last time I saw her.

So that photo of Faye on Facebook was oft-visited during my fallow period at home and even now – especially now – as I whiled away the hours holed up in the Crouch End shitter between call-outs, I frequently clicked to her page to study her pert nose, limpid green eyes and wistful smile. My own profile bespoke my happy marriage to the wonderful Lisa, my successful career in high-end IT systems maintenance/sales and my continuing interest in music. Run that through Google Translate and you get 'tedious fucking bore'. Perhaps I should have added my hobbies and interests – cinema, sport – to highlight the sorry blandness of my existence as I waited to die. I felt uncomfortable about sending a friend request; we weren't friends any more. It would be pushy, presumptuous, voyeuristic. Maybe I should just send her a message. But what if she didn't reply or, worse, didn't remember me?

But, the day after the gig, as I sat ruminating between call-outs to fix the letter 'J' on the keyboard at the hairdressers over the road

(Mane Attraction – hair clip stuck underneath) and replace a bit of cabling at the police station in Hornsey (PC Dildo tried to fix it himself with that special non-stick Sellotape and electrocuted himself), I decided to take the plunge. With breathless trepidation, I started typing:

Hi Faye. So what have you been up to these past twenty years!

That exclamation mark had to go. In fact the whole sentence had to go.

Hi Faye! I was just having a gander around Facebook and found your profile. The years have been good to you! You look younger if anything! Unlike me!

Ok, total shit. *Total* shit. Exclamation mark overload, witless, stupid. I had to do better. I needed to calm down, be a little more business-like. She wasn't that sweet, innocent girl any more, was she? She was forty-two, a grown woman who'd lived a life, done stuff, maybe got married, had a career. I couldn't get away with tweeness or lame, mirthless quips. If she remembered me at all, I didn't want to reinforce her perception of me as a gauche little chancer.

Dear Faye. Last time I saw you was at a party at Brunel (I think). A lot of water under the bridge since then. It'd be nice to hear from you.

Oh for fuck's sake. The (*I think*) was a dead giveaway; '*water under the bridge*' beyond prosaic. Cretin.

Dear Faye. Remember me? Hope you do. You popped into my head the other day because I was singing this song at a gig and – this'll make you laugh – I remembered that I actually kind of wrote it for you and…

Are you out of your fucking mind?

I couldn't believe I was about to do this but, devoid of inspiration, I decided to ask Marcus for his input. Desperate times…'Yoh, Marcus,' I called out. He looked up from a specialist magazine for diode fanatics, the remnants of a Flake tumbling lazily through the filaments of his fuzzy, schoolboy beard. 'Say you hadn't seen someone for twenty-odd years, someone you quite liked. How would you write to them without sounding tacky or desperate?'

'Twenty years? I'd probably say something like, *remember that rattle you nicked out of my pram? I want the fucker back.*'

Marcus laughed like a bear choking on bark. 'Yeah, ok, I know you were *really* young twenty years ago. But imagine you were my age, ok? however appalling that might be. Come on, give it a shot.'

Marcus looked up ruminatively at the suspended ceiling which had more gaps than tiles and stroked his beard with a grubby, food-soiled hand. A painful minute passed. 'Ok. How about *Hi. It's been a while. Fancy getting together for a coffee?*'

Blow me if the big lump hadn't absolutely nailed it.

'Hi Bea,' I said as I floated in that evening, high on my almost instant reply from Faye Lester. The boy Marcus had a gift.

'Hello Mr Kenton,' she prissed. She wasn't wearing her glasses and her mousey hair hung loose, released from its tight bun and, for a split second, I mentally ran that age-old scene in which plain Jane shakes her head, undoes her top button and metamorphoses into a ravishing beauty. Bea didn't actually look that bad, I thought, but I was in a buoyant mood and it was as fleeting a thought as fleeting thoughts get. I'd had no sex for weeks and it was obviously making me bonkers.

'Mike, please Bea.'

'Ok,' she said knowing full well she would never utter the word 'Mike' in my presence.

'Kids ok?'

'They're fine.'

'Good. Excellent.'

Our conversation had reached the end of its natural life. Except Bea suddenly, unbelievably, said, 'Is that yours?' as she eyed the guitar case in my hand. I don't recall Bea ever proffering a remark unbidden. Bea merely responds, miserly with her monosyllables. Maybe she was now wearing contact lenses and her whole life was suddenly bathed in brilliant light, bestowing on the world a whole new Bea, a Bea endowed with colour and personality. I'd dumped the guitar off at the office after the gig in case Lisa was up when I came home, thinking I could bring it home with impunity the following night if I made it before seven. Except Bea had seen it. I had to believe she would revert to type and fail to volunteer the information to Lisa, unless Lisa came up with a question to which the specific answer was: *Mr Kenton walked in with his guitar on Friday.*

'Yeah. Just had it reconditioned.' Might as well embellish the lie I'd told Millie. The guitar thing was going to come out one way or the other so no harm in seeing what it sounded like. Not bad, actually. I climbed the first couple of stairs.

'Oh,' said Bea with an animation never previously in evidence. "Cos I've seen it in the study but I didn't realise it was yours.' Her beady eyes widened. Oh shit, surely not. 'Can you play something?'

What?! Who was this alien? No glasses, hair down, not entirely plain and apparently now inhabited by a particularly playful sprite; or maybe she'd eaten some of the kids' processed dinner and accidentally overdosed on artificial additives. 'Oh, I don't really play any more. I'm selling it, actually,' I twittered, trying to escape.

'Oh go on, Mr Kenton. Please.'

I couldn't throw her off the scent. And it was about to get worse. Millie thundered through the hallway, a flaccid polythene tube of fluorescent blackberry yogurt hanging from her teeth. 'Dad's really good on the guitar, aren't you Dad?'

'No I'm not.'

'He is Bea, he's really good. And he sings as well, don't you Dad? although his voice is a bit rubbish.'

I was desperate now. 'Actually I'm shit.'

Millie gasped with utter delight, her hand over her mouth. 'Dad! That's the 's' word! You always tell me not to say it.'

'You're seven,' I said, although I couldn't help smiling. 'Sorry, Bea, that was inappropriate. It just slipped out.'

Bea's already pallid face blanched. The 's' word had done the trick. Phew. She retreated into her shell and scurried away mumbling, 'I've got to tidy up anyway.'

I'm sure her hair was back in its bun before she reached the kitchen.

I went into the study, placed the guitar on its stand and flopped down into the chair. I woke the slumbering computer and opened up the Hotmail account I'd set up specifically to receive the yearned-for reply from Faye. I re-read it: '*Hi! So great to hear from you!*' See that? Great to hear from me. Actually, 'so' great which, I think you'll agree, is even better. But wait. There was more. '*Love to get together.*' Love to. Already using the 'L' word. Whoa there, Ms Lester! '*Give me a call.*' She wanted *me* to give *her* a call. Faye Lester! And she gave me her number!

Yes, I know, married man and everything, but this was Faye we were talking about, so I was entitled to be excited about such a positive, frothy reply. But, bottom line, it was still just a bit of harmless, innocent fun, a sating of curiosity, a chance to catch up, so why not? Convinced? Me neither.

Bea left a minute early, spooked, no doubt, by my unforgivable cuss. By the time I heard the stopwatch-timed door slam as Lisa entered five minutes later, I was in the bath marvelling at how things had taken such a distinct turn for the better. I ran through the positives as I broiled, starting with Faye, of course, who lingered in the steam longer than was probably appropriate. Then there was the job which, if unquestionably pathetic, had at least restored some structure to my life. Not forgetting my re-nascent musical career. I was going to call it a career, even if others might define it as the tragic hobby of a delusional middle-aged buffoon.

The gig had gone well, you see. I didn't go around the audience asking for feedback exactly (it had swelled to twelve by the time I finished) but three of them came up to me afterwards and said they'd enjoyed my set, while Kevin, who nodded appreciatively as I journeyed through my repertoire, asked for my number with a view to a future booking. Even El Magnifico Eric Trevillion slapped me generously on the back.

My nerves had settled as soon as I started singing, extraordinary that, given my crippling trepidation. My fingers settled on impact with the fretboard, feeling oiled, grooved; my voice emerged both solid and soulful; and my patter was chummy, larky, pitched just right for such an intimate gathering. 'Where's everyone else? Is there a train strike? Shall I wait?' staples I'd refined through years of playing to no-one.

And as others ambled in and took their seats, I was relaxed enough to greet each of them with a gentle quip. The atmosphere was warm, unthreatening, and at the end of each song I was rewarded with a decent smattering of applause. I held their attention, as far as that was possible with waiting staff flitting between tables, orders being taken and cutlery clacking on crockery. No encore, granted, but I left the 'stage,' a tiny patch of floor you'd have struggled to fit Earth, Wind & Fire's socks into, to as rousing a reception as twenty four hands can muster. A triumph? Not exactly, but far from the disaster I'd anticipated. I was back, baby, I was back.

I was sweating profusely now, salt running into my eyes as I steamed the grime and stink of the foetid 'office' out of my pores. Lisa popped her head round the bathroom door and acknowledged me with an odd half-smile before disappearing. Was that a look on her face, one I ought to have recognised? I suffered a little longer in the scummy water, then showered off and washed my hair. Lisa was undressing in the bedroom when I entered, occasion for me to marvel at her taut musculature, silken skin, needlepoint shoulder blades and swan's neck. I could only take in so much at a time; there was much, much more. 'You ok?' I ventured, wrapping my towelling robe around me.

'Fine. Just absolutely shattered.'

'You in tonight?'

'Yeah. Thank God. Just going to chill out with a glass of wine and get an early night.'

'Right.'

'How was your day?' At least she asked.

'Busy. Pretty busy.' She was already glazing over. 'Major crash to sort out at the opticians. No virus protection, idiots. It's just a simple bit of softw…'

'I'm going to take a quick shower.'

'Sure. Ok. Enjoy.'

She made to leave but stopped at the open door. 'Oh, Millie says you came in from work with your guitar? What's that about?'

The kid can forget about Christmas, little snitch. 'Did she?'

'Yeah. Why?'

'Why did she say that or…?'

'Why did you take your guitar to work?' Weary tone. Trouble looming.

'I didn't take it to work.'

'All right, if you don't want to tell me…'

We both knew Millie was scrupulously honest, while I liked a little fib now and then when it was for the greater good. Which this would have been. But I was cornered. 'I just…ok, look. Keep calm, ok? I just got an urge to do a bit of performing again. It was a nothing gig in a piddly little bistro. Twelve people in the audience, right? Nothing.'

Lisa closed the bedroom door, a sure sign that this was going to escalate. She assumed a defensive, arms-folded stance as she leaned against the wall. 'Why didn't you tell me?'

Was she upset because she would've liked to have been invited to my musical rebirth, or was it because a husband tells his wife about things like that rather than fabricating stories about being on call-out? More likely it was because it confirmed my quintessential fecklessness, my predilection for folly, my fuzzy career focus.

'Look, it was just a one-off, after work, twenty minute gig in a dump. Not a bloody career move. I just fancied it, ok?' I said, my voice swathed in self-righteous indignation. I didn't think mentioning that the dump was, in fact, the romantic little bistro where we'd met all those years ago was going to help. 'It didn't interfere with my job which, incidentally, is going very well, not that you really care, you're so wrapped up in your bloody gallery. I mean, do you give a damn that Marcus has already begun talking to me about taking some equity in the business? Huh? Do you?' Equity? Where the fuck did I dredge that one up from? I think it hit home, though.

'Why couldn't you just tell me?' Wrong again. My impending fake shareholding in PC Repairs (Crouch End) Ltd wasn't cutting the mustard.

'Why? Why? Because of this. Because we'd have had this pointless, stupid argument *before* I did the gig instead of after, so what's the difference?'

'It's the deceit, Mike. I don't care that you did the gig. That's your business. I'm your *wife* and yet you go off and…then you cover your tracks with some stupid story. God!'

'That's not why you're angry, and we both know it. But you can relax; I'm not doing any more gigs, ok?'

'I'm not saying don't, Mike. I know you used to love performing. Why shouldn't you if you want to? Just tell me stuff like that, ok? Don't sneak around and leave me to find out from the kids. It's about trust.'

'Trust, yeah, ok. Fine,' I said, sounding like one of them, only more puerile. 'Can we just forget it? It's not a big deal, is it? I don't need this, Lisa. There are more important things to worry about.' Like unsticking the letter 'V' on the keyboard in the Indian across the road in the morning. Butter sauce, I'd wager.

Lisa headed for the bathroom looking hurt and thinking, I'm pretty sure, that her husband had taken yet another misguided turn in the general direction of oblivion.

CHAPTER 9

'What the fuck do you mean?'

Marcus was clearly taken aback by my sudden vehemence. 'I'm sorry, bro',' he said, 'we just feel you're not really…right for this company.'

'What, you mean this tin pot, piece of shit little repair shop? It's not even a company. It's just you and some anonymous bloke who never does any fucking work. Who else is going to go out and do all the shit you can't be bothered getting off your fat arse to do yourself?'

I had a feeling I might be burning bridges here.

'We need someone. It's just…we feel you think it's all a bit beneath you.'

'We? Who's we?'

'Me and Alex.'

'Yeah, Alex, right. *Where's* fucking Alex? How does Alex know this is beneath me?'

'Look, you're a really great guy, Mick, but…we made a mistake. We should've brought in a young kid to train up rather than someone more…mature. You're over-qualified.'

Mick? I was Mick now? 'But I'm doing the work. With my eyes closed.'

'That's kind of the point. We need someone a bit eager who's not going to bugger off when something better comes along, someone who's going to grow with the company. I know you're looking, Mick.'

'Mike, and nothing better's going to come along.' This I knew for a fact. 'I like it here. I'm settled. And I'm not looking around, actually.' I sighed and looked right into his sad walrus eyes. 'Was it the guitar?'

'What?'

'Did you think, there's a guy who'd rather be singing for a living?'

'Due respect, Mick. You're not going to get anywhere at your age, are you?'

'Fair point. Good point,' I said, slightly hurt despite his having hit the nail so firmly on the head. Like I say, the boy had a gift. 'And exactly my point. I'm a stayer. I want to help you build this place up to be the best…' I struggled to imagine what it could possibly ever become the best at, '…computer maintenance company in the Crouch End area…and Hornsey.'

'The guitar had nothing to do with it, Mick. It's about fitting in and…you kinda don't.'

That took the shine off, I can tell you. Even the gathering excitement over my lunchtime rendezvous with Faye Lester took a hit. Ok, PC Repair (Crouch End) Ltd was a shithole, the work was dismal, Marcus was a prat and the job was utterly without prospects. But it was a job. I was earning a small wage for doing something, the one thing, at which I was actually quite good and feeling like I had at least this, if nothing else, to offer.

I think it's called self-worth and, for what it's worth, I felt very little as I checked myself over in the toilet mirror at *Jaques* where I'd arranged to meet Faye. It seemed as good a place as any for a quick catch-up over a light bite, the kind that doesn't get stuck in your teeth or slathered embarrassingly on your chin. I was early, of course, Marcus having finally plucked up the courage to sack me at around eleven, and not before I'd removed some stray bric-a-brac from the printer in the bric-a-brac shop (BricBats (sic)). My brief, fiery defence only lasted five minutes, so I now had two hours to kill, the first of which I spent walking hollow-eyed around Crouch End, a place which now felt alien and unwelcoming, like the hotel you've just checked out of. Kevin didn't mind me wasting the second hour sitting in *Jaques*; at least it looked like he had a customer. It gave me time to ponder this latest black hole and, like all matters of the universe, it left me feeling confused, hopeless and utterly faithless. And now I was about to have a clandestine meeting with a woman who still stirred feelings within me years after they should have been laid to rest. Wasn't I in enough shit? Curiosity was at the root of it, I suppose, but why expose myself to the possibility of re-igniting the flame? Mine only, of course; Faye never offered me more than gentle, platonic affection. And, hang on a minute, I loved Lisa. It was long term love, ingrained, if a little tired, a little under strain. Which made us no different to millions of other couples in twenty year relationships. Underneath remained a solid core upon which we'd built a family unit and made a life for ourselves. Maybe I just wanted to feel interesting and fresh in the eyes of somebody else rather than the aimless, fibbing, floundering nobody I felt I'd become in Lisa's.

I shivered hard, a combination of the cold – there were too few customers to justify wasting valuable resources on heating – and nerves. A droplet of mucus formed just inside my left nostril which I dabbed away with a serviette. Kevin sauntered in from the kitchen and sat at the table. 'Listen. Really liked your set the other night,' he said. 'Fancy doing another one Thursday?'

'Oh, thanks.' In other circumstances, I'd have been pleasantly surprised. 'I appreciate that, I really do, but I think I'm hanging up my guitar.'

'What? That'd be criminal, man,' he said in an accent which only now struck me as faintly Scottish.

'Well, you know, I just wanted to get back on the horse and see how it felt. Mid-life crisis sort of thing. Got it out of my system now.'

'The wife?' he said with astonishing perception.

'My wife? Hah!' I protested, like a man under a thumb. 'Not at all. It's other things, you know…like…yeah, mainly my wife.'

'You can't allow art to be strangled by people who don't appreciate it.'

She ran a bloody art gallery. She *was* art. But there was a strong argument to suggest she didn't appreciate my chosen form. 'Well, you know, it's not just…I mean, it's unsociable hours, late nights, and there's work and the kids and everything.'

'Come on, Mike. Come and do a full set for me Thursday night, forty minutes, fifty quid. I know it's not a fortune, but…you're a musician, man. Music is your mistress. You've got to follow the muse.' I waited for the next tortured aphorism. 'Anyway, Eric fucking Trevillion's let me down this week, so the evening's all yours.'

'So…wow…' I flustered, '…look at you.'

'Look at *you*.'

Faye was being polite. I did forty-two with wrinkles, greying hair, missing teeth, a paunch; Faye did it with porcelain skin, dark hair (she can't have dyed it, not Faye) and luminescent eyes that twinkled, untarnished by the years. Her smile detonated tingles in places that hadn't tingled in a while. She was leaner and taller than I remembered, although as a student she tended to slope around in trainers rather than the steepling black boots she now wore beneath a sharp grey trouser suit. My first task – and this had been worrying me for a while – was to avoid any kind of arousal when she kissed me on the cheek, a battle I'd fought and lost when we last got close. But her kiss felt strangely dry, detached, unsensual, and I survived unscathed. We settled into a couple of *Jaques's* rock-hard chairs.

'No, but you really *do* look terrific,' I said, my cheeks flushing with the banality of it all. Fill the silence. Fill it! 'So you've got some work on locally today, yeah?'

'Yeah, little project at a hotel up in Muswell Hill.'

'Interesting.' I nodded sagely.

'No it's not.'

Kevin arrived at our table, wedged into the draughty bay window area which doubled as the Thursday night stage, to save us from further vacuity. He placed two menus on the table. 'Specials today are the lamb and the cod,' he said, ever more Scottishly.

'Oh, gosh, no,' said Faye. 'I can't eat anything cooked at lunchtime. I'll just have a salad or something.'

'Salads are there,' said Kevin, pointing at the word 'Salads' on the menu, just in case.

'Give us a couple of minutes,' I said, even though I'd spent much of the previous hour learning the menu by rote.

Kevin bowed and retreated, then raised a private eyebrow. He knew this wasn't Mrs Kenton. Faye and I studied our menus with fake industry; it was easier than being the first to start the conversation proper. How, where, do you pick things up after twenty one years? Is there a protocol? This was a whole new person in front of me, someone who bore a strong resemblance to a girl I once loved but who was now a stranger. As I probably was to her. 'So…you're divorced?' I said. Cracking start. Subtle as a force nine gale. But it drew a smile.

'How'd you know that?'

Because I'd looked up her profiles on Friends Reunited and MySpace and searched Google until it ran out of information, that's how. It's all there if you scour, but it was a step away from stalking. 'Heard it from…someone at…know what? I don't know how I know.'

'Well I married a bastard.'

'Of all people. You always got everything right.'

'Not everything.'

'It wasn't Ray, was it?'

'Ray?' she spluttered. 'That loser? No!'

'See? I always told you he wasn't good enough for you.'

'Compared to the guy I ended up with…' Faye stumbled, then steadied herself, '…the guy I ended up with was more interested in his business and his cars and his stupid boy-toys than me. And he also had a bit of a penchant for screwing anything in a skirt…or trousers… in fact anything with a respiratory system.'

'Shit.'

'And it all started so well. Model husband for three years, then… don't know what happened after that. Must have been something I said.' Faye smiled, but there was pain in her eyes. She waved a dismissive hand. 'Ach, water under the bridge. Being single is so much easier.'

'Really?'

'Course. Doing what you want when you want without some… *man*…screwing everything up. Recommend it.' Faye was a little bit pricklier than I remembered. Probably with good reason.

'You've got to be lucky, haven't you?'

'Absolutely. Like you. Married…so it says on Facebook. How long?'

'Long,' I chuckled, but I wasn't interested in talking about me. 'So you're…not with anyone at the moment then?' I said, unlike a lucky man ensconced in an eighteen year relationship.

'Actually, I am. Louis, and he's just a…really, really nice, normal guy. Couple of years now.'

'Oh…because I sort of got the impression you preferred being single.'

'Depends, doesn't it? It's better than being with a bastard.'

I smiled as my heart plummeted into my shoes like a faulty lift. And I know I shouldn't have felt so deflated. I mean, what Faye was doing with her life, with Louis, shouldn't have affected me either way. Not now.

'So what about you? What have you been up to for the last twenty-one years, then?' She might have done a bit more reciprocal research.

'Me? I dunno.'

'Come on.'

'Oh it's all so…ordinary.'

'Humour me.'

'Ok, well…' My voice came out flat. I couldn't help myself. 'I've, er…well ok, so I'm married, as you know, got two smashing little girls, seven and eight, work in IT…sort of…I like sport and cinema…that's about it, really.'

'Sounds…idyllic.'

'Does it?' Oh God. I hadn't prepped for this bit at all.

'Successful marriage, kids, career. What more do you want?

'Yeah, well…everything's…you know…I'm happy.'

'That's great, Mike.'

Did I just say happy? 'Yeah. Lucky man.'

Faye smiled and started studying the specials on the blackboard. Which should have been my signal to move on. She'd read between the lines and tried to bale me out, but suddenly I was having none of it. If she and, whassisname?…Louis…had found happiness, I had to parry her, show her it didn't bother me, that I really was very bloody happy. 'Yeah, well, you know, it's a long time to be married and… course, lots of stuff happens, but it's been great and she's a fantastic girl, Lisa…that's her name, by the way, Lisa…very successful lady, much more so than me.' I laughed, meaning to sound self-deprecating but sounding like a goon.

'Listen, Mike…'

'She's just been made creative director of a big art gallery in town. Works like a demon. A demon. And doing really well, really well. Well deserved, too. Very well deserved.' This was how teachers at parents' evenings talk when praising a child they can't quite remember.

'Which gallery?' said Faye.

'Marc Rouillard. In Mayfair?'

'I know it,' said Faye. 'Very posh.'

'Well, I married way above my station. You probably expected me to do that.'

'No.'

'Me neither.'

'I'd hang onto her if I were you.'

'Yeah. Definitely. Absolutely.'

Kevin finally, mercifully, appeared to take our order. I questioned him in detail about every dish on the menu, a throat-clearing exercise saving me, if only momentarily, from blurting any more rubbish in the direction of Faye. Maybe this cheery interval would make her forget everything I'd just said. She ordered cheese salad while I, having cross-examined the poor man into oblivion, eventually plumped for the ham and cheese toasted sandwich which I figured I could eat without looking too clumsy. Kevin beat a slow retreat, looking confused, bowing obsequiously until he finally disappeared into the kitchen.

We had the place to ourselves apart from an old man in a shabby suit two tables away who sat reading something by Brecht whilst poking at a dry tuna salad. Only the gentle clack of fork on plate punctured the silence, so I launched in with something benign, that old staple: 'people we used to know.' I'm sure Faye was equally relieved to be back on safe ground. Finally, we began to relax, reminiscing, laughing and speculating about the many idiots we both wasted time with at Brunel. We moved on to films – in which I was expert, of course (it's all on the CV) – music and even politics, something we'd both had a studenty dabble at, though we only went on anti-Maggie marches if it was sunny and there were plenty of pubs along the route. Which was not to say we didn't hate her, of course.

The old warmth was now coursing through me, the attraction as strong as ever. Stronger. Unhealthily so. But I was buzzing, just like twenty year old Mikey used to, entranced by this woman he could never have. More than once I had to stop myself from squeezing her hand, settling instead for the odd matey tap on the arm. Even that sent a frisson through my fingers. Was it obvious I was feeling this way? No idea. I couldn't gauge her at all. Inscrutable Faye. She gave me nothing to go on, never did. I tried to match her airy indifference, but couldn't tear my eyes from hers, even when nibbling at my tricky little side salad (shredded, browning endive, two cherry tomatoes, slice of cucumber, river of oil). I was flirting, couldn't help it, and realised this had always been my default mode in her company. I was needy, helpless, foolish. Even now, I just wanted her to like me back the way I liked her. Half as much would do. You'd have thought twenty years, a wife, two kids and a career down the crapper might have cured me.

I'd never been unfaithful to Lisa. In fact, beyond the odd cyberspace liaison with Tyffany and her porno sisters, it'd never really entered my mind. There was a time, soon after Katia was born, when Lisa was devilishly depressed leaving me to fumble uselessly around the periphery, unable to help. I found myself getting close to a woman in the office, Martina, a thirty year old from Poland with beautiful eyes and a seductive accent. She liked me and I was flattered. But nothing happened, not even a kiss. Maybe I just enjoyed feeling desirable again, like I mattered; I knew I'd never follow it up. But this was Faye. She was of a different order altogether. Faye and I had *history*, even if we interpreted it a little differently. This was as close to unfaithful as I'd ever been, and we were only at a table in a third rate bistro eating a fourth rate lunch.

Faye left me on my own for a few minutes while she went to freshen up, a sudden loneliness that hurt and made me realise that this was going to be over soon. Then what? We'd filled in the last twenty years, however sketchily, like long lost friends do. What more was there to say? We hadn't met with a view to anything more. We both had lives to get back to. Me and Lisa, her and…who was this Louis character anyway? What did he mean to her? Was it serious? Hang on. What the hell was I thinking? He wasn't the competition. He was her boyfriend and I was married. It wasn't my place to start interrogating her about him.

'So tell me about Louis,' I said, five seconds into the resumption. Faye had emerged from the washroom, a vision as she strode through *Jaques,* but one patently with other things to do. If nothing else, this might keep her here a bit longer.

'Louis? He's a…a very sweet, generous man and…and I really like him.' Bland, non-committal; it wasn't my business. She checked her watch. 'Think we could…?'

'I'll get it,' I interrupted. Luckily, Kevin wasn't about. 'When he comes back.'

'Sorry, it's just…got to get back.'

'Yeah. Me too, me too.'

Faye stared at the table, sheepish for the first time. 'Mike, I'm so sorry. I haven't asked you anything about work.'

I waved a hand. 'Doesn't matter. Boring as hell. And you've got to go.'

'They can wait another ten minutes.'

This wasn't going to take ten seconds. Let's see. Perhaps I could tell her how, having recently left my high-end IT systems maintenance/sales job after seventeen years to seek a fresh challenge (*having hit the glass ceiling*), I joined a cutting-edge outfit which was aiming to float within five years, and I was the last piece of the jigsaw. I could even offer to show her around our hyper-modern offices one day as she was a surveyor who would appreciate that sort of thing – oh no, silly me, I'd just left them (*we weren't singing from the same hymn sheet*) to seek another fresh challenge.

Shit. Even embellished, it was a sad, sorry odyssey. And it said everything about me. I was never exotic, never special, a serial nobody. What had I ever achieved?

'Tell you what isn't boring, though,' I said, about to play my one miserable trump card, the insignificant morsel that might persuade Faye that I wasn't a complete loser. Did I say insignificant? How many men of forty-two have a singing career? Certainly not me, but it was all I had left, and it wasn't nothing, given that everything else was. Would Faye be remotely impressed? She'd probably remember me playing, unremarkably, in smoke-filled college bars and at one or two evenings-in. But if it didn't do anything for her then, why would it now? Fuck it. It was too late to go back. I had to tell her, *had to*.

'What?' she said.

'This. Where we're sitting. *The stage!*' I boomed theatrically, arms akimbo, hoping this cryptic opening would intrigue her. 'This definitely isn't boring.'

'What?'

'Well they have live music here on Thursdays…'

'Oh. Right,' she said, fumbling in her bag for her purse. I was losing her.

'So, er, guess who stormed it here last week?'

'Go on.'

'You're looking at him.' My face burned; sweat pooled above my top lip. This was unbridled, embarrassing crassness. I was truly twenty again, an immature little twerp trying to impress her with absolutely nothing.

'You're singing again then?'

'Ah-ha.'

'That's great,' she said, sounding like she couldn't have cared less.

'Well, you know. You've got to give the people what they want.'

'Absolutely.' Faye extracted her credit card but I waved it away. 'You sure?'

'My treat.' I dabbed my forehead. *Stay with it*. 'So, anyway…it was my first *live* performance in God knows how long.'

'You were quite good, if I remember.'

'Quite?'

'Yeah. You had quite a nice voice.'

'Well thanks quite a lot.'

Faye chuckled like a mother humouring her stroppy four year old son. 'Good for you, Mike. Seriously.'

'I just got the urge to get up there and do it again and it went really well, amazingly well.'

Faye tucked her credit card into a slot in her purse and looked me in the eye. Was that pity? 'It's nice to be able to do something like that when you're…you know…our age.'

And there it was. I was just a stupid old fool hanging onto something that had long since sailed. 'You don't have to be a young kid to sing, Faye. As long as there's an audience who want to listen…'

'Yeah, no, you're right. Absolutely, Mike. I didn't mean it like that.'

'You should come and see me one night.' There! Gauntlet thrown. 'I've improved since that night everyone pelted me with spit and bottles in the Three Tuns. Not much, but a bit.'

Faye smiled. 'Yeah, well maybe I will.'

Make of that 'maybe' what you will, but it had a strong whiff of finality from where I was sitting.

Outside, we exchanged hollow promises to stay in touch, swapping phone numbers like you do. It made it a notch more personal than social media messaging, but it would still take one of us to actually call the other and I couldn't see that happening. I closed the cab door behind her and watched, mesmerised, as she settled. A warm, pungent fug seeped from the window through which I kissed her cheek. Then the cab chugged away and I'm pretty sure I heard her say, 'Have a great life,' as it disappeared into the mist shrouding Crouch End Hill.

'Chazmeister! The Chazzah!? Anything?'

'Mikeyman. Mikeyyyyyy! Nothing. S'up, my son?'

Boys never grow up, in case you hadn't noticed.

'Fancy a snifter after work?' I said, my hand frozen solid to my mobile phone.

'Ooh, tricky,' he said. 'Tell you what, I can get away around seven-thirty? Too late?'

'Nah! Perfect. I've got to be in town later anyway,' I lied. 'Outside your gaff?'

Chaz was my trusted lieutenant, someone with whom I could discuss anything. I could tell him about things I couldn't tell Lisa because, well, Lisa was most of those things, and she and I were done talking. We knew where we stood, even before she learned of my latest professional calamity.

The truth was, I couldn't go home. I was feeling wobbly, my body no longer centred, like a top running out of spin. Seeing Faye had messed with my wiring. That hour or so with her wasn't nearly enough. I needed more time to look at her, hear her voice, inhale her, so that I could carry her inside me for the next twenty years. Home was the last place I wanted to be feeling like that. It represented everything that was stale and staid and it was about to become my prison once again; the same walls, the same furniture, the same hopeless tomorrow. Even the love of my children couldn't change that.

Chaz emerged from his glassy office block at seven forty-five by which time my lips were purple. I'd got there early, parked myself in Starbucks until they threw me out and waited for him in the perishing cold of Baker Street rather than sit like a lemon in reception. I always felt uncomfortable in places where I had no business. He apologised, gave me a playful hug around the waist, then hailed a cab. I began to thaw out on the way to his favourite boozer, The White Horse in Beak Street, where the small miracle of a free table in a relatively quiet corner made me think life wasn't all bad. Three pints saw us through all the usual infantile banter, before we moved on to: (Me) 'So, how's work going?'

(Him) 'Pretty good' (Translation – I'm the Managing Partner of a Magic Circle accountancy firm, raking it in. It's fucking great). 'How about you?'

(Me) 'Got fired by a twenty-three year old hippy with the brain of a mollusc.' (Translation – got fired by a twenty-three year old hippy with the brain of a mollusc).

'Shit!' said Chaz with a theatrical spit of his Green King. 'No!'

'Back to square fucking one.'

'What happened?'

'I turned forty-two and lost my job, then I lost another, same reason. That's what happened.' I took a steadying sip of alcohol. 'I can't really blame the kid. Would you want to work for your dad?'

'Jesus, mate. What you going to do?'

'Fucked if I know. I mean, that one took me God knows how long to pin down.'

'Lisa know?'

'Christ no. We're on eggshells as it is.'

We shrugged and sighed in unison. I was feeling warm now, a bit fuzzy; I'd drunk enough to numb me up for the ghastly, pride-swallowing moment that was to follow. 'Listen, mate. If you've got anything, anything at all, I'll grab it. I need to get out of the house in the morning and come home in the evening and actually do something vaguely useful in between.'

'Bloody hell, Mikey. I don't know. You didn't want to do the driving.'

I splayed my hands in bitter defeat. It was better than nothing.

'Listen. I'll talk to personnel in the morning, ok? Let's see if there's anything a bit more *you*.'

'Thanks mate,' I slurred, like a sad old drunk

CHAPTER 10

JERRY TAGGART SEEMED like an able young man and a decent enough fellow. Twenty-eight and already the head of Glaziers's IT department, responsible for over forty staff. And I think Jerry thought me a decent enough fellow as well. Or maybe that was Chaz telling him to think that. I didn't care. Jerry wanted me on board, Chaz wanted me on board and I wanted me on board, despite the slight out-of-the-frying-pan feel to the whole thing. Middle-aged, over-qualified bloke reports to young boss; it sounded familiar. But Jerry was a world away from the dishevelled pup Marcus. He was all business, a dapper, sharp young man in an expensive suit, with a geometrically perfect goatee and spiky gelled hair. He wore cuff links – always a sign of thrusting ambition – and was as far removed from the stereotypical techno-nerd as it was possible to be. There was an edge to him, allied to an odd, robotic vapidity, but we weren't here to make friends, were we?

For once, I was in the right place at the right time, Glaziers having just let go an IT systems guy who'd frozen up the firm's entire network for two days. Cost them 'millions,' apparently, so maybe they deducted a few quid from his final pay check. Jerry offered me the job after a mild grilling and I accepted on the spot without even bothering with the pretence of thinking about it. I guess you could now call me a trouble-shooter, someone whose job it was to apply first aid around the intra-office network wherever it was needed, a kind of Rolls Royce version of the 1987 Lada I'd become at PC Repair (Crouch End) Ltd. Here, I would encounter a better class of paper clip stuck under a pricier keyboard. The money was better than my previous pittance, but not sufficient to indulge in the extravagance of the Prêt smoked salmon baguette *every* day.

A Monday start was deemed appropriate as Jerry was away for the rest of the week at the firm's New York office knocking heads with his whiz-kid counterparts, so I had a few days to relax and take it all in.

Chaz took me out for lunch after the interview and insisted I'd got the job on my merits. His nepotism only stretched as far as securing the interview, he said, and I chose not to challenge that assertion, despite everything having been nailed down after forty minutes of superficial ground-covering. This was going to be a hell of a surprise for Lisa, the first really positive thing that had happened to me since leaving Edmonds & White. Not that she had any inkling of the grim depravity of my Crouch End debacle. I'd sexed it up for her on the odd occasions we talked about my career and a visit to that 'office' would only have convinced her I was spending my days in a particularly rancid squat rather than working. In stark contrast, Glaziers's IT department was the gleaming techno-spine of a Blue Chip operation. Something to crow about at last, partial redemption. Maybe we could get back on track now.

I couldn't wait to tell her.

Lisa's squeal of delight as she clamped her sinewy arms around my neck, her legs knotted at the ankles around my buttocks, was ear-shattering. You could say she was pleased. Glaziers *meant* something out there in the wider world, unlike PC Repairs (Crouch End) Ltd which meant nothing to anyone anywhere. Now she could introduce me to people as her husband again. The only surprise was that her display of jubilation came before I'd delivered the news.

'Chaz told me,' she said. 'How the hell do you think I already knew?'

'Chaz? You spoke to Chaz?'

'Yeah, of course.'

'He's *my* friend. Why's he telling *you*?'

'I've known him for twenty years. You don't own him.'

'Yeah, but why was he…?'

'Because I've roped his firm in to sponsor my next exhibition and we happened to be speaking about it this afternoon, ok? No mystery.'

'Well *he's* muscled in on *my* surprise. Little bastard.'

'Ooh, diddums.'

'I've had nothing good to tell you for months and…'

'Oh come on,' she snorted, 'it's great news whoever imparted it. He was excited about it too, couldn't keep it to himself. He loves you. I couldn't wait to get home and celebrate with you.'

And so we celebrated with a bout of sex so fierce (her, not me) I actually drew no pleasure from it. Lisa was masterful (mistressful?), dominant, riding me with a grinding abandon I found off-putting. Halfway through the pounding, Faye floated into my head and suddenly I felt calm, comforted, contented, until Lisa's teeth got hold of my right nipple and all but ripped it off.

We took the kids out to the local pasta joint and, for the first time in ages, we were a family, joshing and joking, chatting about school and the word 'shit' and how we really shouldn't say it, and where we were going on holiday and why things were particularly good at the moment. But I wasn't feeling it. The job was Chaz's nepotistic gift to me, which might have met with Lisa's approval but left me feeling empty. I hadn't merited it. And it wasn't a panacea; it didn't right all the wrongs of the last few months. The blatant superficiality of Lisa's response, the fact that my worth was measured in status and income, was depressing. What about me? Didn't I offer anything beyond my employer's name and five star location? Lisa was insatiable again later that night, bouncing up and down on me as the Carbonara sloshed about in my belly. She was less intense this time, more sensual, but I was miles away, thinking about Faye, worrying about my new job and compiling a song list for Thursday.

It felt good to have some time alone. The next few days were mine. Only a few weeks earlier, I'd dreaded getting up in the morning and making the pathetic commute across the hall to my study where I'd sit wasting the hours. And the Crouch End interlude had hardly boosted my ego. But now I had a couple of things going on in my life, things to prepare for, to look forward to. It was time to set aside my feelings about the manner in which I'd become an employee again and show everybody that I deserved to be there. But I had to get Thursday's gig out of the way first, a gig I'd resolved to make my last. It was essential that I make a go of the new job, my final chance to re-establish myself as a respectable professional. Singing a few songs in a deadbeat bistro every week was inappropriate for someone with such a serious objective. I needed to focus. Or was that Lisa talking? Either way, Lisa and I had to find a way to return to an even keel, for our sake and the kids'. This might be our last chance.

They say children pick up on the slightest tension between their parents but I have to say ours seemed to saunter on with benign indifference to the blatantly obvious. Maybe they were bottling it up. Maybe they would turn to drugs by the age of ten, become anorexic/bulimic and move into a hippy commune in Norwich – or worse, simply move to Norwich and live in a semi and make it a proper slap in the face – but there was no hint of any mental or psychological scarring. We had to make sure it stayed that way.

I wanted to go out with a bang, to leave the heaving, double figure audience at *Jaques* wanting more, to tell them they'd just witnessed my farewell concert and retire tearfully even as they implored me not to throw my gift away. Up in my study, I ran through the Lionel Ritchie canon picking out a few favourites, then delved into the David Gray and Jack Johnson archives for something less enjoyable but arguably more worthy. I assembled my eclectic song list, one I'd have been happy to listen to, much less perform. It was going to be a spectacular finale.

The extraordinary thing – and this was *really* extraordinary – was that Lisa came to the gig. The last time she'd shown anything other than complete indifference to my singing was about fifteen years earlier. Since then, she'd become obsessed with her divine raisons d'être: the pursuit of a serious career; being a serious mother; indulging in serious social climbing, this last ambition part-thwarted only by her seriously disinterested other half. A busking boyfriend was one thing – it had a quasi-bohemian whiff back then, a muted rebelliousness, which would make a hell of a good story when people asked how we met at dinner parties – but a busking *husband* was right off the scale. And, I'm ashamed to say, I simply fell into line. While she was busy insinuating herself into the upper echelons of the art world, I was worming my way up the lower rungs of the IT ladder and doing ok. Material gain and respectability seemed objectives worth striving for. Then along came the kids, the most joyous and life-changing events of my life, but accompanied by the caveat that I was now under even greater pressure to conform, to arrive at the statutory minimum middle-class station and then strive to exceed it. Singing in clubs and cafés was blatantly at odds with all of this. But this was my last gig and all of that was on hold. It was going to be a hell of a night.

Chaz, bless him, made the effort to come along too, but without Denise who was busy doing something, anything, else. Lisa sat beside him at the table furthest from the sticky patch of linoleum on which, soon enough, I'd be standing as the headline act. Yes, me. Headlining. Get in! I had my very own support act as well, though where Kevin dredged him up from – or why – was a mystery. I hated myself for wishing he'd be useless, thus making me look at least mediocre but, fuck it, I couldn't help myself. A good support act can leave the audience exhausted and disinterested in whoever follows; only occasionally will the goodwill carry over to the next act and I didn't want a battle to get the audience onside. So, luckily (and I'm not proud of myself here), Edward Nish was absolute pants. His collection of anal, lugubrious ballads would have sent Leonard Cohen running for a gun to stick in his mouth. I'm not sure if there is a singular form of the word 'applause' (applau?) but that was all he mustered. Brilliant!

It was cold and rainy outside which may have accounted for the near-full house. I'm not suggesting that *Jaques* could never be a destination venue, but with twenty-seven better restaurants within a hundred yards, all without Edward Nish dragging the atmosphere down into Dante's Inferno, I can only assume they were all full. Or maybe word had got round that some never-was was in town armed with his acoustic axe and a slate of easy-listening standards. Either way, the size of the crowd was unnerving. I was already in a state because of Lisa's royal presence, but now this unexpectedly large crowd was desperate for an improvement on the gruesome musical hors d'oeuvres. Oddly, Chaz's cheery presence only added to the tension. He'd last seen me play when we were young bucks and it was all just a laugh. We were so different now, him especially, and I was embarrassed about the middle-aged me singing cheesy songs to my middle-aged best friend.

Just after nine, twenty minutes after Edward Nish's aural assault had finally ended, Kevin sidled up to our table. I'd been sitting there, silent, trembling, hands clammy and cold while Lisa and Chaz chatted away without a care in the world. It was time. I grabbed my guitar from the seat next to me, stood up and took a steadying breath to calm the nausea bubbling in my stomach. Lisa patted my back dutifully and perhaps a little ironically. Chaz, following her lead, offered a matey slap on the rump and a high-pitched Mockney chant to the effect of 'Go on my son' which hardly befitted a man of his standing.

Jaques was buzzing, though I doubt the lively atmosphere had much to do with the imminent appearance of the headliner. Most of the punters had a few measures of alcohol inside them by now and it was Friday tomorrow. I could only bring them down, couldn't I? I weaved between the tables and took up my position behind the microphone. The place quietened. I strummed the strings to check they were in tune (having already checked them forty-eight times at the table), then launched into a funked-up version of Bill Withers's *Just The Two Of Us*. The chords sounded crisp and perfectly formed, my rhythm choppy, tight, on the money, fingers supple, working like a dream. Now if only I could squeeze a decent sound out of my narrowing throat. The moment was fast approaching but I wasn't sure I could hit the note, or any note. I played the intro again to delay it a little bit longer, drawing a few quizzical looks from the Withers cognoscenti, but not Lisa or Chaz who I could see talking at the back. The bloody intro wasn't long enough the second time round either, but I was going to have to launch in. *Here we go…here we go…*

I see the crystal raindrops fall…

It was all right, more than all right. The nerves had laced my voice with a decorative crackle.

…and the beauty of it all…

Yesss! Very nice. Very Withers.

…is when the sun comes shining through…

I was on fire! Everything was working.

I'd just needed a good start, and I got it. I was in the zone, voice spot on, accompaniment solid and secure, and soon the audience joined me in my little cocoon of perfection, absorbed, excited, eager for more; every song met with enthusiastic applause, whistles, cheers. I was too wrapped up in myself and the moment to register Lisa's response, but how could she not be lost in admiration? There he was, dull old Mike, up there wowing a roomful of strangers.

I was into my penultimate song when I made my first mistake. It was only a tiddler, virtually undetectable, but I made it just the same. I missed a chord and lost my way in the middle of one of my own songs, *It's Love, But Not As We Know It*, a fluff which coincided exactly with the moment Faye Lester walked in.

Shit, Faye! Faye, with whom, in this very bistro, I'd had a tryst three days earlier. Faye about whom I'd thought all those thoughts, felt all those feelings. Oh God. Lisa was sitting five yards away and now Faye was here, in this same fuggy room. Ok, nothing had happened, of course it hadn't, but guilt enveloped me like treacle. Faye caught my eye, smiled, then rounded a couple of tables, taking up a position by the bar just a couple of steps away from where Lisa and Chaz were, I now noticed, whispering intimately into each other's ears. I cocked up a few more chords, missed a couple more notes, but I was still running on goodwill. Feet were tapping, smiles beaming and the applause, when I finally staggered over the line with an exultant last chord, was enthusiastic. My eyes strayed as if magnetised to Faye who was clapping with gusto, a broad smile electrifying her stunning face. To her right, Lisa and Chaz were clapping too, but distractedly, focused still on their private conversation. I took a breath, composed myself and spoke into the microphone: 'Thank you. Thanks very much. Flown by, hasn't it? Just time for one more, which I'd like to dedicate to my wife Lisa who's sitting just over there. Lisa?' All eyes followed my hand gesture and turned to look at her as she continued to whisper into Chaz's ear. She suddenly realised she was the centre of attention and snapped back and away from him wearing a look only I recognised as contained fury but which, with her usual poise, she made appear coy and gracious. Faye's eyes were drawn to Lisa, before re-focusing on me. She arched an eyebrow and nodded approvingly. I had, indeed, married above my station.

'This one's called *Three Times A Lady*…thangyou.'

But even as I'd called her out, I knew it was a mistake. Lisa sat there, shiny-faced, wearing a rictus grin as the audience gushed in her direction. No more cosying up to Chaz under that kind of scrutiny. Oh how wonderful, they all thought, how romantic. The singer dedicating a song to his beloved wife. Ahh.

I switched to autopilot as my mind raced furiously. Had I done it to embarrass her out of her irritating fixation with Chaz? Was I angry with her? My last gig, the last time she'd ever hear me perform, and she couldn't be bothered to actually watch. Or maybe I was delivering a clumsy message to Faye. My marriage mattered, and she really ought to respect that, notwithstanding that she wasn't remotely interested in me. Though my mind was a mush, I sang the song perfectly, with power and sensitivity, drawing the biggest round of applause of the evening. Poor Lisa felt obliged to half-stand at the behest of the insistent crowd and acknowledge my sweet gesture. But I read that smile. I was in deep, deep shit.

I ran a gauntlet of back-slaps and congratulations to get to Faye who was still in position by the bar. I shook her hand with stiff formality – no kiss – and thanked her for coming. *What a surprise, lovely to see you, blah blah blah*, keep talking, hope Lisa will tire of burning my back with her laser stare. It was Faye, uncomfortable with the discourtesy, who forced me to turn around and introduce them. 'Lisa. Sorry. This is Faye Lester. Faye, my lovely wife Lisa.' They shook hands coolly. 'Faye and I were at uni together.'

'He's really good, isn't he? Does he serenade you at home?' said Faye. It wasn't the greatest ice-breaker I'd ever heard.

'Fortunately not,' said Lisa through a dry little laugh.

'Oh and this is my old friend Chaz from, like, when we were babies,' I said. Chaz raised himself to his full height. He might as well have stayed in his seat. He shook Faye's hand with exaggerated courtesy. 'Don't know if you two ever met at one of my glorious student gigs?'

Chaz and Faye squinted at each other shaking doubtful heads. 'I'd have remembered,' he said oleaginously.

'Me too,' said Faye studying the little man in front of her. I doubt he had much more hair at eighteen and he'd worn the same thick-framed glasses forever. He'd always looked forty-two. Surely she'd have remembered meeting a middle-aged student gnome. Truth was, he was at LSE among the bright young things while I was a lower division plodder in parochial Uxbridge. But Brunel was mine, the one place where Chaz wasn't smarter than me because I never invited him.

The conversation evaporated remarkably quickly. 'Well, lovely to meet you both,' said Faye, taking a deep, apparently regretful breath as she checked her watch. 'Got to get back. Maybe I'll bump into you backstage at the Hammersmith Apollo some time.'

Lisa and Chaz smiled vacantly, evidently keen to get back to their cosy little natter. I touched the small of Faye's back and we headed for the front door. Outside, I ushered her towards the florist's a couple of doors down where we cowered under a striped awning. Rain pelted its prickly tattoo onto the taut fabric.

'Well that was unexpected,' I said. 'Really great of you to make the effort.'

'I enjoyed it. You're actually pretty good, Mikey.'

'Yeah, well, thank you, but that's me done. Last gig. Good thing you were there to witness it. You can tell your children...'

'Shut up!'

'Really. It's over. I mean, I've got so much on at work, and...the kids and the mortgage and everything...' I was off on that one again, only it rang even hollower now.

'And everything,' she said, her voice flat, sceptical. Faye was no fool. Five minutes in her company and she could tell Lisa wasn't behind me. No doubt she'd observed Lisa's animated conversation with Chaz when, perhaps, she might have been watching her husband sing, and there'd been that sudden dismissive froideur when Faye praised my performance. Faye already knew what I only then understood: that I was packing it in because it was what Lisa expected of me. She turned and spotted a cab heading towards us and hailed it. 'There's my ride.'

'Faye. Er…listen…' I stuttered. Where was Marcus when you needed a mot juste? 'Er…yeah. So, thanks for coming.'

'You said that.'

'Wasn't sure you heard…'

'No, I heard. Look, take care Mikey,' she said as she closed the cab door behind her and chugged out of my life again.

'Thanks for making me look a complete idiot.'

The deep, deep shit I mentioned? I was now drowning in it in the car home.

'I'm sorry.'

'What the fuck?'

'I dunno. I just…it was my last gig, and we met there and…I thought it would be romantic…'

'What, in that dive? You sure?'

'Oh great.' Nice to know she, too, harboured gilded memories of our original coming together.

'I thought we met in that…oh, no, that was…ok, if you say so.'

'Why are you so angry? What's the big deal?'

'A roomful of strangers gawping at me? That's just fucking embarrassing. And it was so bloody tacky. *Three Times a* fucking *Lady*? If you had to do it, couldn't you at least have come up with a decent song?'

'Sorry, did I disturb you?' I said, staging a spirited counter-attack.

'Meaning?'

'You and Chaz. Didn't stop talking for five seconds. Did you even listen to me?'

'Oh do me a…of course I did. We both did.'

'Would've been nice if you'd at least pretended you were interested. And, you know what? It would've been even nicer if you'd said well done. Would that have killed you? You just came under sufferance, didn't you? Thanks for patronising me.'

'I'm not even going to dignify that with a…it was your last performance before the start of a new chapter in your life. That's why I came, to mark the transition. You should be thanking me.' Flinty, business-like.

'Thanking you? Thanking you?! Don't do me any bloody favours, love!'

Lisa rolled her eyes and turned to study the rain spattering the passenger window. She huddled into her coat, shaking her head, as though the whole thing was beneath her.

We were in for another lengthy silence.

CHAPTER 11

An hour seems like a lifetime when that's how long there is to go before Spy Kids 8 finally fucking finishes. A morning waiting in for the washing machine repair man – between eight and one? yeah, right – has that whipped by a couple of lifetimes. And a week is a long time in politics, apparently. But it's arguable that two days isn't a terribly long time in the context of a new job intended to see you through to retirement. Give it time; that's the old adage. And, mostly, that's pretty sensible advice. But, and you have to trust me here, two days was ample. Let me explain. Jerry, my new boss, was – and I hesitate to use the expression because base insults often betray a slack, inarticulate mind – a monumental fucking wanker. If anything, I'm being generous. This was a man so bloated on self-regard, so arrogant, so dismissively condescending that, two days in (actually, an hour in was probably enough), I knew things weren't going to get any better.

The first day in a new job is usually characterised by guarded politeness, tentative stabs at familiarisation, eagerness tempered with a desire to avoid obsequiousness. Even with Marcus, we'd observed these nervous little rituals, despite the lack of formality. And I've been on the other side as the employer, don't forget, so I know how these things work.

But Jerry didn't do first days.

I was early, keen to make a good impression. At 8.45 I knocked on Jerry's door which wrought the instantly worrying response: 'Wait!'

Fifteen minutes ticked by. I knocked again. Another curt order to wait. He knew it was me because he used the word 'Michael' after 'wait' this time. I checked the reception area for CCTV cameras which, at the time struck me as vaguely paranoic but, in hindsight, was eminently justified. At 9.32, he emerged wearing his all-business face, shook my hand with regulation firmness – he knew what a firm grip said about a man – and led me into his office. He sat behind his desk and leaned back in his leather chair. There was no chair the other side. Jerry didn't do meetings. Jerry did instructions.

'Don't knock twice, Michael. If you've knocked once, I know you're there.'

This was not promising.

'Sure,' I said, eager not to cock things up this early.

Jerry's suit was so sharp, he probably trimmed his goatee with it. His left wrist bore an ugly but expensive chronograph watch and I noticed a small silver stud glinting in his right ear. He looked at his monitor and started manoeuvring his mouse around a Glaziers liveried mat. 'So, here's what we're going to do,' he said without looking up. 'I'll give you the tour, show you your cubby-hole and then you'll get to work, which means you doing the jobs I give you. That's what I do, that's what you do. It's simple, it's efficient. As long as we understand each other, we'll get on just fine.'

I did understand him, but didn't wholly concur with his conclusion. Still, it was all about goodwill at this early stage, despite my misgivings. 'Ok. No problem.'

Jerry shot up out of his chair, strode past me in a blur of aftershave and marched out of his office. 'C'mon, let's move,' he said as if schooling a recalcitrant poodle.

Jerry had evidently spent some of his quality time immersed in the box set of *The West Wing;* he'd mastered the walk and talk, fizzing with information and detail, yet still able to hurl rebukes at any staff member who'd earned his opprobrium. We stopped occasionally to marvel at the sheer ingenuity of 'The System,' *his* system, its brilliance extolled with cloying self-congratulation. He introduced me cursorily to various members of his team (was I supposed to remember forty names?) before depositing me at a pretty young secretary's terminal which he ordered me to strip down to check out the motherboard. It felt like an IT GCSE.

In retrospect, I should have trusted the inkling I'd had about Jerry at the interview, an instinct that here was a man so up himself, so obnoxiously self-regarding, it would be impossible to tolerate him for any length of time. But he'd been faintly charming as well, and I allowed myself to believe it could work. I was desperate, after all. Only now did it occur to me that maybe he'd been on best behaviour because the Managing Partner was behind the introduction. And maybe I was only here because Chaz, whatever he'd said to the contrary, wanted it, not Jerry. So it was possible I was feeling the backlash. More likely, Jerry was just a serious prick who treated everyone like shit on a shoe.

My second morning was distinguished by Jerry's snippy instruction to pop out and buy him a coffee. Not any old coffee, mind, but one whose precise composition was already a muddle long before he'd finished reciting it. The word 'latte' was definitely in there amongst the drivel, so I plumped for one of them with non-fat milk and a chocolate topping. The first sip told him I'd messed up and he insisted I write down the re-delivered instruction with a warning to make sure I didn't cock it up again. Now, I don't want to paint a one-dimensional picture of Jerry here because that would accord him one dimension too many. He was semi-dimensional at best. Aside from his obvious technical competence and steely efficiency, I discerned not a single redeeming personal attribute. I'd worked for and alongside people with scant regard for the niceties, whose man-management skills were virtually non-existent, but always, even if a hammer drill was required, I'd eventually winkled out a scintilla of humanity which, with time and patience, might be nurtured. An excavation beneath Jerry's surface would reveal only the blackest void. I looked to my colleagues in the IT unit for some support, for any sign that they, too, were appalled by the man, but the next oldest member after me was twenty-nine. Perhaps being less old-school inured them to this posturing, macho professionalism. They found Jerry easier to tolerate or maybe take with a pinch of salt.

The work was reasonably challenging and, even after a couple of days, I'd added some new skills to my increasingly bitty CV. It got me up in the morning and procured a little respect from Lisa who was just about communicative. But the die had been cast. I knew the alternative was a return to the aimless, endless days in solitary, staring vacantly at my computer monitor, a misery compounded by Lisa's profound disgust, but even that struck me as attractive by comparison. Two days, then, is all it took for me to decide to leave. Two days. An interminably long time as a serf in Jerry's kingdom.

On my first and only Friday, Chaz popped his head round my door. I say door. More an opening in the partitioned sliver of floor space I'd been allocated, which afforded me insufficient room to reverse my chair to get my legs out from under my desk without cracking a knee on something hard. I like to think Chaz was a little shocked and possibly embarrassed by the sight of his old friend cooped up in a space which would have had the animal rights lunatics throwing petrol bombs if the same indignity were visited on a dog. If he was, though, he hid it well.

'Jerry likes you,' said Chaz, swallowing a chunk of lamb so tender, so heavenly, it merely caressed the teeth on its way through.

We were in the executive dining room. It's who you know.

'Jerry doesn't *like* anybody.'

'He thinks you're up to it, on your early showing.'

'Up to what? Fetching his newspaper? Popping his suit into the dry cleaner?'

'He is a bit of a character,' chuckled Chaz.

'No. He's a bit of a cunt.'

I don't use that word, I really don't.

'You'll get used to him,' said Chaz who was clearly finding this all highly amusing.

'You see,' I said as a hunk of meaty heaven slid, butter-like, down my gullet, 'people like Jerry simply exist. He's a fucking android, Chaz. He can't relate.'

'We like him. Not personally, obviously – that's not possible. I know he doesn't exactly exude warmth, but he does a bloody good job. The system he's built is the best there is and he maintains it brilliantly, so we never have to worry. Anyway, you don't have to like the people you work with. No-one likes me. Do I give a fuck? Do they? No, we just get on with it. As long as we're all making money.'

'I don't work with him. I work for him. That's different, isn't it?'

'Ok, but once he believes in you, once he trusts you, you'll get along fine. Honestly. Give it time.'

I shook my head. I couldn't look him in the eye: 'Chaz. Mate. Listen. This isn't going to work.'

'Course it is.'

'No. You're not listening. I'm really sorry.'

Chaz placed his knife and fork on his plate in a perfectly geometric 'V' – bloody accountants. His supercilious smirk had V for vanished. He was about to come over all portentous. 'Michael,' he said with managing partner gravity. I'd never heard him utter my full name before. What happened to Mikeyyyy!? 'I put my head on the block for you. We wouldn't normally even look at a bloke your age…'

'Well that's illegal for a start.'

'Listen!' This was a whole new tone. You think you know someone. 'I had to persuade my partners you could do this. That wasn't easy. They prefer eager, young hot-shots in that department, not middle-a…' I'd have twatted him if he'd finished that sentence. 'Look, Jerry could've brought in any number of kids instead of you. I told him to do this as a personal favour to me.'

'*You got it on your merits, Mikeyyyy.*'

'So I lied,' he said without looking remotely sheepish. 'Look, you asked me to help. I didn't come to you.'

'Fuck, Chaz. Listen to yourself.'

'And you're here now, so don't be so fucking ungrateful. Stop living in your head, Mike. You've got to look at the bigger picture.'

'Did you just say 'bigger picture?' Shit. There's no hope.'

'Pack it in, Mike. Stop being such a feckless, selfish tit. Take responsibility for once. It's not just about you. Other people are affected, I'm affected. God, no wonder Lisa's sick of you.'

There are staggered silences, there's stupefaction behind which only a yawning vacuum can exist and then there was this.

'Shit, I'm sorry Mike. Mike?'

Chaz reached across the table and touched my forearm. I was too numb to withdraw it. I stared hollow-eyed at a couple of sauce-soaked potatoes on my plate which, a minute ago, had looked irresistible.

'That was completely out of order,' said Chaz. 'And it wasn't true.'

I gulped in some air like I'd been under water for three minutes.

'Yes it fucking was.'

'She never said that.'

'Didn't she?'

'She just said, in passing, that she was worried about you, that…she wanted you to make a go of this, not mess it up, so that things would be…better for both of you.'

'She said all of that…to you?'

'At the gig. It was just, you know, old friends talking.'

'About our relationship?'

'In passing.'

'She's sick of me.'

'She. Did. Not. Say. That,' said Chaz so pointedly, the words must have speared his tongue.

'Thanks for lunch,' I said, placing my hands on the table and standing with a theatrical flourish. My kicked-back chair slid away and toppled over, clattering into the table behind me. The conversational buzz faded to nothing and all eyes focused on me. If I hadn't been feeling so utterly undermined, I might have enjoyed the attention. I strode out without looking back.

CHAPTER 12

So that was that. No option, really. Call me naïve, but I hadn't imagined that Chaz would take it so badly and genuinely thought he'd let me hang around until I found something else. But it had been a personal affront. I returned to my micro-cubicle, collected my few possessions and flounced out. If being demeaned by a twenty-eight year old tosspot with the personality of a sofa was a blow to the ego, at least I had the compensation of having embarrassed Chaz in front of his peers. Yep, my best friend, I'm talking about. These last few days, he'd revealed himself to be someone I hardly knew. It wasn't just that pear-shaped lunch that changed a perception gleaned over thirty-five years. What about that little wretch virtually blanking me as I performed my final gig so he could spend the evening with his tongue down my wife's ear? And his apparent largesse in helping me secure the job at Glaziers was merely the action of a despotic puppeteer flexing his muscles to belittle me and impress Lisa. Little man finally getting one over the guy who always got the girl.

Lisa scorned the suggestion that something was going on between her and Chaz with a venom more poisonous than any she'd ever sunk into me before. How dare I? They were friends and potential commercial partners, no more. That must be how she knew about my walk-out before I had the chance to tell her myself, the news having been delivered over the 'business' hotline between wife and ex-best friend. Who rang whom? And what business did Chaz have mentioning it to her? We argued briefly and fiercely before Lisa stomped up the stairs and locked herself in the bathroom, though not before delivering a volley of abuse from the landing so profane, even Millie was taken aback.

Methinks she did protest too much. Ludicrous as it might seem to any right-thinking person, I couldn't help but be convinced that my beautiful, intelligent and highly desirable wife was, indeed, engaged in some sort of relationship with a bald midget with a face like Munsch's Scream on a particularly stressful day. The evidence was inescapably credible. Him: fabulously wealthy and about to grace Lisa's beloved gallery with major financial patronage; respected, serious, top of his profession; indisputably canoodling with her at the gig; married to a harridan; knew Lisa was sick of me. Her: sick of me; easily seduced by anyone of status, especially if he was prepared to invest in the real love of her life. And, there was something else, something that had been nagging at me for a while: he knew about Lisa's new job when she'd told me it was a secret. Oh, God. How hadn't I *seen* it?

But how could she? I mean, fancy him, sleep with him? Seriously. Ok, it's superficial in the extreme to focus on the man's physical inadequacies (I used to tell him he was small but strong, slim but sinewy – he could forget all that consolatory bullshit now), but come on. With him? Even with all those fringe benefits. In fact, how could anyone, even Denise, desperate spinster though she undoubtedly was when he swept her off her feet (as if *he* could lift *her* – ha!). Look, I have nothing against small people – I used to be one myself – but here was a man in whom his maker had lost interest or simply run out of components. I'm not a man's man, never have been, but I'm man enough to assess another's looks objectively and without a hint of homoeroticism. If you're good looking, I'll say so. Brad Pitt? Beautiful. See? Not Chaz, though, a seriously unattractive human being. Imagining any man in bed with Lisa would make me vomit. But Chaz? That was going to take my intestines with it.

We both knew it was time for me to leave. It was just a question of the mechanics. Our marriage had reached rock bottom and carried on plummeting through the crust towards the fiery inner core. I was at home all day again with nothing to do and even less to hope for and I was doing nobody any good. If they'd been blithely oblivious before, the kids couldn't help but notice the heightened tension, the frequent periods of non-communication, the frosty courtesies just sufficient to get us through another day. Millie's swearing was out of control and her behaviour, at school and at home, was a cause for concern.

Meanwhile, Katia had withdrawn into herself. An independent and insular child at the best of times, it didn't take much for her to become fully self-absorbed once her parents could no longer be trusted to act like adults and take proper care of her.

The one thing about which we remained civilised was my impending departure and its attendant terms and conditions. We had to be practical, sensible, non-contentious. The joint account would be maintained; I would redouble my efforts to find another job; I'd look after the kids most weekends and see them as often as possible during the week; we were not going to file for divorce any time soon, if at all. This was a cooling off period, a chance for us to reflect on what we wanted to do with the next thirty years of our lives. Nothing rash, nothing irreversible.

The girls reacted to the announcement much as expected. Millie dissolved into tears and sobbed inconsolably throughout several conciliatory visits to her room. She was eventually persuaded that it was all going to be fine and that Daddy would be around lots, and would drop everything, even the football on TV, and come straight over whenever she wanted him to. Katia was stoical, reasoning that, however sad, it might be better for everyone if I left given how bad things had been recently. Later, as I tried to get comfortable on the sofabed in the study, I heard her sobbing in her room. I went in and sat on her bed. 'Don't cry, lovely. We'll be fine,' I said, stroking her damp forehead.

'Yeah,' she said, wiping a lump of snot from her nose with her pyjama sleeve, 'but how am I going to get to my skating lesson now if you're not here?'

Ever the pragmatist.

'I'll still take you, Kattie. And I'll see you every Saturday and we'll spend lots of time together.'

'Really? *Every* Saturday?'

'Course. I'll always be your Dad, won't I?'

'Yeah. I suppose so.'

I searched the internet and spoke to various letting agents who, unsurprisingly (and I hesitate to stereotype here), were as thick and unhelpful as most of the recruitment agents on whom I'd wasted so many man-hours. I was just another bloke looking for digs, another boring client, another data entry. It was proving surprisingly difficult to find a suitable two bed flat in a decent location close to home at the right rent. Lisa was effectively paying for everything now, so I was on a budget. Most of the reasonably priced flats around Chiswick were dumps, more suited to impecunious students prepared to share a toilet with fourteen others and steal each other's cheese from the fridge. Been there, done that. At nineteen, sleeping on a spring-free sofa in a dingy Uxbridge basement, surviving on baked beans, eggs and Rowntrees Fruit Pastilles was a bit of a lark. It seemed a less attractive proposition now having got used to my comfortable four-bedder in Chiswick. I needed somewhere the kids could come and stay without catching fungal diseases from the walls or dying from hypothermia. If staying with Dad was a hateful experience, we'd grow even further apart.

Eventually, I found a tiny, utilitarian apartment in a dismal, pre-Brutalist 30's-built block overlooking the Hanger Lane Gyratory System. Do you know it? It's quite the beauty spot. From my living room window, I could see the roundabout with its gloomy, post-war tube station at the centre and two of the world's busiest, slowest arterial roads converging like viscous slime around it, roads clogged with traffic from morning till night, then through the night and into the next morning; its legacy, a pall of choking carbon dioxide so pungent, so dense, you wouldn't be able to see a health warning at three yards much less be saved by it. Welcome to global warming's epicentre, its spiritual home. Dotted around the roundabout beneath the grubby flats, as moribund a selection of shops and restaurants as you could hope to find anywhere in the western world. I couldn't imagine anyone – other than the locals whose lungs and senses were beyond redemption – bothering to stop off and spend money in one of them. Better to drive 30 miles up the M40 in the wrong direction and find a service station.

My flat, with its rusting metal window frames and drab magnolia woodchip walls, was perched above the April Moon Chinese restaurant. The smell of Soy sauce and cheap cooked meat was organically ingrained into the plaster, but the place, if damp, was basically clean, practical and not far from home. And, if the call ever came, I could commute to and from a central London office in minutes.

I moved out one Thursday morning while the kids were at school. I don't know how to say goodbye at the best of times and walking out of the door as my children waved me off would have left me in a wretched heap. I piled as much of my rubbish into the Honda Civic – so grudgingly donated by Edwards & White – as was legal and set off, my throat swollen shut as I fought back the tears. I eventually drew up outside April Moon and sat in the car for a moment staring up at the soulless red brick building that was to become my new home. It was then that I lost all control. I cried, wailed and railed at the ineffable sadness of it all. The end of an era. I was no longer Dad, no longer a husband. I now had a new, indeterminate status, at best, a guest in my own home. And as for me and Lisa, who was I kidding?

It was over.

My first visitor was – and I was as surprised as anyone – my good old mate Chaz. He'd heard about my leaving, funnily enough, and couldn't rush round fast enough to give me a bit of company on what was going to be my first difficult night alone. Wasn't that what friends were for? Actually, they were for not shagging your wife. I didn't want to let him in, of course, as much because of his perceived culpability in all of this as my shame at being reduced to living in a place one step up from a cardboard box under the Hammersmith flyover. But I relented, grudgingly, after he pleaded with me not to let thirty-odd years of friendship go by the wayside. At least I should hear what he had to say for himself. He entered my joyless abode and perched himself on the plastic crate I'd stolen from Katia's room having first emptied out a plethora of deformed, abandoned dolls and arranged them on her shelves. I leaned against a wobbly old MFI table not designed for the purpose. We studied each other like two men who'd just been introduced after a lifetime on opposite sides of the Iron Curtain.

After a few seconds of cringing awkwardness, he launched into an apology for his behaviour, his lack of sympathy, empathy and understanding, his failure to do the right thing by me. He should have listened when I told him how unhappy I was at Glaziers rather than taken it as a personal and professional slight. It sounded rehearsed but undoubtedly heartfelt. And then he moved on to the far touchier subject of Lisa, admitting they'd become closer because of Glaziers's sponsorship of the gallery, but insisting nothing was going on between them; the very thought made him sick. Sick? He was too ugly and she too beautiful for him to have the gall to even fantasise about it. But, again, he sounded genuine. I had to believe him, needed to.

So what could I say? Maybe I should have sought forgiveness for being so ungrateful, so impatient, so puerile, but I wasn't in the mood. I was too raw, full to the brim with self-pity, and didn't want him there whatever the truth. Marooned in my emotional fug, I could see no crossable bridge, no reconciliation. I thanked him for coming, but in a formal, distant voice I hardly recognised and, for the first time, shook his hand as he left, thinking I might never see him again.

The flat was partly furnished with an ancient job-lot of creaking, softening pine which qualified principally as rotting timber. I figured it was just a case of re-arranging this pile of crap until it felt like home. If only. But this was the present and the future. Maybe it was all there was and would ever be. An unemployed, unemployable man, separated from the woman he'd loved for eighteen years, estranged from his children who meant everything, living in a fume-filled hovel. Perhaps the first night alone was not the best one on which to make that judgement, but as I lay sobbing in my tiny, curtain-less bedroom, a fierce orange light blazing into the tragic little space as traffic thundered by outside, I never felt more bereft. Sleep was elusive – how would I ever sleep again? – so I got up and padded across the raspy, bare carpet into the frigid lounge and slumped onto the sofa, a bad idea as the wood-to-cushion ratio was massively in favour of the former. My tailbone cracked against the rear cross-strut and I let out a furious 'Fuck!' followed by a minute of agony-appropriate invective as I tried to walk it off. I hobbled to the sink, filled the kettle (the rusty old spare one from our garage) and flicked it on. In the corner of the room, bathed in scummy light, stood my guitar case looking abandoned and unloved. It needed me. I shuffled over, picked it up and unlocked it, the latches cracking open with a reassuring snap. The guitar's deep red wooden body radiated warmth like my only true friend. I took it out and sat on a tubular steel stool with retractable steps, a convenient platform on which to rest my foot and cradle the curve of the guitar on my thigh. I tuned up and started strumming. It sounded so good, so pure, so like home. I settled on a four chord riff, started humming and, within minutes, composed my first new song in fifteen years. Enthusiasm mounting, just like it did when this was all I really cared about, I jumped off the stool and rustled through a box for a pad and pen. Lyrics, never my strong point, came to me unbidden. I was crashing through the artistic dyke, my head flooding with inspiration. Let's face it, I had a whole world of misery and self-pity to pour into that song – a double album's worth – and the catharsis was energising, at least for as long as it took me to finish it.

An hour later, exhausted, I lay the guitar down for the night feeling no better about my overall predicament, but vindicated in my belief that, if nothing else, music has the power to release you from emotional turmoil, however temporarily. I curled up on the knobbly sofa and covered myself with my dressing gown. Somewhere in the back of my mind, as I drifted into scratchy unconsciousness, I knew I'd regret dozing off on a piece of furniture which, in another age, would have been an instrument of torture, but maybe I deserved to be punished before I could even contemplate redemption.

CHAPTER 13

I'M THE FIRST person to hyperventilate when I see lone, middle-aged men sitting in their cars watching young children emerging from a school. But that was me, cowering behind the steering wheel across the road as I waited for Katia and Millie to frolic through the school gates. Lisa and I had agreed that it would be sensible not to mess with their emotions and possibly interfere with their school work by popping up unexpectedly. Better to ring ahead and make a date. But I'm a dad. Dads, in the main, want to be with their kids. If wasting the day in my Hanger Lane hell wasn't sufficiently soul-destroying, the post-school hours between four and eight – minus the accompaniment of their chattering, excitable voices, their curiosity and humour, their proclivity for incendiary fury followed by sweet tenderness – was a living death. So I took to driving to Chiswick every day to observe them for the minute it took for them to leave the school and file into Lisa's BMW – one of her many gallery perks – with Bea at the wheel. They always looked happy, chatty, animated, and while on the one hand this filled me with delight, I think I'd have preferred them to look distraught, with painted signs around their necks reading: 'Come Home Daddy. Mum's a bitch.'

But she wasn't. A bitch, I mean. She was a good mum and they knew it. We spoke two or three times a week initially, mostly cordially, but the calls waned and we did little more than acknowledge each other on Saturdays, alternate Sundays and the odd weekday when I collected them from school. Finding somewhere fascinating to take your children once a month is hard enough. Try doing it twice a week, or more. We ran the gamut of museums and London attractions, ventured out to the Cotswolds and Brighton, even had a go at swinging from trees in an adventure park. But it became a strain and, as my vapid life withered still further on the vine, I found it increasingly difficult to summon the requisite energy and enthusiasm to keep things fresh. Soon, we were settling for crappy films followed by a McDonalds or something less nutritious. The conversation began to feel forced – how many times could I ask them how they were getting on at school or what they'd been up to all week? It's surprising how little common ground there is between a forty-two year old adult and children under the age of ten, even his own. When we were a family, there was no compulsion to make conversation. Life simply happened, a natural ebb and flow. My time with them grew shorter as the entertainment on offer grew thinner. I loved their company but, increasingly, I felt they could do without the disruption of compulsory weekly expeditions stretched out to fit the hours we were supposed to spend together. I'd drop them off and watch them race to their rooms like mad things, free at last, pleased that it was over, and knew I had to take a step back. I didn't want to relinquish my access to them, knowing also that it might count against me later, and nor did I want to be uninvolved, but even though I was still clocking up more hours in their company than Lisa, it was becoming increasingly stressful. They wanted to get on with their own little lives with minimum disruption. No point punishing them for our inadequacies.

Lisa's career continued to soar. The parties, the schmoozy dinners, the globe-trotting were multiplying exponentially while my career (sorry, my 'career') had smashed through the buffers and into the station concourse, like in that Die Hard film, the one Lisa refused to see with me. In desperation, and for something to do lest I go bonkers, I found myself a part time job advertised on one of those suspicious, hand-written cards in the newsagent's window. Peter Schofield ran a little business-to-business telesales company which he operated from the lounge of his vile 1930s semi. Just a couple of minutes' walk from my flat, it was nevertheless in a relatively quiet road with no direct views of the Hanger Lane Gyratory System which must have played havoc with its valuation. My twenty-two hour week involved indulging in inane and largely unproductive conversations with apathetic and occasionally aggressively disinterested targets. Peter, a stout man in his late thirties, who sported the full range of M & S Argyll jumpers for men twice his age and half his girth, was mostly too wrapped up in his own activities to manage his team properly. There were usually eight to ten of us crammed into that seedy room, and we spent much of the day chatting. Most of my colleagues were students and foreigners and the atmosphere was largely jolly. If nothing else, it enabled me to live outside my own head for a few precious hours. The money was abysmal, sufficient to give a single man a smidgeon of financial independence, but too insignificant, if we divorced, to merit more than a judicial snigger in the financial shake-up.

I kept the flat tidy, a fairly simple task given the absence of children and my preference for food straight out of a box. I've always been a bit of a stickler for a clean bathroom and properly disinfected work surfaces and, in fairness, I wasn't lacking in available time to ensure that my usual standards were met, nay exceeded. I welcomed my trips to the launderette every other day. It was somewhere warm and quiet to go with a newspaper. Keeping up with current affairs whilst doing something both productive and essential? That's multi-tasking, my friends. I watched TV, jogged most days around Gunnersbury Park, caught up with all those books I meant to read, sang a few songs and kept myself clean. A basic life, a life without colour or definition, a bit like an own-brand bag of sweets from Superdrug.

My phone wasn't exactly ringing off the hook, or whatever it is modern phones do. Chaz's calls were unwelcome but nobody else seemed that interested in what I wasn't doing, and I managed to maintain a measure of muted civility without encouraging a resumption of the friendship. My mother, initially distraught about the break-up and its effect on the girls, resorted to platitudes about it 'being for the best' after I ruled out the possibility of a reconciliation. She called every other day, supportive as she'd always been despite my having given her so little to be proud of. And occasionally, if I was particularly down on my luck, she'd drop off a crate of plastic containers heavy with inedible soups and stews. But otherwise, I waited for the kids' mid-week call to raise my spirits. Millie was always garrulous until she lost focus or a cartoon started, but Katia became increasingly reluctant to come to the phone, preferring to shout the odd 'hi, Dad' from a safe distance. Rightly, she reasoned it was better to save up her news so that we could discuss it all in about four minutes at the weekend. I played the occasional game of squash with a couple of guys at the local leisure centre – Tim, an interior designer with a Trump-like quiff which occasionally came loose and threatened to take an eye out, and Gordon, a ferociously sweaty BBC cameraman who I usually let win rather than risk bumping into and getting splattered. We'd have a drink afterwards and indulge in a little shallow conversation, but nothing more. They were both married with kids and living in relative harmony and I…well I wasn't, so they avoided what should have been comfortable topics of conversation for fear of upsetting me. We pared it down to football, beer and an occasional leer.

So there you go. Forty-two, friendless, alone and bordering on pathetic. What a catch.

Of course I thought about calling Faye, but our last meeting had ended messily. And I'd have to tell her that Lisa and I had split up, which would sound opportunistic, desperate, like I was saying the coast was clear. Which it wasn't. She had a boyfriend. That, and the fact that she never fancied me in the first place. And, more importantly, I couldn't help labouring under the delusion that Lisa and I might still get back together. Calling Faye would be to admit – to myself – how I felt about her, and I couldn't allow that to interfere with the possibility, however remote, of reclaiming my family.

Kevin's fey Scottish brogue, made feyer by the sibilant hiss of my mobile phone, its prima donna protest at having to function in the pervasive Hanger Lane smog, was as unexpected as it was welcome. The Irish folk singing combo, Craic, who were due to headline that night had cried off at the last minute and he was desperate. He was prepared to pay me the same as he was going to pay them, a fee intended to reward an entire band just for little old me! Sadly, Craic had been prepared to split sixty lousy quid three ways but it would, at least, be a significant advance on my previous fee. The man was begging. What was I to do? I'd been at the coalface for seventeen years, acquiring the hard-nosed negotiating techniques and business acumen now serving me so handsomely in my role as a part time telesales marketer with a pan-Ealing client base, so naturally I haggled. I insisted that the post-gig meal comprise two proper courses rather than just a bit of left over pudding. He folded under the pressure and the deal was struck. I had intended to go into the office – sorry, Peter's lounge – to put some hours in but, unaccountably lifted, I decided to rehearse instead. The guitar in my hands, vocal cords rippling, purpose coursing through me, it was truly a joyous couple of hours and I could hardly wait to get up there and share my gift with my audience.

A bright, clear day became a bitterly cold March night punctuated by horizontal snow flurries and drifting fog, limiting my audience, at its peak, to seven. That, though, wasn't their fault; I couldn't take it out on them. At least they bothered to turn up and I owed them a performance. My sixty quid fee would be somewhat disproportionate to the night's takings, and with my free two-courser on top, Kevin was taking a hit. It can be a tough old world, show business. What we lacked in numbers, though, we more than made up for in intimacy. We were all in this together and an unpromising prospect turned into a lively and pleasant evening. The appreciation was warm and genuine and I felt I'd done a good thing, given that Kevin had asked me if I wanted to pull out. In fact, he may have begged me to pull out, but I'm way too professional to do something like that.

I finished my set and strolled through the audience to receive seven individual accolades; it was probably too embarrassing for the other six not to throw some praise my way after a lonely old fellow at the first table shook my hand and likened me to the young Elton John. I sat down at the table nearest to the bar at the back and waited for Kevin to serve up a grudging plate of lamb stew. At the next table sat a slightly rotund man of, I guessed, fifty-five with a jet black widow's peak which didn't fit his face and screamed Just For Men. At the back, his hair was gathered in a shapeless bush rather than a mullet, untamed by the wet-look gel he'd slathered all over it. He wore a white, collarless shirt with dressy, silken stripes, silver buttons and huge matching cufflinks, a thrilling ensemble gift-wrapped in a black waistcoat with a satin rainbow lining. I'd gathered he was American when he congratulated me on my set, but he looked more like a cruise ship magician from Barnsley. Opposite him sat an attractive, dark-haired woman of about thirty wearing a contrastingly uncomplicated white blouse and jeans. They were huddled over the table talking, clearly about me, their constant glances in my direction a dead giveaway. Fame, eh? I smiled at them once or twice as I chewed on Kevin's sinewy lamb which, pre-slaughter, had probably spent some time working as a steroidal professional bodybuilder, but was in no mood for a conversation. Still they looked over as I battled gamely on, but I was all smiled out and decided to don my blinkers at least until pudding was served. A few minutes later, I was aware of them rising and moving towards me. Ok, fine, one more handshake, but then I really just wanted to be left in peace with my soggy lemon meringue pie. I lay down my spoon and prepared myself for a pat on the back, or an autograph request perhaps, but instead the man asked if they could join me for a minute. I couldn't say no, could I? We'd be nothing without the fans. He extended his right hand which bore at least three diamond encrusted rings.

'Ben Stern,' he said in an accent acquired, I guessed, in the Bronx, though admittedly I was working off a tiny sample.

'Mike Kenton,' I said, half standing to shake his hand.

'Good to meet ya, Mike. Oh, where are my manners? Elaine Sturgis, my assistant.'

I shook Elaine's slender hand, her pretty hooded eyes crinkling as she smiled. 'Hi,' she said. American? Not enough to go on. They sat down opposite me and Ben opened the batting.

'Great show. *Great* show. You've got a pretty good setalungs.'

'Thanks.'

Ben reached into the top pocket of his waistcoat and plucked out a card which he handed to me.

Benjamin A Stern
Chief Executive
President Records

Underneath were two addresses, both on Broadway, one in New York, the other in…Crouch End. President Records's London HQ was in the converted church – just off the Broadway, in fact – where numerous pop luminaries had recorded a string of hits during the eighties and nineties. It was no more than three minutes' walk from where we were sitting.

'So, here's the thing,' he said.

Elaine opened a spiral notepad which Ben consulted as he spoke. Was this to be that recording contract I'd yearned for? And only a mere twenty years too late.

'Your third song tonight…'

'Er…'

'*In Love We Trust*,' piped Elaine. Londoner. Possibly north of the Thames. Or south.

'Yeah…*In Love We Trust*. Loved it. *Loved* it.'

'Thank you.'

'We heard you play it last time we were here. Great tune,' said Ben beaming a fine row of veneers. '*Great* tune.' *Toon.*

'Thanks again.'

'Ok, here's the thing…' he repeated. 'I'm a record producer – maybe you hearda me?'

A non-committal half-smile seemed politic. The head shake was involuntary.

'Ok, why should you?' Ben chuckled with the disappointed mirthlessness he'd probably been choking on for years. 'I was a musician like you a thousand years ago, back in the day. Played in a few bands, wrote a coupla songs. Never got too far till I started producing. Right off the bat, I got involved with The Llamas? Heardathem?'

'Everyone knows The Llamas.' They'd had a few hits without ever really breaking through.

'Celia Weston? Barry Lane? The Capsules? Produced them all.'

And I knew them all – vaguely – British acts who'd flickered briefly and quickly drowned in the cesspit of pop oblivion.

'I set up over here just after Glam Rock died. Small label, but we got some pretty hot names. Hey, hearda Nate Kyle?'

At last, he'd actually struck a meaningful chord. Nate Kyle had had a number one hit a few months earlier with a soulful ballad. 'Yes, of course.'

'Well he's the kind of act we're looking to produce now.'

'I see.'

Ben paused, leaned forward and shrugged. 'Can I level with ya?'

'Level away.'

'Nate Kyle you ain't.'

'If only I was black and twenty-three.' I scooped the final lump of pie off the plate and slid it into my mouth.

'You're a little…mature?' *Matoor.*

'Old's fine.'

Elaine smiled and appeared to scribble this nugget down in her notebook.

'Ok. You're old,' said Ben, 'but you can write, man. *Whoo*, can you write! And…ok, here's the thing.'

The thing again.

'That song…'

'*In Love We Trust*,' I prompted.

'Yeah. Ok. Well how would you feel about entering it in the Eurovision Song Contest?'

I spat a tiny chunk of lemon rind onto the back of my hand. 'Well…that's a bit of a…the Euro…what?'

'Here's the thing. The BBC approached me a while back to ask if one of my acts wanted to put up a song. You know Howard James?'

'Lead singer with…errr…that band with the…'

'The Cupid Stunts.'

Geddit? The BBC wouldn't play any of their stuff until they got over themselves. I mean, if they were going to let Frankie fellate…

'Coulda been huge, bigger than, I dunno…Queen. But Howie, well, he likes his booze and his pills and his weed. Crazy fucker. Blew it all. Talented writer, *great* singer, that's the tragedy. Fuckin' idiot…oh…'

Elaine smiled again, reprovingly this time, and tutted. Were they a couple? I hoped not. That wouldn't have been fair or right. She was too young, too attractive; not beautiful in the conventional sense – her nose was too wide, her jaw too square, her eyes cloaked beneath puffy lids, but the sum of the parts transcended these individual imperfections.

'She don't like me cussing.' Ben shot her an enigmatic smile. What did it mean? 'Anyway, the BBC thought it'd be fun to bring him back, stick him in front of the country and see what happened. Curiosity value, I guess. Sometimes it works, sometimes it don't. So they came to me…because no other idiot will manage him.'

'So *he's* doing a song…for Europe? The wild man of rock?'

'Not exactly,' said Elaine. 'He can't write any more. He brought us a couple of songs and they were…'.

'Fuckin' abysmal,' said Ben, forgetting himself. 'You'd have to be The Darkness on speed to even think about inflicting that kinda shit on the public.'

'That bad?'

'Worse. But they still want him out front, so we've been looking for songs. And, man, we've listened to a shitload…but they're either crap or the composers don't want them on Eurovision. They'll let him record them but, you know…like, God help them if they make a million writing a Eurovision winner. Embarrassing, huh? Artistic fuckin' integrity. Do me a favour. Assholes.' Ben touched a finger to his lips and smiled at Elaine like a cheeky schoolboy.

'We were in here a couple of weeks ago when you were playing,' said Elaine.

'Just catching a bite, you know?' Ben interrupted. This was his story. 'And then we heard you and that song and we started thinking. The thing is, we had nothing else for Howard to sing and Eurovision:You Decide is coming up, like, next month.'

'You've lost me.'

'The qualification show to pick the UK entry? BBC tried a few other ideas – as if fuckin' Lloyd-Webber's gonna write something worth voting for. Or that other guy?'

'Pete Waterman,' piped Elaine.

'Yeah. Forty number ones, can't write for shit. Go figure.'

'So now they're starting with the singers and getting them to write something,' said Elaine. 'Mostly acts who are already popular around Europe. Howard never went away in Germany, Scandinavia…'

'Winner goes to the final in Paris in May,' said Ben. 'All we need now is a fuckin' song. But I think we got it, uh?'

Elaine nodded. 'S'why we asked Kevin to get you on again,' she said. 'To hear it again, to make sure.'

'He blew off some Irish pricks for us.'

And I'd thought I was Kevin's go-to guy.

'Look, I wrote it down last time,' said Elaine pointing to a page in her note book. 'See? *In Love We Trust*. We've heard nothing better. Not even close. It's the one.'

The song I'd written for Faye Lester. Was this an elaborate practical joke? Where were the cameras? 'So…you want to give my song to Howard James…to sing on Eurovision?'

'Nutshell,' said Ben.

'And what about *my* artistic integrity?' I said, just in case I *was* being filmed. I was in on it. Ha.

'Fuck, man! You don't got any, singing in a joint like this!' Ben was playing his part wonderfully well, too well. I was beginning to think he was for real.

'It was just a joke,' I mumbled, having exposed the vast Atlantic humour divide like a raw nerve. Assuming I'd been joking.

Elaine leaned towards me. 'We're desperate. That's the honest truth.'

I frowned in mock offence. She didn't get me either.

'Oh! No! I don't mean we're so desperate that…no, I mean…'

'It's ok,' I said, waving a hand.

'It's a really good song, Mike. Isn't it, Ben?'

'Fuckin' A'

'But we're tight for time. The BBC are going to blow us out if we don't come up with something in the next couple of weeks. It'd be a huge opportunity lost.'

She sounded like she meant it. Maybe it was time I started buying into this ridiculous fiction. 'Let's just say I was interested; it's not the kind of song Howard's known for, is it? It's too poppy, too mainstream,' I said, looking this gift horse squarely in the mouth.

'The guy's not a kid any more, Mike,' said Ben, 'he can't pogo, can't even spit. This is grown up Howard, mature Howard, on the wagon Howard. Sure, we'll rock it up to suit his voice, but he could surprise everyone with this, especially himself.'

'We really need to make a decision now, Mike,' said Elaine, 'otherwise we'll have to go with something else, something not as good.'

'Look. Here's the thing,' said Ben. 'God's truth? Howard will go to pieces again some time soon. Guy's gonna wind up in a sewer whatever happens, but if we can squeeze this out of him, get a hit, raise our profile, start attracting some better acts...you know?'

'Very altruistic.'

'Yeah, yeah, yeah,' continued Ben, 'it's heartless. But it's business. That's all it ever is. That's why artistic integrity is a crock. We can all make some money here if we're smart. And you...you won't have to sing in shitholes any more.'

I shrugged. Maybe they were a couple of local perverts who got a kick out of this kind of thing and followed it up with a bout of ferocious intercourse. Each to their own, of course. But they sounded so earnest, so desperate. Hmm. So, ok, thinking out loud here, has a Eurovision song ever picked up the Mercury Prize? Oh shit, they had me, didn't they? And I wanted to be had.

'We won't be able to credit you with the song but...'

'Hang on. What?' That snapped me out of my reverie.

'Howard will take the credit. That's the whole schtick this year. Singer/songwriter. But you'll get a cut. A good cut. And, like I say, it's about the doors that'll open after...'

But I'd stopped listening. Maybe artistic integrity was a crock, but this didn't even sound like good business. I was being used. If Howard won, all the fuss would be over him, not me. For every Abba, there are a hundred Estonian/Norwegian/British flops who've wound up collecting shopping trolleys in the supermarket car park. I, the uncredited, anonymous composer, might make a few short-term quid under a confidential agreement with Ben, but unless he was going to offer me a song writing contract as well, I'd be lucky to get a job oiling their wheels. Or worse, wind up back here in *Jaques* singing, till kingdom come, to seven people who only came in to get out of the rain. But – and this was all I had – Ben was on his last chance, so much so that he'd turned to a complete unknown, someone else on his last chance. I'm no negotiator, no salesman – that much we know – but this was my sole bargaining chip.

'So what's my cut?' I said, all nasty-cop eyes, but wobbly inside.

'Hey, don't worry Mike, we'll talk about that…'

'Talk about it now.'

'Wow, tough guy.'

'I don't want to get shafted.'

'No-one's gonna shaft you, Mike.'

Americans always overuse your name, don't they? Especially when they're shafting you.

'Ok,' he said, his face beginning to glisten. He'd anticipated fawning gratitude, not a negotiation. 'Basically, and I'm just talking basics here…you'll get…I dunno…we're looking at…just north of twenty per cent.'

That didn't sound enough. 'Of what?'

'Of the whole thing. We're talking record sales, downloads, royalties, residuals. It's a good deal.'

'Oh, well where do I sign?'

'C'mon, Mike.'

'And who creams off the eighty per cent?' I knew nothing about anything, but this was manifestly unfair. I think.

Elaine looked uncomfortable and jotted a note which she shoved under Ben's nose. He forced a smile. He could see he was dealing with a player. 'Ok, forty per cent. Final offer. We've got overheads, Mike… promotional costs, musicians, producers, the whole schmeer. Your cut's from gross, not net, but we still gotta pay all that shit.'

I stood up and grabbed my guitar case. I'd pushed him from twenty to forty in five seconds. It had gone way better than my Virgin negotiations. I couldn't remember feeling this bullish since 2003. I extended my right hand which Ben ignored. 'Tell you what. I'm going to think about it and then I'm going to call you tomorrow. How's that?' Ach, tomorrow? Too keen. 'Or the day after. Whatever.'

'We need to know now,' said Ben. 'We've got a fu...'

'Tomorrow, if you can, Mike. Time is of the essence,' said Elaine.

As I drove home, the slushy rain spattering the windscreen too insistently for my ailing, shredded windscreen wipers, I pondered my strategy. Wasn't this a dream come true? Shouldn't I have grabbed this opportunity at any price? So, I wasn't going to get the credit. Did that matter? This was about one song and getting paid for it. I could never prove it was mine; I'd never written anything down, never deposited a tape at the bank and the few inebriated *Jaques* customers who'd heard me sing it would never remember who, where or when. Not forgetting that Ben's lawyers would gut me with a hunting knife if I attempted to assert my authorship. So this was all about the application of sound commercial principles, business expediency. Best case scenario, the song wins Eurovision and sells millions – stranger things; more realistically, Howard records it, sells a few copies and I'm a few thousand pounds to the good. I could use the money to set up a small IT consultancy or – ok, fuck that, but at the very least I'd be less dependent on hand-outs from Lisa until I got a job I really, really fancied. What's not to like?

But still that insistent little voice, the one that had shouted so loudly twenty years ago, wouldn't be silenced. Maybe, with a following wind and the luck of a triple lottery winner, this venture might yet open the door to the one industry I'd always dreamed of working in. I'd only ever had a job, a career, but music was my passion. Jesus, what if Ben told me to go screw myself? What if he didn't like the uppity Brit playing hardball? What had I done? As if my dying marriage, distant children, neutered career and miserable abode weren't sufficiently stress-inducing, I now had another reason not to sleep.

And, of course, I didn't. I lay there fidgeting, turning it over in my mind until the sweat threatened to drown me. What the hell was I playing at? Maybe it *was* all a scam, but what if it wasn't? Was I scared? Had I spent all my life praying for this opportunity only to run away from it when it landed on my doorstep? I finally dropped off around five, waking at seven feeling groggy and displaced. In my semi-conscious haze, I imagined everything was ok, that the nightmare was over, that Lisa's smooth leg was draped over mine, that the kids were bickering about nothing on the landing. Then the building trembled as some monstrous pantechnicon rumbled past and I opened my eyes to that same threadbare little room.

I got up and made myself a cup of builder's tea; two bags with sufficient caffeine to kick-start a fossil. I'd finally decided, at some lonely, chilly point in the middle of the night, that I *was* going to call Ben, a resolve designed to persuade my over-revving head to shut up for a minute so I could get some kip. I knew the fact that he envisioned my song as Eurovision fodder suggested it was essentially meritless, but if he was right, if it sold like hotcakes (and/or bratwurst and/or snails and/or paella) maybe he'd acknowledge my genius for lowest-common-denominator pap and let me loose on his stable of second division acts. I could write album tracks forever.

I began to feel positive, energised, up for the task. I'd been validated as a song writer, never mind by whom or why. It was a good thing, something to build on. I dressed, nipped out to get the paper and settled in for the morning on a chair by the kettle. No telemarketing today, not with my musical career finally in the pre-launch phase. I was a bit too starry for that kind of drudgery now. My heart beat hard all morning, not fast, but with weight, gravity, as if to remind me how important this could be. I didn't want to call Ben too early; chapter one, page one, para one, Negotiating Made Simple: don't be too eager. But what if he was spending the morning scouring the planet for another song? Maybe he'd find something even crappier than mine at half the price.

Eleven o'clock. Couldn't settle, couldn't find my inner calm. But I couldn't call then, on the dot. That would be too obvious, a dead giveaway, like I'd mapped it out. I'd try at eleven thirty seven, an arbitrary time, thus demonstrating my complete indifference. That'd show him what kind of a player he was dealing with.

God, those thirty seven minutes were taking a fucking month.

Eleven thirty. Oh fuck it: 'Hi, can I speak to Ben Stern please?'

'Who's calling?' said a disembodied Mockney voice. Female, I think, but a smoker.

'Mike Kenton.'

'Does he know what it's concerning?'

'Yes.' Of course he fucking does.

'Just a moment.'

There was a click, followed by a dreary dirge presumably by one of Ben's hack protégés. Awful. And I had to listen to all of it. And the next track. And the beginning of the one after. Ben was playing hard to get. Or he was in the toilet.

'Putting you through,' said the voice.

Click. Click. *Come on!*

'Mike!' bellowed Ben, forcing me to pull the receiver away from my ear.

'Morning Ben.' Starchy, English, formal.

'So, we've got a deal, right?'

'Well…ha…not exactly…no…well yes…' I was turning into Ronnie Corbett.

'That a yes or a no?'

'It's a yes, but…'

'Good job! Whoo!'

'…but we need to talk about the cut…and everything.'

'Listen, Mike. Get your beautiful, talented British ass in here and we'll get everything signed and sealed. We're not gonna have any problems, you and me. Hey, whyntcha come for lunch?'

President Records's enclave was surprisingly stylish, considering their Chief Executive's criminally misbegotten fashion sense. I'd expected to be met by garish, over-the-top tat, flashy décor, shiny brass door fittings, a couple of cheap chandeliers, that kind of nonsense. Instead, both inside and out, the place was a pleasing mix of tasteful modernity and Gothic grandeur. The reception area was unexpectedly large and crisply furnished with sleek leather sofas, glassy, minimalist tables and banks of expensive looking hi-tech equipment. The original reticulated windows lent the offices a majestic ambience, the sturdy, bare stone walls at once cold and comforting. Ben welcomed me with a bear hug – I went rigid, being from London – and took me on a tour of the studio suite which comprised a large, main chamber with a magnificent grand piano at its centre and several racks loaded with guitars, percussion instruments and electric keyboards; a couple of small, glass-walled vocal booths nestled at the back; the control booth was compact and dominated by a vast mixing desk alive with faders, lights and knobs. Above it sat three linked Apple Macs and a set of burly, high spec speakers. In an age when any idiot can record a hit using thirty-five quid's worth of software and a PC in a bedroom, it was a relief to see that Ben did things properly. Call me an old fart.

We took another door out of the control booth and into Ben's office which maintained the generally tasteful theme, save for a self-congratulatory wall of photographs of him, shiny-faced, in his more hirsute heyday, shaking hands and making pally with a variety of music biz nonentities. He guided me to an expansive cream leather chair which swallowed me whole. Without saying a word, he pressed a button on an elaborate remote control, unleashing a song which boomed out of a pair of speakers behind his desk. It was pretty catchy, a mid-tempo number with real heart that had me nodding and tapping my fingers appreciatively on my knee. Ben pressed 'pause' after a minute or so, arched an eyebrow and asked me for my opinion. I told him I liked it, that it had energy and a memorable hook, thereby completely undermining my negotiating position. This, it transpired, was the song he was going to go with if I didn't want to play ball. I couldn't very well hold out for a hundred per cent now, but forty-seven, the number I'd finally and arbitrarily arrived at was attractive enough for Ben to type into a document on his PC. Shit, still too bloody low. He swivelled his screen to show me some projections on a spread sheet. I stood to make a chunky sum of money, subject to Howard liking the song, getting a good producer on board, the BBC accepting it, winning Eurovision: You Decide and storming Eurovision itself. The odds, admittedly, were long.

Elaine arrived with a tin foil platter of de-crusted sandwiches, a few bottles of lager and water and a glutinous looking fruit based drink for Ben. This wasn't going to be the most lavish of celebratory lunches. Elaine sat on a leather chair opposite me and crossed her legs, a pleasing swish emanating from her denim clad thighs. I caught her eye and lingered there for a moment, hoping for some sort of sign that the air was rich with sexual chemistry – we can't help it, remember – but she quickly turned her gaze to her ubiquitous notepad and started writing. Nothing much had been said; maybe she was drawing a cartoon of a man about to swallow the stupidest deal of all time. Ben had already prepared the contract, a little presumptuously, I thought, but then he'd completely out-manoeuvred me so who could blame him? I read it to the accompaniment of the same song on a loop, lest I forget what I was up against. I needed to get a professional opinion, I said, but thought it looked ok. Ben gave me twenty-four hours, but assured me he wasn't being bullish or trying to screw me over, which made everything fine then. He just needed to make a quick decision, he said, simple as that. No other agenda. I trusted Ben in the way America trusts Iran.

A few hastily swallowed sandwiches later and the meeting was over. Ben slapped me on the back, done-deal fashion and told me to call him the following day. Elaine led me down a gently curving staircase, our footsteps echoing off the cold, stone walls, and reached the door to the street. Despite the lack of compelling evidence, I took her invitation to go out for a drink some time *to celebrate* as a clear indication of her nascent attraction to me, though it might have been more compelling if she'd simply asked me out there and then. Was she merely doing the Devil's work and tightening the presumptive screw?

I didn't know any solicitors, although if things continued on their current downward spiral, I'd soon have to make the acquaintance of at least one of this odd breed of professional when Lisa filed for divorce. What do you do in these situations? I mean, when someone wants you to relinquish your ownership of a song so that someone else can sing it in the Eurovision Song Contest? Do people specialise in that branch of the law? Not if the Yellow Pages was anything to go by. I couldn't find a single *Eurovision song: signing-away-all-rights-thereto-followed-by-eternal-obscurity* expert. Not one. I'd need a sharp showbiz lawyer for sure, but had no idea where to look. A sudden inspiration prompted me to call the Law Society who gave me the names of several firms. But which one to choose? And how would they react to my simple opening question: are you cheap? by definition, a stupid question. Though not to me, because money was tight and I wanted to avoid involving Lisa in this folly by asking her to shell out for a £350 per hour smartarse in a Savile Row suit who'd find a way to take 10 hours over a three page contract *and* charge a couple of grand for stamps and photocopying. The sad truth was, I couldn't tell Lisa anything. My Eurovision odyssey was not something she would celebrate. For her, any involvement in this annual kitsch-fest would be embarrassing, something she'd go to great lengths to conceal from the culture cronies and sophisticates who populated her world. I didn't want to have to explain it or justify myself to her. Given the improbability of anything coming of it, I could live without her icy opprobrium.

Yet she ought to take a measure of pride, if not in the achievement itself, then in the fact that I'd got off my backside and made something happen. After all, wasn't my professional demise and subsequent inertia at the root of all this animosity? Even if she had no regard for my musical ambitions or abilities – and she didn't – surely if I made some money or signed a song writing deal, it would repair some of the damage, give us a platform, allow us to at least think about reconstructing the family unit. But I was confused, hurt, depressed and wasn't sure what I wanted any more. Yes, I needed my girls back, but not necessarily on those terms. Maybe I just wanted to bloody show her I could do something. Did I still love her? God, I had no idea. That wasn't even the point. In the end, I had to make this work because it was all I had to cling onto, a last chance saloon at which there was a bit of a run on the booze.

I was getting nowhere in my search for a solicitor. I made several calls but rarely got beyond reception, perhaps because my opening query about 'ball park' fees followed by a whispered 'shit' after they hit me with it, rendered further discussion redundant. Promised return calls were slow to materialise. You'd have thought solicitors, of all people, would be quick to latch onto any prospect of generating fees, but perhaps my patent anxiety, pitiful financial constraints and the fact that I used phrases like 'I only need a tiny piece of advice' or 'it'll only take five minutes, if that,' deterred even the most voracious of them. One who did come to the phone couldn't see me for two days, and another said he couldn't help but would speak to a colleague when he returned from the Maldives in a couple of weeks' time. Good luck to him, but I couldn't wait.

Desperate times called for desperate measures. There was only one man I could turn to. Chaz. His was the only name I could muster from my slim lexicon of well-connected friends, but I was damned if I was going to call him. He wouldn't exactly be blown away by all this Eurovision nonsense. He'd find the whole thing laughable, beneath him. I could hear him scoffing now, up in his rosewood-clad office suite. He'd always been the first to help, whatever the problem, but having allowed business and pleasure to combust, I perceived him differently now. I felt he enjoyed feeling professionally superior because, in every other respect, he was quite the opposite, a little man with myriad complexes, locked in a flat, childless marriage. I wasn't feeling particularly charitable towards him, I think it's fair to say, and I wasn't about to forgive and forget. Oh no. I'm a grudge-bearer, right up there with Iago, if you know the guy. But I was in a situation, here.

Glaziers's building in Baker Street is a ghastly thing to behold from the outside. A product of the architecturally bankrupt sixties, it resembles a play set of featureless interlocking boxes with not a single embellishment to liven it up. Inside, though, it's quite a different story, the firm having lavished millions on the say-so of one of their clients, a high profile TV star interior designer with unfeasibly long hair who'd made a name for himself fucking up people's homes. I stood in the doorway of the Santander just along from Glaziers's entrance dressed in my smartest jeans, a neatly ironed white shirt and the half-decent woollen jacket I'd bought in French Connection a year or two earlier. My balls were freezing off. It was lunchtime, but I'd arrived at eight hoping to catch Chaz on his way in, forgetting that a driven little bastard like that with nothing much else to live for probably arrived way earlier than that. Having miscalculated, I took off around nine and had a damp little cake for breakfast in a nearby Starbucks, before wasting a couple of hours wandering up and down Oxford Street. I knew Chaz liked to get out for lunch if he could; I was banking on it, if my sophisticated plan to 'accidentally' bump into him without the whole thing looking staged was to work. It would be funny (both ha-ha and the other one) and open the door to a muted but beneficial – for me – rapprochement. All this without having to climb down off my high horse and eat shit. Clever stuff, I think you'll agree.

Men in suits, couriers in leathers, women in skirts – people with things to do – filed in and out, faceless, anonymous, going about their business. But Chaz would be an instant spot, a tiny man in a sharp bespoke suit, a man I knew like a brother. At around one fifteen, a large, top of the range Lexus drew up outside. This was my moment. Chaz bounded out of the front entrance, all urgent importance. I had twenty yards to make up while he only had to cover five. I started jogging, but he was jaunty, almost at the car door. I picked up speed. As he was about to slide inside, I thundered past and barged my shoulder into his. The poor little man careened into the open door, bounced off it and hit the pavement. I stopped and turned, all stunned amazement. I was good at this. Chaz was sitting there, on his backside, bemused, blinking. I darted back towards him and looked down at him sitting there like a baby, legs akimbo.

'Chaz?' I said, then, 'Chaz!' I'd nailed the relevant range of vocal inflections perfectly. 'Fuck.' I leaned down to help him up but was muscled roughly out of the way by the chauffeur who scraped him off the floor.

'Mike? The fuck you doing?' he gasped, dusting himself down.

'Chaz. Sorry. This is unbelievable. Jesus! I've got a meeting up the road and I'm running late, of course, and…I can't believe this! Bloody hell.'

Chaz manoeuvred the chauffeur gently out of the way. 'What meeting's that?'

Had he seen through me already? 'Oh it's…nothing…a record company.'

'A record company?'

'You won't believe me if I tell you.'

'Tell me anyway.'

'One of my songs, it's…this is fucking embarrassing, mate…it's being entered in the Eurovision Song Contest. There, said it. Bloody ridiculous, I know.'

'You're joking! How'd that happen?' A weird smile began to warm his ashen face.

'Oh…guy saw me sing at…that place,' I said, waving airily, 'record producer…liked one of my songs, next thing you know…I know, it's naff, but what the hell?'

'The Euro-fucking-vision Song Contest!' he blurted. Here it came. I braced myself for the ridicule. 'Fucking brilliant! Love it. Never miss it. It's a ritual.'

You think you know someone.

'What you talking about, love it?'

'Yeah, me and Denise…in a post-modern, ironic sort of way,' he said without convincing. Suddenly I had noxious visions of him and Denise bopping in their blue satin jumpsuits and white platform shoes whilst marking their scorecards. 'Why not? We make a night of it, have some people over…'

'How long's this been going on?' I said. This sounded more warped than swinging.

'A few years.'

'And you never invited me.'

'You? You'd just be sitting there taking the piss and we're serious… in that post-modern ironic way I was talking about. And Lisa? I mean, can you imagine her watching that for three hours? *She's* cultured.' Chaz laughed. 'And now you're in it! Fuck me! Magic.'

'Well, ok, hold your horses,' I said, 'not yet. First it's Eurovision: You…'

'…You Decide, yeah. With Gordon O'Hara. Brilliant.'

'Actually, you know what? You got a minute? You could help me with something.'

'Shit,' he said checking his watch, 'I've got a bloody meeting I'm late for because some nutter mowed me down in the street.'

I whipped the folded document from my inside pocket, 'Just have a quick look at this for me will you? It's the contract. Tell me what you think. I've got to give them an answer today.'

'It's not really my…'

I winced and gave him my best 'everything-hinges-on-this' shrug.

'Ok, I'll have a look. Maybe I can run it by a mate of mine. Alan Welby. Solicitor. Owes me a favour; owes me lots of favours actually, the wanker.'

'Any chance you can get back to me by, I dunno, three?'

Chaz blew out his cheeks, then slapped me on the shoulder. 'Yeah, course. I'll call you.'

I'd intended to use Chaz, to take advantage of his contrition, rather than manipulate a reconciliation. The memory of him and Lisa virtually necking at my gig and his self-important arrogance when I raised my concerns about the loathsome Jerry still stuck in my craw. But maybe I'd been too hard on him, lashing out at my closest friend when, in reality, he'd had little to do with my descent into hopelessness. He'd strenuously denied an affair with Lisa, thought the very suggestion risible, and I had to concede that the evidence was less than sketchy. And I could see how I must have embarrassed him when I started moaning about the job he'd gone out of his way to secure for me. It was ungrateful, ungracious. It wasn't his fault I couldn't get along with Jerry. No sane person could, but others, more sensible than I, let it wash over them. He'd stuck his neck out for me and I'd chopped his head off. I'd sought a nepotistic favour, then crossed the line and placed an intolerable strain on our friendship. Yet I was the one who'd strutted off in high dudgeon. I should have hung on in there for a few months, taken it like a man, and slipped away quietly when no-one was looking.

Now Chaz was kowtowing to me, desperate to re-rail our relationship when he'd done nothing much wrong. Ok, he was a bit full of himself, an otherwise insignificant man keen to have his success acknowledged. What was wrong with that? It never bothered me before. And I couldn't help but find this newly discovered obsession with Eurovision, if a little tragic, oddly endearing.

Any call from Lisa was a surprise now, even one as routine as this. She wanted me to collect the girls from her sister's house in Hammersmith on Saturday morning as she was going away on the Friday and wouldn't be back until Sunday. Bea didn't do overnighters, so Rachel, a chubbier, less up-tight version of Lisa, was helping out.

'They could stay with me on Friday,' I said.

'No. Too much hassle with picking-up and homework and food *and everything.*' Don't you start.

'It's not a hassle…'

'It is.'

So that was that. Move on. 'Where you going?'

'Barcelona. I'm meeting an artist over there, Jorge Ortiz, whose work is absolutely breatht…sorry, I know this is boring for you.' Yes, it was all a bit highbrow for the Philistine. How on Earth had we ever got together in the first place? 'Plane gets in on Sunday at 4 so drop them off at 6.30ish?'

'Look, it's not a hassle,' said the Philistine, pissed off about his wife controlling everything. 'I mean, you could at least have discussed it with me.'

'Yes,' she said, 'I could.'

Ominous silence. 'What?'

'It's just…your place is a bit…'

'A bit what? You've never been here.'

Another silence, stony this time. Then it hit me. The kids didn't want to come.

'They're happy to stay on Saturday nights, Michael. It's just, you know, two nights is a bit much for them.'

'I'm a bit much for them. That's what you're saying.'

'Don't be stupid! The flat, I mean. They just think it's a bit…small.'

For two little tiddlers? When I were a lad, it would have represented luxury on a grand scale. Actually, no, it still would have been a shithole.

'Jesus,' I mumbled as the prospect of losing the girls altogether began to bite.

'They love you, Mike.'

'Yeah,' I said, coughing to release my tightening throat.

'Oh come on, don't be silly.'

I put myself in their tiny shoes. 'They're right, it is a bit small. And not very nice. Can't blame them, really,' I said. I couldn't bear for Lisa to hear me sound broken and summoned all my bravado. 'So. Anyway. Barcelona, eh? Very nice.'

'It's just work. I won't get to see anything.'

'When were we there?'

'Barcelona?'

Oh God. Keep calm. 'Before Katia was born, wasn't it? Yeah, you were pregnant with her.'

'Course. Yes.'

I was silent. Had that trip been expunged from her memory? What else was gone?

'Ok, I forgot. I'm sorry, Mike,' she added, finally on the back foot, 'and it was lovely, a really great weekend.'

It was a midweek trip, but I wasn't about to nit-pick. Lisa's voice had softened momentarily and it sounded nice, how it used to. But it was soon back to business. 'Anyway, is that all ok for Saturday? About 9.30?'

It was nearly four by the time Chaz called. I'd decamped to Crouch End and was entrenched in another of its hip coffee shops – *The Bean Thing*, God help me – anxiously reading the Standard. I'd taken the precaution of calling Ben earlier to tell him I was coming in later on to sign. Chaz sounded enervated. 'Mike, sorry. I'm running around like a madman. Stepping into another fucking meeting in a minute.'

'Haven't you made enough money yet?'

'Denise said she'll let me know when I can stop. She's already spent everything I'm going to make in the next five years.'

A private joke. Denise was frugal. It was Chaz who liked to splash out on boats, foreign property, gadgets and insanely expensive hi-fi equipment.

'Anyway, listen,' he said, 'the contract's fine, legally. Alan had a look over it. Nothing sneaky. I presume you're happy with the terms?'

'Er…yeah.'

'Because I think – as does Alan – that you're getting a bit screwed here. You wrote it, it's yours. You should get the lion's share, not them.'

'It's that or nothing. They've got another song they can use and it's probably better than mine.'

'Ok, mate. If you're happy. Listen, sorry to rush. Gotta run. Catch up later, yeah?'

I heaved myself to my aching feet, waited for my head to stop spinning and stepped out onto Crouch End Broadway. Fluffy snow was falling in apologetic flurries and the air was frigid. I huddled into my coat and moved at pace towards Ben's office. He welcomed me like a long lost relative, squeezing the air from my lungs. Stop with the bear hugs already. With scant preamble, he produced a bound copy of the contract which I struggled to sign with my cold-stiffened hand. Ben countersigned and the deal was done. Just like that. Elaine came in on cue with a bottle of champagne which we finished rather too giddily.

On wobbly legs, Ben led us through to the control room to watch a hapless female singer with half-cocked dreadlocks fluffing notes in the voice booth with tragic regularity. We all smiled encouragement at her through the window, which only flustered her further. Even Ben, who specialised in never-will-be's, couldn't disguise his pity. The producer, a wafer-thin man with long, lank hair which covered his eyes like an Afghan dog, looked to be about thirteen. He seemed unconcerned by the singer's vocal waywardness. Perhaps he'd tweak it through the Vocoder later on or, better, just find someone who could sing. Ben introduced me to Gilbert, the 'hottest young producer in the country right now.' Gilbert didn't seem overly embarrassed by the accolade and extended an elegant hand for me to shake, eschewing eye contact. I'm all for the firm, manly, corporate grip, but I was too afraid of rearranging his metacarpals if I went in too hard. Gilbert returned his attentions to the increasingly emotional singer, whose thick coating of Gothic make-up couldn't hide her tears.

'Hannah Field. Gonna be a huge, huge star, *huge*,' said Ben, though you could see even he didn't believe it.

Gilbert shushed Ben without looking up, drawing an indulgent smile from his erstwhile boss. Ben put his finger to his lips, pointed at Gilbert's nodding head and mouthed 'genius' to me. From Ben's subsequent gesticulations, I guessed the great Gilbert was going to produce my song.

Back in Ben's office, over another bottle of bubbly, he assured me that Gilbert would respect the song and my musical integrity, that he would make it sound unique, perfect for Eurovision yet still geared to the contemporary, music-buying public. Howard James was excited about it too (even though, it seemed, he'd never actually heard it) and there was every chance the song was going to be a big, big hit. *Big* hit.

Did Ben ever stop talking shit? *Ever?*

I stood just inside the main lobby and rubbed away a small porthole in the misted glass of the front door. The snow was beginning to settle on the pavement and people were scurrying home, coddled deep inside their coats. A procession of headlights reflected brightly in the glistening Crouch Hill road surface, merely wet now but it would be ice by midnight. It wasn't too inviting out there, but I felt lifted, as though I'd finally committed to something, even if my involvement from here on in was going to be patchy. Maybe the champagne was making me a little buzzy too. I was ready to brave it when I felt a hand on my shoulder and turned to see Elaine in her long woollen coat.

'Nice out,' she said.

'Yeah.'

'Heading home?'

'Suppose so,' I shrugged.

'Fancy a quick warmer first? Or a bite?'

'Er, well, to be honest...'

'It's ok, don't worry. I'm not making a pass or anything.'

'No. Sorry. I know. Why would you? Ha ha. It's just...it's not that I don't want to.' Where the hell was I going with this? Shit, I was scared.

'No?'

'No. I mean, I'm married. Which I know is irrelevant, because you're not making...shall I shut up?'

Elaine hooked her hand through my arm and tugged me gently through the door. 'Let's just go and get a hamburger, all right? Then you can go home to your wife. We're in business now, that's all. We've got things to discuss.'

I wasn't particularly hungry, if truth be told. Yes, I forced a massive sizzling bacon burger down my face, together with some thick cut chips and fat-smothered onion rings, but I could have done without it. As, indeed, could I have passed on the Banoffi Pie and ice cream. Elaine had a sensible looking tuna salad without making me feel in the least bit guilty. My growing paunch bore testimony to my current lack of discipline. The conversation was light, free-flowing, interesting, amusing, engrossing. This was what I believe was called 'having fun,' the rudiments of which I had completely forgotten. I wasn't sure if I was flirting exactly, nor if something was happening between us, but a frisson in my midriff spent all evening despatching little sparks both north and south. Elaine was the type of woman I'd always gone for before settling for perfection. Unconventionally attractive, she had an easy, unruffled charm, a sharp mind and a healthy smattering of cynicism. As the alcohol set in, the line between business and pleasure became a bit of a blur, for me at least. Hadn't I made this mistake before?

'Howard is a complete arsehole, everyone in the business knows it, but he's always sold records. Who knows why? Never over-estimate the public, someone said. Was it Simon Cowell? Even when he's been completely out of his tree, turned up in a gutter somewhere, he's never lost them. They're curious about him. He's got, I dunno, an aura. And now we've got him doing Eurovision.' Elaine chuckled in astonishment. 'I mean, it's so absolutely weird, it's got to work, hasn't it?' Her cheeks dimpled, her eyes crinkled and I wanted to lean across and kiss her wonky lips.

'I hope so.'

'He's the one guy who can do Eurovision without losing credibility. And, with the right song – and this *is* the right song – we're going to make some money. *You're* going to make some money.'

'Well it wouldn't hurt,' I said. 'I just don't want this to be where the story begins and ends.'

'Listen,' said Elaine, leaning forward, her elbows splayed on the chunky wooden table, 'if this works out half as well as we think it will, Ben's not going to let you drift off into obscurity again.'

'Oh, cheers.'

'Sorry,' she laughed.

'No. That's fair. Look at me. This is what obscure looks like.'

'Have you been working the circuit for long?'

'I used to sing around the place twenty-odd years ago, but I've only just started again. For the hell of it, really. I mean, I've got a sensible job, and everything. I.T. All very dull.'

'What does your wife think?'

'Oh she's very supportive. Amazing woman.'

I was off again, praising Lisa to the skies, trying to put Elaine off the scent. I'd done the same with Faye. I don't think it was guilt. Maybe I just couldn't let go, or maybe I didn't want to jeopardise the possibility of gluing the broken pieces back together. It might even have been Elaine's lack of interest in me (cf Faye) that was making me so defensive.

'Good,' she said. 'That's important. You need to have the people who love you right behind you.'

'Absolutely. And my kids are going to be really excited.'

'Kids?'

'Two little girls.'

I stopped short of producing slides from my wallet and setting up the projector, but I'd now completed the job of repelling this compelling woman forever. Kids. That was the clincher. I was getting my rejection in first to save her the trouble.

'Ahh. That's great,' said Elaine, settling back into her chair. 'They're going to be so proud.'

She hadn't met them yet.

We stood beneath Elaine's pitifully inadequate folding umbrella at the top end of Crouch End Broadway. The snow had turned to insistent, biting sleet and taxis were in short supply. Finally, a yellow light began weaving its way down the hill and I stepped into the road to flag it down.

'You take it,' said Elaine.

'Don't be silly,' I said, 'I'll take the train or a bus or something.'

'Where do you live?'

'Hanger...near Chiswick.'

'Fine. We'll share. I'm in Ealing.'

'You sure?'

'I'm sure. Ben's paying.'

The taxi stuttered along the wretched North Circular, slowing to walking pace as it passed the eternally teeming Ikea and the Wembley Stadium arch, lit and imperious, a few hundred yards behind it. Things had turned slightly awkward, the conversation drier than desert sand. I'd portrayed myself as the contented, gainfully employed family man, but Elaine was doing something to my innards and I think she knew it.

The Hanger Lane roundabout was heavily backed up, giving me time to consider whether to jump out there or maintain the fiction that I lived in Chiswick. It was a tight one. I decided to stay in the cab, partly to postpone my return to the chilly wasteland of my flat, partly to inhale Elaine a little longer. As we finally extricated ourselves from roundabout stew, she directed the surly driver to turn off to the right and take a complex back-doubles route culminating at a grand old block of flats on Haven Green.

'This is me,' she said without making a move to open the door.

'Here?'

'Yeah, right here. This place.' Elaine smiled sweetly and began fishing in her purse. She pulled out a £20 note. 'Here, take it.'

'No!'

'Ben's paying, I told you.'

I took the note, but had the grace to feel ungentlemanly about it. Elaine looked at me and we both smiled through a sudden prickly silence. Twenty years ago, the next question would have been, 'do you want to come in for coffee' but…

'Do you want to come in for coff…?'

'That'd be nice.'

Coffee was the last thing anyone of my generation actually drank when the invitation was taken up. It was very un-English. Still is, of course. It was usually a cup of tea, a Penguin and a quick grope without waking her parents. In fact, the cup of tea was often as good as it got, the Penguin a bonus. Significantly more sophisticated now, I took the glass of red wine Elaine proffered, followed by another and another and soon began to feel pleasantly fuzzy. Her flat was small but stylistically grand, her landlord's classic furnishings offset by a few tasteful modern pieces she'd bought herself. The lounge was cosy, its walls adorned with wonderful pencil sketches of the human form which Elaine had drawn as an art student. I imagined Lisa appraising these stark and simple images with her gimlet eye, her mouth turned down at the corners as if she was sucking anchovies. She was into odd shapes and structures, modern abstract impressionism – or something – and looked down her nose at straightforward realism.

Elaine and I sat, cross-legged, facing each other on the carpet, our stilted hour in the cab long forgotten, replaced by easy familiarity and conversational flow which belied our scant acquaintance. The boozy warmth pulsing through me prompted a deepening urge to leap on top of her and kiss her mesmerising, wine-moistened lips. I somehow resisted, hoping she'd make the first move. I was in for a long wait.

I'm not too good with alcohol – as my little mishap at Lisa's gallery would testify – but mixed with this rare contentment and gut-deep desire, I found myself welling up, a confusing and unwelcome emotional response which I hoped I was concealing. I didn't want this night to end, but at around 5, Elaine got up, stretched and said she needed to get some sleep. I was welcome to crash on the sofabed. Given her clear message, I should have gone home but reasoned that I was bound to stagger onto the wrong bus – if they were even running at that time of the morning. Walking was out of the question;

I didn't trust myself to make the mile and a half trek back up Hanger Lane without ending up in a puddle of vomit on the verge. And a mini cab struck me, perversely, as extravagant. What was a boy to do, especially one who wanted to stay just in case? I recall undressing, a little prematurely I think, down to my tee-shirt and underpants and feeling mightily uncomfortable for a few minutes, my hairy legs quivering in the cold while Elaine pottered around rustling up bedclothes and pillows. Then nothing until I awoke at around 8.

In Elaine's bed.

CHAPTER 14

Morning. Bright, crisp, dry. And sober enough to brave the walk home, thereby taking in the delights of an entire stretch of Hanger Lane in all its frost-tainted, litter-strewn, rush hour glory. It took less than twenty minutes and helped clear the residual fug from my aching head. My flat was cold and forbidding, as ever, lacking the barest rudiments of comfort no matter how many times I rearranged my stuff. I made myself a strong, un-English coffee and stood, in my coat, looking blankly out at the endless lines of traffic edging, like thwarted ants, around Hanger Lane roundabout. Cars dipped into and out of lanes they perceived to be moving faster than their own to no great advantage. It was a rush hour without the rush, a crawl hour, a slug hour, people rushing absolutely nowhere.

Elaine hadn't been there when I woke up. She'd left me a note saying she had to get to a meeting and that I should make myself breakfast and let myself out whenever I wanted. The note didn't mention whether we'd had sex. I'd checked myself over, of course, and found no tell-tale signs, no leakages or incrustations, but that wasn't necessarily conclusive. I had no idea how I ended up in her bed, no idea if I kissed her or touched her, no idea what she felt about me, but nothing was going to stop me wallowing in my sweet imaginings. I waited until ten to call her and, naturally, she wasn't available. I was still feeling a little heady and slightly nauseous, but contemporaneously excited, edgy and delightedly guilty. I couldn't sit still. Had to speak to someone.

'Chaz! Chazza! Mate. Whassup?!'

'Mike. Can't really talk.'

'Need to see you, mate. Need to see you.' I was closer to the legal limit than I thought but unable to do much about it. I must have sounded insane.

'Anything up?'

'Need to talk. Need. To. Talk. C'mon!'

166

'Today's a bastard,' he said. 'Tell you what. How's about a game tonight? I could do with a workout.'

Squash? All that running and bouncing? A squirt of bitter bile hit the back of my throat. 'I dunno, feeling a bit delicate.'

'You pissed? You sound pissed. You're not bloody drinking now, are you?'

'No! Had a couple last night, that's all. I'm fine now. Fuckin' top.'

'Are you in?'

Oh shit, go on then. 'Eight?'

'I'll book the court.'

I left two more messages for Elaine, neither of which she returned. Ben called later in the day to discuss my coming into the studio the following Friday to sit in on the recording of the instrumental tracks. I didn't have the balls to ask him where she was. I met Chaz at the club at 7.45 by which time I'd slept off the queasiness and even managed a couple of slices of dry toast and jam. I slaughtered him, of course, but couldn't muster the additional energy to gloat. He tried to jolly me along – abusive banter was integral to this ritual – but gave up after a while. Late on, and with the distracted air that allows muscle memory to do its stuff, I swung at the ball and caught it so sweetly I barely felt the vibration go through my arm. It whipped off the back wall with an almost silent beauty and back towards Chaz's left cheekbone. He was sorely under-equipped to deal with such murderous perfection. He crumpled onto the wooden floor, pole-axed, unconscious and terrifyingly still. I ran across the court and slipped my hand under his slick, sweaty head. His cheek was bleeding and a huge blue welt was forming beneath his eye. And he wasn't moving. I'd only gone and killed my best friend. Jesus, I'd already lost a wife…

After what seemed a lifetime, but was probably only a few seconds, his eyelids flickered and he began clutching at his face. He blinked, his eyes finally focusing on his assailant.

'Fuck,' he grunted.

'Still my point,' I said, dripping sweat onto his prone torso.

'No, I'm retiring hurt so technically, it's a draw.'

And he meant it.

I helped him off the court and into the bar where the barman handed me a first aid kit. I stuck a plaster over the wound and gave Chaz a handful of ice from a bucket on the counter to press onto the throbbing lump. I've never truly felt sorry for Chaz – he's just too bright, too damn successful – but just occasionally, and in the most irrelevant and trivial ways, marginally superior. But right now, as I scanned his damp little body swimming inside a shirt and shorts he probably bought in the Lillywhites boyswear department, I felt a pang of sympathy. It lasted fourteen seconds.

'Just bought a pad in Florida,' he said, a propos nothing.

'Florida?'

'Yeah. It's a bit of a tax dodge, really.'

He was throwing money at his burgeoning global property empire just to get rid of it.

'Well bully for you.'

'Sorry, mate. Shit. Didn't mean that to sound so boastful. I was only going to say, why don't you go out there? On me, flights and everything. My way of saying sorry properly. 'Cos I was an absolute shit.'

'No you weren't. I was a spoiled brat.'

'A phenomenal prick, actually. But the offer still stands.'

'Why?'

''Cos you're having a tough time, you're living in a cesspit, you've got no money, no career…'

'Ok, but apart from that.'

'…and it's fucking freezing here. So go and get some sun, recharge your batteries. Point is, you need to be strong for Eurovision.' Chaz clenched a tiny fist.

'Yeah, 'cos it's an assault course. All those songs and singers and Estonian girls in tinsel skirts…' I shook my head at my Euro-git friend. 'I've just written the song, Chaz. They won't even want me there, assuming we even get that far. You read the contract.'

'What about new material? That song wins, never mind the contract. You're gonna be hot. They're not gonna let you slip away into the night. So go and be creative. Write the follow-up hit.'

'Cart? Horse?'

'Told you before, think positively.'

'I'm not being ungrateful, mate, but I prefer to be lonely and cold and poor somewhere near my kids. Anyway, I need to be around for the next couple of weeks. We're in the studio next week and then it's going to be hectic until Eurovision:You Decide.'

Chaz nodded. He understood. Sort of. 'Ok. Got to concentrate on winning it first, haven't you? You can always go there after you've blitzed Europe.'

I smiled. Maybe I'd go when – if – I had some money of my own. And someone to take with me. 'Yeah. Thanks mate."

'So, come on, what's Howard James like. Tosser?'

'Dunno yet. They've got to wake him from his coma to lay down the vocals at some point.'

'You playing on it?'

'They've got proper musicians for that, and a whiz-kid producer who can make a fart sound melodious.'

'Backing vocals?'

I shook my head.

'So, apart from writing the song, what *are* you doing?'

'Consulting.'

'The fuck's that mean?' I shrugged. I had no idea. I'd just made it up. 'They all right, this record company?'

'Yeah. Guy who runs it is a bit second division – I mean, you've never heard of anyone he's produced – *but* he manages Howard and the BBC are insisting on having him, so…oh, and there's this woman there called…' I faked a stumble, 'Elaine? Yeah, Elaine. She's the guy's PA but I think she's the one who really makes the place tick. Elaine.'

'So when are you…?'

'Good looking lady, as it goes.'

'Ah-ha. So what about the…?'

'Gotta say, I quite like her. Not, like *that*, obviously, although in a parallel universe, all things being equal, I'd…but, you know, she's very bright, very…helpful.' Helpful. Yes, that's what I said.

Chaz stared into my eyes laser-fashion. 'You fucking her?'

'For Christ's sake! I'm still married. Just about, admittedly…but you know me better than that.' I'd been trying to confess – to what I'm not sure – but now I was atop my horse, High Dudgeon, up on the moral high ground, where it was all very high.

'Well you went all glassy-eyed, so…'

'Yeah, she's nice, big deal, but I haven't written off my marriage, I can tell you that for free.'

'Good. Glad to hear it.'

'Nothing's going on with me and…whatsher…Elaine. Ha! Jesus, come on!' I chuckled incredulously. 'As if.'

'Got it.'

'It's not over between me and Lisa. Not by a long chalk.'

'Well I hope you guys get back together, I really do. Nothing would make me happier.'

'Yeah. Thanks. Me too.'

Chaz checked his watch and jumped up off his chair. 'Shit. Listen, mate, I've got to go. Up early tomorrow. Off to Barcelona for the weekend. It never fucking stops. Let's talk Monday.'

What could I say? Chaz was my best mate again, assuming I was prepared to overlook the fact that he was going to Barcelona to fuck my wife the following day. And the day after that, most likely. I sat in stupefied silence as he sped off to the changing room, a glass of lager in my limp hand, staring into the crowd congregated by the bar. They all seemed happy enough. Plenty of laughs and smiles. Was it only me whose life was so irredeemably shit-soaked? Yes, I had the Eurovision thing to give me something to live for and, arguably, I'd met a woman I liked enormously with whom I may have had some sort of physical conjunction. But these lone swallows did not even make a wet spring. If Elaine was interested in me, I was flattered, if not a bit excited, but I wasn't seeking a relationship with her. I'd been vulnerable, lonely and, ok, maybe technically adulterous, but despite this smidgeon of moral ambiguity, at least she wasn't my best friend's wife. I wanted my family back. I wanted to be in amongst the cut and thrust of the daily routine, the grind, the normality. I wanted to be Dad, not a dad, and a husband to my wife…I think. But these simple dreams had disappeared over the horizon as I listed, holed below the waterline.

'Fuckin' great! Fuckin' amazing!' Thus spake Ben in considered and perceptive appreciation of a guitar riff on *In Love We Trust*. Gilbert nodded, but then he did that most of the time. It was impossible to tell what he was thinking as he slid faders and twiddled knobs to infinitesimally minimal effect. The guy had musical dog whistle receptors. Inside the recording booth, a thin man with a shaven head was experimenting with guitar licks over the blanket of bass, drums and synth which had been laid down by three bored-looking session musicians that morning. Elaine wandered in from time to time to offer her own critique, which was infinitely more acute than Ben's, throwing the occasional awkward smile my way; we really needed to talk. *In Love We Trust* sounded like a song I vaguely knew, but not the one I'd composed. The chord structure and lyrics were essentially the same, but the sweeping synthesised violins, grand piano (effect) and fake brass gave it a depth and breadth entirely alien to my original man-and-his-guitar version. Maybe Gilbert was a genius, or maybe he was a complete prick making mincemeat of a decent song. Until Howard James deigned to grace us with his presence, it would be impossible to know for sure if it had legs, and even then…

I'd been in recording studios a few times, mostly (and we're going back a bit here) limited four track facilities that smelt like smoking rooms. I'd cut a few demo tracks with friends, but it was a case of maximising the potential of each precious track by singing and playing as many instruments on each as humanly possible before dubbing everything down into an incoherent mush. Prehistoric, unlike the software that has revolutionised the recording industry in recent years with its endless variations, gizmos and effects, sufficient to make you delirious with choice. Gilbert seemed to be on top of it all but, in the end, the song's the thing. And if it isn't, it should be. Still, there was no more exciting or exhilarating environment for someone who'd always dreamed of making recording studios his principal place of business.

The session ended after six and I felt wired. I'd been too preoccupied with the process to allow images of Chaz and Lisa grinding themselves into oblivion to sully my day, but they might decimate my evening if I returned to my drab little tomb to cogitate. A Friday night piss-up struck me as the ideal way to maintain my high before slipping into unconsciousness without touching the sides. I passed Elaine's tiny office on my way out and tapped on her open door. She looked up and returned my smile, but quickly refocused on her screen.

'Bye, then,' I said, starting for the outer door.

'See ya,' she replied, still transfixed.

I took a step back and closed her door. I was almost at the stairs when I heard a muffled voice. 'Fancy a drink? I mean, if you can hang on ten minutes.'

I stopped, mulled momentarily, then continued on my way, the outer door swinging lazily into its jamb behind me. The one bum note of the day had been played by Elaine and I'd harmonised it pretty bummily myself. Two adults barely able to look each other in the eye all day and only able to communicate once backs were turned and doors were closed.

I set off up the mountainous Crouch Hill towards the station. Overground to…somewhere, then the Tube to, fuck knew where else. I'd improvise; I was bound to find a pub eventually. The air was dry, icy, and bit into my already chapped lips. I reached the underlit station foyer and bought a ticket from a machine. I turned to walk through the barrier and saw Elaine standing on the platform, smiling. God knows how she'd ghosted past me.

'I said, fancy a drink?'

I hate the West End, I really do, particularly on Friday nights when the shackles are off. So much needless shouting and whooping, groups of smokers and drinkers outside pubs blocking streets, people jaywalking and swearing at hooting cars. And that's at 7pm. Four hours later, it's Dystopia.

But tonight I craved the energy and buzz of W1, as opposed to Hanger Lane, the antithesis of life itself. Elaine and I steered a path from the studied frostiness of the day towards something approaching the intimacy of our night together. And, loosened by a couple of drinks or eight, I was finally able to ask that nagging question. Her response, charmingly prefaced by a farcical splutter into her wine, shattered all doubt.

'Sex? Oh do me a lemon!'

'Ok, so how the hell did I end up in your bed?'

'You stumbled in. I don't know if you were looking for the toilet, or whether you were disorientated, but you just collapsed on the bed. So I left you there. I didn't defile you, ok?'

'Phew, thank God for that.' Stupid little wipe of the forehead.

'Repulsive idea, eh?'

'No! Oh, no, I didn't mean that at all. I just meant…'

'*I'm married, I've got kids.* Yeah, blah, blah, blah. Boring.'

'Sorry.'

'Oh gawd, don't apologise. Look, no offence but you're not my type.'

She didn't really mean that. 'Ok, if you say so.'

'Mike, watch my lips. Seriously. I mean, I like you a lot, just not like *that*. You're the polar opposite of the kind of person I go for. You couldn't be any less my type.'

Either she doth protest too much or…no, she bloody meant it. Well at least that was that sorted. Except, knowing what I knew for certain now, I wished something *had* happened. Then I'd have felt almost even with Lisa, a puerile and primal response I know, but valid in my warped estimation.

I checked my watch. Somehow it had gone eleven and although Elaine and I could have bantered into the early hours, I had to pick up the kids in the morning and didn't want to be late, much less hung over. Outside, we battled for a cab with the waifs and strays, finally stopping one in Wardour Street. I stood aside and guided Elaine inside, closing the door behind her. I leaned through the window and kissed her wind-cooled cheek, reminding me of my last brush with Faye a few weeks earlier. Faye. I'd thought about her, a lot, mainly with regret. I'd let her slip away, even if she was never there for the taking.

I really liked Elaine, but Faye…Faye was special.

Here's a tip. If you're thinking about a family outing to the Science Museum, make sure it coincides with a major royal wedding, a World Cup Final or the immediate aftermath of a nuclear war, otherwise be prepared for an interminable wait in the middle of a heaving scrum. In the rain. With your pissed off kids. Who'd rather be watching their Shrek 2 DVD somewhere warm. I'm not much good when I finally get inside either. The yawning starts almost immediately and ten minutes in my watering eyes can barely focus. This does not, I hope, betray Philistinism on my part, though Lisa might argue. It's just my body's natural reaction to the energy-sapping shuffle through vast, airless rooms surrounded by other people's squabbling children, as if my own aren't enough. I like looking at the exhibits, I really do, but I can't handle the enforced lingering. I can take in a lunar pod or a 1950's Hoover on the move; no need to stop. It's all very fascinating up to a point – which usually arrives after four minutes – but then I want to run, screaming all the way down Kensington Gore.

Forewarned is forearmed. A clear strategy was essential. So I picked the kids up insanely early amid searing protestations – Lisa's bleary-eyed sister wasn't too happy with me either – got there in a flash, parked up and joined the queue somewhere near Wolverhampton. Hey presto, mere hours later, we were inside. We decided to start with a much-trumpeted laser light exhibition which, it transpired, comprised lots of coloured lights beaming mainly at walls. I then dragged the kids to a little exhibition of vintage household appliances. It was the only bit I ever enjoyed, probably because no-one else did and it was always relatively empty. 'See that phone,' I bored, 'we used to use those. We actually had to dial numbers. With our fingers. Never mind buttons, or speed dial or address books.'

'Yeah Dad. Very interesting. Can we, like, get some chocolate?' said Katia. 'Just for energy.'

'Not yet. Hey, look at that mangle. See, nowadays we have dryers, but my mum used to go in the garden and…'

You make your own fun, don't you?

Afterwards, we ate in a staggeringly expensive burger bar in Knightsbridge before making our way back to my flat via the multiplex cinema in Ealing where I slept through a mind-rotting American high school 'comedy'. The kids were in no hurry to reacquaint themselves with my charmless abode with its miserably inadequate TV, curtainless windows and yellowing furniture. It was purpose-designed to depress. But they didn't complain, at least not to me. Maybe they were under instructions. We ordered in some Chinese from downstairs (Katia only ate the rice even though she had me casually order four other dishes) and watched, if memory serves, the Shrek 2 DVD. For a change. At around ten, I settled them into my bed and sat chatting with them until their eyes drooped. I kissed their buttery cheeks and turned out the light. Back in the lounge, I unfolded my creaking sofabed and lay propped against the unforgiving pine headboard watching the football.

I flicked off the light at midnight and wept myself to sleep.

CHAPTER 15

Everyone, it turns out, was right. Howard James was a complete tosser. He hadn't changed much since his multi-coloured hair days, except that there was less hair to multi-colour now. From his high forehead down, his face was worryingly gaunt, pallid skin stretched to breaking point over the sharp architecture of his face. The bridge of his nose looked about ready to collapse. One severe cold should do it. His teeth were crooked and yellow and he was dressed in the same long-tailed purple overcoat he wore in his heyday. But, somehow, he could still sing. The instrumental tracks had been teased rather magically by Gilbert into a sumptuous melange of strings, horns and percussion. The guitar solo worked beautifully and with Howard's unique, reedy vocals overlaying this confection, my song sounded, well, fucking fantastic. Too classy to win Eurovision obviously, but maybe good enough to make the charts.

Howard barked orders from the booth, demanding more echo, less treble, more Coke (Diet – he was all business in there), a tuna sandwich with celery and mayonnaise and cheese and onion crisps. He barely registered my existence. I doubt he even knew I was the song's composer, much less cared. I was just some bloke nodding in the corner, although Ben had introduced me as a musical consultant, which sounded grand albeit my consultancy services were not sought once throughout the entire process. I wondered whether Howard actually believed he'd written it, perhaps in a drug-addled trance. He certainly claimed proprietary rights over the final mix, although I knew the sanguine, unflappable Gilbert was going to do whatever he bloody-well pleased with it later on when Howard was busy tripping in his Hertfordshire mansion. The session ended just after four and Howard, Gilbert, Ben, Elaine and I went out to celebrate with tea and inedible organic cakes in a Bohemian little cafe opposite the studios. The inscrutable, mute Gilbert was lost in his mental remix while the rest of us chatted excitedly about the next couple of weeks leading up to Eurovision:You Decide – the TV promo, the press, the photo shoots and so much else. Howard disappeared after downing his Earl Grey, re-emerging ten minutes later, his nose dusted with fine, white powder, to wolf down a pastry before being chauffeured home by a terse little man in an expensively hired limo. Ben was pushing the boat out on this one. This song had better do some business, I thought; we all thought.

I didn't return to the studio with the others, electing to head back home. Elaine had twinkled all day, her conversation, her coy, private, smiles, her endless good humour rendering me woebegone and confused. She didn't like me like *that,* did she? Or did she? Maybe, just maybe, she was beginning to see me in a different light. Was that even possible? I knew nothing any more. Whatever might or might not have been bubbling under with Elaine, I had to confront Lisa and/or Chaz at some point. I needed 'closure' (yeah, sorry). I knew, though, that I couldn't take Lisa on at the house, not if the kids were there; frankly, I wasn't sure when I'd be ready for such a traumatic conversation whatever the venue. Chaz, on the other hand, was small and not actually that strong or wiry, and so while he may have been able to parry my line of questioning with his gift for methodical reasoning, I could just beat it the fuck out of him.

My laptop glared brightly in the gloom of the living room, if you could apply the word 'living' to any room in that flat. It was giving me a headache. I was glued to Faye's Facebook page and marvelling at her photo for the umpteenth time. My little arrow flickered over the '+ New message' button for an age, challenging me to left-click, taunting me. I wanted to send her a message, just to know that, for the brief moment it would take her to read it, I'd be in her thoughts. I wanted to tell her that my marriage was over, that I was an unencumbered single man again and that I'd like to see her. But then counsel for the sane argued that I was barely a friend, and I'd pissed her off anyway. But what if I told her about my Eurovision adventure? Surely that would elicit some sort of positive response, something pleasant and congratulatory. So what if my contract forbade me from telling anyone I'd written the song? Faye wasn't anyone, and who was she going to tell? It was something, and maybe it would squirt some oil on the rust-stiffened hinges of that door. On the other hand...

I sat and I stared, and I stared and I stared.

I was never going to click on that button.

I only have to say the word 'squash' and Chaz is there in his baggy, Corinthian shorts hitched high above his shapeless waist, bouncing nimbly on his Green-Flashed toes, full of hope and intent. Sucker. Doesn't he know he hasn't beaten me in fourteen years (since I tore ankle ligaments chasing a short one – he was 7-0 down at the time and claimed it)? I arrived deliberately late and didn't apologise. We met on the court, no preamble, no pre-match banter. He was already sweating, having got in some sneaky practise while he waited, like it was going to do him any good. I forsook a warm-up and insisted we get under way. I immediately took command of the 'T', thwacking the ball from side to side while he scampered fruitlessly around behind me like a hamster in a wheel. Just when he thought he'd got the measure of me, I'd chip one in short and wait for him to scramble it back before smashing it away for a winner while he stood stranded and breathless by the front wall. I varied it occasionally, pinging a couple of straight ones along his backhand side, the ball adhering to the wall, forcing him to smash his racket frame trying to gouge it out. This was fun. I let him have one point in the first set (he mis-hit one which died in the nick and I couldn't be arsed to chase it), none in the second and one in the third (he actually hit a decent shot which kept low). He was drenched with sweat as we entered the fourth set so I stepped up the pace. I even took my jumper off. I toyed with him for a while, then brought him in close so that I could barge him 'accidentally' to the floor. I'm not a violent or physical man, but I suddenly understood the simple, primal pleasure of knocking a man flying. That beefy moment of impact, the grunt as air is bullied from the lungs, the clatter of limbs hitting solid wood. I wanted some more of that. The next barge sent him spiralling into the side wall. He yelped and dropped his racket, then stood there in a crouch, buttocks against the wall, rubbing his protruding shoulder bone for a minute. Chaz was too proud, too competitive to tell me to cool it which rather played into my hands. The next rally ended with a nasty little drop shot and I strolled to set point with a sumptuous wrong-footing volley. I started the final rally by bringing him in close again, and had him buzzing around me, mosquito-fashion, for the next few shots. He was within my swinging arc and, after he'd scooped up a dolly, I took a ferocious swipe and caught him square on the hip with the end of my racket. It made a fearful crack and my old wooden racket snapped. Chaz collapsed clutching himself in agony. I glowered over him, dripping sweat into his face and said: 'That's going to hurt next time you fuck my wife.'

Men? We're just stupid kids who never properly grow up. Male adulthood, with all its familial and financial burdens, is a front. Underneath it all, we remain pre-pubescent. I remember having a fight with a kid called Paul Knight when I was about nine. Knight was the school yobbo; you didn't mess with him. But I knew I was strong and fast and, crucially, twice his size, and even though I was regarded as vaguely academic rather than Neanderthal, I wanted to take him on. I provoked a fight on the field at the back of the school, making sure my classmates were there to witness it. We pushed and jostled for a bit until I karate-chopped him on the back of the neck. Knight crumbled and I strolled away triumphant and preening, kudos enhanced. But afterwards, when the glow of victory had faded, I experienced an unbidden self-loathing, a recognition that I would never fight anyone ever again, reasoning that there were better ways to prove you were tough, albeit I'm still looking. And, on a practical level, I've always felt that if you have to take some pain for ultimate gain, you can keep the gain. I prefer to rely on an acid tongue and scathing sarcasm, on the strict understanding that I'm pretty quick on my feet if things turn nasty.

But beating up Chaz was easy, well merited and, I'm ashamed to say, rather satisfying. For all his money and status and smug contentment, for all that he was screwing Mrs Kenton, I left him as nothing more than a pathetic heap of humiliated bones.

CHAPTER 16

THERE'S SOMETHING HEART-WRENCHINGLY poignant about a wizened man in his fifties frolicking around a frost-coated field on a bitter April morning in a linen shirt and outdated frock coat. Trust me on this one. Howard James was not blessed with manifest physical grace, elegance or fluidity, but he was game, I'll give him that. He mimed to *In Love We Trust* with gusto, take after freezing fucking take, in barns and outhouses, by icy streams and in misty copses. Quite whose idea it was to cart a film crew, fake backing band and poor old Howard to a remote swathe of countryside in Berkshire, I don't know, but he was clearly a sadistic prick. I was struggling to make the link between a song about trusting in the inherent beauty of love to make a relationship work and the frozen, dung-laden greenery in which we were all suffering, but perhaps I lacked the aesthetic sensibility to fully appreciate it. The final scenes were shot in a stone-built farmhouse with an oddly ineffective log fire burning in the period fireplace, while Howard cuddled a girl half his age on the hearth. It was vaguely offensive, but by then I wouldn't have cared if he'd been wrestling naked with John McCririck in a vat of vomit. I just wanted this day to be over. Ben was on hand to keep the spirits up, although I'd have appreciated him more if he'd arranged a warm Winnebago for those not involved or, better still, smacked the director across the jaw when he first unveiled his vision. Elaine drove up in the afternoon and we spent much of the time giggling at the insanity and being shushed by the director, a middle-aged man with an earring for whom feature films would forever be a distant dream.

Elaine drove me home and I thought it only sensible to tell her where I actually lived rather than have her drop me off miles away and face a nose-numbing walk home. Our conversation as we trundled along the A40 was, for once, rather prosaic. Fewer giggles, more straight talking. Somehow she'd guessed that the idyllic family life I'd trumpeted was no longer extant, although quite when I'd signalled the fact, I don't know. Perhaps I'd confessed during my drunken stupor, or perhaps it was the fact that I'd been so obviously attracted to her. Either way, she would have figured it out as soon as she caught sight of my miserable bachelor pad, wouldn't she? I tried to convince her that I was better off being single, that Lisa and I needed space, that it was healthier for the kids not to be in a house where tension reigned and she accused me of rationalising. Which I was. Frankly, this female intuition thing was beginning to get on my tits.

The car heater had only managed a weak whisper of tepid air and we were both in need of warming up, so I invited her up for a hot drink. She declined. She had to get home, she said, to ready herself for some sort of music biz bash and, if I'm honest, it was a bit of a relief to have the evening to myself. I just wanted a hot bath and a chance to reflect. Later, as I lay there steaming the ice out of my pores, it dawned on me that I'd played the part of the vulnerable, emotionally confused man to perfection. I'd mis-read Elaine's signals. Ours was the burgeoning relationship of Platonic soul mates, not potential lovers. And that was fine with me. As much as I liked Elaine, as much as we got along, it didn't add up to anything. I mean, never mind that I wasn't her type; something was missing. Something like feelings.

My answerphone was blinking furiously in the gloom of the living room when I padded in huddled into my dressing gown. I pinned the ratty curtains I'd manufactured from a couple of old sheets to the window frame, flicked the light on, then the kettle, and dragged my fan heater to within an inch of my legs, setting it to maximum. A nasty, burnt wool smell filled the room. I pushed the 'play' button.

'What's the fucking matter with you, eh? How long have you known me, you tit? I just wouldn't do something like that. I just fucking wouldn't. But…'

The tape ran on and I thought Chaz must have hung up, until: 'But there is something you need to know.' Another long pause. 'Look, I'm not going to do it in a bloody answerphone message. Call me, ok? And stop being an arsehole.' Long pause. 'God you're an idiot.'

Bleep.

'Fuck off,' I muttered bitterly.

181

Another Saturday, another day to fill with Millie and Katia. This was the plan: after the pick-up, we were heading straight for a squalid little bowling alley in Hammersmith, then onto McDonalds ('it's our little secret, ok?') then, if it stayed dry (and even if it drizzled) Kew Gardens (they were going to love that, weren't they?, looking at flowers) and finally back to my flat for pizzas and a DVD. Probably Shrek 2. I felt for the poor little sods.

You don't have to be away from your own house for long for it to stop feeling like home. Everything was familiar, the walls, the doors, the furniture, the bits and pieces lying around, the smell, but it wasn't mine, not any more, not for me. I sat in the kitchen waiting for Millie to pack her little pink rucksack upstairs. Lisa was in the shower (as she always seemed to be when I turned up) and Katia was at the kitchen table humming as she studiously filled in a crossword in a kids' pop music magazine. She'd only recently taken an interest in music and was now obsessed. Next week it would be computer games. I just hoped the following week – and for that matter, month, year and lifetime – it wouldn't be boys. I know what boys want. She was struggling with a couple of clues, so I pulled my chair around the table to sit next to her. To the right of the crossword page was a composite photo of the British Eurovision contestants with the gangly Howard standing in the centre, looking like the others' wacky and rather sinister old uncle. Either side of him, strewn awkwardly across a variety of chairs and sofas were, variously: a black hip hop outfit wearing, even I knew, naff white headbands; a female duo (one ugly one gorgeous – which one could actually sing? Hmm); a sugary male/ female combo; a little boy who'd been a one hit wonder a couple of years earlier; and a bubble-gum band which had failed to make it through the auditions on X Factor. It was quite a mix. One thing I did know was that Howard had a modicum of talent, which probably set him apart and made him favourite to come last.

Millie finally joined us and saw me looking over Katia's shoulder at the magazine. 'Dad,' she laughed, 'you're too old for that, silly.'

'No I'm not. Music doesn't have an age limit. I like lots of pop groups that you like.'

'Like who?'

'That's not important. But why shouldn't I?'

'Er, 'cos you're old?'

It was cogent and unarguable, but I gave it a go.

'A, I'm not old and B, I'm not old.'

'A and B, yes you are,' said Millie as she disarranged the fridge in search of a blackcurrant Froob.

'What about the Eurovision Song Contest? That's pop music and it's watched by millions of people. They can't all be young, can they?'

'Eurovision?' she said, her eyebrows slanted in pity. 'Dad. That's absolute shit.'

While the girls ate their dismal thin crust Margheritas in my drab little lounge, transfixed by a green cartoon monster with an accent from God-knows-where, I settled for the dry ham sandwich I'd bought in Sainsburys a couple of days ago, my own gaze firmly on the blinking answerphone light. It had to be Chaz again and I was in no mood to listen to his whining self-justification. He'd also left two voicemail messages on my mobile and a text, none of which I'd returned. When was he going to get the message?

CHAPTER 17

It WAS EASY to get swept up in the excitement. The TV appearances, the press interviews, the PR gatherings. I went to everything, eager to soak up this fame by proxy. I may never have this opportunity again, so what the hell? Howard never questioned my presence – in truth, the man was incapable of basic social interaction – and barely grunted in my general direction when Ben introduced me at each event as though for the first time. I was the music consultant. How could he keep forgetting? I hovered in the background wearing an amused little smirk, offering the odd sarcastic comment whenever Elaine was around, like it was all a bit beneath me. I think it was important, to me if nobody else, not to be seen to be taking the whole thing too seriously. I was above this trivial competition. I had artistic integrity. But it was serious; I had nothing else. I preferred not to think about the empty road that lay ahead of me if this all turned to dust. Ben seemed happy to have me around as long as I remained benign, and I continued to enjoy Elaine's company even if any hint of romance was dead in the water. There was no time for that kind of nonsense anyway. Too much else going on.

I was still putting in the odd telesales shift, but finding it increasingly difficult to concentrate, my mind forever floating off into the world of celebrity, applause, awards, idolatry. What if we won? I couldn't help asking myself that question as I sleep-walked through countless, by-numbers conversations with my disinterested marks. We'd have a massive hit on our hands, compelling Ben, surely, to draft me in to write Howard's follow-up album in addition to songs for all the other artistes on the roster. With my reputation as the next big thing growing, I'd be flown out to LA and New York to write with and for Prince and Stevie and maybe even the great man himself, Lionel Richie. There'd be red carpets to cruise at the MTV awards and the Mobos (I know I'm not especially black, but you don't have to be apparently) and I'd have a string of girlfriends plucked from the worlds of pop and fashion. And then, I suppose, natural progression would lead to the composition of Oscar winning film scores; Tom would ask for me by name. I'd be the go-to composer, the man. And you know what? I was going to keep my Hanger Lane shithole despite owning fabulous houses and apartments in every glamorous corner of the globe. It'd keep me grounded, remind me of the hard times. And it would also be quite handy for Heathrow, my gateway to the world, my playground. I'd install state-of-the-art studios in my pads in NY (Dakota Building), St Tropez (up the hill from Elton and Posh) and the Bahamas (an island next door Branson's).

'Good morning. How are you today? My name's Michael Kenton from PBJ Accounting. I'm calling to ask whether you'd be interested in outsourcing your bookkeeping to...hello? Hello?'

I'm hopeless with sombre news. My first reaction is to giggle. It's nerves, I think, not a sign of disrespect. Lisa's father passed away in his sleep. That's the way to go, isn't it? So they say. Personally, I'd rather go just after making love to the young Kim Basinger followed by a full English, but that's me. Lisa called with the news as I was about to nip over the roundabout to Raj Temple for a lonesome curry. I uttered a few 'I'm sorrys,' and 'maybe it was for the bests,' but only through suppressed, hugely inappropriate laughter. I don't think she noticed. He'd been battling prostate cancer for a few years so his demise was not unexpected. Even so, it's always a shock, isn't it? I liked the old buffer in a distant, far-from-matey way. We didn't share many laughs or play golf together; there was no sporty banter or whispered, nudge-nudge asides about women. But we got along and never rubbed each other up the wrong way, a pleasant, formal relationship with a thoroughly decent man. I wanted to go to the funeral to pay my respects regardless of the state of play with Lisa and she and I acknowledged the need to demonstrate a unified front. Her mother knew nothing about our problems and Lisa, understandably, didn't want to burden her with it now. We had to arrive together, stand together and leave together. I wasn't looking forward to the journey but at least the kids were coming along to provide a pressure valve. I had no intention of discussing the state of our marriage, much less Chaz. There would come a day when I'd confront her about that little twat, but this was not the right time. Indeed, nothing was going to be said – at least not by me – until after Eurovision: You Decide.

Funerals never move me. When my own father died four years ago, the ceremony was an unnecessary adornment. He'd gone and I knew how I felt. I didn't need to celebrate his life with a dry speech in a cold chapel nor make public my sadness. You keep those things in your head and your heart. And I bristle when I hear the pat generalisations about parents and children, about goodness and reward, about achievement and contentment from people who barely knew the deceased.

The trip to the crematorium in Shepton Mallet was uneventful. Lisa seemed to be holding it together, coping. I wouldn't have expected anything less. The girls struggled to maintain sobriety in the back of the car, but what do kids understand about death? Death's for old people. Let them worry about mortality. The service was mercifully short and the whole thing over and done with in less than half an hour. There were too many more funerals on the list to dawdle. Death is a business like anything else, and we've all got a stake in it. Lisa accepted condolences with her customary grace while I shook countless hands, bent to receive the dry, papery, lavender-scented kisses of elderly female relatives and maintained mournful eyebrows till they ached. Testimony to Lisa's standing in the art world was the attendance of scores of colleagues, artists and clients as well as one or two celebrities who caused quite a stir during the service. Wasn't that David Thirwell, the hirsute and eminent presenter of many an arts and culture show? That was definitely Dame Harriet Lewis, the actress, blowing her restructured nose in the corner. And fuck me if that wasn't old chocolate-voice himself, Don Ellwood. Did he remember me, the vomiting spouse? He bestowed his sly, oily wink on a privileged few, but not me. Instead, I received a cool handshake, a blank expression and a muttered, yet profoundly theatrical, 'I'm so sorry.' We didn't have a lot else to talk about. He was rather warmer with Lisa, giving her his trade mark squeeze on the hip as he kissed her cheek. Lisa smiled, her eyes a-twinkle, face glowing. I couldn't remember the last time I engendered that kind of response from her. If ever.

Everyone trudged back to Lisa's mother's magnificent house in Crapnell (no tittering) for tea served up in bone china thimbles, and a range of one-bite-and-they're-gone sandwiches. I bundled the kids upstairs to watch TV in the spare bedroom, their patience having worn dangerously thin after so much enforced reverence. Kids need to shout and create a little havoc or, at the very least, watch something mindless to stop them going haywire. Back downstairs, the low, respectful mumbling was occasionally punctured by the booming, look-at-me voice of Don Ellwood whose beautifully realised 'expression tragique' (made that one up) signified his very real grief. The disingenuous tit. Around seven, Lisa commenced the longest goodbye in history while the kids and I sat patiently watching her in the hallway. Sober relatives exchanged muted farewell handshakes and kisses while the art crowd indulged in hollow mwah-mwahs, gushing thank-yous and dramatic tears. At last we were about ready to leave I thought, but Don Ellwood ushered Lisa into the kitchen where he appeared to deliver an impassioned pep talk, followed by a longish but not quite inappropriate hug. Lisa patted his lapels as she gazed dolefully up at him, eyes moist, then turned to join us. As if dictating terms to her dog, she strode past and beckoned us to follow. Which we did.

We were silent for most of the return journey, apart from the odd cutting remark about some aunt's garish dress or some family friend's inapt remark. Lisa's observations sounded flat and tetchy. Five years ago they'd have come across as sarcastic, hilarious. Back at the house, we tumbled out of the car and I crouched on my haunches to give the girls a hug and a kiss. They were like tense little muscles, itching to get inside, especially as a steady rain was now falling. I ushered them halfway up the front path before their patience expired. Duty done, they sped into the hall and flew up the stairs. Lisa stood at a respectable distance behind me as this sad little scene played itself out, then took my hand.

'Thanks for coming. I appreciate it.'

'Of course. I wanted to be there,' I said.

'Well, whatever, thanks.'

'Sure.'

She released my hand and started to walk towards the house, but stopped at the front step. Was she waiting for me to speak up? I didn't have an awful lot left to lose. 'Look, I know what's going on so…it's all right…well it's not all right, but…'

'This is not the time, Mike.'

Which was a good point. 'It's never really the time, though, is it?'

Lisa stepped into the hallway.

'So, I'm going to get a solicitor,' I said. 'Ok?'

'Do what you want, Michael.'

I got back in the car and drove away, stopping thirty yards down the road when I was out of view. I stared hollow-eyed at the rain as it lashed against the windscreen, my eyes now watering as profusely as the sky. I was doing a lot of weeping lately. I hadn't planned any of that, but standing there looking at that alien woman, it tumbled out and it felt right. I had to take control of things now. I'd been a passive bystander observing my own demise for too long.

Nobody likes solicitors. I mean, why would they? Not even their wives and children think much of them, probably. A jaundiced view, maybe, but it's based on bruising experience, not lazy stereotyping or tabloid-style prejudice. I've had a few brushes with them along the way, you see, and always come away feeling like a little piece of myself has gone missing, my faith in humanity shaken to the core. I'm sure there are some smashing solicitors out there, fine, trustworthy, principled men and women who stand up for what's fair and equitable and who seek a reasonable fee for work done. Yeah, right. Look, it's just that those I've dealt with have been one or more of: greedy, thoughtless, pompous, unreliable, unpleasant. There was the local guy who handled our dispute with a neighbour over the maintenance of a fence, a trivial little matter which had, rather embarrassingly, spiralled out of control. Lisa had a bee in her bonnet; don't look at me. Cost of mending the fence, £137, paid, eventually and grudgingly, by our neighbour; our solicitor's fee, £580. He cited research as the pricey culprit, and had apparently allocated an hour to writing the single paragraph warning letter. There was another, an odious City slicker from a Magic Circle firm who, against my better judgement, Pete had called in to update our standard maintenance contract. £3,700 + VAT, that cost the company. On examination, he'd merely copied our existing documentation, changing a couple of words here and there. His weasely justification was that he'd had to consider our entire contractual position vis a vis clients before concluding that we were already adequately protected, omitting to mention that he'd seen us coming. I imagine he had a deskful of mugs with witty legal aphorisms like: *Lawyer, n – Someone who prepares a 10,000 word document and calls it a brief* and *Hell hath no fury like the lawyer of a woman scorned.* The only one missing would be: *You don't have to be a cock to work here…but if you ain't, you won't make partner.*

As with my search for a specialist Eurovision lawyer, I had no idea where to start, having never got divorced before. Astoundingly, given my age and the middle class circles in which we mixed, I only knew one divorcee. Faye. What an opportunity lay before me here; as soon as I asked her for the name of the solicitor who handled her divorce, she'd know I was a single man. Bang. Result! Never mind that she didn't fancy me, didn't even like me much, was in a relationship and had a hundred other reasons not to take my pathetic bait, this was a one-off last chance to make her see sense.

My message was short and sweet (it took over two hours to compose):

Hi Faye. Hope you're well. Bit of bad news, I'm afraid. Lisa and I are splitting up. It's amicable, if that's the right word! Anyway, just wondering whether you could give me the name and number of the guy who handled your divorce as I think you mentioned he was pretty good. Love, Mike.

I spent an hour over '*love*' but went with it in the end. What harm could it do? I also took about forty-five minutes pondering the bit about her saying her solicitor was pretty good because she hadn't, but without that fib the whole thing would have been transparently groundless. I clicked 'send' and waited. Ten minutes later, there was *still* no reply. Oh, shit. I'd really pissed her off. An hour later – nothing, and still nothing an hour after that. I eventually trooped off to bed deflated and dejected. Why hadn't she replied? An acknowledgement would've done. I was never going to sleep now. My smart phone had no internet connection this deep into the grim underbelly of Hanger Lane, and I hadn't got round to setting up broadband, so I was stuck with an ancient modem and a too-short lead which wouldn't stretch to the bedroom forcing me to get up after twenty minutes to check, and again thirty minutes later. Nothing, nothing, nothing! At 3.30am, I concluded that unless she was now living in a different time zone, she was unlikely to be checking for messages for at least another six hours.

I drifted into a sour dream set in a freezing funeral parlour. Inside, the handful of mourners were dressed in black, their faces ashen and featureless. Only Lisa's face was recognisable, characteristically beautiful behind her gauze veil. She smiled but all her top teeth were missing. She guided me to the coffin. Inside, a well-dressed man lay there with a tear on his cheek. The man was me. He/I got up, wiped away the tear, smiled, and strode out of the parlour without looking back.

There's probably some pretty elementary dream analysis bollocks to be taken from that (apart from the teeth – inexplicable that). Either way, I can tell you I was fucking freaked out and jumped out of bed at six in an icy sweat. I settled in the living room nursing a mug of tea, the fan heater char-grilling my shins, leaving the rest of me frozen. I'd never paid much attention to dreams, but this was a pointed message if ever I saw one, from me to myself: it was over, properly over but, far from being dead and buried, it signalled my glorious rebirth. I felt pretty charged up about that – whether Faye replied or not.

Chaz had finally given up trying to contact me – I'd been screening all unknown numbers on my mobile in case he tried to sneak through the back door by using someone else's, and I was leaving all landline calls to the answerphone. I suspect he even rang the doorbell a couple of times, but without a peephole – and as an inveterate ignorer of unannounced callers – I couldn't be sure. I didn't have time for him and his 'innocent' explanation. I'd have thought more of him if he'd had the balls to tell me the truth from the off. Even so, I'd been feeling nauseous about the squash court debacle. What did violence achieve apart from momentary macho triumph? I'd have been better off squealing to Denise about her miserable infidel of a husband, though she might have killed him and I didn't want that on my conscience. Let her find out the hard way like I did.

But regardless of the rights and wrongs, the cheating and the deception, I'd come to accept that I wasn't blameless, and it would have been naïve to think that my personal travails of the last few months were solely responsible for the collapse of our marriage. It ran much deeper than that. Still and all, couldn't Lisa have screwed someone else, anyone else? That's what really hurt. And it had obviously been going on while we continued to maintain the façade of an on-going, viable marriage which, I assume, meant she was having sex with both of us over a period of time. Not something I wanted to spend too much time contemplating.

'Hi Mike. I'm well thanks. Sorry about your news. The guy's name is Matthew Roberts. Don't remember mentioning him to you but, anyway, here's his email address. Best, Faye.'

I scoured this message for an hour analysing its many positives. *Sorry about your news* – so she was upset on my behalf and maybe wanted to get together to talk, to help me through this tough time; *Don't remember mentioning him to you* – which could mean that she wanted to get together to fill me in about him before I called him. *Best.* Ahh, that was the big clue. No regards or sincerity, only her best, one step below *Love*. This merited a reply but I decided to wait. It was going to require some serious thought.

I emailed Matthew Roberts and received a fairly instant response which concerned me. It's the same with builders. If they can start next week, they can't be any good. I arranged to meet him the following morning at his offices in Maida Vale. Meantime, I thought a shift at the 'office' – for want of a better word – was in order given my imminent fleecing by the aforementioned Mr Roberts. Telesales had lost much of its allure for me since, well since the first minute, but even more so since my brush with the glitz and glamour of the music business, but needs must. Why hadn't Chaz or his useless solicitor friend advised me to insist on a clause providing for an advance on royalties? the useless bastards. Maybe because they knew Ben would tell me to go screw myself? I had to maintain a modicum of independence from Lisa, but I was going to be reliant on the divorce settlement to keep me financially viable given that telesales was probably my professional pinnacle, a thought so depressing, it was tempting to call Jerry and ask if I could buff his cufflinks on a full-time basis. Exciting as my Eurovision adventure was, deep down I simply didn't believe it would lead anywhere, whatever Ben said about the song's potential. He was a bullshitter, a serial low achiever, a small time operator who'd carved out an unspectacular niche for himself within an industry that was fast leaving him in its slipstream. He peddled minor artistes and has-beens, making a living out of back catalogues and compilations, peppered with the odd novelty hit. He had no musical vision, no master plan. He just went from day to day, snapping up bargains and grasping minor opportunities. If the song won, either Eurovision:You Decide or even the whole thing, I still wasn't going to get the credit or recognition, so unless Ben was going to throw me some bones, my musical résumé would make my IT CV look stellar. And even Ben's very finest bones would be little more than a few tracks on obscure albums selling in single figures. A healthy dose of realism like that can be quite refreshing sometimes. Other times, it can make you reach for the bread knife.

Matthew Roberts was the antithesis of every solicitor I'd ever met. His hair was unfashionably long, the back nudging distressingly into mullet territory. He wore jeans and trainers, an open-necked denim shirt and some sort of tribal necklace of the type people stopped wearing in 1979, unless they're Richard Hammond. More like an out of touch A & R man than a serious purveyor of legal services. His office was a dank cell in a faded Edwardian mansion block, piled high with files and bundled papers tied with pink ribbons. His secretary, a woman in her mid-thirties with neon-cherry hair and stately cheekbones who, it transpired, was his wife, operated out of a cupboard next door. He called her his PA, but only when she was in the room.

I told Matthew everything, with much emphasis on Lisa's infidelity with my best friend, their deception, the hurt. It was cathartic, moving Matthew to adopt a practised nodding mien, eyebrows knitted in a tight, empathetic knot at the top of his nose. He'd heard this kind of stuff before, of course, but he responded sensitively and patiently, a counsellor as much as a lawyer. He had his feet up on his desk as we spoke, but I didn't hold that against him. It was *his way* and he was on *my side*. He walked me through the legal steps, the likely responses and the time it would probably take to settle. He also said that bitterness would inevitably flow. Au contraire. I explained that Lisa and I were amicable, that we were going to be sensible and reasonable, that the kids came first.

'Yeah, ok, but that's all bollocks in the end,' said the now jaunty Matthew. 'No such thing as an amicable divorce. I know you think you're going to do this without rancour, but somewhere down the line you'll be arguing over who gets the Teasmaid. It always happens. But that's what I'm here for. I'm basically a pragmatist, Mike, so I'll try and steer you round the bull and make sure you see the bigger picture.'

'Honestly, I just want enough to get by. She's the one with the money and she's entitled to keep what she makes. As long as the kids…'

'Ok, stop you there. You need to get real, Mike,' he said. 'Guiding principle? Go for everything to get something. And by the way, who's helped pay the mortgage all these years, who's helped buy the kids' clothes, who put up that set of shelves in the lounge? You.'

'Actually, it was a Polish bloke called Wotjek.'

For a guy with such a happy-go-lucky appearance, he was a shade humourless.

'You've made your contribution, Mike, you're entitled to a fair reward.'

'Ok. Look, Faye says you're good, and I trust her implicitly so…do your stuff.'

'Fees, Mike. How are we for fees? I'm not the most expensive solicitor in the world, but I've got to eat.'

'I'll be ok.'

'I mean, ultimately, all the fees come out of the pot, but I'm going to need to keep ticking over.'

'Sure,' I said, knowing full well that, at some point soon, Lisa was going to instruct a snake who would advise her to open a new bank account in her sole name and leave me to service Matthew's fees out of my miserly telesales income. He'd drop me faster than I could say 'Legal Aid'.

Hi Faye. Saw Matthew Roberts the other day. Seems excellent. Thanks so much for the referral. He says it's going to be a fairly miserable ride but I don't have to tell you about that, do I? Anyway, thanks again. Best, Mike.

CHAPTER 18

I'D ONLY EVER been to a television studio once before. I was about nine and my dad had somehow wangled me a ticket to sit in the Tiswas audience. I loved it and even got flanned by the Phantom Flan Flinger. Actually, the kid next to me got flanned, but I got a collateral flanning when a squirt of goo flew off his head and hit me in the throat. Brilliant! I was fascinated by the cameras and lights, the undergrowth of chunky cables, the monitors, the studio manager fussing about in headphones, the sheer organised chaos of the whole operation. I resolved then to be a TV producer, although I had no idea what that meant or entailed, and bandied that career aspiration around at school for a good year thereafter. It lent me a certain kudos. I mean, I'd spent the morning with Chris Tarrant and Lenny Henry and spoken to a number of people on the team who'd said I should get in touch one day now that I'd acquired such an intimate understanding of the whole TV production thingy. And, which is more, my son, I got flanned. Top that. The whole spoke-to-people, get-in-touch thing was a fabrication, of course, my sole tangible memento of the day being a lump of dried goo which I tried, and failed, to preserve in a jar. I was eventually trumped by a little git in the year above who had a part, an actual part, in a kids' TV drama about kids on bikes, biking everywhere and having bike-related adventures that kids generally didn't have – on bikes or any other mode of transport. My TV production career paled into insignificance and I put it, sensibly, on the back burner in favour of a future in investment banking, thank you very much, whatever the hell that was. I did attempt to revive my interest, writing to the BBC when I was about seventeen to enquire about getting onto their trainee producers' course, but it involved living in far flung places around the UK like Coventry, learning the ropes and earning fuck-all, so I let it slide.

Ben sent a cab to collect me from Hanger Lane just after eleven. I'd have been perfectly happy to take the Central Line to White City – it's only a few stops from Hell – but he insisted I arrive in style. Or maybe he'd got a two-for-one with Luxor Cabs (Hornsey) Ltd. As I waited to be collected from the flashy glass-fronted BBC reception area in Wood Lane, I spotted a couple of newsreaders, an aged singer whose name I couldn't recall and a sickly-sweet children's TV presenter I'd once bad-mouthed in front of the kids. Your average star-struck stalker/psycho would have a field day sitting there.

Sarah, a pretty girl in her early twenties who was desperately trying to disguise her Home Counties accent by dropping a few 'h's' and scrambling her 'f's' and 'th's', led me through the revolving security turnstile and on through a warren of corridors until we reached the old reception area where I took another seat. Minutes later, a virtually identical but, I'm almost certain, different girl arrived to escort me into the studio. I was deposited at the side of a large auditorium from where I could see three limber black guys wearing white towelling headbands and tight tee shirts flouncing with ersatz aggression through a tortuous routine to the accompaniment of a thumpingly dull hip hop track. Sarah-clones with clipboards flitted hither and yon and, fleetingly, Gordon O'Hara himself popped his head round the studio door before disappearing, covering his ears with his hands. I didn't think it was possible to rap out of tune, but the guys on stage were giving it a hell of a go.

I was spellbound. Above me, banks of monitors suspended from metal rigging displayed the hapless, dripping trio from various angles. To the rear, a huge control booth teemed with people. Cameramen jockeyed around the stage finalising positions and angles. No flans, but this was way better than Tiswas. Elaine, appearing out of nowhere, tapped me on the shoulder and motioned for me to follow her. We negotiated another maze of corridors and arrived at a dark wooden door halfway down a long corridor. Elaine knocked and Ben answered. The dressing room was narrow and long, furnished with a couple of stained orange sofas, fitted wardrobes, a table groaning under the weight of bottled water, snacks and sandwiches and the obligatory mirror with bulb surround. A shower/toilet cubicle nestled at the back. Howard was conspicuously absent, but wasn't due on stage for forty-five minutes for his first run-through so panic hadn't yet set in. Ben slapped my back. 'Hey, like this place? This is all down to you, baby,' he bellowed.

'I like it.'

'Everything's riding on your song now.'

'No pressure then.'

Ben roared disingenuously and slapped my back again. He was nervous and overcompensating. 'No pressure! Get this guy! Don't worry, we're gonna enjoy this, ok?'

'Ok.'

'Sandwich?' piped Elaine.

'Maybe later,' I said, watching the cheap white bread curl in real time. I reached for a bottle of Evian.

'Well listen, Mikey,' said Ben (Mikey? I was Mikey now?). 'Just chill. You want anything, press zero and some lah-di-dah chick'll come tend to your every need.' Ben paused as the lame, tasteless leer formed in his head. 'You know what I mean? Hope you brought protection.'

Ben roared. Elaine shot him a disgusted look, one she must have given him a million times before.

'Cheers. I'm fine at the moment.'

'*I'm fine at the moment,*' he mocked in an accent indistinguishable from his own. 'You're so damn British. I been living here twenty-five years and I still get a fuckin' buzz from all that reserve.' *Resoive*. The man was adrenaline-crazed.

Ben paced the room, his megawatt grin and desperate conversation failing to mask his growing concern. Howard still hadn't arrived and, worryingly, his driver had called in to report that he'd not been at his west London flat when he arrived to pick him up. Howard, of all people, needed some stage time to make sure he knew what he was doing. He was a legendarily undisciplined performer, someone who often sang half his set from the balcony or the front row of the stalls, anything to be different, dangerous. I always thought it was choreographed and it probably was, but that kind of shit was unbecoming of an old man on live prime time TV. Tonight he needed to pander to old ladies in Hull, nurses in Norwich, bookkeepers in

Balham. Their votes were vital. His, and a few other careers, hung on his likeability and professionalism.

Three o'clock came and went. Ben had exercised considerable diplomatic skills to engineer adjustments to the rehearsal rota, but the director, a sallow, diminutive man with an etched frown, had lost patience and declared the run-through over at three fifteen. He wanted to start the second and final run-through in ten minutes. Having missed the first opportunity to rehearse his routine, Howard was about to miss his last. Ben was in pieces. He'd been calling Howard every ten minutes to be parried by an infuriating outgoing message, sung to the tune of one of his late 80s hits, while Howard's equally perplexed personal assistant, Ged, had been filing regular reports of his fruitless chase from one sad gin joint to another in search of his idiot client.

Howard finally tottered in at four, looking cadaverous and vacant and stinking like a skunk marinated in alcohol. His voice was reedy and tremulous, but I wouldn't say he was acting any more stoned than normal. Ben tried to maintain a semblance of calm as he chatted to Howard, knowing he couldn't afford to anger or upset him this close to kick off. Howard seemed nonchalant and unaware of the havoc he'd wrought. His story, for what it was worth, was that he'd been at his girlfriend's flat in Bayswater and was convinced he'd told Ged to arrange for the BBC car to pick him up from there. His mobile phone had been switched off because he was low on battery power and didn't want to waste it. It hadn't occurred to him, apparently, to call Ged or Ben from 'his girlfriend's flat' to find out what was going on when the car didn't show. Blatant bullshit, every word.

Howard urgently needed to spend an hour in the shower scrubbing down with a Brillo, but there wasn't time. He was due on stage immediately. He clapped his hands, said something tragically Spinal Tap ('Let's rock,' I believe) and marched out of the dressing room, his hands on the shoulders of the Sarah-clone who'd been given the unenviable task of collecting him, like a boxer making his way to the ring. Ben, Elaine and I trudged along in his reeking slipstream, pinching our noses and shaking our heads with a tangible sense of foreboding.

Once inside the auditorium, Howard galloped towards the stage and, forgetting he was fifty-three and as athletic as a warped stick, leapt up and tripped over a feedback monitor. He landed face first but didn't linger on the floor. He sprang to his feet, brushed himself down without a hint of embarrassment and said, to no-one in particular, 'Whoo! I'm ready, man. What do you want me to do?'

Whatever he was on was working. For now. Elaine buried her head in my shoulder and groaned, 'We're fucked,' which I think nailed it pretty accurately.

Ben, looking nauseous, nevertheless stapled a super-smiley grin to his sweaty face and marched confidently up to the stage, conveying the false impression that everything was all right with the world. He spoke confidentially to Howard who nodded and 'yupped' and said 'ok man' a few times, then smiled at the floor manager, the director and anyone else wearing a look of vexed concern (ie everyone). Ben made an 'O' with his thumb and forefinger and winked at the producer in the control box whose face resembled that of a drowning man who'd just realised he was also bleeding to death. Gilbert, hitherto detached and other-worldly, rose from a stool in front of a crew of jobbing musicians and raised his arms. They responded with a collective been-there-done-that-and-it's-shit look, raised their instruments and prepared for the off. Gilbert whipped his arms up vertically and they launched into the opening bars of *In Love We Trust*. From such unpromising beginnings, it was an amazing rush to hear the song played live – and brilliantly – by such a large, professional ensemble. We held our breath as Howard pogo-ed on the spot, knees crossed like he needed a piss, waiting for his cue. Was he going to hit it? Was he going to remember the words?

> *Every day, I want to tell you I need you*
> *And I look in your eyes to see*
> *If you need me too*
> *'Cos I believe, as I must*
> *That we can be together*
> *I hope that in love we trust*

All right, shut up. Don't you think I know that, in the cold light of day, just sitting there on the page like that, the lyrics look unconscionably banal and cretinous? But when Howard sang them with his dry-throated wail, they sounded heartfelt, profound, even. He had a way of investing words with emotion that you couldn't teach. I'm not ashamed to say I welled up. I looked at Elaine through the mist and saw that she was trembling, but probably with relief that Howard was actually there and apparently capable of pulling this off. I put my arm around her and she dabbed away the single embarrassing tear which was snaking down my cheek. Howard belted out the final chorus with gut-wrenching conviction, then took a simple bow as the violins and horns conspired to make the last chord soar. He took another bow, this time with a sweep of the arm, and another, throwing his head back to the sky before falling forward again like a rag doll. He was actually rehearsing his bow, the prick. The entire studio – technicians, Sarah-clones, the producer, the still-grimacing director, everyone – applauded wildly. I don't know for sure whether any of the other contestants had been rewarded with a similar ovation, but the ones I'd watched on the dressing room monitor had simply mooched off to the sound of the studio readying itself for the next act. Ben rushed across to Howard, jumped onto the stage and all but snapped him in half in a bear hug. He turned to me beaming a beatific, veneer-perfect smile. We were saved.

Weren't we?

Howard lay comatose on his dressing room sofa. His six minute performance had understandably left him drained. With only an hour to go till showtime, he would soon have to be roused. Given the copious drool and crusty white residue lining his lips, I wasn't about to volunteer. Ben spent much of the intervening time rebuking Ged in an apoplectic whisper for failing to ensure Howard was delivered on time and in full working order. I felt sorry for him; Howard was as slippery and inchoate as mercury. Late in the afternoon, Gordon O'Hara popped his head around the door to wish Howard luck, his (allegedly) newly reconstructed Irish nose wrinkling at the stench of smoke, booze, sweat and smack now woven into Howard's DNA. The rest of us had become inured to it, although whenever Elaine and I wandered off for one of several turgid BBC coffees, we had to steel ourselves for re-entry. But I was too enamoured of the magical scent of light entertainment to let a stink like that bother me. I was going to savour every moment, record and log the sights, sounds and even obnoxious smells of this day, to sustain me through the dark, lonely days I knew were bound to follow. For even as I revelled in the thrilling electricity of the day, my mind wandered to the gruesome image of Lisa and Chaz rutting naked on my bed, and how that one vile act (probably several of them) had drawn a line through my marriage and deprived me of my best friend. I would never again walk into my own house to receive the casual, throwaway hugs of my children on a wet Tuesday night. It would be by appointment only from now on, imposing a formality upon my relationship with them that would inevitably erode all spontaneity.

With thirty-five minutes to go, Ben was pacing furiously, sweat pooling on his upper lip and soaking the armpits of his dated silk shirt. The fickle, essentially useless Ged had scarpered and was no longer answering his phone, leaving Ben to rouse the still unconscious Howard. Ged had probably left the building and, if he had any sense, show business and the country. Gilbert drifted in and out of the dressing room expressing concern, in his own muted, monosyllabic way, about the state of the reeking Howard who was stretched out, legs askew, a stream of viscous saliva dribbling onto the fatally ruined orange sofa. Only by setting fire to it and disposing of the ashes thirty miles out to sea could others be spared. And I, too, was beginning to panic about the level of performance we could expect from the wreckage. This was going to be the only time one of my songs would be heard by an audience larger than seventeen. I couldn't bear to let that opportunity get away.

'We've got to wake him up!' urged Elaine, aware that she was stating the obvious but too panic-ridden to care.

'Shit, Elaine. You think I don't know that? *You think I don't know that?!*' snapped Ben, glancing at Howard's filleted, prostrate form. 'Motherfucker!'

'He can't just wake up and go on.'

'I know, I fuckin' know.' Ben, though, was edging further away from the gurgling, disgusting Howard.

'Well I'll do it, then' said Elaine.

'No! Don't!'

'For God's sake, Ben.'

'Jesus. Why did we have to use this fucker?' winced Ben, slumping into a chair, head in hands.

'It was him or no-one. And now we're stuck with him so, step over the…gate…whatever…'

'Step up to the plate,' whimpered Ben.

'Yeah. Ben! Come on! Stop feeling sorry for yourself.'

Elaine grabbed Ben's elbow and hauled him upright. He went floppy, head bowed, pouting.

'Ok, ok,' he said, wrenching his arm free. 'You guys take a walk. He won't want to see a lot of faces when he wakes up. I'll have him ready, ok?'

Elaine and I looked at each other, shrugged and left Ben to his grisly task. She went to the Ladies, leaving me alone in an unusually quiet corridor. No Sarah-clones screeching into walkie-talkies, no techies rushing about like manic androids, no Ben, no-one, just me and the quiet hum of the air conditioning. How I ached to call Lisa, despite everything, to tell her to watch the show. It would make no difference, of course, but for twenty years she'd been the first person I called when there was news, good or bad, the only person in whom I confided everything. I guess she confided everything in me until the gravity and import of her secrets made that impossible. I wanted the girls to watch too, to be proud of Daddy, but I didn't think they'd quite understand what I'd done or how I was involved in something so remote from them. And Eurovision *was* 'shit' after all.

Elaine re-joined Ben in the dressing room to bolster the poor bastard, but I chose to stay outside. The smell was something I could no longer tolerate, much less the angst and anger inside. I glimpsed a couple of Sarah-clones and the exasperated director at Howard's side as the door closed. They were all wasting their time; Howard was irrevocably unconscious. I wandered off, certain now that the jig was up, and lost myself in another maze of BBC corridors before somehow pitching up at the studio door. Inside, the audience was settled and in the throes of being warmed up by a large man in too-tight jeans. We should have been in the holding room backstage by now, along with the bouncing headband boys and the sugary pop plodders, but the show would have to go ahead with five rather than six songs. Gordon O'Hara was going to be on waffle overload tonight.

I returned to the dressing room and put my ear to the door. I heard a whooshing sound and the muted voices of Elaine, Ben and even Gilbert. I knocked. Elaine answered and her face told me what I already knew. Her melancholy eyes drifted to the back of the room and I followed their route. No sign of Howard on the sofa now. Ben stood facing the wall, head bowed, shoulders slumped, while Gilbert sat staring at nothing. I walked towards the shower cubicle, pulled back the screen and looked inside. Howard lay slumped in the shower tray, water powering onto the top of his head, highlighting the patches of skin where his wiry hair was thinning. His eyes remained resolutely closed. I looked back at Elaine who shrugged in abject defeat.

'Get up you motherfucker!' yelled Ben in a sudden fit of righteous anger. 'Get up! Get the fuck up!'

Ben spun and took three quick strides towards Howard, growling like a bear. I think he was ready to kill him, which would have been a little Pyrrhic but nonetheless cathartic. I bravely tried to hold him back but he was too pumped, too strong. It took Gilbert to step in and flip Ben away from the cubicle with some sort of judo move. He was full of surprises, that boy.

'That's not gonna help,' said Gilbert in an alien display of articulacy and forthrightness.

'Leave him, Ben,' said Elaine. 'It's over.'

'We're fucking finished,' muttered Ben. 'Finished.'

A Sarah-clone – I think it was the original Sarah, but don't quote me – pushed through the door. Elaine walked over to her, placed a consolatory arm around her shoulder and confirmed that we'd tried everything. Howard wasn't going on. Poor Sarah would be the bearer of the bad news to the director. She looked like she'd rather eat splintered glass.

A groan came from the shower cubicle and we all turned to see if it signalled a last minute reprieve. Instead, a dripping Ben emerged with a wicked smile that had Schadenfreude written all over it. 'Couldn't even rouse him with my foot in his balls.'

Well at least Ben felt a bit better.

Elaine and I sat in the draughty old reception area staring at a flickering wall of plasma monitors. There wasn't much to say as we waved goodbye to the chance of a lifetime with wistful resignation. It was eight o'clock and the opening titles of Eurovision:You Decide were just flashing across one of the screens. The cheerful smile of Gordon O'Hara hove into view, followed by shots of a wildly enthusiastic audience. Beside O'Hara stood a slim, blonde girl, better known for hip music shows and yoof TV, wearing a shimmering, semi-Gothic outfit which screamed 'still credible, say what you like'.

'Why am I so upset?' said Elaine. 'You shouldn't gamble everything on someone like Howard and expect to win.'

'Doesn't matter, does it? You'll go back to making compilations and I'll go back to singing for my Tiramisu. It's all about the art, anyway, not the money.'

'Now we both know that's bollocks, don't we?'

'Yes we do.'

O'Hara introduced the first act, the ugly/beautiful girl combo, *neither* of whom, I had ascertained during rehearsals, could actually sing a note. I wondered aloud how the director was going to handle the fact that they were a song short, but Elaine said that O'Hara, along with the panel of C-list celebrities hauled in to pass comment, could talk filler shit till the cows came home. Howard was originally due on second last and I suppose, deep down, we clung to the remote hope that he might yet recover in time, but when we returned to the dressing room he lay dripping on the sofa, out cold and groaning as he cupped his testicles with a bony hand. Ben was staring, hollow-eyed, at his visibly ageing reflection in the mirror while Gilbert rocked gently on a chair, knees drawn to his chest, adrift in Gilbertworld.

Sarah-clone came in and sat next to Ben who didn't bother adjusting his sulk for this conversation. They mumbled to each other for a few minutes before Ben sprang to his feet and snapped, 'Are you shitting me? Look at me. I'm sixty-two years old for Chrissakes. I haven't stood in front of an audience in thirty years.'

Sixty-two?

'Well couldn't you, you know, do it now? Just this once?' whinnied Sara-clone.

'Get out of here!' bellowed Ben. 'Mother*fuck*!'

Elaine stepped in to save Sarah-clone from further abuse. 'Ben! Don't shoot the messenger. Sorry, he's a little upset,' said Elaine to the shaken young Old Roedeanian.

Ben was instantly contrite and planted an unwanted kiss on Sarah-clone's cheek. 'Honey, sorry, I can't do it. I lost my nerve. Long story. That's why I do what I do. I can't sing in front of my own mother, God rest her soul.'

And then it happened. Elaine and Ben turned to me in slow motion. Nothing needed to be said.

'Oh no. Shit no. No way,' I said, hands raised, backing away until I collided with the door.

'Why not? It's your song. Who else can sing it like you?' said Elaine.

'Man, do it for me, for Elaine, for your family, your kids, do it for the sake of this contest.' Dramatic pause. 'Do it for Britain.'

I don't think he left anyone out.

'Oh for…I can't! You could fit my aggregated audience since I was eighteen into the front row out there. Never mind…six million!'

'Eight,' said Sarah-clone with instant regret.

Ben ground his veneers. 'Six, eight? Big deal. It's just a camera.'

'No. Absolutely not. I'm not…ready.'

'Perfect,' said Elaine. 'That's to your advantage. Imagine if you'd had time to think about it. Now you can just go out there and do it. Just pretend you're in that little bistro.'

I gulped, Scooby Doo-fashion, blinked a few times and collapsed onto the nearest chair before my legs gave way. Elaine and Ben looked at me, all puppy-dog-eyes and pleading, winsome smiles. Sarah-clone tilted her head to one side and mouthed 'ah, go on' and even the de-tranced Gilbert mustered some fleeting eye contact. Head and heart started crowding in on me. Terror, excitement, trepidation, fear of failure, doors opening, doors closing, redemption. I thought of Lisa, Chaz, my mother; Faye popped into my head – what would she think? And, of course, my children? Was I going to be an eighty-year old bore recounting for the umpteenth time how I let this one slip by, how I coulda been a contender?

'Oh, fuck it,' I said.

Trust me, twenty-five minutes was plenty of time to think about it, and plenty of time to shit myself. I probably knew I was going go on as soon as Ben and Elaine looked at me. I just needed to go through the motions, to buy myself some time to absorb the sheer magnitude of what I was about to do. I'd been protesting when, all along, a little voice had been screaming at me to stop being such a bloody idiot. Understudy becomes star for the night – it's as old as the hills – and I was Little Mikey Nomark, about to play the part of the humble, reluctant protagonist in the best Hollywood tradition. Star for one night only.

A Sarah-clone rushed me down some new corridors towards make-up, all the while conducting a bellowed conversation on her walkie talkie. 'His name's…sorry what's your name?'

'Mike.'

'Mike,' she said.

The reply was belligerent and unintelligible.

'Surname?' she said, looking ever more suicidal.

'Kenton. Mike Kenton.'

'Mike Kenton!' she screamed.

Elaine held my cold, clammy hand as the make-up girl fussed around me, smothering my face with skin-tone which seemed a little redundant as I already had my own, albeit it was currently at the sheet-white end of the spectrum. Elaine was constantly checking my expression in the mirror, smiling encouragingly, and I could see how much this meant to her. Make-up done, Elaine hooked her hand under my elbow, helped me up and looked me up and down. I was still wearing the fraying-at-the-cuffs denim shirt I'd arrived in. Elaine tugged it out of the trousers into which they'd been tucked all day – I'm forty-two you know – and shook her head. 'Ok, this needs an iron,' she said as she started to unbutton it. I held my flaccid stomach in as she pulled it off my back and handed it to a sullen woman who was slumped in the corner looking slightly put out at having to fire up the steam iron again.

Throughout this preparatory process, I was cracking lame, nervous jokes about my hair needing a cut and blow-job, how I wanted the cameras to get my good side if only I had one, checking to see if mikekenton.com was still available – you get the tragic gist. Elaine and the make-up girl tittered and gushed, my first and probably last taste of being humoured and pandered to like a star with an ego to feed. It wasn't doing much for my nerves. My heart was exploring escape routes out of my chest, my breathing shallow and rapid, my throat steely and constricted. How the hell was I going to hit a single note?

I didn't want to think about performing live in front of five hundred people with a TV audience of – Scooby gulp, cotton wool mouth – 8 million. That way madness lay. Elaine was right; I had to treat it like *Jaques* only with better lighting and a microphone manufactured this century. I started a quick mental rehearsal of the song but got no further than the first line. What the fuck was it? I knew it like the back of my hand, but all trace of it had deserted me. Maybe it would come to me once I got up there in front of those eight million people. Yes, that's right, it would all flow then once the pressure was off. Piece of piss.

The warm ironed shirt was returned to me and I put it on, fumbling with every button. I was still in my almost-matching jeans which completed the rather sad uniform of the dress-in-the-dark Gap-Dad I'd become. 'Nope, you can't wear those,' said Elaine. 'You look like Shakin' fucking Stevens.' She'd never sworn before. It was getting to her. 'Off.' I obeyed. I was putty. She disappeared for a few minutes leaving me sitting on the faux leather make-up chair in my pants. *What's the first fucking line?*

Elaine returned with a pair of black trousers and ordered me to stand up. Behind me, a pool of sweat in the shape of an arse crack sat steaming on the chair. She held the trousers out for me like I was her seven year old son and I stepped into them. They, too, were warm and a little damp.

'They're Ben's. Sorry. Best I could do.'

I instantly recoiled, a cold wave of nausea rippling through my stomach. I might have had a sweaty arse, but I didn't want it anywhere near where Ben's had been. But there was no time to protest. I'd have to disinfect later. Forget Ben's arse, I told myself, forget it! Now…

The first line. Come on, brain, try and bloody remember…

The make-up girl lumped some gel into my hair and swept it up into a ludicrous quiff. I shook my head in despair, which she took as a signal to muss it into little, electric-shock spikes. I plastered it back down and teased it into a vaguely acceptable, forty-two year old man's style, of which she clearly disapproved. It was my bloody hair, though, wasn't it? I was going to decide how shit it should look in front of those eight million poor souls. Eight million. Oh God. I stood up and checked myself in the full length mirror behind the door. There stood a middle-aged man with a matt tan face, oily hair, an over-pressed shirt and fear spurting from every pore. The make-up girl blotted some beads of newly-formed sweat from my nose and forehead with a tissue and reapplied some slap, but this was a losing battle.

Like an executioner's assistant, Sarah-clone arrived and told me it was time to go. I looked at Elaine who smiled reassuringly. 'I'm not ready. I'll never be ready,' I said.

'Knock 'em dead. I'll be right here when you get back.' She gave me a hug and caressed my cheek, before Sarah-clone grabbed my arm and guided me into the corridor to meet my fate. My limbs felt barely co-ordinated as we entered the studio, like I was in the wrong body altogether and we'd all made a huge mistake. The headband hip-hoppers were just starting up, their percussion vibrating through the floor and up into my petrified soul as we neared the stage. A few more steps and I'd have nowhere to run, nowhere to hide

Dead man walking.

We were live, yet somehow O'Hara had been told, and absorbed the fact, that we had six songs again instead of five and that the arsehole who was supposed to sing it wasn't going to and that some complete amateur nobody was stepping in to save the day and his name was Mike Kenton who wrote the song anyway so that was even better. He conveyed all this in his seamlessly casual Irish lilt, omitting 'arsehole', I think, to the expectant audience. What a pro. I didn't even cotton the fact that I was now being credited as the composer. I was just thinking about the first line. *Which was what, exactly? Fuck!*

I watched, glassy-eyed, from the wings as O'Hara wound up his schtick. He said something about making me welcome and giving me a chance as this was my first TV appearance, every word piling additional tonnes of pressure on my lyric-free head. Most of my senses had already shut down, so by the time he announced my name, I was effectively comatose. Applause, some cheering; a cold, clone hand in the middle of my back applying gentle pressure; unable to move like an obstinate horse in its stall; more pushing, harder. And then out I stumbled, instantly bemused by the noise and the lights and the shiny stage. I'd been told to look for a mark on the floor where I was supposed to stand at the beginning and end of the song, but didn't absorb the information, forgot to look out for it and wouldn't have seen it anyway. I couldn't focus on anything. I was vaguely aware of cameramen racing around trying to reposition themselves. They hadn't rehearsed this either. I held a radio microphone in my hand – how the hell did it get there? – and some instinct told me that the intro was almost over and it was time to sing.

What was the first fucking line?

Whatever it was, I missed it, my jaw flapping like a dying fish as nothing came out. First line, no vocal. I didn't panic. I was too scared to panic. But then the familiarity of the melody sparked an almost atavistic moment of clarity. I raised the microphone to my lips – Pavlov dog style – and started singing. It just came out. And once I'd broken the ice, I forgot about the lights and the shiny stage and the fact that I was now singing one of my little songs to eight million people. My voice sounded like it should and, God help me, the lyrics were now flowing as if on autopilot. Well of course; I wrote them, didn't I? And I'd sung them a hundred times. Now I was moving around the stage, the cameramen scuttling this way and that to keep up. I smiled as my confidence grew and even allowed myself the luxury of throwing a few shapes, carefully avoiding anything that might resemble a Dad Dance just in case the kids *were* watching.

I was reaching the end now. Why wasn't the song a bit longer? I could go on all night. The audience was with me, no longer that hostile death squad of my worst imaginings. Surely the eight million were feeling it as well. It was my song, the song I'd written for Faye, and I was singing it to the nation. Bloody hell!

So obviously you're waiting for something to go catastrophically wrong, aren't you? I would be. But nothing did. Sorry. I finished with an unwavering final note, standing on the newly discovered mark, looking into the camera. I was born to do this, a natural. Gilbert waved the orchestra to a swooping halt and there was a moment of scary silence before the audience exploded. Cheering, whistling, whooping, the works. I stood there beaming, arms akimbo, chest heaving, a little lump dancing in my throat. O'Hara was at the side of the stage waiting to ask the panel for their invaluable opinions, but the ovation continued, building if anything, and he waved his arms to try and calm them down. They were having none of it. I bowed, still smiling like an idiot, trying to look a little bashful now – *hey, come on, what's all the fuss about?* – but I couldn't have been more disingenuous. I was eating it up. And then I spotted Elaine and Ben in the wings. Ben was punching the air and I could hear him shouting above the din: 'Fucking awesome, *fucking awesome!*' Elaine's eyes were glistening, her hands together in satisfied supplication. I waved my hands in my own humble attempt to calm the audience, but was complicit in all this. Humility aside, I'd blown the place apart and would happily have let the applause ring on forever.

O'Hara finally threw some superfluous questions at the panel whose responses were almost drowned out by the febrile mob. I was wonderful, the song was fantastic, I'd done an unbelievable job stepping in like that. The audience lapped up every accolade, cheering and clapping like…well, Americans. I left the stage carried, metaphorically, shoulder high. The birth of the kids apart, I can't remember ever feeling more elated.

Back in the dressing room I couldn't stop shaking; perspiration pumped from every pore; I was enervated, disorientated. Elaine kissed me, Ben kissed me, Sarah-clone shook my hand and even Gilbert anointed me with a single pat on the back. I guzzled down litres of water and slaked a sudden fierce hunger by forcing several wooden sandwiches down my face. Well-wishers, programme executives, the producer, the director, all sorts of Sarah-clones flitted in and out. It was overwhelming, this moment in the sun, something I'd never dreamed of or bargained for. I'd turned up as the humble 'music consultant', there to witness Howard taking the plaudits, but I was going home with the glory. Even then I think I knew this was ephemeral, that it had no value, no substance, but for a brief moment I felt the breath-taking power of celebrity; everything centred on me, everyone else was irrelevant.

I wanted to ring anyone who'd ever doubted me, who'd thought I wouldn't amount to anything. It would take all night. And then I wanted to call everyone who'd ever loved me, stood by me, believed in me, a necessarily shorter list. This was my moment, however short-lived it might prove to be, and I wanted the world to know – and then maybe rub it in a bit.

I was feeling light-headed and a shade nauseous having eaten too much too quickly, and I asked Ben if he could clear the room so I could have a minute or two on my own. Like an on-side bouncer, he ushered the disappointed throng out, promising them further access to me in the green room. Only Elaine remained once the hubbub subsided. She flopped onto the uncontaminated sofa opposite me and closed her eyes with a profound sigh. I swiped my mobile phone from the dressing table and flicked it on. The screen was alive with icons denoting texts, emails and messages. I dialled into my voicemail account and was immediately assailed by my mother's screeching, frantically excited voice, although she still managed to deliver a rebuke for failing to forewarn her. There were messages from a couple of old school friends I hadn't seen in ages; Matthew, my solicitor (wonder what he was going to charge me for watching); Kevin, who wanted to congratulate me and ask if I'd deign to do a celebrity spot at *Jaques;* various relatives I only ever bumped into at weddings and funerals; and, needless to say, Chaz, his voice a mixture of wonderment and pain. There were texts from my dentist ('can't wait to drill one of those famous teeth'), a couple of estate agents I'd last dealt with three years earlier (opportunistic motherfuckers), some people from my old office and one or two of the lost souls from the telesales wasteland. There was even one from Marcus, expressing ironic admiration while making it clear that he'd only glimpsed me on the big screen in the pub. I wondered how many of these people would have owned up to watching a show with a nil credibility factor had there not been this opportunity to bask in my dim reflection.

I scanned more texts until, finally, I found the one I'd been praying for:

'That was you, wasn't it? OMG, as the kids say, apparently. Why didn't you tell me you were going to be on the telly? Call me if you're not too famous. Got to go now and register my vote for that hip hop band. Love Faye.'

I needed to be somewhere quiet, somewhere I could draw breath and take everything in; somewhere I could call the kids, my mother, maybe even Lisa, and definitely Faye. But there was no prospect of doing any of that. I'd been left to my own devices for precisely five minutes before being dragged into the green room. The fizz and fuss surrounding me was already becoming oppressive. The other acts and acolytes were drinking and networking somewhere in my periphery, but I, very definitely, was the centre of attention, besieged by back-slaps, kisses and the incessant ruffling of my gel-hardened hair. People bellowed at me, Sarah-clones fussed around me, Ben showed me off like a proud father. Too much, too much.

There was a sudden hush and the crowd parted like the Red Sea to allow Gordon O'Hara access to the man of the moment. He shook my hand and offered some sage words about how my life was going to change and how to cope with it. He used to be a dog handler, or something – I wasn't paying proper attention – and he'd had to adjust to being 'O'Hara,' so he knew what he was on about. Some of the judges followed him over and we laughed and joshed like old mates. I was in, and once you're in, you're in. Until you're out, I suppose. Elaine made sure she was always in my field of vision. Her nods of reassurance and private smiles sustaining me through this madness. For the first time that evening, though for the thousandth time overall, I noted how attractive she was, and tonight she was a-twinkle, euphoric, pleased for me, pleased for Ben. I'd made a new friend, a real friend, something you don't expect when you're my age (forty-two). And, who knew? Maybe I'd be more her type after this triumph.

It wasn't long before the boiling cluster of celebrities, hangers-on and sundry movers and shakers were bellowing at each other rather than at the new star. *They* didn't take long to lose interest. But at least it gave me the chance to slip away from under their noses. Back in the now empty dressing room I rang home, if I could still call it that, and Lisa answered. Her voice was stone which didn't necessarily indicate whether she'd seen the show or not, but as we edged through our stilted conversation, it was clear she hadn't. I asked to speak to the kids but was informed they were both in bed. Then I heard Kattie's sleepy voice in the background asking who it was, so Lisa, who never got in the way of my relationship with the girls whatever she thought about me, put her on.

'Hi baby,' I said, 'how are you?'

'I'm good, Daddy. How 'bout you?'

'I'm really good. You sound tired.'

'I am a bit.'

Simon Lipson

'Well, I love you, and I'll see you on Saturday.'

'Love you too.'

'Bye, darling.'

'Dad?'

'Yeah.'

'Hang on.'

I could hear Katia leaving the echoey environs of the kitchen and padding into a room with flatter acoustics. Privacy.

'Dad?'

'What's the matter, sweetheart?'

'My friend Amy just called me.' Yes, her own mobile phone at eight. Blame the mother. I do. 'That's why I'm up. You know Amy? She's the one with no front teeth and a ponytail.'

Amy could have been any one of a dozen of Katia's classmates. 'Of course.'

'Well, I think she's gone completely crazy 'cos she said you were just on telly and I was like, what? And she was like, yeah, really, it was your dad and I was like, don't be so stupid and she was like, I'm not being stupid, he was, like, singing in some competition?'

Bea was, like, letting them watch too much American trash and I was going to have to step in at some point. For now, though, I had to deal with Kattie's curiosity. I knew for sure that my photo was going to be on the front pages of any number of tatty tabloids in the morning, win or lose. 'Ok, listen. Here's what happened. I wrote a song and someone liked it and wanted to enter it in this song contest so I said yes. I wasn't supposed to be singing it, but the man who *was* supposed to be singing it was ill, so I stood in for him. That's all.'

'Yeah, right.'

'Well, ok, but that's what happened. It was all very last minute so I didn't have time to call you to tell you to watch.'

'Come on Dad. That's like a fairy tale. I'm nearly nine.'

'I know, I get that, but it's a fairy tale that came true so…'

Lisa entered whichever room Katia was hiding in to tell her it was getting late. Then followed Katia's off-mike, eight-nearly-nine year old's version of events as relayed to her, followed by the unmistakeable

214

sound of the phone being snatched from her hand.

'What are you telling her stupid stories for? Now she'll never sleep.'

'That's what happened. Sorry if it's going to embarrass you. Don't worry, you won't have to explain me away for much longer.'

I hung up and switched off my phone.

Yes, I know, over the top, too shirty. Maybe it was the adrenaline, but more likely it was that all-too-familiar tone, the tetchy one she reserved for me, and I had no time for it. On reflection, I should have given her the benefit of the doubt. I knew her better than that. She didn't think much of my musical skills, but she wasn't grudging or spiteful. Once I'd explained everything she'd have been happy for me, but I'd allowed my scrambled emotions to obfuscate reason.

I sat there a little longer, hoping for few minutes' peace, but someone was rapping on the door. 'Hang on.'

'Oh, thank God you're there.'

'Out in a minute.'

'No, need you right now!' she shouted. They'd sent an assertive clone. 'Results show in fifteen minutes.'

'Ok! Toilet! One minute!'

There was a time when I'd have used those precious sixty seconds to call Chaz. Now, the idea seemed sad and ridiculous. But there was one call I had to make.

'Faye?'

'Michael!'

She was fit to burst.

'Hi.'

'That has to be the most surreal five minutes of my entire life,' she said.

'Mine too.'

'I was ironing a blouse for work and I only had that rubbish on for background noise – sorry, not rubbish, but, you know – anyway, up pops this face and I thought, shit, that cannot be Michael!'

'What can I tell you?'

'You kept that one quiet.'

'I'm a sly one.'

'I even recognised that song. You played it at that place.'

'Top marks.' And I wrote it for you.

'So now I know a celebrity. How cool am I?'

'Honestly? Not *that* cool.'

'No, true, it's only you isn't it? But seriously, Mike, well done you. Proud of you.'

'Thanks.'

'Hey, were you miming, 'cos the voice was really good?'

'It was all me, in the raw.'

'Well I've always said you've got a good voice, haven't I?'

'No.'

'Ok, I haven't, but I've kept meaning to. God, what if you win?'

'I haven't even thought about it.' Which I realised was true. I hadn't landed since coming off stage. There was another, furious knock at the door and now Elaine was shouting at me to come out.

'Minute!' I bellowed.

'You being called away now you're so important?'

'The results show's going out in a minute. I suppose I ought to be there.'

'No, hide. It'll be more fun.'

'Yeah, but…my mum's watching. '

'You were always a good boy, Mike, just a bit of a…well you know.'

I didn't and I wanted to find out, but was interrupted by more knocking, fiercer this time, and the screaming voices of at least three people in deep panic.

'So…can I call you maybe?' I ventured.

'You just did.'

'No, I mean…'

'Of course call me. Take me out for a meal and then I'll be snapped by the paps and be in Heat. I'd better buy some decent shoes.'

I laughed. 'Me too. My Hush Puppies have seen better days.'

'Good luck Mike. You're gonna win you know.' Faye paused. 'Really great that you called.'

So? Shall I keep you in suspense a bit longer? Do you give a toss? Ok, here's what happened. I stood on the stage with all the other acts and we pretended we were all mates and were going to be happy for whoever came out on top. They replayed excerpts of each song (mine got the loudest cheer), then O'Hara and the blonde sidekick started reading out the results in reverse order. For the suspense. The hip hoppers didn't make the cut, but at least that gave them a shot at regaining their credibility back out on the street – that or being slain for their disservice to an important musical art form. The ugly/ beautiful girls also got the chop, followed by the male/female duo and the one-hit wonder. It was down to me and the bubble-gum pop band in their deliberately not-quite-matching-but-matching-anyway outfits. They'd actually delivered a catchy little ditty and danced their socks off and I seriously wouldn't have begrudged them the win. Well, I would, but they seemed like a worthy group of kids who probably had a better chance of impressing the European audience than me. We stood on either side of O'Hara and the blonde as he ramped up the tension, backed up by some manically portentous music.

'And the winner is…'.

It was a landslide.

If the mêlée surrounding me after the first show was overwhelming, it was nothing compared to the smothering I endured after the results show. My cheeks were kissed raw by a phalanx of over-familiar people I'd never met before; everyone talked at me about going to Paris for the 'big one' and how they were all behind me; hangers-on congratulated me to within an inch of my life. Over in the corner of the green room, Ben graciously accepted the plaudits and spoke in his broad, patriotic Bronx about how we were going to win the whole fucking thing for Britain, while Gilbert perched on a chair like a little bird swigging a Bud as he stared into some personal abyss. He knew this wasn't about music and that, of course, was *all* he was about. Meanwhile, Elaine flashed her lop-sided smile and bestowed honeyed charm on all who entered her aura.

I was spent by the time Ben ushered us all into a large black car outside Television Centre while flashbulbs exploded all around us. We pitched up at some club in the West End, its glittering lobby dense with photographers, second rate footballers and third rate soap stars (by definition) all poised to welcome the singing hero; Ben had doubtless been on the phone to his PR person as soon as the results were in. He was not to be underestimated. Ben hand-picked three journalists and dragged them into the car. He'd given me a brief Not Putting Your Foot In It For Dummies master class on the way over. I was to talk only about the song, my musical influences and my aspirations for the final. Nothing personal, nothing controversial. And I did my best, honestly, but simply wasn't sharp or experienced enough to play this game and win. Or even draw. I parried a few early questions, the softener-uppers, then got too comfortable with my friendly, earnest inquisitors, one of whom sneaked in a question about how my wife and kids were feeling tonight. I took the offered bait, naturally, while Ben and Elaine were momentarily out of the car chatting up a vaguely familiar singer, and explained that my kids were delighted and that although I was separated from my wife, I'd spoken to her and she was very happy for me. Bits of which were true, of course, but I'd blown it, something I should have realised as soon as they drooled onto their notebooks.

Being a useless drinker who can't take excessive noise, I'm not really built for night clubs. Faye was right about me. I was always an old fart, despite my rock and roll pretensions. After an hour of bellowing and being bellowed at – I now had all sorts of fabulous new best friends who would remain so for, ooh, minutes – I was fading fast and I gestured to Elaine that I'd had enough. She led me to a quiet room at the top of a flight of steel stairs which I presumed was reserved for special guests. We talked briefly and incredulously about the evening's events before the car she'd ordered arrived to whisk us away. We emerged from a back door into the chilly night; only one photographer had second-guessed us, but he got nothing thanks to Elaine's quick thinking in draping her jacket over my head as we ducked into the car. She insisted we go back to her place reasoning that the press would probably have sussed out my address by now and be lying in wait. On the way, I picked up a message from Lisa who'd watched the results show. She apologised, although God knows what for. I'd been the arse, not her and, when I returned her call, it was me who blathered in humble contrition. She sounded cheery, maybe even slightly taken with me, making me feel less of an oaf for my earlier boorishness. I'd spent the last few years falling below her expectations and I'd let her down, not because I'd chosen a career that offered so little, but because I hadn't tried to improve my lot. Being a good father and a faithful husband was a given. Settling for mediocrity was my sin. I told her to close the curtains and keep herself and the kids out of sight. The press would be after her and she should avoid engaging with them. She said not to worry; she knew how to handle the press – well of course she did – and she would make sure Bea understood the importance of protecting the kids at all times. We said goodbye like we used to, with warmth, not just words.

Elaine and I talked over a pot of tea. I was still fizzing, partly because of my whirlwind fifteen minutes in the spotlight but mostly in response to my having stepped off the gangplank into foreign waters. It was too late to swim back to shore. Scary, yes, but utterly thrilling. Elaine counselled me on what to expect, but I could think of nothing more exciting than emerging from obscurity to become the focus of the world's lens. Maybe that's overstating it. This was only Eurovision, for Christ's sake, not the G8 summit, but why not revel in whatever attention came my way rather than shrink from it? Elaine left me to my misguided designs and went to bed. There was never any question of sleeping anywhere other than on Elaine's spongy little sofa. I hadn't changed just because I'd been on the telly, hadn't become more attractive, more desirable. And why even think of complicating our relationship with something as pointless as sex? Can't believe I said that. I was a coiled spring that night despite my exhaustion and, frankly, sex would have been a nice way to top things off. But not with Elaine. Our friendship was the thing and it would have been meaningless and gratuitous. I was better than that.

And, minor detail I know, she didn't want me.

I lay there replaying every moment. From zero to…well something a bit more. One minute O'Hara was that really famous bloke off the telly, the next he was shaking my hand and cautioning me about the vagaries of fame. I was a guy who fell asleep watching crap like Eurovision, not someone who appeared on it. But tonight, millions of people had watched little old me. More than that, they liked me, or at least they liked my story, and I was now fastening myself in for the ride of my life.

CHAPTER 19

IT WAS ALL very well expecting it, but seeing my sweaty, beaming face on the front page of the Mirror ('A Star Is Born'), The Star ('The Old Ones Are The Best'), The Sun ('Stand In, Stands Out!') and even The Times (tucked away, smirkily, on page seven – 'Substitute Scores a Hit') was still a massive shock. Especially with that blatantly Photoshopped double chin. Or maybe they'd all got the wrong angle. I'd taken a cab back from Elaine's at around seven and jumped out at the dingy indoor bazaar opposite my flat to buy the full range of dailies and some semi-skimmed. The owner didn't recognise me even after I casually held my front page photo up beside my face, but then he never remembered me from one day to the next. I'd hoped there'd be no early risers in the press corps, but two men with grey faces and rumpled coats popped out of a car outside my block and bounded towards me. I believe the correct response in such circumstances is 'no comment' but I asked them if they wouldn't mind fucking off. In my defence, this only came after the one with the Dictaphone asked me why my marriage had fallen apart. It was ill-advised, of course, and no doubt an asterisked version of my invective and a photograph of my sour, sleep-starved face would appear the following morning as the backlash began, but I hoped I had a few more weeks in the upward cycle of goodwill before they started the demolition process in earnest.

Inside, my answerphone was blinking wildly. It had actually run out of recording space, not something I would normally expect to happen if I left it untouched for a year. There were countless messages from friends and relatives as well as the press (how the hell do they find out your number? You'd think they hack people's phones, or something). I rang the people who mattered, telling and re-telling my story without tiring of it. Both my mobile and landline phones trilled all morning and I did my best to screen unwanted calls, but in the end I just let them ring out unless I was absolutely certain who was on the other end. I caught up with Lisa around nine. She'd been followed to the station and onto the train, but managed to shake the parasites off somewhere near Bond Street. The kids had been smuggled out of the curiously unattended wooden door at the back of the garden by my mother and had not been tailed. At least, she didn't think so. Perhaps a separated wife was more instantly newsworthy than a couple of kids, but I feared they'd be targeted when they tired of Lisa.

Ben called, slightly after the horse had bolted, to tell me to say nothing to the press. I asked to speak to Elaine to thank her again for looking after me, but she was on another line and Ben said she'd call me back in one minute. Thirty seconds later, the phone rang and I picked it up without thinking.

'Hey.'

'Fuck's sake, don't hang up!' yelled Chaz.

I was tempted, but opted for stony silence.

'Listen. I am not, nor have I ever slept with Lisa.'

'Lousy grammar, Bill Clinton, but just as disingenuous.'

'But I haven't! Ok, look. I didn't want to do this over the phone, but you've been such a fucking juvenile…'

'Why don't you just f…'

'Lisa…she's…ok, listen, she's been having an affair…'

'I fucking know that, don't I?' I snapped. 'Bye, bye.'

'Not with me, Mike. Understand? Not with me!' Chaz paused, hardly able to bear the responsibility of spitting it out. He took a nervous breath, then delivered the coup de grace. 'Don Ellwood.'

'Yeah, really,' I blustered, but already knew it was true.

'It's been going on a while.'

'You're such a little…'

'Three weeks ago I had a meeting with her at the gallery about the sponsorship deal, got there early, walked in on them in her office. Kissing, Mike.'

'That's conclusive, is it?' I said, the earth shifting irrevocably beneath me.

'No. Her admitting it to me was conclusive.'

My shoulders slumped. 'Ok, well, that's *quite* conclusive.'

It made perfect sense, of course. The doe-eyed, coquettishness whenever he was around, the intimate little touches, the hugs, the flirtatiousness. How had I missed it? Or been so wilfully blind? Swiftly substituting the grim mental image of weasely little Chaz for that of the handsome, muscular superstar sweatily humping my wife didn't make me feel any better. Worse, if anything. How could I hope to compete?

'She said they'd been seeing each other for a few months and I wasn't to say anything to you. But now I have, because I want you to stop blaming me and because you're my mate.'

I was shaking, couldn't swallow. 'If you were a mate, you'd have told me sooner.'

'Oh do fuck off, Mike. You wouldn't let me anywhere near you. She said *she* was going to tell you when the time was right, whenever that was going to be, but she obviously hasn't, so…'

'So you stepped in. Cheers.'

'I never wanted to hurt you, Mike, but it's been driving me insane. I just need you to know it wasn't me. Our friendship's important to me, even if it isn't to you.'

My eyes were stinging. It was all I could do to force the words out. 'It is. Course it is.'

'I'm sorry for you, Mike, but you should know me better than that, arsehole.'

'Yes, yes I should.' I held the phone away from my face so he wouldn't hear me sobbing. I was numb, which didn't prevent my vanquished machismo from helpfully pointing out that she must have been having sex with me and Ellwood at the same time. I felt dirty and disgusted, and suddenly angry enough to recover my composure. 'I owe you an apology, don't I?'

'Er, yes.'

'I know.'

'Well?'

'What? Now?'

'Yes now.'

'Ok. So…well, the thing is, ok, I am,' I'm a man, remember. This kind of bollocks doesn't come easily.

'That's it? God almighty. That was shit…oh go on then, you're forgiven, you fucking tit.'

'I'm bloody pathetic, aren't I? Can't hold onto my wife, no job, didn't trust my best friend…and, I mean, as if she'd sleep with *you*.'

'Cheers.'

'Seriously, I'm just ridiculous, a complete waste of space.'

'Normally, I'd be the first to agree but, with respect, no man who wins Eurovision:You Decide can ever be ridiculous in my book.'

For the first time in several hours, I'd forgotten about my trivial little victory. 'Yeah. Doesn't seem such a big deal now though, does it? Not when you've been cuckolded by the next James Bond.'

'Are you mad? It's the biggest fucking deal of all time. You won! You're going to Paris. For the Eurovision Song Contest! You are *the man*. I'm getting a posse together. I'm not missing that.'

'Face it, we'll never beat the Balkan bloc or the…Baltics or whatever.'

'The French managed it last year. And you've got the advantage of not being French. We can take them!'

Ben sent a car to pick me up at ten. The press boys, whose number had grown significantly, were looking a bit cold and bored as I exited my building, but they perked up a bit when I told them I'd give them proper interviews later on when I got back. I was lying, of course, but teasing them was so much fun.

Elaine ushered me into Ben's office and, as feared, he enveloped me in a massive, Paco Rabanne-scented bear hug. I could feel a headache coming on. Sitting elegantly in one of Ben's fine leather chairs was a formidable looking woman of about fifty with swirling black hair and fiercely plucked eyebrows. She wore a sturdy tweed skirt suit which accentuated her broad hips and even broader shoulders. She stood, surprising me with her immense height, and we shook hands. 'Good to meet you, Michael. Mary Dillon. Congratulations,' she said in a thin voice that belied her appearance. 'You must be absolutely chuffed.'

'It's a bit surreal.'

'Well it's going to be that and a lot more besides for the next few weeks, so we need to be prepared. That's my job, to guide you through the minefield.' She flashed a sweet smile but was visibly girding her not inconsiderable loins. 'Press snapping at your heels?'

'All over me.'

'Well, they're a venal, nasty little pack when they're hungry, so we're going to feed them a few scraps to make sure we keep them onside, ok?'

'Mary's the best, Mike, *the best*. Listen to her and you're gonna be just fine.'

Mary acknowledged Ben's accolade with a confident smile. 'A few simple rules and we shouldn't have any problems.'

Elaine brought in a tray of hot drinks and a selection of goodies from Dunns, the exquisite bakery just across the road from the studio. I'd been too excited to eat anything of substance since gorging myself in the green room and the aroma of the coffee and plump, buttery croissants triggered a sudden ravenousness. I tore off a flaky chunk and stuffed it into my mouth as Mary outlined her action plan. In essence, I was forbidden from speaking directly to the press unless she was within two yards of me. Three yards? Don't even think about it. If they did corner me unaccompanied, I was to say 'no comment' and absolutely not, under any circumstances, rise to any bait. Telling them to fuck off, therefore, appeared to be somewhat of a misjudgement on my part. Mary showed me the evidence on The Sun's website and wagged an admonishing finger at the silly boy.

A little later, Ben took me aside and shoved a stapled sheaf of papers into my hand. 'New contract. Standard sole composer. You baled us out, baby,' he said, slapping my shoulder, which was now beginning to bruise from the constant battering. 'We told the world who really wrote the song, so we don't need to pretend Howard had anything to do with it. Motherfucker's blown it with me big time. Breach of contract et cetera, et cetera. I'm gonna sue the shit out of him.'

'Not really worth it, is it?'

Ben flapped his arms at my rhetorical question. 'Anyway, now it's out there, we need a piece of paper to reflect it.' Ben jabbed at the contract in my hand which I speed-read. It named me as the composer and the royalty provisions seemed ok, but I told Ben it still warranted a professional eye. He heaved a wounded 'what, you still don't trust me?' sigh. No, I still didn't.

Mary called Lisa to give her a similar briefing. I imagined my distracted wife sitting there nodding wearily, being taught to suck eggs. That was just before I imagined her breathless beneath the slick, tanned, hairless body of Don Ellwood. I had to confront her with it at some point, but was pleased to have so much else going on to justify delaying that awful conversation. Mary said she was going to leak some basic, anodyne personal information to the press and it went without saying that she'd handle the issue of the separation with practised sensitivity; we were still friends (were we?) and, like any caring, devoted parents, we were putting the children first. It seemed obvious to me that Lisa's dalliance was going to come out – how could it not? We're talking Don Ellwood here. Through gritted teeth, I divulged this sensational tidbit to Mary. Who already knew. Of course.

First up, then, would be a series of photographs showing me in relaxed mode at home (ie an appropriately furnished studio rather than my scum-hole). There'd also be fly-on-the-wall-yet-artfully-posed shots of me, guitar across my knee, scraps of paper everywhere, spit-soaked pen between my teeth, beavering away at the emotionally draining art of song writing. The world would learn of my refusal to admit defeat, about how I'd overcome the odds to fulfil my lifelong passion. All news to me, this shit, but it sounded great. This little PR package would keep the press sated for now, leaving the coast clear to get our teeth into the stuff that really mattered. Most urgently, I had to get into the studio to record my own version of the song. We'd then shoot the companion-piece video and have some new photos taken for the CD cover and the press who would soon need something fresh to gorge on.

Most urgent, at least as far as my 'hand-picked' style gurus were concerned, was a trip down the Kings Road to get myself a decent wardrobe (a first), some 'happening' shoes (no idea) and a funky haircut (what, pray tell, was wrong with Mr Topper?). Quite who hand-picked Lorna and Sophia, an almost identical pair of over-excited fashion snobs, or why, was a mystery, but they were tasked with dragging me in their toffish wake as they attempted to de-daddify me. This tedious suiting and booting was punctuated by a PR masterclass from Mary who put me through my paces in preparation for appearances on a host of TV and radio shows. It was all about promotion and awareness to boost record sales and gain momentum going into Paris. The simple shtick: 'the stand-in who took Britain by storm.' If we could make Europe aware of my poignant yet uniquely heart-warming struggle, record sales could go through the roof, although I'd be up against other contestants who might have equally gripping tales to sell – maybe an ex-soldier who cheated death but lost his guitar-playing fingers in Bosnia, or a Finnish mother of nine (years old) with something terminal. In the X Factor age, tragedy is everything.

Mary, no slouch she, had scheduled a swathe of radio interviews for that afternoon and stretching long into the evening. A host of local stations around the country wanted to talk to me but as we couldn't waste time sitting in a studio, Mary arranged for these to be conducted by telephone to coincide with my downtime in the cab. She wasn't too worried about the quality of the line; the very fact that I would be live and on the hoof only added to my everyman myth. That said, I'm not the best of passengers in lurching, liberty-taking, diesel-fumed metal boxes and my interview with a radio station in Liverpool was cut short to allow for the ejection of copious stomach contents from a window.

I turned out to be a decent interviewee, or so Mary said. Apparently I displayed just the right blend of articulacy, wit and, if I may be so humble, humility. I was good at this. Who knew? Informality combined with an inability to take anything seriously hadn't served me too well in my previous career, but it was a boon in this one. Mary remained in my eye line at all times to ensure I didn't stray into difficult territory. A raised eyebrow here, a wince there kept me on track.

Perhaps I shouldn't have been surprised when Jonathan Ross's people called my people to set up a short interview followed by a live rendition of the song on his Saturday night show. But, I mean, come on, Jonathan Ross! Before that, I was scheduled to make several more appearances on national and local radio as well as BBC1's Breakfast, Daybreak, some moronic show on E4 and Lorraine. That, plus newspaper interviews, features in the TV listings magazines and possible spreads in Hello, OK, Woman's Own and Time Out. It was endless and bewildering. I'd assumed there'd be a minor media storm, but I realised I'd been thinking more in terms of a light shower.

I slept at Elaine's again, having first eaten too much at an odd Moroccan restaurant, drunk too much alcohol and talked too much about myself. I was out in an instant, too far gone to toss and turn. It had been all-consuming and I still had to summon the energy for the far more demanding days ahead. There'd been no time to reflect, no time to gather myself, no time to analyse my chewed-up personal life. But whatever else happened, I was determined to keep my Saturday morning date with the kids. It might be truncated, possibly interrupted, but if I let that go, I could wave goodbye to reality. Being newly owned by the public, I wasn't going to be able to pick them up from the house, nor spend another stultifying day shuffling around museums, eating crap in McDonalds or hunting for the Shrek 2 DVD in Blockbusters. Someone would be following with a camera and I couldn't put them through that. I had to find a way to keep things normal for them, and I would, dammit.

It was while stiffening this resolve that Mary called to say I was block-booked for Saturday.

I had fifteen minutes to kill before my Friday afternoon interview with Richard Bacon, a rare moment of tranquillity in the maelstrom. I made my excuses to Mary, sneaked off to a BBC toilet, locked myself in a cubicle and dialled the familiar number with cold, nervous fingers. Lisa answered, her voice surprisingly fluffy and upbeat. This wasn't the time to mention Ellwood; rather to revel in her sunny mood while it lasted. I explained that I couldn't make it on Saturday – she understood – and asked her to put me onto the kids. They were deliciously unimpressed with my instant stardom. On the contrary, why hadn't I just refused to do it, it was *that* shit? Why couldn't I have, like, written a song for like One Direction or Dappy – whatever that was – someone who could sing *and* was cool? Wasn't I embarrassed about being in all the newspapers? They were. They'd even taken some light-hearted stick at school. I was no hero to the under-tens. I promised them I'd do something way cooler after the contest was over to spare them further embarrassment. I'd like to say they were too young to fully comprehend what was going on, but in fact they were too worldly-wise, too au fait with the sheer nebulousness of fame to be fazed by it.

And then I called Faye.

I was pretty good on Jonathan Ross. There I go again, but I was. I was made for this, if nothing else. Wossy took the piss out of my age, my squareness and the naffness of Eurovision, while I reminded him that he was older than me, his hair was dated and that it wasn't called Euwovision. And he'd been a judge on some Eurovision show a few years earlier, so who was he to scoff? I garnered a few laughs, raised a few eyebrows and splashed around in the goodwill flowing down the banked studio seating like a waterfall. Wossy shook my hand and I turned to acknowledge the enthusiastic applause. A wobbly, out-of-body moment followed as I caught sight of my shiny face in a giant monitor. Who was that man and how the hell did he get here? On Jonathan Ross. It made no sense. In a moment of scary prescience, I knew I'd look back on this one day and find it impossible to believe it had ever happened.

In the green room, I mingled with a dazzling, miniature poodle-hugging American film actress and her massive, fussing entourage, a chubby British comedy actor (no entourage, lots of cakes) and a slightly whiffy Indie band who'd closed the show. I'd sung my song from the sofa – an acoustic version comprising the first couple of verses and a chorus. And very intimate it was too, like being in *Jaques* again if you ignored the studio audience, the millions watching at home, the cameras, the lights, Wossy…

Chaz had somehow blagged a ticket and I sneaked him into the green room like my own little miniature. After an abortive attempt to add the actress and the fat boy to his client base, he joined me, Ben, Elaine and Mary at Locatellis where, had I still been Michael Kenton, IT Nobody, I'd have struggled to get a table any time before global warming finally turned properly nasty and fried the planet. I'd eaten furiously in the green room, post-show hunger apparently another new phenomenon to which I'd have to adjust, and still had room for a plate of pasta before Chaz and I made our excuses, leaving Ben to foot the bill. This was all on highly optimistic credit. Mary chased me into the street and made me swear not to speak to anybody about anything before allowing me to get into Chaz's car. He drove us to Hanger Lane where I introduced him to the delights of April Moon. All that savoury food had left me gasping for something sweet and where better than here, with its faded chintz, dowdy décor and uncomprehending waiters, to gorge on soggy banana fritters and vanilla ice cream? Seemed like no-one else had the same idea, so it was mercifully quiet. No press either, their relentless pursuit foiled or at least on hold. I passed Chaz a copy of the new contract Ben had asked me to sign and he was only too pleased to give it the once over. I think it made him feel connected, an integral cog in the vast Eurovision wheel.

No longer fearing my seething opprobrium, Chaz opened up about Lisa. He'd suspected the viperous Ellwood for a while, having bumped into him more than once at the gallery before stumbling in on the fateful kiss. Ellwood had initially struck him as a natural charmer with a genuine appreciation of art, but his appreciation of Lisa was clearly the point. I'd witnessed them flirting first hand but chosen to brush it under the carpet and would probably have continued with this self-delusion had Chaz not spoken up. The whole Barcelona thing was a red herring I'd cooked and swallowed. Chaz had flown out to start discussions about setting up a new office there. Lisa's trip was completely coincidental.

'It's my fault, really. This whole thing,' I said, trying to make light. 'I vomited all over his jacket.'

'Oh. Now it all makes sense,' said Chaz.

'*I'm so sorry. My husband's a terrible embarrassment. What about a fuck to apologise?*'

'Well hopefully the jacket's knackered.'

I swirled an oily globule of banana around my mouth. 'I know I've been bloody aimless for God knows how long, but she could've at least talked to me first.'

'What, and got your permission?'

'Yes. *Would you mind awfully if I screwed around a bit with James Bond?* I mean, that's only civilised, isn't it?'

'Basic manners.'

'Why didn't she tell me she was *that* unhappy?'

'You're saying you didn't know?'

I shrugged. I'd known for years.

'Why didn't you tell her *you* were unhappy?' said Chaz.

'I wasn't.'

'Yes you were.'

'Yeah, ok, I was, but I had my head in the sand. Separating's what other people do. It's so…drastic. And, I mean, what about the girls? I couldn't contemplate not having them around.'

'And now?'

'Now…now I realise I loved her out of habit. I was lonely with her and I'm lonely without her but…I haven't missed her for a second. I've missed 'home', I've missed the girls. Not her. That make any sense?'

Chaz nodded. He always got me. At least someone did.

'It still hurts,' I said, 'hurts like hell, but that's just my ego getting all het up. It's a delicate little flower.'

'I think I know,' Chaz said, offering a wry smile.

'I miss those kids so much…being part of them and their little worlds. Yes, I get my Saturdays and the odd Sunday, but it takes us half a day to get to know each other again and it's all over before it's started. And I'm left having to get through another week on my own in this fucking shithole.' I looked up. Only a yellowing Artexed ceiling separated us from my living room.

'Well all that's going to change. Ok, not everything, but I mean, whatever else happens you're going to make some dough, aren't you? You'll move out of there and find somewhere appropriate to a Eurovision legend and you and Lisa will sort things out like the sensible adults you are…well she is. And the kids will be the absolute priority. Can't imagine Lisa making things difficult on that front.'

'No,' I said, dreamily immersed in the simple joys of tucking them in, feeling their soft, tired kisses drying on my cheek, their cool, soft skin and tangy, shampooed hair. 'Kids…they're magic, they really are.'

There I went again, insensitive to a fault. Didn't I know how much Chaz and Denise wanted kids of their own? Well didn't I? God. I winced at my faux pas but Chaz, ever the diplomat, rescued me from my own crassness.

'We're trying IVF again. Might as well, eh?'

'Can you afford it?'

'Depends how many test tubes we fuck up,' said Chaz. 'Maybe we'll crack it this time.' The pain was etched into his pale face like a tattoo.

'I meant can you afford kids? School fees, braces, laser correction, boob jobs, car insurance…?'

'Better start saving up, eh?'

Chaz and I took the long trek back up to my flat; a sharp left turn, through the security door with the broken lock and a trudge up a single flight of narrow, cat piss drenched stairs. A couple of hacks with snappers in tow who'd evidently arrived while we were eating, slipped in behind us before the door clicked shut. I asked them – politely, note – to leave, but Chaz was having none of it, gurning for the cameras and giving them an exclusive on this 'gay lovers' tryst' before slamming the door in their faces. Over tea and Kit-Kats, we watched my Jonathan Ross interview on the knackered old video recorder I'd rescued from the loft, me mostly through my fingers. There's nothing worse than hearing your own voice, except seeing yourself using it. We sank a few bottles of lager and chatted until two, when Chaz got up and slipped his coat on. At the front door he turned to look at me with a disturbingly fluttery-eyed smile. I thought he was going to kiss me. 'I'm glad we're, you know…'

'Yeah…me too.'

Then Chaz opened his arms and stepped towards me. He was going for the full man hug but stopped just short as I flinched. We'd never hugged in thirty years. I don't think we'd even touched each other in all that time other than accidentally or whilst one of us, me, was beating the other one, him, up.

'Go on, fuck off,' I said.

'See ya, arsehole.'

The interviews were becoming tedious, repetitive and unwelcome, but I had another slew to endure on Sunday morning. Mary picked me up at eight and said I could have the afternoon off if I was a good boy. She handed me a buff file of the day's press clippings and said they were 'mostly pretty good', and suggested I bear in mind that the only thing worse than bad publicity was no publicity. Hmm. I'd hoped to sneak in a visit to the kids, but had to make do with a quick call from the car to get my fix. They were going to a cousin's party in the afternoon so I wouldn't be able to see them then. Or was that an excuse? Ben called as we approached a small studio in Dean Street to say he'd set up the video shoot for Tuesday and he confirmed, following a forensic interrogation, that we wouldn't be going anywhere near a petrified meadow. I guested on a phone-in for a radio station in Newcastle down an ISDN line and sang the song acoustic style. Three further interviews followed before I was whisked across to Absolute Radio's studios to appear on the Martyn Lee show. Absolute Radio used to be Virgin, apparently, and I had a story to tell about them, didn't I? Ruined my career, those bastards. By 1pm I was shattered and sick of talking about myself. And, seriously, how many times can you spout the same fabrications?

I had a quick bite to eat in a Wardour Street brasserie with Elaine who'd arrived to lend her support. I relished our easy intimacy, made easier by the lack of sexual tension. And I admired her patience as, like a bar room bore, I re-traced my sorry tale: how I'd got to forty-two with so little to show for it; how things had gone so sour with Lisa; my fear of losing the kids. Elaine, hitherto not especially effusive about her personal life, let rip, revealing that she and Ben had had a relationship which had ended a few years earlier, something I'd sensed when we first met. Ben continued to pine for her but there was no going back for Elaine. She was a well-educated Home Counties art student who'd gone off the rails for a while and got involved with all sorts of ne'er do wells. She'd been a rock chick cliché, done drugs and rehab, and it was Ben who rescued her from complete meltdown. But with that came a proprietorial claim which made him possessive, obsessive and jealous. She broke it off to save them both. A couple of years later, Ben asked her to come and work for him, no strings. She was connected, knowledgeable and hugely capable, a strong administrative hand on President Records's tiller. And, to his credit, Ben had honoured his promise to keep his romantic flame doused. But I'm pretty sure he still goes home every night and bashes his head against the walls in unrequited frustration.

I got back to the flat around three and settled in with a mug of tea and the press clippings to wallow in all the nonsense about some singer called Mike Kenton. There were some decent stills of him performing on Eurovision: You Decide and one paper had even unearthed a photo of the be-mulleted, twenty year old Mike when he was, briefly, the lead singer in a college band. The Sunday Mirror carried a photo of him on a grimy staircase beside a short, bald man with the headline: 'Eurovision Mike Walks on the Wild Side!' but the story made light of my 'outing' having identified Chaz as the married (and therefore probably heterosexual) managing partner of Glaziers and Mike's best friend. Some less flattering reports variously guessed at this guy Kenton's culpability in the break-up of his marriage, that he suffered from stage fright and might make a sorry mess of things in Paris, that he'd abandoned his kids, that his favourite colour was yellow, that he preferred brunettes with plastic boobs, that he was a serial failure with a low IQ, that he was known at school as Farty Mike. I was beginning to feel a bit sorry for the poor bastard, to be honest.

Sunday remained relatively quiet until Lisa called asking if I fancied putting the kids to bed. I was in the car in thirty seconds. There were no obvious signs of long lenses when I left the flat or arrived at the house. Maybe I'd peaked. I was only a Eurovision entrant, after all, not someone important like Jordan or Gazza. Here today, gone tonight. The girls were tired but effusive. The party had been shhhi…useless and the food all vegetarian rubbish because Harry's parents were, like, weird. The chips with their skins on were, like, ok but not as good as the ones at Macs. We drank hot chocolate together in the kitchen before they headed upstairs for a bath. I followed a few minutes later to tuck them both in, telling Kattie some stories about my Eurovision adventure and reading Millie a few pages from a Shrek book. She was going to grow out of this fixation, wasn't she?

Lisa was waiting for me in the kitchen when I came downstairs. She usually hustled me out of there as soon as possible, but this time she offered me tea and pulled back a chair for me to sit on. I sensed this was the moment to finally get everything out in the open.

'I'm not contesting the divorce,' she said, dunking an M & S tea bag.

'Good. Me neither. Nothing to argue about, is there? And it's not good for the kids if we slug it out.'

'I mean, ideally, I'd like to keep the house and have them stay with me so they aren't uprooted, but you should be able to see them whenever you like. Keep your key if you like but, obviously, ring first.'

'Yeah. Fine. Sensible.'

My, we *were* being mature. When was this going to turn ugly?

'You'll get out of that vile flat soon enough, won't you? Now you're a superstar,' she said, offering a cool, stunning smile. 'Maybe get somewhere they can stay with you in a bit more comfort?'

'That's the idea. Although I am getting quite attached to woodchip wallpaper and rusted window frames now.'

'I can understand that,' said Lisa, sounding a bit like her old self. She reached across and put her hand on mine. 'I'm sorry, Mike. I've been a complete bitch.'

'True.'

Lisa took a deep breath. 'Look, I know you know about me and…'

'How?'

'Chaz told me.'

'Can't that fucker keep anything to himself?'

'I made him. He's not very good under pressure.' Lisa's face went all sad at the edges. 'I'm not in love with him.'

'Who could love Chaz?'

Lisa smiled. 'Don paid attention to me. It was nice.'

'I get it, Leese,' I said. I hadn't called her that in a while. 'I knew things weren't right. Why didn't I try and talk to you like a normal human being? I thought our problems would just miraculously resolve themselves.'

'We were both dissembling.'

'Exactly. Whatever that means. Maybe neither of us thought it was worth fighting for.'

'You think so? It was good once, wasn't it?'

'Yeah, but…something happened along the way…fuck it, sorry, that's Earth Wind and Fire.'

Lisa chuckled. 'And now, after we've made a mess of everything, you're finally doing something fantastic with your life. I quite fancy you now. Shallow bitch, aren't I?'

'Nah. All the girls fancy me now. I've got my own groupies…at least three of them are under seventy.'

Lisa leaned across the table and pecked me on the cheek. 'You'd better go before I ask you not to.'

I stood up and we studied each other for a moment before embracing. God, it felt so good, so natural, to hold her again. The familiar contours of her body, her unique, sexy smell, her moist breath coating my neck. My heart raced and something dislodged inside my personal universe, an old, forgotten feeling, one I wasn't ready for. I backed off and made for the front door. Was I hoping she'd stop me? She followed me down the hall but let me go without another word. I turned, waved from the gate and headed for the car.

I drove back to my flat with watery eyes and confusion raging. Was she suggesting we try again? Was that something I even wanted? I didn't know anything about anything for a change.

And then Faye rang.

The thing I particularly like about Faye is – everything. Smart, funny, beautiful, thoughtful, informed, mature. Most of which I'm not. I have my qualities, of course, but I think I understood why Faye never went for me. Just too many gaps in the CV to be a viable long term partner; a fairly sensible, well brought up boy, but one with no clear defining purpose who, instead, dreamed of a career in pop music. The fool! Still and all, why did she go for that creep at Brunel? And if he *was* good enough, where did that leave me?

The prospect of seeing Faye again was both uplifting and depressing. Just to spend some time in her company was reward in itself, but it was tinged with the emptiness of knowing nothing I could ever do was going to make her want anything beyond a very occasional, very platonic relationship. Chemistry is a tough nut to crack. You can't magic it up and we always fell short. Not that she wasn't fond of me, or that we weren't physically attracted, or that we didn't once have a flirty, zingy thing going on, but it didn't add up to a whole number for her. We were friends, never lovers; Faye, a girl friend, never a girlfriend. So the best I could hope for was to become her friend again, albeit a besotted, unrequited knot of frustration like Ben.

She shimmered like some glorious apparition in the doorway of La Lumiere restaurant in Richmond, flicking her windswept hair unselfconsciously, yet without ostentation, from her face. There was nothing 'look-at-me' about her, nothing arrogant. I almost didn't want to reveal my whereabouts, preferring to drink her in from my vantage point across the room, but she spotted me and I stood up to greet her. We kissed each other's cheek, the merest touch of her cool, damp skin against mine triggering the usual frisson. Her saliva began cooling on my face, a living gift evaporating all too fast. She sat down, smiled and took a second to catch her breath.

'Hi,' she said.

'You look great.' Already? Save it, idiot.

'Oh shut up.'

She blew a jet of warm air past my ear. 'Sorry I'm late. Unbelievable traffic, nowhere to park and the…I'll shut up.'

'You're here, that's all that matters.'

She nodded. 'I'm here.'

Yes she was. Right in front of me. If only I could bottle this and stick it in the fridge.

There are some people with whom you can have a reasonable and cogent conversation whilst thinking about fifteen different things. Not Faye. She commands absolute focus, especially if you're besotted. Eyes like magnets, a voice like golden syrup, wit and nous evident in every sentence, and a smile like a gilded invitation to kiss her delicious lips. And she didn't know any of this. She was just being herself. Back when we were teenagers, my inexperienced self believed her to be the perfect woman. The intervening years had eroded that certainty. Maybe it had simply been youthful infatuation unsullied by harsh reality. Yet here we were, twenty years on, with so much muddy, turgid water under the bridge, and nothing had changed, for me at least. I felt faintly ridiculous as I sat there, heart pounding, muddled, befuddled, inadequate, a gauche kid again. I so wanted to reach across, take her hand and simply fly away, like Peter Pan, to somewhere nobody could touch or separate us. It's foolish, I know, to deify someone. I'd put Lisa on a pedestal as well, but if I've learned nothing else, people let you down in the end and it's as well to maintain some perspective.

I don't recall anything I said in those first fifteen jittery minutes; my conversation can only have been sketchy, disjointed, discursive, but Faye kept smiling that smile of hers, making me laugh, drawing me out until, with a little help from the wine inveigling my bloodstream, I relaxed. Which was probably how I had the gall to ask her how she'd allowed herself to marry such a shit. The question saddened rather than angered her. Her judgement had failed her, she said. He'd seemed like the soul mate she'd been searching for, the perfect man, and couldn't let go of that idyll even as he philandered and misbehaved. What kind of man could do that to her, to Faye? Why hadn't she left him immediately and found someone worthy of her? Faye didn't have any answers. She'd just let things get away from her, become marooned, closed herself off from reality and the possibilities beyond her miserable lot. I empathised, albeit my circumstances were entirely different. Lisa could never be bracketed with Faye's appalling ex. We simply ran out of steam and I should have seen it coming, but maybe it's easier to do nothing than challenge the status quo.

So Faye wasn't perfect, didn't have everything covered. She'd fucked up. It was a bit of a shock, to be honest. But as shocks go, it was nothing compared to…

'Married? Really?' I tried to muster a smile, a couple of thin words of congratulation, but couldn't squeeze anything past my childish pout. I sat back, shoulders slumped, shattered, already deep into a crushing, terminal sulk. Louis had proposed on a weekend break in Amsterdam. Got down on one knee beside a canal, the fucking, ingratiating cliché.

'I'm so excited,' said Faye.

'Yeah, of course. Why wouldn't you be?' I said with the numbness of a man having a conversation with the speaking clock. 'One knee. Wow.'

'He's a terrific guy. You must meet him.'

'I must?'

'Yes. You'll like him.'

I wanted to kill him.

'Ok, now I know I didn't mention this before but…brace yourself.' Faye paused for comic effect. 'He's an actuary. Sorry, I know, boring! But he's not. He's a real laugh.'

'I bet. All those actuarial tables and pensions and things.'

'I mean, what's more important is that he's the polar opposite of Rob, you know? He's not going to screw around. He's steady, he's reliable, I can trust him. Exactly what I need after that bastard.'

Louis certainly boasted a splendid melange of sturdy attributes. But what about that special feeling, the one I had for Faye?

'Rob was never home, never called, or if he did, you could hear the lies slithering out of his mouth. Louis calls me twice a day, sends me flowers, looks after me. He's solid. Don't look at me like that, Mike. I know you think it's pathetic, but after everything I've…look, sometimes solid's what a woman needs.'

I nodded, humbled and defeated by this block of solidity. 'You must love him a lot.'

'He's a great guy, a really great guy.'

Having your entire world implode is bad enough, but try it when all you've got to go back to is a dank, mildewed grotto overlooking the Hanger Lane Gyratory System. It transcends hell and transports you into a whole new dimension of utter desolation. Take it from me. I know what I'm talking abo…sorry can't hear myself slosh around in morbidity for that three-thousand-tonner hurtling towards Reading outside my window.

In need of a friendly voice, I called Chaz, but only got a sleepy Denise who was polite but, unlike every other Australian ever born, frosty. He was in Rio de Janeiro on business, the poor bastard. I wasn't going to foot *that* phone bill. I rang Elaine who was in bed and probably didn't appreciate being woken up, but she was kind enough not to let it show. We talked about Eurovision, my impending divorce, the next day's activities, but not Faye. I lacked the vocabulary to even begin to articulate that scenario. If you can call nothing a scenario. We finished up and I put the phone down.

And then there was silence. I couldn't even hear the traffic.

It's all relative, you understand. Misery, I mean. It's about how *you* feel, not what others think you should be feeling. So it would've been no use telling me that I had Eurovision coming up and that I was a little bit famous and extremely lucky to be following my dream. That's not life in my book; that's only what I happened to be doing with my time. It was superficial, a low-grade pursuit, a minor achievement. It had no bearing on what really mattered. Of course my kids loved me – and me them – without qualification; I had a soul mate in Chaz and a rock in Elaine; I even had a career of sorts. I'm not blind to all that. But in the end we all need that special someone to love, and mine was lost in perpetuity.

Tomorrow I had to record the vocal and the latest plan was to shoot a shoestring video in the studio. Mike Kenton raw, the man and his music. There would be no frolicking through frozen fields in a cheesecloth shirt, thank fuck. But how the hell was I going to raise the smile to win European hearts?

CHAPTER 20

I WAS LOST in music. Someone ought to write a song about that. Maybe a disco number. Gilbert, who I now acknowledged to be a semi-mute genius, extracted a performance I didn't think I had in me. I'd always sung songs as they came out, never worrying about emotion or feeling or any of that old bollocks. But Gilbert, with an esoteric array of inspired grunts and gesticulations, forced me to think about inflection and timbre, about complementing the drift and swell of the backing track with volume, tone and phrasing, about lending weight and nuance to lyrics in ways I'd never dreamed of. I was pretty proud of the final mix. It didn't even sound like me, which wasn't a bad thing. Gilbert had churned my voice through his magic maze of software, creating a perfectly balanced, expertly syncopated vocal performance. A camera crew fussed around me as unobtrusively as possible, filming me in action in the booth and as I chatted in the control room, drank tea, ate biscuits and went for a piss, for all I knew. We were going to give the world the real Mike Kenton, the laid back, unguarded, cool-as-you-like, unpretentious urinating charmer from nowhere, even if it took us a hundred takes to get it right.

So, yes, I was lost in music and all the attendant paraphernalia and thus able to keep the demons largely at bay. The bilious lump in my stomach was saving itself for later when I only had silence for company. Meanwhile, Mary buzzed around the place, mobile phone fused to her ear, my heart sinking ever lower as she bellowed out each new media commitment. An interview here, a supermarket opening there ('there' being Croydon, just to cheer me up). Britain was right behind its have-a-go hero and the fascination, fuelled by Mary's remorseless PR assault, was showing no signs of abating.

Towards the end of another exhausting day, Matthew Roberts called to say that the legal formalities were in train and that he had already opened negotiations with Lisa's solicitor, Derek Scott, a plummy nerd who fluttered around the edges of Lisa's chinless Oxbridge coterie. He cropped up at the odd party and was pleasant enough, the kind of man I humoured but never bothered to befriend, but he didn't strike me as someone to fear if things turned nasty. Naïve? Almost certainly. I told Matthew about the agreement Lisa and I had reached and emphasised that we wanted to remain amicable. He scoffed. I told you. Solicitors.

Jaques was absolutely teeming. Well it would be, wouldn't it? what with the UK's Eurovision contestant headlining. Hastily prepared photocopies of a newly word processed menu sat gathering candle wax on every table, Kevin having upped his prices by about 50% on the strength of the anticipated demand. I agreed to do two shows so he could arrange a second sitting. I owed him that much and had no intention of asking for a fee. Mary said we could 'exploit the hell' out of my generosity, but that was never my motivation. Kevin added more tables, making an already poky room pokier, with sardine-style standing room by the bar for anyone prepared to eat and drink without using their hands. It was almost certainly illegal, but he was entitled to a bumper night.

I'd come straight from a turgid afternoon chat show on Channel 4 and arrived feeling mentally drained and emotionally cleaned out, but the enthusiastic response to my first song, the genuine warmth and goodwill, eased the tension from my muscles and adrenaline took over. I don't recall enjoying a gig so much, and even as I rattled through my repertoire for the first time, I was looking forward to the second show.

I rested up during the break in a small, stinking room above the kitchen, which I shared with industrial sized cans of cooking oil, overflow freezers, some suspiciously green substance in Clingfilm and a batch of filthy saucepans. With only half an hour to recharge, I gobbled down a massive steak sandwich, an alpine mountain of chips and a knee-high side salad kindly supplied, gratis, by the ebullient Kevin. There'd have been leftovers if he'd served that lot up to a famished chain gang. Bloated but replete, I clambered past the pots, pans and cans strewn on the narrow staircase and re-entered the restaurant from the rear to a ripple of anticipation. Elaine had found a tiny pocket of space to the side of the bar and pinched my bum as I passed her. I turned, smiled, then threaded my way through the micro-gaps between the tables and chairs to take up my position behind the microphone. There was a palpable electricity in the room as I stepped up and introduced myself, rather formally, forgetting I was no longer Mike Who? I strummed the intro to *the song* to a rapturous reception which only faded halfway through the first verse. I've never lived to perform, but when an audience gets behind you like that, I can understand why some people breathe their love like oxygen. I was floating now, my voice mellifluous, resonant, tuneful, Gilbert's sage insights adding new polish and professionalism. The first audience had been enthusiastic, but this lot erupted at the end of *In Love We Trust*, their fervour almost sucking the air from my lungs. I winked conspiratorially: *Hey, come on, I'm still one of you, just an ordinary guy who'll be signing autographs afterwards.* I drank it in, savouring the moment, wishing I could take this feeling home with me, knowing it would be a chimera as soon as Hanger Lane enveloped me in its loveless embrace. But I had a set to finish and I was surfing the wave. A complicated riff got the second song under way. I launched into the vocal buoyed by a confidence I'd never felt before. I was emoting, living the music, flying. Until my eye alighted on a couple standing at the bar and I completely lost my thread.

Faye. And beside her, a tall, thin man with a massive Adam's Apple, a military haircut, rimless glasses and a sensible M & S shirt, one button undone, not two. Tucked in. Louis, if I wasn't very much mistaken. Trust me, I'm not stereotyping here; take the straightest die, straighten it, then straighten it a bit more and, hey presto, you've got yourself a Louis. I may have missed a couple of lyrics as I lost my way, but the audience was too pumped to notice and I somehow recovered my poise. I wasn't going to let anything ruin this evening, not even the sight of a palpably unsuitable man with his arm around Faye. My Faye. No, not tonight, not when I was having the gig of my life.

'Gosh, an actual pop star,' said Louis with what would, from anyone else, but not from him, have been a drizzle of sarcasm. 'It must be great.'

'Not really,' I said.

'Come on Michael,' said Faye, 'you're having the time of your life.'

'I'm certainly having a time in my life; just don't think it's *the* one.' I shrugged, as you would following such an asinine remark. 'I've had worse.' Like you sitting there with him slathered all over you.

'Beats working in an office, I bet,' said Louis, poshly, straining for insight.

'Well, anything beats that,' I said trying not to sound like I was taking the piss. It was hard. 'But, you know, each to their own. You probably enjoy it, working in an office?'

'Hate it,' said Louis with a stern face, which gave way to a braying laugh. 'Only kidding. What am I saying? I bloody love it. I was made for an office. I am office. Look at me. Where else could I work? I couldn't do what you do if you paid me.'

'And you sing like a castrated cat,' said Faye.

Oh, Louis loved that! More equine snorts, followed by a dopey head butt into Faye's neck. Stop it, you two, for fuck's sake, you're killing me.

'It takes a bit of guts to stand up there in front of all those people and bare your soul like that,' said Faye, who had the good grace to look slightly embarrassed by the antics of the Straight Die Man.

'Not really.'

'Well I reckon it does,' agreed lapdog Louis.

'He's being modest,' continued Faye. 'I mean, you know if they like you or hate you straight away, don't you? You can hide away in an office for ten years without anyone really bothering you.'

'S'true. I know I did,' I said.

'Well I'm proud of you Mike,' continued Faye, who looked at Louis and said: 'He was such a dreamer at college. Nobody thought he'd amount to anything.'

Cheers.

'He honestly thought he could be a musician! Idiot!' added Faye, drawing another disturbing honk from her narrow-throated beau.

'Well you're doing all right now, aren't you?' said Louis. 'Doesn't matter *when* you make it, as long as you're young enough to enjoy it when you do (comedy pause)…and you just about are.'

Louis's rancour-free chuckle said everything. He was a good man, a kind man, an earnest man, a man without side. What the fuck was Faye thinking? That ex-husband of hers had a lot to answer for. He'd sent her so far the other way, she was about to marry an ironing board.

Louis was back to serious mode again: 'I think it's absolutely fantastic, I really do, Michael. Good on you. I hope you win. I'm certainly going to be watching.'

I wanted to hate him, but I couldn't. No-one could. And I could see in his eyes how much he worshipped Faye. He was never going to shit on her. I couldn't blame her for attaching herself to this paragon.

Jaques began to empty, but not before I was back-slapped and hand-shaken until it hurt. Do surgeons or UN peacekeepers or Save The Children volunteers or nurses saving lives in Africa receive such fawning admiration for all their important work? I doubt it, but then how many of them have scaled the Olympian heights of not just composing but also singing a vapid Euro-pop song? Not many, I bet. Our glasses were empty and Louis was ready to go, but not before he toodled off to the toilet for a *Jimmy Riddle*. I kid you not, that's what he said. I looked at Faye for any sign that I'd been had, maybe a smirk, a tell. When was Louis going to spring out shouting: 'Gotcha!'

'I told you he was a nice bloke, didn't I?'

'And you were right. Charming.'

'So, you'll come to the wedding? It's in August.'

'Course I will. That'd be great.'

'Bit cheeky, but would you do a couple of songs for us? I don't know any other famous musicians I can ask.'

I smiled through a silent cry of anguish. 'I'd be delighted.'

My mobile trilled as I lurched up the North Circular. I parked up to take the call, of course. Doesn't everyone?

'Hi.'

'Elaine. Hi. Where did you get to after the gig? I was looking for you.'

'Sorry, couldn't stay. Just wanted to say you were bloody great tonight.'

'Well thank you,' I said.

Elaine paused. She had something on her mind. 'So, I was talking to Faye.'

'Faye?'

'You know, Faye? The pretty one you can't take your eyes off. That Faye'

Ok, now I did pull over and park up.

'My ex-boyfriend knew her ex-husband. We're going way back,' said Elaine.

'You...and Faye...were friends? That's what you're telling me?'

'Didn't say that. We just saw each other around the place, you know, parties, the odd get-together, that sort of thing. Rob...her ex, I mean, we're talking absolute horror. Arrogant, self-centred...ugh. Pig. I avoided getting too matey with them, you know?'

I was stunned.

'So she said you were at college together.'

'Yeah.' It was all I could manage.

'You had a bit of a thing for her, didn't you?'

'She tell you that?'

'No.'

Elaine waited for me to respond, but hers was a particularly potent form of female intuition obviating further embellishment.

'Mike?'

'Gotta go.'

You know how, when you were a teenager and you got dumped by a girlfriend (or boyfriend – this applies to everyone, so pay attention) and it hurt like hell but you were friendly with one of her best friends and you kept pumping the best friend for information, hoping your ex-girlfriend would confide something vaguely encouraging in her that might give you cause for hope? Just me? Well anyway, that's kind of where I was with Elaine. She knew Faye, however distantly, and Elaine obviously knew how I felt about her, so maybe, just maybe, she could talk to Faye and see if she might let slip anything to suggest she'd made the most horrendous mistake and actually desperately wanted me to ride by on my white charger and whisk her away to a faraway forever land.

These are the kind of idiotic thoughts that churn through the tortured mind of a restless man lying on a bed of nails with the sound of juggernauts raging relentlessly past his bedroom window.

'Dad! Dad! We saw you on MTV,' bellowed Millie down the phone.

'Did you? Was I any good?'

'No, absolute shit. But it was, like, great 'cos we had Lauren and Mandy round and when you came on we said that's our Dad and they didn't believe us, so I got the photo album out and showed them some pictures of all of us together in Nice that time and then they believed us and they were like, no way!'

'Really?'

'Yeah.'

'Well listen. Now I'm so important and famous, I'd really like you and Kattie to come to the Eurovision final in Paris. How about that? I'll take you backstage and you can meet all the famous singers...'

'They're not famous to us, though, are they? They're all foreign?'

'Ok, but it'll still be amazing.'

'Is Mum going?'

'I don't know, sweetheart. Maybe. But if not, maybe grandma will bring you. Hey, you can go on the Eurostar.'

'What's that?'

'It's a fantastic train that goes under the Channel and goes straight to Paris.'

'A train? Boring.'

'Well...ok...but it's very fast.'

'Is it?'

This was proving to be a tougher nut to crack than I'd anticipated. 'We'll see the Eiffel Tower...and...the...lots of other fun things.'

Little lamb wouldn't recognise any other Parisian landmarks. Like I could think of any.

'Ok,' said Millie. 'Maybe.'

A 'maybe' that turned swiftly to 'no' after Lisa explained they'd be watching from the Wiltshire weekend retreat of one of her best clients. But they'd be with me in spirit.

Matthew Roberts was right. Of course he was, the smart-arsed, trainer-footed little prick. We were only in the early stages and already there were skirmishes in the foothills. Derek Scott was playing hardball on behalf of Lisa who surely knew nothing about it. He didn't want me to have open-ended access to the children 'or anything of the kind'. Who was that privileged bastard to say when I could and couldn't see my children? And he was suggesting I pay maintenance to Lisa. I'm not joking; it was in a letter which he'd actually signed. Obviously I was more than happy to pay my share towards the kids, but Lisa didn't need half of what would be left over after that (can you divi up zero?). Apparently Derek was under the impression that I was earning serious cash from my late-blossoming career and he felt Lisa should get her slice. Which, of course, reminded me that I hadn't received a penny from Ben so far. The song was due for release in two days' time and Chaz's lawyer friend had inserted a clause providing for a £20,000 advance against future sales. I called Elaine and asked her to look into it and an hour later a cheque arrived by courier for the full amount. My God she was good. No wonder Ben worshipped her, although probably slightly less ardently after she forced him to sign it.

So now I was flush.

And nowhere near happy.

CHAPTER 21

W<small>HEN WAS THE</small> last time a Eurovision song got to number one? Eh? Well don't look at me. Waterloo? Boom Bang a Bang? Puppet on a Wotsit? Who cares? But I was at number one now. Me. Mike Kenton. *In Love We Trust.* Insane!

Ben had pulled out all the stops to get the song in the shops – and online for downloading, as is, I believe, the young people's preference these days – before Paris. He'd wilted under the sheer weight of public demand, the old philanthropist. It was flying off the shelves/servers and Ben was hopping around his office shouting 'Ker-ching!' rather too energetically for a man in his sixties. He was going to do himself a mischief. For the first time, Ben wanted to talk about life post-Eurovision, specifically how we were going to cash in on my success. This was all, ahem, music to my ears. First off, he wanted to start preparing an album so that, as soon as Eurovision was over, we'd be ready to follow up and not give the public a chance to forget me. 'Outta sight, outta mind, fella,' was his latest mantra. He didn't say whether the album would comprise a tepid collection of standards or original material or both, and I don't think he thought it mattered. It wasn't about quality or content, just being out there. All the worthy, artistic bullshit would come later once I was established. Think Will Young. Then we had to organise a UK tour, followed by some dates in Europe. And then, according to Ben, still lost in his delicious reverie, my 'quintessential British MOR sensibility' could be adapted for the American market and we could *all fucking retire.*

I was happy to ride this bandwagon – a bit of global superstardom never hurt anyone – but I thought he was letting his wallet run away with itself without checking that there were a couple of chips of sanity in the little zip-up compartment. This was but one song riding high on the back of the 'last minute stand-in' story which was undeniably romantic and compelling but had nothing to do with whether the British public was actually interested in my music. Did they know I'd written other songs? Did they care? Mike Kenton, specifically their perception of Mike Kenton, was the reason the public were interested, and as long as the newspapers fanned the flames, it was good for business all round. But I could see my smiling face wrapped around tomorrow's fish and chips. This is Britain, after all. Today's hero, tomorrow's Eddie the Eagle. I wondered when they'd dig up that old skeleton – you know, nine years old, the Sherbet Dip-Dab? More likely, they'd rake up some marital muck and trump that with stories about abandoning my kids to pursue my musical career. They'd already seeped some of that kind of poison into the atmosphere without detrimental effect, but after Eurovision, whatever the outcome, I'd be fair game. Nothing could do more to guarantee the instant decimation of my popular appeal, unless they faked some photos of me in a public toilet wearing a pini. So I was probably going to be the ultimate one hit wonder, sooner than anticipated if I completely bombed in Paris, which was more than likely if those bloody Balkans and Baltics ganged up on me.

Mary was still fizzing around, determined not to miss a single opportunity to PR me to the hilt. In the pipeline: more photo sessions, more interviews, an appearance on Weakest Link Does Eurovision (oh God) and so much other stuff, my head was spinning off my neck. I tried to rein her in, to convince her that I needed to concentrate on Eurovision so that I didn't let the country down (I did actually say that – sorry) but she was way past Eurovision. It was almost an irrelevance now.

It had become impossible to enter or exit my flat without being door-stepped or snooped on. One ingenious photographer hired a van with a platform hoist, the sort of thing the local council use to replace lamppost bulbs, so he could shoot through my first floor window. You've got to take your hat off to these guys, and if I did, the photo of my flattened funky haircut would be in tomorrow's paper. So I finally replaced my too-short gossamer sheets with daylight-blocking Argos blinds, courtesy of a rare spare morning spent mostly spearing my hands with a screwdriver and swearing savagely at my own incompetence. I gave the photographer a smile as I triumphantly tugged the cord with my bloodied fingers and lowered my new cloaking device. He snapped that too and, yes, it appeared in the next day's tabloids. Why do editors buy that kind of crap? What possible contribution can a shot of a smirking nobody through a filthy window make to humanity? Why don't they stick to tits?

More damagingly, it had become almost impossible for me to pop over and see the kids without a hullabaloo. The press had been camped outside the house for days in the hope that I'd turn up. The scrutiny was driving Lisa mad. They'd sussed the escape route out of the garden and had even snapped her through the window of the gallery. The girls were quite amused by all the attention and not the least bit fazed and, in fairness to the press creeps, they never stooped to publishing photos of them other than a couple from behind. What, exactly, did they think I was going to do that might render a picture newsworthy? Go through my front door? Fascinating. Emerge from the same door with my kids? Fuck me, the world simply had to know. Mary had forbidden me from speaking to or inciting them, so I fed them wan smiles and Paul McCartney-style thumbs-ups in the hope they'd be too anodyne to print. They weren't.

But I was growing tired of being spied on, of being penned in, of devising new ways of giving them the slip. It was time to call in my fixer. Chaz, managing operations from somewhere in South America, sent a car one evening and I chose my moment to slip out of the flat with a bag of clothes and toiletries. The driver, a huge man with jug ears and a neck wider than his head, was a self-confessed fan of the Die Hard franchise and told me he'd have no trouble losing anyone stupid enough to follow us. The fucking maniac proceeded to screech around like a demented dodgem, probably for the hell of it as I'm pretty sure no-one was actually behind us. We arrived at Chaz's Richmond mansion in what seemed simultaneously like seconds and a lifetime, to be met by Denise looking unusually rosy-cheeked. She smiled, gave me a cool hug and directed me to a large bedroom with an en suite bathroom the size of my flat, the one next door and the two upstairs. I unpacked and washed my face, then went downstairs to the cavernous, marbled kitchen where a mug of tea of indeterminate provenance was waiting on the counter. It was a bit spicy, a bit cold and wholly repulsive, but Denise was trying her best to be the perfect hostess and it would have been churlish to ask for something drinkable. It occurred to me then that, in all the years I'd known her, Denise and I had never actually been on our own together for any length of time. It was predictably prickly and awkward, made all the more so by our silent, almost choreographed sipping to give our lips something to do. Finally, Denise put her mug down and tried to bale us out.

'Your life is a bit crazy at the moment, isn't it?' she ventured.

'That's not the word,' I said, not knowing what the word was.

'You were great on that show, by the way. Didn't know you had it in you.'

'Me neither.'

'I've always just thought of you as Chaz's…'

…waste of space, puerile, crap-talking crony who's been engaged in an unarticulated battle with me for his affections for the last fifteen years…

'…best mate. And my mate too, of course. You *and* Lisa.' She almost choked on that faux pas. 'Sorry, I mean…' I waved her apology away. 'What I mean is, it's weird because, well you know, you've always just been that steady bloke who works in an office, type of thing, not some…national treasure.'

'Ha! I like that. Not sure I qualify as a national treasure with my shelf life. Here today…'

'You're just getting started. Come on. Be positive.'

She had a point. That's the Aussie spirit for you.

'So what's next?' she said.

'Dunno. I just zone out and do as I'm told. Be there, do that, don't eat that, stop picking your nose, say this, don't say that. They're driving me mad.'

Denise nodded. 'Mmm.'

'It's…tough. You know?'

We were already running out of steam. More mutual sipping was called for, even though I'd long since finished my nauseating brew and was reduced to chewing the tart leaves at the bottom.

'Anyway…' I said.

'Anyway…' she said.

Silence.

'So…I'd better go upstairs and get some rest. Doing a radio show later, and a TV thing so…'

'Sure. Sure. I'm going out now anyway, but call Nadia if you need anything.'

'Nadia?'

'Yeah – oh, didn't Chaz tell you?'

'Tell me what?'

'We've brought in an au pair.'

In more insensitive mode, I'd have said something crass about au pairs usually being employed by families with kids to look after, but even us faux pas specialists have an edit button. We just have to remember to hit it in time and, for once, I did. It had been a close call.

'It's all right, Michael, I know what you're thinking. Look, it's a big house and I needed some help around the place, that's all. Just didn't want to call her a maid. Bit pompous, especially coming from a convict, eh mate?' Denise broadened her accent, comedy spilling unbidden from this dourest of visages.

'Right, got you.' I took a final slug of leaves. 'Maybe you could call her an auxiliary home help or live-in personal assistant-cum-cleaner-cum-cook, or something.'

'Yeah, good suggestion. Let me sleep on it.'

I didn't see a lot of Denise after that. She stayed out of the way when Chaz was around, leaving us to indulge in the kind of adolescent farting about we'd never grown out of. Only now, we could do it in boundless comfort, watching crap on Chaz's 60 inch plasma splayed on a sofa softer than a cloud, scoffing junk food and drinking beer. Cocooned in this splendour and invisible to the hacks, I finally relaxed. And I loved seeing Chaz let go. Success had bought him an opulent, regimented lifestyle, along with status and respect, but he ached to go on occasional day release and let that mischievous little boy out to play. He just needed someone to catalyse and condone the idiocy, and I saw that as my responsibility. We steadfastly avoided discussing trivia like marriage break-ups, infidelity and infertility; there was too much important ground to cover. Football, women, McDonalds v Burger King, Dominoes v Pizza Hut (involving extensive hands-on testing), Eurovision. It was endless. I was still flying off to fulfil my various media commitments and, when I could, taking the opportunity to slip home and see the kids, usually in the little window between their coming home from school and Lisa's return from the office. The press generally knew where to find me but Chaz's driver, all tyre squeals, late-braking and handbrake turns, ensured they never tracked me back to his sanctuary.

Bea was still calling me Mr Kenton, but there was a coy little twinkle in her eye now. Once that tiresome little man trying to eke a smile out of her, I was now the guy with his face plastered all over the papers. I think she was a bit star-struck. I invited her to Paris – in fact, I was inviting everyone I knew, without knowing for sure if I could get them in – but she had an exam to study for so, thank you very much, Mr Kenton, but not on this occasion. Maybe she'd be fully qualified at whatever mysterious subject her eternal studies equipped her for and thus free to go wherever she pleased by the time I returned to Eurovision, Cliff Richard-fashion, in fifteen years' time.

The kids were well used to the idea that the bloke who told them off for being naughty, kissed and consoled them when they hurt themselves, played chaotic board games with them on the bed, drove them to parties – that bloke, Dad – now had a famous face. And they remained fabulously unimpressed. There could never be anyone less cool than me whatever anyone else said, but they rather liked the idea that this piece of public property who was fêted for a talent mysteriously unacknowledged for the last twenty years, was *their* dad and no-one else's. Not pride, exactly, more ownership allied to minor bragging rights.

The photo in the Daily Mirror of Lisa and Don Ellwood smiling toothily at each other at some glitzy function probably wouldn't have bothered the girls, but the suggestion that Mike Kenton's wife was now stepping out with the famous actor certainly did. The headline alone probably gave them – and everyone else – the gist: *Mrs Eurovision's Secret Romps With (The Next?) James Bond.* I'd known all along that the press would be keeping a close eye on Lisa and she'd been at pains to avoid all physical contact with Ellwood in public, but the tabloid press weren't stupid (ok, they were, but not when it came to sniffing out a lurid story), and they winkled it out. The photogenic Lisa might find herself under greater scrutiny than me if she wasn't careful. I told Kattie and Millie that Ellwood was Mum's good friend from the gallery, something Lisa had also explained to them, and that the newspapers had made something out of very little. But the press weren't going to let this bone go and, at some point soon, we would have to ease the girls into gentle acceptance. The divorce was shitty enough, a tough one for them to swallow, but me being Eurovision's Mike Kenton and Lisa being Don Ellwood's latest arm candy exacerbated an already complex situation. We all lap up the kind of prurient detail best kept behind closed doors – it's human nature – and no-one was going to worry too much about how this might affect a family.

I didn't win Weakest Link Does Eurovision, by the way. That honour went to one of the guys out of Brotherhood of Man. You'd never have thought that someone who sang '*Save All Your Kisses For Me,*' in a C & A jumper would have a brain but, as my mother would say, don't judge a book by its cover or, in this case, a balding man by his comb over and wardrobe. I got down to the last three, which I thought was a decent effort for someone with a lazy 2:2 from Brunel.

Chaz was a busy man, a man in huge demand, meaning he wasn't around as much as I would have liked. The Barcelona project alone consumed days of his life and, for a spell, he only seemed to come home to collect fresh clothing. I was starting to feel uncomfortable accepting his hospitality when he was so rarely there. I was busy too – one day I might be singing live on Chiltern Radio, another opening the Altrincham branch of Lidl – but when I was there, stuck in my room or cleaning out the fridge or marooned in front of the mega-plasma while Denise sat in another room, I felt like I was overstaying my welcome.

It was time to go back to my sty.

My answerphone was pregnant with messages, most of them of no interest. If you haven't given them your mobile number, chances are they're people who don't matter. But Faye had left message number fourteen, and she did. She'd rung the same evening I'd returned to the flat and, when I checked my mobile, she'd left a message on there as well. I'd had it switched off for a while to avoid being bludgeoned by Mary into making a personal appearance at a bowling alley in Watford or a photo-opp at the Hull Leisure Centre, something I now regretted as Faye wasn't answering now. A couple of hours and four desperate calls later, I tracked her down.

Jaques seemed as sensible a place to meet as any. On the 'stage' where it had all started stood a lugubrious Welshman called Joey who sang songs mostly in Cymru. I don't know why. His repertoire of dirges would have been enough to drive even the most sanguine of souls to a dark place where even suicide wouldn't help. Luckily, no-one was listening. Faye, for once, looked less than radiant. She wore no make-up, her skin looked sallow and her hair unkempt. But this was Faye and Faye was always beautiful.

'Thanks for coming,' she said.

'Hey, come on,' I shrugged with jokey magnanimity. She barely smiled. We'd only spoken briefly on the phone the previous night and she'd sounded unusually flat.

Faye fixed her pretty eyes on mine. 'I want your advice.'

'Sure. I'm particularly good on motherboards, CAT 5 cabling and where to find the Yoplait in Tesco.'

'Shut up, you idiot,' she said without malice, 'I'm serious.'

I knew that, but I was the worst shoulder to cry on. Emotional immaturity and lack of depth were my stock in trade. I mentioned I'm man, I think, and you'll find that most of us suffer from these personality lacunae. We're much better at being stupid and making jokes. Oh, and if this involved never seeing me again, I definitely didn't want to bloody hear it.

Faye gathered herself. 'It's Louis.'

'Is he all right?' Maybe he was dead. Things might be looking up.

'Louis? Oh, he's fine.' Did she just roll her eyes? 'He's always fine.'

'So?'

'Straight to the point, ok?' Faye cleared her throat, steadied herself. 'Shit, this isn't as easy as I thought.'

'Take your time.'

'I...ok, I don't know if I want to marry him. There.'

'What?'

'I can't see myself spending the rest of my life with him.'

'Look, sorry, but why are you talking to *me* about this?'

'Why do you think?'

I didn't think anything. I didn't dare. Faye fixed her eyes on mine and flickered a melancholy smile so brief it was hardly there. Had I been so insecure, so lacking in self-confidence and self-esteem that I'd missed the signals?

'I really don't know,' I said, my heart racing twice as fast as it usually did when I was in in Faye's company, which was already dangerously fast.

She reached over the table and took each of my hands in hers. 'You are a stupid, stupid bastard,' she said, her voice trembly, like she was in a car going too fast over bumps. It threatened to be the most romantic thing anyone had ever said to me.

'You mean...? Sorry, no, what *do* you mean?'

'Oh don't make me spell it out, Mike.'

'What, you? and...me?'

Faye nodded. It was the moment I'd been waiting for, for...well, forever, give or take. Now what was I supposed to do? You're never ready, are you?

'But...ok, help me out here. You spent three years giving me the run-around, treating me like a kid with a hopeless crush...then...oh yeah, then twenty years went by, nearly forgot, and suddenly you're getting married to Mr Solid.' Faye shrugged. I had her bang to rights. 'Not forgetting *oh, Mikey, will you sing at the wedding*. You see where I'm coming from?'

'Yeah. Sorry about the singing thing.'

'I mean, granted I'm not that bright, but at what point was I supposed to gather that you…I don't know…you…?'

'Wanted us to get together?'

'What does that mean, anyway?'

'You know what it means.' Faye swallowed hard. 'I've got…you know, feelings for you.'

'And what does *that* bloody mean?' I was in a bit of a state by now, I think it's fair to say. Confused, excited, agitated and really fucking angry without knowing quite why. Time to lash out. 'Suddenly I'm famous and you come running out of the woodwork. Is that it?'

'Oh fuck off, Mike, you fucking arsehole!' Faye's chair scraped the floor as she sprang to her feet. Everyone in *Jaques* turned to check out the commotion, all one of them. 'Fuck you.'

'Come on, sit down…'

'Know what? It's the naffest show on the planet, and the people who *sing* on it are…I mean, I should be embarrassed I feel this way about you. God, Mike. You'll be all washed up in six months. Get real.'

That hurt. 'Six months?'

'If you're lucky.'

I checked for any sign that she might be joking. She wasn't. 'Ok, but you can see why I…you know…'

Faye shook her head. No, she couldn't see why I…you know. Rather, she was still debating whether to storm out. She stood there panting for a moment until her angry, heaving chest settled.

'I'm sorry,' I mumbled.

'Idiot,' she said, sitting again, grudgingly.

'Ok, but let me see if I'm getting this. Whether or not you marry Louis is dependent on me?'

'No, I didn't say that…'

'Because that's not fair, is it? It should have nothing to do with me. I mean, will you still marry him if I tell you to take a running jump?'

'Don't know. Maybe.' Her eyes were misting over now.

'That doesn't sound like you at all, at least not the Faye I thought I knew. You wouldn't do something stupid like marry someone you don't love just because someone you…have feelings for…rejects you.'

'So you're rejecting me?'

Oh fuck! I was being principled all of a sudden when I should have been genuflecting, thanking her for finally yielding and sweeping her off to my Hanger Lane love nest without further ado.

'Faye, listen, ok? This is difficult.' I looked heavenwards seeking inspiration, but found only the knotted, pine-clad ceiling. 'I loved you from the moment I set eyes on you. And I think…I think you knew that and maybe you enjoyed it a bit too much. And you gave me nothing back.'

'I was your friend.'

'Well, yeah, and of course I valued your friendship, but you knew I…that time you kissed me? Why? I think it was because you could, and I sort of hated you for that. It was taking advantage, pumping yourself up at my expense.'

'I was absolutely pissed that night.' Faye squeezed my hands again. I was thrilled she'd even remembered it. 'I was behaving like a moron. That wasn't me.'

'It was like being patted on the head and given a biscuit.'

'If I hurt you…'

'Oh, you hurt me, and it took me ages to get you out of my system. Ages. Even after I married Lisa, I always wondered what you were doing.' I'd spent years rehearsing versions of this conversation, knowing it would never happen. Now I was fumbling around off script. 'And…and…

'And what?'

'Truth is, I never did get you out of my system.'

Faye broke into a gentle sob. 'I'm such an idiot.' She leaned closer and spoke in a quavering half-whisper. 'I knew there was something going on between us, of course I did, but Little Miss Practical here thought you were a bit too much of a dreamer, with your music and your plans to go off after graduating and perform all over the world. Remember? There wasn't any future in it.'

Now she mentioned it, I was that mouthy fool, an otherwise sensible boy desperate to impress. And I did get as far as Sheffield once, albeit to re-wire a network. On reflection, maybe bragging about my fantasies to Faye was a defence mechanism.

'So I stuck with that drip Ray,' she continued, 'because I knew he'd never let me down. See? Even then I needed certainty and stability in my life. You…you were my friend, my best friend, and I thought if we crossed the line…look, I was going to lose you anyway, so why even allow myself to get hurt?'

'I wouldn't have let you down.'

'Course you would. You were a baby. Even if you didn't go anywhere or do anything, you'd have wanted to see what else – who else – was out there. Maybe I would, too. Eventually.'

'I only wanted you.'

Faye smiled and shook her head. She was probably right. It was easy to worship her memory, much harder to seriously believe that a college fling would have turned into anything more. What do you know at twenty-one? There's too much ahead of you, too many things to do, too many possibilities. None of which invalidated the authenticity of the feelings I had for her then, still had. Nor those, it turns out, she still had for me. First love. It's a persistent little bastard.

'I used to think, if only we'd met when we were thirty, we'd have been ready.' All those years thinking about her, she'd been thinking about me too. Insane! 'I looked for you, you know. Found you as well.'

I arched an astonished eyebrow. 'When?'

'Dunno. A few years after we left Brunel. You were with Lisa by then so I didn't…and then I married that evil bastard.'

'Fucked that one up, didn't you?'

'With knobs on. But I wouldn't allow myself to believe I'd made a mistake, of course. Too perfect to be pitied or proved wrong. Me to a T.'

'Jesus, Faye,' I said, dabbing a snaking tear from her cheek, a tear for which I took full responsibility. Which felt good, by the way. 'Perfect Faye, eh? Blimey, what happened?'

'Then, when you contacted me, I thought maybe…maybe things could be put back in the right order. But, well obviously you were still married, you had your kids, great career…'

Ahem.

'It didn't look promising,' she continued, 'but I was hoping…' she looked guiltily at the table, '…you were separated, or Lisa was dying or something.'

'Hah!'

'Ok, maybe not dying but having an affair? Oh, I don't know.'

'You were a couple of weeks early.'

'Anyway, I thought you seemed happy enough, and I had Louis and he was safe as houses, so I decided to soldier on. The things-could-be-worse principle. I couldn't let myself want you, so I just sort of… closed for business.'

'But I told you I was getting divorced.'

'Yeah, later, but I'd made up my mind by then, settled for what I had.'

The pretty Spanish waitress came over and asked in an esoteric version of English if we wanted anything else. We pissed her off by ordering a couple of coffees, cutting into her siesta.

'So?' I said, my mind like the ancient Apple Mac in Hair Repair on Crouch End Hill, unable to fully compute. 'What now?'

'You tell me.'

'God, Faye! It's not up to me.' I was angry again, angry and baffled, and suddenly on the verge of something unthinkable.

'I know, I'm sorry. Forget I said that.' She started fumbling in her handbag for a tissue to mop the teary rivulets sliding down towards her quivering mouth. 'It's not a choice between you and Louis. It really isn't. It's just about you.'

My throat was clogged and I had to swallow hard to hold back the deep sob welling inside me. 'You know what you're going to get with him, don't you?'

'Down to the very last second.' She stared off into the distance, her eyes drained of energy.

'Well…that's something. It's not nothing. That's good, isn't it?'

Faye nodded disconsolately at the prospect. She'd already written the book in her head and knew the ending.

'I mean,' I went on, trying to sound solicitous but coming apart at every seam, 'you and I might not work out and you'll have dumped him and ruined everything for yourself and it'll be my fault. I can't let you screw your life up. And anyway, I'm going through the divorce, I've got the girls to think about, the bloody song contest. I don't know what my life's going to be like from now on. It's all up in the air. I'm still everything you've never wanted.'

'Ok,' said Faye studying her hands as they shredded a damp tissue. 'If that's how you feel. I understand, I really do.'

Wish I did. 'I think it'd be better…it'd be better if…' I stood up and tottered, the blood pin-balling around my head, the remaining fragments of my heart beseeching me to sit down again. But I couldn't. It had to be this way. I needed to get out of there before I passed out. I fumbled in a pocket and pulled out £40 which I slapped on the table. 'Do you mind if I…just go?'

Faye shook her head. 'S'ok.'

'I love you,' I said, stooping to kiss her damp cheek. 'I always will.'

It would be my next song: *Song for Faye, Part Two, The Fuck-Up*. The song I would sing through tears forever.

Chivalrous? You think I was being chivalrous? Oh do stop it. I was just terrified. Faye was my paradigm, the ideal woman, the soul mate Lisa had never quite been. Love isn't about sharing common interests or making each other laugh or anything so measurable. They help, of course, but they aren't the nub. With luck, you'll recognise love's irresistible alchemy when it comes along and let it have its way. And I wanted to, more than anything. But, here's the thing, as Ben would say. What was going to happen when she realised I couldn't make her happy? I wasn't that funny, interesting, musically ambitious young boy she once fell for (without letting on, the cow). I'd turned into a plodder, a man who'd accepted mediocrity and made it his creed. Eurovision was an illusion; it didn't change who I'd become. What if that boy was lost in the mists of time and gone forever? She'd be off, if she had any sense – and she did, in bucket loads – and who could blame her? And me? I'd be a shell, devastated, with nothing but my kids to live for and they, over time, were only going to need me less. I'd come to terms with not having Faye a long time ago. I'd finally parked her memory somewhere safe, where it couldn't do me too much damage; I'd coned her off. If I let her back in now, I'd have no defence against the inevitable emotional decimation. So I was playing it safe, meeting the pain head on, taking it on the chin up front rather than risking the inestimably greater agony of losing her.

Just because love is undeniable, doesn't mean you have to embrace it. Not if it's going to kill you.

CHAPTER 22

A week to go before Paris and my life had transcended hectic and slipped towards chaos. The weeks since Eurovision: You Decide had flown by, and so much had happened without the luxury of distance to allow me to digest things objectively. Engulfed and overwhelmed, I was splashing around, swallowing water, trying to hang on.

May! Spring! Whoo-hoo! So went the theory. But the weather was still miserable, with a pervasive gloom that glowered at me both inside and out. The flat was typically cold despite the boiling cauldron of traffic outside and, curled up under a duvet in front of breakfast TV, I could barely face the day's myriad radio, TV and personal appearances stretching out before me like an endless, rain-spattered road. I shuddered. What had I got myself into? I'd always wanted to be a famous pop star, but not for the fame; for the pop. I wanted the world to appreciate my art (yes, art, ok?) to be someone whose name was synonymous with high calibre output, like Elton John or Paul McCartney. Even as a young musician, I harboured such high-flown ideals even though I'd probably have settled for a fleeting, Gary Numan-esque moment in the sun. I'd always believed that if the music isn't up to it, it isn't worth putting out there. Quality is everything. And today, at three fifteen, I was due to open a leisure centre in Penge. Penge! What did that have to do with anything? You see, naïvely, I hadn't properly bargained for this, nor the continued intrusion into my private life. What on Earth made me think that it should come without a price? And talking of stark realities, I was still only a novelty entrant in a superficial and musically vacuous contest which traditionally left a bloodied trail of failure and terminal obscurity. My credibility was already compromised. There I was hoping I might forge a serious musical career, knowing all along that any future, beyond Eurovision, was an inchoate concept at best. For all of Ben's bluster, was he really interested in developing me as a singer/

songwriter? He was all about seizing opportunities, jumping on bandwagons, short-termism. And if Ben couldn't use me, who else would?

And of course there was Faye. I hadn't stopped thinking about her for a single agonising millisecond since our final sad parting. It was gnawing me to death from the inside out. I'd wrapped myself in emotional bubble wrap to insulate myself from the pain of her probable rejection somewhere down the line, but surely this pain, this open sore, was infinitely worse. What had I done? Was there a part of me, I wondered, that rejected her because I thought the door might still be open with Lisa, the door back to being plain old Dad again? Or was I just too shit-scared to grasp the opportunity to take a fantasy and try and make it real?

I was exhausted from another interminable PR Saturday and my diary was almost solid until Wednesday when we were due to travel to Paris, so I asked Mary to clear Sunday afternoon and evening so I could spend some time with the kids before the mayhem really kicked off. After a couple of horrible local radio slots, I picked them up at twelve thirty and took them for lunch at a bustling Italian restaurant in Camden. Both had Spaghetti Carbonara, Millie fastidiously removing every last lump of bacon and depositing it on the side of her plate. From there, we walked to Regents Park to go rowing (tantrums, a lost oar, deliberate splashings, several 'shits') after which we chucked the Frisbee around for half an hour until they'd each caught it once. But I couldn't relax, couldn't help feeling irritable, manfully though I tried to hide it. Not manfully enough, as it turns out. That old saw about kids? It's true. They pick up on stuff, although mine didn't have to dig too deep on this occasion. There's something wonderfully grounding about being told to *chill out* by two under-tens. In unison. I laughed and chilled as instructed, but I still didn't feel like me, like Mike, like Dad. Everything was teetering, about to spin out of control, and the only certainty I had left was the unquestioning, uncomplicated love of my kids.

We got back around eight-thirty and the girls draped me in warm, exhausted hugs before dragging themselves up the stairs with exaggerated, comic floppiness. Lisa was in the living room reading Living Etc, with Property Ladder or possibly Grand Designs on in the background to make sure she didn't miss anything. We smiled at each other briefly but I wasn't in the mood to talk and followed the girls upstairs instead. Millie brushed her teeth in under twelve seconds, a record, while Kattie changed into her pyjamas before cutting Millie's time on the Braun in half. Millie, now wearing her little pink nightdress, clambered into bed and I sat beside her. She smiled, sleepy-eyed, and wrapped her arms around my neck. I kissed her plump, velvet cheek and laid her down on the pillow. She was asleep before I switched the light off. It was the same routine with Kattie, who smelt of toothpaste and the fabulously expensive strawberries she'd half-eaten at the restaurant. As we cuddled, I felt her arms go loose and heavy around my neck and I knew she was already in dreamland, too exhausted for the usual rough and tumble. There's nothing, simply nothing, to touch the simple joy of hugging your own child, especially when she's rag-doll tired. It was something I'd taken for granted but now yearned for every night.

Downstairs, Lisa was in the kitchen filling two glasses with red wine. She tilted her head, her signal for me to follow her into the living room. The rustic table lamp we'd bought – at her insistence – at a flea market in Dorset a lifetime ago glowed in the corner. I settled beside her on the lumpy leather sofa we'd bought – at my insistence – at DFS last year. How the hell did I slip that one past her?

'How are they?' she said.

'Fine. Shattered.'

'Good day?'

'They're going to give me a bad report, I think. Maybe 'G' for effort, but definitely 'U' for achievement. I was a bit uptight.'

'Well you've got a lot on. They'll understand. They were thrilled to get to see you at all with all this madness going on.'

'Yeah, well…'

Lisa sipped her wine. She was edging towards something, I could always tell. 'So, when are you going to Paris?'

'Wednesday.'

'That's a bit early isn't it?' Weary nod. We had three days of nonsense to endure before the big night. 'Excited? You must be. Course you are.'

'I'm just bloody exhausted.'

'The adrenaline will get you through. Don't worry, you'll be brilliant.' She patted my thigh. This was her version of a bowler's run-up. 'Anyway, I was thinking…' here it came, '…why don't I come over with the kids?'

I stared into my glass. This was no time to catch her eye.

'I'm not…I mean,' Lisa had rehearsed this but even she, with all her polish, all her guile, was finding it difficult. 'I mean, it'd just be nice to have your family there, wouldn't it?'

'Are we a family?'

'We'll always be a family.'

'But,' I laughed incredulously, 'we're not, though, are we? We're family. There's a difference.'

Lisa placed her glass on the coffee table and edged closer to me. 'We could be. *A* family, I mean. If you wanted us to be.'

Why do all these decisions fall to me? I don't do decisions, not the important ones that require maturity, intelligence and judgement. 'God, Leese.'

'Yeah, I know. Bit of a bombshell.'

'I mean, we've gone through a lot of shit, haven't we? It's not easy to pretend it never happened.'

'I know. I'm sorry.' 'She never aplogised.'

'I don't just mean you and…whassisname. It's everything, isn't it? The last ten years.'

'We've got a lot of talking to do, and a lot of forgiving.'

Lisa's eyes reddened. The last time I'd seen her cry was when I put a thumb through a painting she'd just bought. I couldn't remember the last time she'd cried over me. She slotted her cool hand into mine. 'Look Leese,' I said, 'I need to…let me just get this week out of the way, ok?'

'Sure. Of course. Absolutely,' she whispered.

'So…I'm gonna go, ok?'

I stood up and Lisa, still holding my hand, raised herself to her feet. I started for the hallway, but she tugged me towards her and nuzzled her head into my shoulder, her full weight now pushing into me as her hands locked behind my back. I didn't feel like wrapping my arms around her, but didn't want to reject her either. She looked up at me, her eyes now spilling bulbous tears.

'Stay.'

'What?'

'Stay. Just tonight. I want to be with you.'

'Leese…I…'

She pushed herself up onto her toes, opened her mouth and clamped her succulent lips onto mine. She thrust her tongue into my mouth flushing a familiar, zingy warmth through my veins, simultaneously draining the fight from me. I stroked her back, then slid my hands down to her pert bottom and pulled her into my groin where my penis jutted out like a tempered steel bar, only harder. Penises, eh? No subtlety. I cradled her head in both hands and dragged her into me, into my mouth, into my heart. The bedroom was but a few urgent steps away.

But then, somehow, I pulled back from the brink and pushed her gently away, a feat of superhuman fortitude. 'I don't think I'm ready for this,' I rasped.

'Oh yes you are,' she said, cradling the ludicrous tent in my trousers.

'He's ready, but I'm not,' I said.

Lisa pouted and let me go. 'Ok. No. I understand. I'm sorry. We'll talk next week? After the…'

'We'll definitely talk.'

CHAPTER 23

PARIS IN THE springtime. People love it, apparently. Not me though. It was pissing hard, it was cold and I was utterly drained. I don't think the Eurovision rule book is prescriptive as to mind-set, but I'm pretty sure mine fell some way short of ideal for the purpose of appearing live in front of two hundred million people in three days' time. Eurovision is all about beaming, carefree smiles and glittery outfits, not gloomy old geezers with intractable personal issues.

If I hadn't been inundated with wall-to-wall media commitments in the days following Lisa's astonishing proposal, I'd probably have hidden out in my Mum's shed, spiders and all, until it was all over. It took an enormous effort – and a little tough love from Elaine and Ben – to maintain a patina of geniality, but at every personal appearance in every nondescript town, at every fatuous, repetitive press call, I was a but hair's breadth from running out in front of the first available bendy bus. I couldn't escape that insidious, nagging voice: *what are you going to do when this is all over, eh? You're a no-one who got lucky, and we all know what happens to them – Steve Brookstein anyone? He can't get a job serving in a pub where they have live music.* I know, I know! *And what about Faye?* it whispered malevolently, *screwed that one up, haven't you? Tit.* Shut up! *You still want that divorce? Really? She wants you back. Say no and your kids will become strangers, forget who you are – and you can kiss goodbye to every penny you ever had.* It had more: *how the hell are you going to serenade Europe with all this shit swilling round your head? Eh? Eh?* I couldn't afford to let the voice gain a stranglehold. I tried throwing myself into my commitments, keeping myself occupied, praying that fatigue would take me during the lonely hours, sparing me the tossing-turning torment.

We travelled to Paris by Eurostar on the Wednesday morning, following a shamelessly staged, flag-waving send-off at St Pancras. We were doing it for Britain. I forced a plastic smile for the rented crowd and snappers, but ached to climb aboard and stow away in a luggage compartment. Anonymity, though, wasn't part of the package. This was a public parade all the way to Paris. Well-wishers, autograph hunters and even the stewards – ostensibly selling overpriced, undrinkable beverages – were all involved in this photo opp. What curiosity they'd satisfy when they got to the pub. *What did he really look like close up? Was he nice? Is that a bald patch on his head? Isn't he just a middle-aged, nothing-special, waste-of-space fartarse?*

Elaine, Ben, Mary and the cocooned, be-earphoned Gilbert were my immediate travelling companions, but our entourage also included a bunch of mostly camp, colourful oddballs whose precise individual roles were unclear to me. Mercifully, they were booked into the next carriage, but each took turns bending my ear with fabulous ideas and complex instructions, all of which I resolutely failed to absorb. Clothes, shoes, hairstyles, things to say in French to the French, things not to say, places to eat, places to be seen. Did any of this matter?

I'd hoped to have some time to myself in my room at the rather stately Hotel de Vigny in Rue Balzac, right next to the Arc de Triomphe, but as soon as I'd unpacked I was set upon by the entourage, like ants around a buttery breadcrumb, and whisked off to Le Zenith, the 6000-seat concert hall where the final was due to kick off in three days' time. After a short and terrifying journey through the frantic Parisian maelstrom, we were escorted into a gaping auditorium which was, I felt, a shade more salubrious than the venue for my last 'arena' gig – the students' union at Brunel University twenty-one years ago, a sticky-floored, under-lit cave which accommodated 300; I attracted 28, all friends. Gilbert scuttled off to talk to (mumble at?) the musical director, a moustachioed man with uncompromisingly dyed-black hair called Jean-Claude (naturellement), a scary-looking rake who was at least seven feet tall. Meanwhile, Elaine, Ben and I, plus a handful of nameless entourage, were given a brief tour of the venue by a tiny, charming woman called Emilie, whom Jean-Claude could comfortably have packed away in his suit bag. Scores of French Sarah-clones, TV execs and technical staff darted to and fro taking instructions through headphones or barking frantically into walkie talkies, while a team of essentially pot-bellied blokes shifted cables and equipment hither and yon. We were led into a cavernous backstage area decked out with white leather sofas, tables and easy chairs, a glorified, televisual green room where we, the performers, would sit with our coteries as the scores came in and where, inevitably, I and every other western European hopeful would be beaming defiant smiles as the Balkan/ Baltic axis crushed all hope. With hundreds of performers and musicians taking part, there simply wasn't the room backstage to accommodate us all in our own dressing rooms. Instead, everyone was allocated a toilet-sized cubicle squirrelled away amongst a warren of Portacabins in the car park to the rear, an area which also housed a village of marquees and Winnebagoes. How the hell was I going to find the stage unassisted?

I waited for most of the day to do my walk-through, a complex feat which demanded that I stroll onto the stage, find my mark and stand around for ten minutes while the cameramen took instructions. I was asked to demonstrate how and where I planned to move during my performance (I'd made no plans) before being shunted off and replaced by three Lithuanian people (men, I think) in grotesque masks and silver Lurex tights who, I hope to God, were labouring under the mis-apprehension that this was a dress rehearsal. Either way, I gave them a wide berth. After stapling a disingenuous smile to my face for some photos – I was inured to all forms of frippery by now – I managed to slip away and snatch a brief nap in my cubicle in a standing up position. At 7.30, I did a live link-up from the venue with Radio 5 and dealt wittily (well I thought so) with some thoroughly otiose questions submitted by listeners who all needed to get a life. But this was essentially a day of waiting, watching, yawning and occasionally marvelling at the breath-taking scale of the operation; I felt like a rather tiny and, in the great scheme of things, insignificant part of this giant, useless mechanism.

Around eight, a courtesy car dropped us back at the hotel where I showered and changed before accompanying Elaine, Ben and Mary to a dubious Thai restaurant (well, you know, when in Paris) chosen by the enthusiastic Ben who, having sampled several bottles of wine, mercifully lost consciousness thus curtailing a hitherto unabridged anecdotal review of his eighties escapades with various nonentity bands. Sadly, he'd already covered the sixties and seventies in forensic detail by then. Mary who, off duty, was surprisingly light and frothy company, hauled Ben to his feet around midnight and dragged him outside and into a cab. Elaine and I were still self-mutilating with some hellish espressos and decided to follow on later. A couple of months earlier, I mused, I'd been singing to a handful of people in a Crouch End dive. Elaine had been there then and she was still here now, by my side, our insane journey having reached a point neither of us could have imagined. She was my rock, someone I could lean on, complain to and joke with as the madness raged all about me.

I leaned back, eyes clenched, as another agonising slug of lava burned its way into my stomach where it co-mingled and conspired with myriad just-digested mystery meats and spices to return a sizzling spurt of acid up my gullet.

'You ok?' said Elaine, touching my elbow.

'Fuck!' I rasped. 'Got any Rennies? Shit! Fuck! No!'

Elaine laughed. It was only Ben's swearing she couldn't abide. 'I meant, are you ok?'

'As in, generally?'

'Yes'

'Fine…course…absolutely fine.'

But Elaine knew what I was going through and raised those intuitive eyebrows of hers.

'That obvious, is it?' I said.

'Open book, Mike.'

'Well, you know, it's all so…bloody stressful.'

'Divorce? Still going through?'

'Yeah. Well. No. I dunno.'

'Right.'

And then I told Elaine about my last conversation with Lisa, omitting only the trouser-tenting kiss. 'So, now you're the most famous man in England,' she said, 'she wants to get back with you. Or am I missing something?'

'I thought she'd be completely appalled by me doing Eurovision – I mean, it is shit and trivial and she's, you know, substantial and cultured

– but all this adulation and fame, it seems to have turned her on. I'm not that useless lump who used to take up too much space in the house any more.'

'You can't go back to her, Mike. That's not a basis for a relationship.'

'But she said…'

'It doesn't mean anything. None of this is real, but you're still Michael Kenton. You'll always be that useless lump.'

'Well, thanks.'

'In her eyes, Mike. Doesn't matter what happens to you or your career. When you go home, that's who you'll be, once she gets over herself.'

'Maybe I can change. I've got to. It's my last chance.'

Elaine shook her head, glugged the cold gritty dregs at the bottom of her cup and grimaced.

'I've never stopped loving her,' I said, 'not really. I don't know if I like her all that much any more, but I can't help how I feel.' Where the hell did that lot come from?

'Oh bullshit! I don't buy that,' snapped Elaine. 'Jesus, Mike.'

'What do you know…?'

'It's not love, Mike. It's familiarity, it's the Devil you know, it's safe and convenient, but it's not enough. You go back to her and that's just you admitting you're scared of the future.'

I opened my mouth to protest, but Elaine was irresistible.

'And you're right to be scared. But you've got to decide; is this when you make that change? Or do you hang onto something broken in the vain hope you can fix it? Because, ultimately, you can't.'

'She'll have to change too…'

'Oh come on! It's not about her, and it's certainly not about love. It's about you being Dad again, isn't it? Doesn't take a genius to see that. And, yeah, I get that. But this isn't the answer. Maybe for a while it'll be ok, but in the long run? Look, you can still be Dad, but on your terms, not hers. That's the real change you've got to make.'

I blew the air from my lungs. 'Fuck.'

'That mean I'm right?'

'I don't know. I don't know anything.'

273

And then, unbidden but not unusual given my recent predisposition to tears, I started to weep, the alcohol having tipped me beyond the point where men are abashed. Elaine shuffled round the table and put her arm around my shoulders.

'You can't go back to her,' she whispered. 'You must know that.'

'If it's the only way I can be with my girls…how much have I got to miss them before I…jump off something high?' I whimpered between staccato, blubbering sobs.

'They'll always be the biggest part of your life. You've just got to work out the details.'

I fumbled in my pockets for a tissue before Elaine thrust a napkin into my hand. I sat up, wiped my face dry and waited for my juddering chest to settle. 'Do you think you can stop being right for five minutes?'

Elaine pulled me into her shoulder and laughed into my ear. 'Sorry, don't think so. It's what I do.'

I took a deep, deep breath. This needed a steady nerve. 'Ok, listen, there's something else.'

Elaine leaned back and considered me with such gravity, such intense concern, I suddenly felt like telling her it was only a genital wart and I was getting some cream for it.

'Oh God. You're gay?'

Her gravity had been a piss-take, an attempt to lighten the mood. I snorted a bubble into the snot dribbling from my nose and grabbed another napkin to blot it. 'That would be easy.'

Elaine was laughing too. 'Well go on then, surprise me.'

'Ok. Brace yourself.' I cleared my throat. 'I am in love. Proper love. Just…with somebody else.'

Elaine placed a hand on my shoulder and pushed me gently away. 'Listen to me, Michael, ok? You're not.'

'Oh, fuck! Not you. Sorry. I mean, don't get me wrong, in another universe, if things were…' No, different tack required. 'What I mean is, you're already my joint best friend and that's not to be sniffed at, bearing in mind how important I am in a pan-European context. But, no, I thought we…?'

Elaine spluttered and broke into a broad grin. 'Your face!'

'What?'

'Oh for God's sake, Mike. I'm pissing about. We're way past this, aren't we?'

'Yeah, course! Just mucking about. Ha!' Idiot. Now for the attempted save. 'Although I'd have given it a go. You know, just for the sex.'

'Ahh, how romantic.'

Elaine's smile was brief. There were more important things to discuss. 'So come on then. Let's talk about Faye.'

'That obvious?'

'That night in *Jaques*? She was the only person in the room.'

'Think everyone noticed?'

'Probably. And when I told you I knew her. I mean, you nearly lost it, Michael. Didn't take a genius. That thing you had for her never went away, did it?'

'Not really.'

'But she's still getting married.'

'Thanks for pointing that out.'

'To that streak of piss? Might be a good idea if you stopped worrying about your unfaithful wife and started thinking about Faye.'

'Ach, it's all too complicated.'

'No it's not. It's simple. Tell me, does Faye know how you feel?'

'She's always known,' I said with the resigned, isn't-it-just-bloody-typical shrug I'd perfected. 'Turns out she feels the same way.'

'I know.'

'Stop it, already!'

'It's all in the eyes, Mike. You were the only person in the room for her.'

'All the good that did me.'

'Have you tried to stop her? Getting married, I mean.'

'She gave me a chance...but...I made a complete Horlicks of it.'

'You complete and utter moron. How?' said Elaine, incredulous. I think my stupidity was beginning to wear her out.

'She wanted *me* to tell *her* not to marry him. But I couldn't do that, could I? Wasn't my call.'

Elaine shook her head. It was time for her to make things simple for me. 'You. Absolute. Fucking. Clown. *Course* it was your call. She was desperate for you to say it.'

'I was being…chivalrous?'

'You were being a dickhead.'

Right again. 'Maybe.'

'Well that's you all over,' said Elaine. 'See, at some point, you've got to take a chance. You can't have everything mapped out.'

I smiled oafishly. 'So what the hell do I do now?'

Another numbing, draining day at the coalface. If Wednesday was Eurovision lite, a gentle introduction to its peculiar charms, Thursday was full fat. It was all about getting the song and, more particularly, the choreography right, and my entourage was growing increasingly vexed at my inability to put one foot in front of the other with anything even approaching co-ordination. My choreographer, an impatient, mid-forties wraith called Jo, just wouldn't let up as we battled nature – alongside a hundred other contestants – in a small rehearsal room above the auditorium. I did my best to evade her, but she was canny, tracking me down to my three inch by two inch box in the morning and, later, the car park where she found me cowering behind some dustbins like a fugitive. Jo specialised in shouting and clicking her fingers; I specialised in tripping over my own shadow. You see, *my* vision was that of a dignified, middle-aged but nonetheless youthful looking man, standing stock-still behind the mike stand and singing a song, my choreography stretching, at a push, to an occasional smile. Jo, however, wanted me to take the mike in hand and wander. *Her* vision included grisly mugs to camera, sly winks, hand-claps and a couple of showy shuffles, all of which I was wilfully incapable of carrying out. Desperate, I asked Elaine to get her off my back and, following a series of fractious negotiations, a compromise was agreed – Jo would take the next train home and I would stand there like a stone and sing on Saturday night. Star power.

With Jo out of the way, I had little else to do but eat, drink, test my French on the sweet Ukrainian contestant (she didn't understand a word, bloody nitwit) but mostly get seriously agitated, partly through boredom, mostly because I was thinking about what Elaine had said. Here I was, stuck in Paris with this idiotic contest to get through, when I needed to be at home sorting out my life one way or the other. The impotence was maddening.

I finally got the call to go on for my technical rehearsal at five, by which time my energy level was as low as my tension was high. I sang badly, distractedly, off tune, off the pace. Even Gilbert gave me a bit of a look. That bad. But I got through it, somehow. I still had to hang around afterwards in case any technical glitches needed un-glitching, but we were eventually released around seven. Ben took everyone (including the Jo-less entourage) to a thrashing, garish bar in Montmartre where we drank unspeakably vile cocktails and ate grease. I was in no mood for it – my voice was already creaking under the strain and could take no more – so I left early and took a cab back to the hotel before I lost it altogether. Back in my soundless room, ears ringing, I flicked on the TV to see if my hearing was still intact – it was, just – and took a shower. Feeling cleaner but no more refreshed, I ordered a tea to make me feel more at home. With milk. Oui, Monsieur, milk. No, not hot milk. Jesus wept. It arrived in a huge pot with a yellow label sticking out, indicating one small, overworked Lipton's teabag that would've struggled to infuse an egg cup. I left it to brew for twenty minutes to no great effect, drank the tepid piss anyway, then lay on the bed to check through my texts and voicemail messages. The kids had sent me a raft of sweet, misspelt good luck messages and a photo of them blowing kisses; Chaz had rung to say he and his 'posse' were getting the 11.27 train on Saturday and wondered if I was going to have a spare minute to meet up beforehand (no); Lisa left a short, shuddering message to say she was thinking of me and was looking forward to talking next week. I flicked the light out and lay there watching Sky News for a while, feeling tired but not sleepy, then channel-hopped until I alighted, quite by chance, on some soft porn. Lo and behold, wasn't that Jasmine, one of my internet acquaintances? Hard to tell, but she had a very similar anus. Maybe they were related? I smiled, recalling that patch of dead, wasted time when all I could do was sit staring at my computer, day after soulless, jobless, aimless day. It seemed like yesterday, yet a lifetime away. I toyed with the idea of re-acquainting myself with Jasmine – or her sister – in a private way but, on further consideration, decided she just wasn't doing it for me. I was empty. I turned the TV off, hoping the darkness, warmth and airlessness would transport me to some calm and pleasant dreamland. But even as I drifted off, Lisa, Faye, the kids, Eurovision and my whole cocked-up life butted in and conspired to give me another sleepless night. Cheers.

Friday was like Thursday, only with chips and a heavy pudding on top. Things were getting noticeably more serious now (Eurovision, serious – yeah, I do see the irony). In the morning, I linked live to Breakfast on BBC1 and, with my eyes puffy and red-rimmed, tried to feign the requisite chirpy enthusiasm about the following night's jamboree. *Wow, gee, can't wait, we're gonna do it for Britain!* Then we (me, Elaine, Ben, remaining entourage) trudged into Le Zenith, less alluring by the minute, and sat around getting nervous as I waited for my morning call. The stakes felt tangibly higher, the conversation distinctly professional now. Even the cheeky little Latvian duo, dressed from head to toe in yellow satin, looked a bit edgy. One of them even stopped smiling for thirty seconds. We were running the show once in the morning, when we'd just be going through the songs, and again in the afternoon, this time in full regalia, replete with dance moves, looks to camera and the compères churning out their laborious pigeon-English shtick.

So, imagine this, if you will; you're trapped in a large, cold, featureless building surrounded by tortured, terrified, self-absorbed foreigners and a frantic production crew, with nothing decent to eat and nothing to do…and you're being forced to sit through the fucking Eurovision Song Contest. Twice. Sadly, there were enough technical hitches to write a manual on what not to do if you're thinking of staging a pan-European television event. By three, there was no sign of the morning rehearsal coming to any kind of conclusion and tempers were fraying to breaking point. What little notice I took of the opposition heartened me to the extent that I was going to be one of three people who could actually sing on tune. What I lacked in glamour, charisma, looks and manic costumery, I made up for in relative musical competence, not that previous Eurovisions suggested anything but a direct correlation between talentlessness and success. The main opposition appeared to be the panties-and-not-much-else female singers from Greece, Serbia and Belgium, a sad little balalaika-based combo from Belarus (sympathy vote), a ludicrous heavy rock band from Norway and a couple of third division boy bands singing in fabulously fractured English.

I'd hit it off with the Irish entrant over the previous couple of days. Annette O'Leary was a rather beautiful and refreshingly mature woman who had enjoyed a long and successful career in Ireland but nowhere else. She was a class act with a pure, trilling voice and her song was a ballad of genuine quality. She had no chance. I'd also developed a bit of an understanding with the Dutch entrants, two relaxed, long-haired loafers in their mid-twenties who liked to talk football, something I can do all day and most of the night. Johann Cruyff is always a good starting point in any conversation with the Dutch, I've found. And, in fairness, most of the other entrants were pleasant enough, but it was difficult to forge anything other than the odd passing acquaintance. The consensus, though, was that the contest was a bit of fun which might garner some useful exposure. The winner might gain substantially, but everyone was going to go home with their credibility enhanced or shattered depending on where they came from – unless they came from Britain, in which case they should simply surrender themselves to the tabloids and pray that the ride back to nowhere was relatively painless.

In the evening, after a couple of brief radio interviews from Le Zenith, we made our way back to the hotel where Elaine and I had a snack in her room. I should have been buzzing. A couple of months ago I was Jo Schmo known only to his family and friends, and *they* didn't give much of a shit. My own kids could barely stand the sound of my singing voice. Yet tomorrow I was going to appear on TV screens all around Europe, singing a song conceived and composed by me. Buzzing? Not especially.

Saturday. The Contest. Oh shit.

Chaz called just after I'd come off stage around four, having completed my final, worryingly jumpy dress rehearsal. He was staying in the George V, a five star hotel on the Champs Elysees. He couldn't find one with six. He'd come over with Denise and a couple of his Eurovision cronies, having blagged a bunch of tickets from his contacts. Chaz had contacts. We talked about meeting up at some point, but I was walled in now until it was over, so we made a vague arrangement to try and find each other afterwards. Chaz didn't seem overly bothered. He was fulfilling a boyhood dream, one he'd harboured since Cliff and Lulu flew the flag with such distinction.

Rehearsals never feel like the real thing. That's why they're called rehearsals. You can afford to slip up, take it easy, have a laugh, no matter how many people are yelling at you, no matter how high the stakes. But now, mere hours from the off, my nerves were beginning to jangle. The next one was for real. I remember looking into the gaping auditorium at the end of my final run-through and surveying the 6000 empty seats in front of me. I couldn't imagine them full. Nor could I take in the fact that the fifteen cameras I'd learned to ignore would be beaming me live to an entire continent just waiting for me to fuck up. It took a bit of getting my head around.

I showered in a flimsy backstage cubicle (slightly larger than my dressing room but a swinging cat wouldn't have got out of there alive) and emerged shivering, nose dripping incessantly, hands ice cold. And I couldn't stop yawning. This was my body having its say and it wasn't at all happy with all this stress. With rigid fingers and a little help from Marta, my delightfully insouciant Romanian dresser, I changed into my battle costume – black, regular fit jeans with a slate grey tee shirt beneath a tailored black jacket. Very Miami Vice c 1986 (though I resisted rolling up the sleeves and revealing the red silk lining). Eurovision fashion exists just outside the mainstream, in the way that the Sun is positioned just a couple of miles from Earth. I looked tragically MOR, like a junior employee of a large company told to dress smart/casual to join the boss in a corporate box at Wembley. Lorna and Sophia had ultimately embarrassed a nation with a proud fashion heritage.

We were now confined to the holding area backstage where most of the acts were jumping about excitedly, particularly the boy and girl bands and anyone in a stupid costume. The German entrant, a balding man of about thirty-five with a Zapata moustache and too-tight Lederhosen, was typical of the breed. He was going round giving everyone hugs and kisses, while everyone, in turn, was trying to duck out of his way. The excess jocularity was understandable; we were all shitting it and it helped let off steam, but it was no less irritating for that. Annette and I were among a small minority of acts too mature (ok, old) to indulge in anything flamboyant, preferring to observe and smile with the indulgent tolerance of parents watching their kids fall over at Tumble Tots. The Dutch boys, all whoops! and whoas! whizzed past shouting: 'Frank Lampard. Shit, eh?' to which I could only nod in firm agreement.

Ben was hyper, dashing from one entourage member to another to check on the kind of minutiae over which neither he nor they had any further influence. Elaine tried to restrain him without notable success, although she did manage, at my request, to keep him out of my face. He settled for the odd thumbs-up and across-the-room exhortation of '*you the man*' which I could just about tolerate. Elaine flitted back and forth, a butterfly, bestowing calm wherever she landed. Me? I was now channelling my energies, trying to zoom in on what needed to be done. This was not the time to be thinking about home, Lisa, Faye, even the kids. I had to go up there and give it a proper go. It might be my first, last and only hurrah, and I was determined to make the most of my two and a half lousy minutes in the sun.

I wasn't due on until near the end and had an hour and a half's wait for my judgement day. I'd rather have got it over with, but this wasn't my party. Too much time gave the nerves room to manoeuvre, to grab me by the throat and make the very idea of singing seem futile, no matter how focused I might be. The last thing I needed was a dose of Ben, but he finally broke through Elaine's protective cordon and gave me a manly pat on the shoulder. At least he avoided showering me in bullshit. I made a couple of little circuits around the waiting area, exchanging the odd wordless shrug with the other artistes, but most of them, though smiling and waving vainly at the cameras – we hadn't bloody started yet – were visibly petrified. Even the Dutch boys, hitherto stereotypically laid back, could only manage a mock salute as I passed them. Not even a vicious word or two about Ashley Cole. Annette was talking to the Serbian entrant, a shaven-headed man in a waistcoat who I knew had no English, and I'm pretty sure Annette had no Serbian but, as I discovered when she beckoned me over, they were talking in Drug, a language I didn't understand. He'd slipped her something to help her get through the ordeal and was now winking at me, holding out a cupped hand, urging me to take the proffered gift. I declined and left them to it. Annette – motherly, sisterly, Irish heroine Annette, of all people, taking an upper, or a downer or something. As a one-drag spliff-smoker myself (nineteen, vomited, couldn't see for two days), this was a bit hard to condone.

A female assistant producer with a megaphone got up on a chair and bellowed at us in severely, possibly deliberately, broken English to shut up and settle down. In retrospect only, the time had flown by and the show was suddenly bearing down upon us. The room fell eerily silent, ratcheting up the tension to breaking point, before the familiar Eurovision theme music thundered through two huge columns of speakers at either end of the room. Several large screens around the holding area came to life, displaying the glitzy opening credits which went on for a couple of days before finally ceding to a shot of the rather beautiful blonde presenter and her less beautiful (but still rather gorgeous) male co-presenter. Exaggerated and elongated applause, of the type commonly generated by floor managers rather than enthusiasm, forced the pair to smile until their teeth dried. Finally, they launched into a painfully over-rehearsed bit of banter, conspicuous for its deathly witlessness. Intended jokes whistled into the air like damp rockets, landing low and harmlessly in some humour-free abyss. I suppose it's pretty difficult to try and be funny in fifty different countries, so they compromised by being funny in none. We waited like coiled springs for the camera to go live and invite our opening salvo of mugging and waving at Europe. Smiles were nailed on, hands readied above the shoulder line, last minute sweat dabbed away. The assistant producer gave us a signal, red lights flashed on cameras and we were away, like greyhounds out of the traps. All hell broke loose, nerves finding some release in this display of hysteria. The attention-seeking German started another 'impromptu' round of hugs and kisses, while the first act, an orange-skinned Spanish songstress in a one-piece thong-type thing which had been stretched without mercy to provide Band Aid-level nipple cover, waited anxiously, desperately trying to moisten her tinder-dry mouth, beside the stage. She was hopping up and down, looking into the ravenous black void of the auditorium and then back at the rest of us for support, but we were all busy thanking God she was on first. She ran on like a foal as the music played under her, missed her first note by at least three tones and instantly lost confidence. The rest of us cringed, in part because of her shrill tunelessness, but mostly because, there but for the grace of God went we. Car crash; I couldn't bear to watch. She never got within spitting distance of the melody and her swarthy, flamboyant musical director lost a little dash, a little confidence, as the song progressed to its awful climax. Maybe he'd set the orchestra off in the wrong key? Elaine, standing fifty feet away among the various entourages and well out of shot, caught my eye seeking out a reciprocal snigger, but I didn't dare tempt fate by indulging in Schadenfreude. I was going out there to face the Euro-firing squad myself, wasn't I?

So we were off to a stinker. Juanita, for that was her name, had pushed the anxiety level of every performer – cocky German included – into heart attack territory. I was not immune; far from it. Every muscle felt like stone, my chest tight, my throat parched, and I still had that interminable wait. My symptoms could only worsen. As the torture continued, I attempted to return to my cubicle, just to escape the rising lunacy in the holding area, but was prevented from leaving by a burly man in a dinner suit who'd had garlic for tea. I protested in vain and slumped back to my appointed seat, weaving past the hysterical yet-to-performers and the enervated thank-fuck-it's-overs. It was supposed to look like a party back there, but it was a fucking asylum.

The tough-looking Israeli trio, rising above the nerves and bullshit, went on to belt out a jaunty sing-along, giving Elaine a brief moment to rush over and pass me my mobile phone. On the screen was a message which I struggled to read without my glasses. I blinked, stretching out my arm to accommodate my failing forty-two year old eyes:

'*Hi. I'm in the audience. Kids here too. Good luck. Go for it. Love Lisa x*'

Elaine gave me one of her looks. You know the one. 'That's just so you know your kids are here.'

I raised my hands defensively. 'Ok, ok,' I said, but felt oddly lifted. It wasn't just the kids being there. Maybe things were coming full circle for me. I'd hit rock bottom, scraped along for a bit, but had now begun the slow climb back towards respectability. Maybe Lisa had been on her own journey of self-discovery, learning, ultimately, that she needed to be with me to square her own circle. Ok, it was a convenient analysis but, at that moment, when detailed introspection was a bit beyond me, I was rather drawn to the notion. Lisa didn't want me back just because of my new status; she was many things, but never shallow. Hadn't she called things off with the infinitely more famous Don Ellwood? Didn't that prove the point? Sometimes you have to go looking for love and maybe she'd found it where she least expected, back down that old familiar road.

I re-read the message.

'Well?' said Elaine, already intuiting my wavering emotions.

'Well nothing. Lisa's out there with the kids and…that's really great.'

'Shit. Shouldn't have shown it to you. I thought your children being here would lift you, but now you're just thinking about her.'

'I'm not. Stop it.'

'Listen. Just go out there and make those girls proud,' said Elaine. I'm sure 'girls' didn't include Lisa.

The show plodded on, like the great, unstoppable dinosaur it was. Acts came and went; notes were missed by spectacular margins; tears were shed in abundance (by some of the girls, too); multi-lingual invective abounded as flawed vocalists sought to blame everyone but themselves. Some acts scored heavily with the audience, others garnered sympathy. In typically French fashion, the home audience gave their own entrant the bird just because she couldn't sing or dance.

And my slot was looming ever closer. With fifteen minutes to go, I was bundled out of the holding area by a group of earphoned assistants in official orange bibs, and whisked off to the dark little passageway which led to the stage. Peering round a fake plaster column, I could just make out a tiny triangle of audience, a nonetheless forbidding sight. I was on after the Italians, four slim boys in Freddie Mercury white vests who were pirouetting and gyrating like the great man himself, only without moustaches or any discernible charisma. They were making do with honest endeavour accompanied by a thumping drum and bass cacophony. They finished with a concerted, echoey *hey!*, right arms aloft, heads down, chests heaving. The audience loved them. The champions elect. How the fuck was I going to follow that? A middle-aged man singing a mid-tempo song which, ok, had wowed the discerning punters of Crouch End, but was manifestly lacking the requisite boom-boom-oomph to appeal to the taste-free zone that was Eurovisonland; a man who, despite the sterling work of a professional choreographer, possessed no moves whatsoever? 400,000,000 eyes, give or take, were about to focus on that loser in a few short minutes. I felt very, very sick.

I looked behind me into the holding area, hoping someone was going to call the whole thing off; if only France could rustle up another revolution and get it started smartish. But I was alone, facing the most terrifying moment of my life. No way out. A short piece of film played in (a pointless, touristy sequence showing humdrum London landmarks, followed by me mugging cretinously to camera) while I took up my position on the stage. The audience seemed distracted, fidgety and deeply bored during this kerfuffle, but I was more concerned with the fact that I couldn't remember the first fucking line. Again. I started fishing for it, playing the intro over and over in my head, hoping to find the trigger, failing. And then someone said something about the UK and there was some applause and cheering and the intro proper started up. Oh shit! Oh fuck! I looked out into the audience and saw that they were already swaying, waving flags, expectant. It was coming up…the moment when I'd have to sing.

Got it! Got the fucker! Remembered it in the nick of time.

I was away, on cue and, miraculously, on tune. You never know how your voice is going to sound until it actually leaves your throat even when you're singing in the bath but, fuck me if mine wasn't as solid as it's ever been. No tremors, no croaks, no squeaks. I concentrated on the sound emanating from the feedback monitors and it was clear, crisp and tight. Beyond that, floating on a disembodied echo, I could hear my voice booming into the vastness of the auditorium and wondered if it sounded as good to the audience as it did to me. I was on autopilot, all negative thoughts now pummelled to dust, the nerves helping, not hindering my performance. Confidence coursed through me, so much so that I even tried – and failed – to pick out the girls, Lisa and Chaz from the vast sea of faces in front of me. I was thinking clearly, fully aware, registering every element of this extraordinary experience so I'd be able to mentally replay it on cold November nights. The audience was with me, going for it, moving as one, smiling, trying to latch onto the chorus. I breezed into the last change up and then the final chorus. I'd only just started, surely. Where had the last two and a half minutes gone? I hit the last note, threw an arm into the air, closed my eyes, tilted my head back and totally lost myself in the moment.

And then it was over.

The music stopped and there was silence – Oh God! – followed by a deafening cheer and tumultuous applause. I lowered my head slowly and peered out into the auditorium, chest heaving à la The Freddies. Everyone was standing; arms were waving, air punches being thrown; balloons and streamers crowded the vast space above the audience. Across in the 'orchestra pit', Gilbert let slip a coy smile – he had teeth! – and he nodded at me with something approaching a human expression of contentment. The cheering continued into the next piece of film which covered the orange bib men as they hustled me off stage and wheeled on a six-strong group of Danish girls wearing skin and not a lot else.

Elaine threw her arms around me and kissed my sopping face as soon as I re-entered the holding area. She squealed something joyful and unintelligible into my ear, then led me back towards my seat. Some of the other acts clapped as I floated by, mentally factoring me into their equations. Maybe the old fella in his steady-Eddy jeans was a genuine threat. I was shaking, sweating like a geyser, adrenaline pumping through and seemingly out of me. Then something heavy and clammy crunched into me from behind and clamped itself to my torso.

Ben.

'Fucking hell, man! Fuck! You fucking did it!' he screamed, his hot, whisky breath coating my face.

'Was I ok?' I said, manoeuvring myself out of the line of fire.

'Ok? Ok? Fucking 'A' man! Let me get you a drink! You want a drink? What do you want?'

What I wanted was for him to sod off. I needed to sit for a minute and recover the composure last spotted about three days earlier. 'Anything sweet.'

Ben bounded off towards the performers' bar, slapping any back within a five yard radius. Elaine watched him go, her smile a mixture of affection, indulgence and disgust.

'Well?' I said, like I didn't know. 'Come on. You can tell me the truth.'

Elaine pointed at Ben, now all but engulfed by glitter-clad Euro-bodies around the bar. 'Like the man said.'

I smiled, the tension finally lifting, though it would be a while before my heart regained its natural rhythm. It was over, done, dusted. All that anticipation and preparation. I didn't think for a minute that I'd have to go back out there and sing the song again. I was already thinking about tomorrow, Lisa, the kids, and what the hell was going to happen now.

A frantic, raven-haired presenter in a pink babydoll nightdress started leaping around the holding area with a bored-looking camera crew in tow. Her role, it seemed, was to gauge reaction as the scores came in, wackily interview the participants in pigeon-Euro-bollocks and maintain continuity as the wheels of this lumpen vehicle ground on towards their final, who-gave-a-fuck destination. We watched on the giant screens as the presenters, still chirpy but all out of scripted quips, introduced the first set of results, delivered by a shiny-faced man from a dungeon in Athens. The female presenter explained – for the ninth time – that the first 1–8 points would be added automatically shortly after each spokesperson hove into view, the vital 9–12 points being given one by one to make it feel like something important was afoot. We scoured the scoreboard to see where Greece's minor points had gone. Norway had one, Belgium two, Ukraine three, Belarus…who cared about the small points, especially if you didn't get any?

'Ok, now for the big ones,' said the Greek man with a fluorescent grin. 'Estonia, nine points.'

Huge cheer.

'Estonia, nine points,' echoed the female presenter.

'Turkey, ten points,'

Huger cheer.

'Turkey, ten points.'

'France, eleven points.'

Pandemonium.

But hang on. That was the eleven, right? Oh my God! I was going to get the twelve. This was unbelievable!

'And twelve points goes to…'.

The room fell quiet. Everyone hoped against hope.

'…Italy!'

The Freddie Mercurys leapt, as one, into the air, punching it wildly, screaming, hugging, barely holding back the tears, their damp, hairy armpits seemingly everywhere. Elsewhere, rictus grins prevailed atop drooped shoulders. Come on, it was only the first set of results – there were about fifty more to come. But we knew, all of us pointless ones, that it was a doomy omen.

I didn't get a point until Norway, the fourth country to deliver its verdict, generously made me their least favourite of their favourites. One point. Germany, surprisingly, gave me eight, France, even more surprisingly, ten, but the writing was on the wall long before the end. The Italians and the Latvians were skating away with it. It was going to be nip and tuck all the way and as for who would nick it, only those two gave a fuck.

Elaine, having escaped the bouncers, stroked my arm as the results continued to limp in, while Ben slunk away to get comprehensively pissed. No more whoopin' and a-hollerin' from him. But I was fine, honestly. Once I knew I wasn't going to win, or even come close, I accepted the fact and let it go. It was out of my hands. The points that came my way were still welcome, still appreciated, but no-one was going to remember the losers. I was going home tomorrow, back to reality. There would be some minor press coverage, a day or two of post-match analysis, but my story was already old hat and would buy me no additional goodwill in the public consciousness. Anything I achieved from here on in I would have to earn. If I got the chance.

Gilbert sloped over to pat me on the shoulder and mumble incomprehensibly in my ear before ghosting off into the ether again. The holding area had grown rowdier as the final few results rolled in, the stir-crazy throng itching for it to end so they could start pumping epic quantities of alcohol into their systems. But Elaine and I were oblivious, cocooned in our own little world, chatting as though we were in some half-full café in Hornsey. She confided that she was thinking of taking up a role in America with her brother's advertising company. I was still in a fairly delicate, post-show emotional state – I was an *artistic* person now, so it was allowed – and felt my eyes sting at this news. She gave me a cuddle and said that nothing was settled yet. I made a mental note to speak to Ben to try and persuade him – if I had any clout left with the big buffoon – to give her some executive responsibility and double her money or risk losing her. Utterly selfish, of course, but you don't make many true friends in adulthood I've discovered, so I felt blessed to have what I had with Elaine. She got me, and me her. What price?

I came a respectable eleventh, placing me well above the majority of recent British contestants, a feather in the cap of the utterly fatuous variety. The Freddies had seen off the Baltic/Balkan threat quadruple-handed. They leapt onto the stage in their sodden, now transparent vests to receive their award and give an even more frenetic and tuneless rendition of their song to close the show. Balloons and streamers flew, people swayed, faces beamed. The other acts were invited to stand at the back of the stage to join this amazing celebration of Euro-joy and one-ness, but most of us declined. One of the Dutch guys walked past me, punched me on the shoulder and said: 'Wayne Rooney, eh? Fucking nutter, but what a player. Hey, come to Holland when we play England next time, uh? We'll look after you, man.' I smiled, shook his hand, and then he was gone.

Finally, at long last, the show finished, the music stopped and the audience started filing out. Backstage, an army of caterers was busy re-stocking the bar and several tables with drink and a sumptuous array of finger food, while a gang of hefty roadies shifted the furniture to the sides of the holding area to clear a space to party. The acts and their entourages, free at last, were exuberant, over-excited and way too loud, at least for an old fella like me. Annette wobbled past, drink in one hand, something small and orange in the other, slurring and barely able to stand, and we hadn't even got started yet. She joined the equally dissolute Ben at the bar and they were soon deep in conversation, no doubt shouting disjunctive codswallop at each other.

I slumped in a small armchair pressed against a wall and closed my eyes, trying to shut everything out. Elaine had said I should do my duty, stay for half an hour tops, then go find my kids and take them for a burger somewhere in Paris. And then I felt a tap on my shoulder. If that was bloody Ben again, or the Dutch bores, or slobbering Annette, I'd…

I hauled my head forward and opened my grudging eyes. In front of me stood two little girls dressed like teenagers, their shy, smiling faces and rosy cheeks the most gratifying, thrilling shock to my system. They jumped onto my lap, Kattie's plump knee only just avoiding fatal contact with my testicles, and we cuddled fiercely, the twisted rope of tension running through my core now fully unravelling as I breathed in their familiar scents. They nuzzled into my neck, their squeaky voices piping excitedly into my ears, and immediately, and yet again, hot tears breached my defences and cascaded down my cheeks. I hugged them to the point of asphyxiation, only loosening my grip when Millie yelped: 'Shit, dad, you're killing me.'

Blinking into the mayhem, I made out a figure a few yards in front of me standing, legs apart, arms to the side, like a gunslinger. Lisa smiled gloriously, my flooded eyes making her teeth twinkle like stars. She looked fabulous in a shimmering black dress which somehow made more perfect her already perfect curves. Her head was cocked to one side as she witnessed the scene, a look of delight etched within the flawless geometry of her face. The Hobbit-like Bea cowered behind her, dressed in regulation brown cords and a chunky, zip-up sweater.

'You were really good, Dad,' shouted Millie into my ear.

'Was I?'

'Yeah. You were, like, the best? The others were, like, absolute sh…'

'Millie!'

'You were easily the best, Dad. You should've won,' chimed Kattie, rather more gravely.

'But it doesn't matter,' said Millie, ''cos we still love you, like, soooo much?'

'Sooo much,' said Kattie.

Lisa took a couple of majestic strides towards us and gently tugged at the girls' shoulders. 'Come on, give Daddy some air.' I waved my hand. They could stay there all night and right through the next day as far as I was concerned, but slowly they shuffled off my lap to be replaced by the rather more cumbersome Lisa. She looped a silk-skinned arm around my neck and kissed my sopping cheek, then nestled into me, her fabulous mane cascading down my chest. She smelled edible.

'You were brilliant,' she purred.

'Ach, come on. It's only the bloody Eurovision. And I came nowhere.'

'Not the point. You did it, you got up there and you did it.'

Lisa manoeuvred herself off my lap and leaned down to give me another kiss before unfurling her wondrous frame to its full height. She studied me for a moment, her face wearing a look I hadn't seen in years – pride? – then said to the girls, 'Come on, we'd better get you two back to the hotel. It's very, very late.'

The kids moaned, but not too vociferously. They'd obviously had an exciting day and were now beginning to droop. Lisa beckoned Bea over. The girls took turns planting sweet, wet kisses on my face, before Bea, who was barely capable of looking me in the eye, so overwhelmed was she by my fleeting elevation to Euro-superstar, took them by their little hands and led them away, both of them waving over their shoulders as they disappeared into the crowd.

'So, where you staying?' I said.

'Hotel George V.'

'Oh, so's Chaz.' On another day, I'd have jumped to the wrong conclusion.

'I need a drink. I'm gasping,' she said.

'Me too. Someone was getting me one, but…'

'I'll get it. Diet Coke, or are you into the hard stuff now you're a rock and roll hero?'

'Sod it, what the hell. Ordinary Coke. With sugar *and* caffeine.'

Lisa smiled. 'It's a bit of a scrum over there,' she said, glancing at the bar. 'Might be a few minutes.'

Her lips brushed mine again, then she was off, gliding as if on casters towards the bar. On the opposite side of the room, vaguely nibbling on something covered in puff pastry, stood Elaine, gimlet eyes fixed on me, brows arrowed judgementally towards the bridge of her nose. She'd done all she could, she seemed to be saying. Now it was up to me to follow my heart, to make the right choices. I acknowledged her with a nod, hands splayed, shrugging hopelessly.

Was there really any other decision?

I sat, alone, away from all the noise, staring wistfully into the empty auditorium through the now gloomy passageway leading to the stage where, a couple of hours earlier, I'd stood like a condemned man. It already felt like a dream. Then I turned and saw them, a short, bald man alongside a strapping blonde woman with Amazonian shoulders. To anyone else, they might have been mother and son, but I knew instantly it was Chaz and Denise. He'd wangled after-show party passes, the sly bastard. Chaz really knew a lot of people. I stood up, caught his eye and waved them over. Chaz beamed, danced his way daintily between the heaving throng and flew into me like a child taking a running jump at his dad after school. It was, I'm ashamed to say, a proper man-hug which, under any other circumstances, I'd have resisted but, tonight, I let slide. Denise, bringing up the rear, kissed both of my cheeks and muttered something congratulatory in my ear.

'Fuck me,' enthused Chaz. 'What a night! I'm never watching this on telly again. Ever. You've got to be here to really experience it.'

'So you enjoyed it?'

'Yeah!' he said. 'Why the fuck didn't you win, you useless bastard?'

'Well, at this level of competition, it's all about the vests.'

'Next time, mate, next time.'

We battled our way over to the bar where Lisa was in animated conversation with Harry and Verity Dawson, the Posh and Becks of celebrity cooking. What the hell were they doing here? Others in her immediate coterie included Graeme Jarman, the newly announced Bond (Don Ellwood had just missed out, which was a shame) and Enzo Matterazi who, apparently, is to fashion what God is to pretty much everything. Lisa was in her element, beguiled and beguiling. I caught her eye briefly to check she was ok; she responded with a cursory, distracted nod before flashing another of her dazzling smiles at her new best friends.

I grabbed three glasses of plonk from a table and, with Chaz and Denise in tow, negotiated a path back towards the passageway and then out onto the stage. We sat on the gleaming, streamer-littered floor, staring out into the vast, echoing chasm where a fleet of theatre and technical staff was already making serious inroads into the tidying-up operation. Glittery confetti, flags and burst balloons were bundled into black bags; cables disconnected and rolled onto massive coils; scaffolding unscrewed and dismantled. So much effort and care had gone into putting everything together and it would all gone in a matter of hours.

Chaz was grinning like a kid who'd been given Hamleys for his birthday. 'What's up with you?' I said.

'Can I tell him?' he asked Denise. She looked doubtful, but smiled and decided to let him have his moment. I think, beneath that tough Aussie veneer, lived a softie who wanted to hear how it sounded. Chaz patted her tummy. 'We're with baby!'

'Fuck!' I yelled, 'we're not!'

'We fucking are! With. Baby!'

Chaz cuddled the giggling Denise and, Lord knows I'm not a physical or demonstrative man, but I crawled over and embraced them both, tipping the three of us over. 'I am...so thrilled for you two,' I said. 'Now that...that is the best news I've heard this year. You finally cracked the code!'

And I honestly couldn't have been happier than I was at that moment. 'No more of this for you, Bush Girl,' I said, playfully removing the wine glass from her hand, though I noticed she hadn't drunk any.

We talked until our glasses were empty, then Chaz jumped up, the monkey finally off his back, and headed back into the melée for refills. Denise, feeling awkward, decided to follow him on the flimsy premise that she'd changed her mind about having an orange juice and now wanted a Coke. I leaned onto my elbows to watch her go. Through the passageway, I could see the party still going at full blast. And there, holding court at the centre of a group of famous faces, household names and global stars, stood a dazzlingly beautiful woman. She was thrilled to be in their company, as were they to be in hers, peas in a pod. I sighed. Tomorrow night, we'd be at home in our pleasant Chiswick semi wondering what to have for dinner. And on Monday, I'd ferry the kids to the school bus stop in the piss, while Lisa would slog her way into town on the tube. And then...and then I'd probably spend the day sitting in my study wondering what to do with the rest of my life. Probably. Was all of that enough for her? Or me?

At the back of the stalls, a door opened, sending a dim shaft of light a couple of yards into the centre aisle. In the doorway, I could just make out the silhouettes of two women. They talked for a moment, then one of them turned and left. The other started making her way down the aisle. Her gait struck me as familiar. I got to my feet and walked to the front of the stage, peering under my hand to shield my eyes from a single brilliant spotlight at the back. I took the four steps down onto the floor of the auditorium and walked up the aisle to meet her.

'You ok?' I said.

'I'm fine," said Elaine, 'you?'

'Yeah.'

'Where's the wife?'

'Oh, she's back there,' I said, jabbing a thumb over my shoulder. 'Likes a party, does Lisa.'

'I noticed.'

'Elaine.'

'Sorry. Not my business.'

I stroked her cheek, loving her – like a friend – for caring so much. 'So? What you doing now?'

'Back to the hotel if I can rustle up a car. Not my cup of tea, this.'

'Mine neither, but I'm a bit lumbered.'

'Well you try and enjoy it. You've earned it. Call me when you get back, yeah?' I nodded. 'Whatever else happens, I promise I'm going to make sure Ben doesn't waste all that talent.'

'Aw shucks,' I said, embarrassed. 'Thanks.'

Elaine had something else to add.

'What?'

'Nothing. It's nothing. Look, I'd better go,' she said.

Elaine kissed me on the cheek and left through the same door through which she'd entered. A cool, sweet swish of fresh air wafted over me as the door settled against the jamb. I turned and headed slowly back down the aisle towards the stage. A few steps on and another swish caressed the back of my neck.

'Michael?'

What had Elaine come back to tell me?

'You were really great tonight,' said Faye.

'Oh my God,' I spluttered, spinning, hoping I hadn't mistaken her voice.

'Well, I had to come, didn't I? I was there when you were a nobody.'

I wobbled towards her, my legs suddenly boneless. 'How…I mean, what…?'

'Elaine got me a ticket. Bit of a last minute thing in the end.'

'You were out there?'

Faye placed her hand on my shoulder. 'Hey, you're a star.'

I cupped my hand over hers and smiled, my heart thudding like a mad thing. 'You were going to leave without letting on you were here, weren't you?'

'Yeah. But Elaine made me change my mind out there so…she's very persuasive.'

'You could say that.'

'Well, it would've been a bit churlish to come all this way and just disappear without saying hi. And goodbye.'

An ache settled heavily in my chest. I could hardly breathe. Faye smiled with joyless eyes. 'Elaine tells me you're getting back with your wife. Which is great.'

'And you and Louis?'

'Well, we're…getting married, as you know.'

'Yes, I do. Equally great, by the way.'

Lisa slumped into an aisle seat. 'No it isn't.'

'It isn't?'

'I can't marry Louis, can I?'

I shrugged, still, inexplicably, unable to give her the right answer. I sat in the seat in front of her and swivelled to stare into her soulful, doleful eyes. 'Have you got somewhere to stay tonight?' I said.

'I'm going to catch the next train back. No big deal.'

'I've got somewhere to stay.'

'Lucky you.'

'So now you have. It's too late to go back now.'

'Can't do that.'

'Lisa's staying somewhere else. And, look…we're not definitely getting back together. We've just, you know, talked about it.'

'And?'

'And…' My next words spilled out, the most natural and heartfelt I'd ever uttered, the absolute truth. 'I know we can't.'

'What?'

'We can't. Because I don't want to.'

'What *do* you want?'

'Knowing what you *don't* want is always easier, isn't it?'

Faye nodded. We were in more or less the same boat. 'So...when are you going to tell her?'

I hadn't yet considered the mechanics, but the certainty that ending it was absolutely right, that it was what I wanted, buoyed me. 'Soon... tomorrow. You?'

'Oh sod it. I've already told him, haven't I?'

I blew a shaft of air from my cheeks. 'How did he take it?'

'Louis? How do you think? Stoically. British-ly...is that a word?'

'No. Don't know.'

'He shook my hand...shook my hand!' Faye snorted. 'You believe that?' I did. 'Wished me all the very best.'

We laughed and Faye stroked my forearm. 'Surprised he didn't send you a memo. *Dear Madam, an honour knowing you, yours faithfully...*'

Faye's smile crumpled and sadness invaded her limpid eyes. We sat there looking at each other, hoping the right words would come. 'So, anyway, suppose I'd better go...' she said at last.

Words, but not the right ones. Not even close. My throat started swelling as I blinked back the tears. 'Thing is,' I said, my voice thick, gummed up, 'I could never go back to Lisa. So much shit has happened that...' Rubbish. That wasn't it at all. Say it. 'Actually...'

A syrupy tear serpentined lazily down Faye's cheek.

'I *do* know what I want,' I said, 'That's the thing. I've known for a while. I've just been a bit too stupid to admit it to myself. I mean, there aren't many times in your life when you know what you...'

'Shut up, Mike, just shut up,' said Faye, half-crying, half-laughing. I stood up, stepped into the aisle and knelt down beside her, taking her cool hand in mine. 'Ok. So let me summarise. See, I could never go back to Lisa because...well because...'

Faye gulped and stroked my face, smiling that smile, prompting the right words this time. I squeezed her hand.

'Because of you.'

Acknowledgements

I owe debts of gratitude to all the people who have listened patiently, humoured me and laboured through my several drafts. For his incredible encouragement, belief and support, I want to thank my Dad, Harry. Thanks also to my wife Lynda for tolerating me and my kids (who did nothing useful but whose younger selves inspired Millie and Kattie).

I feel I should also list the many eminent and erudite friends, colleagues and professionals who have devoted their time and expertise to this project, but no-one springs to mind. Everything in this book has come directly from my own warped imagination or – where facts have needed to be scrupulously correct – Google. Thanks boys.

Thanks also go to my sister Marian. She knows why.

Needless to say, any similarity of any of any characters to persons living or dead is entirely coincidental – with the obvious exceptions. Likewise, corporations and organisations.

Next from Simon Lipson:

Standing Up

Steady-Eddy Colin Moran, is still waiting for partnership thirteen years after qualifying as a solicitor. Everyone has zoomed past him, including younger brother Zach. Professionally mired, divorced and struggling to handle feisty 14 year old daughter Clem, Colin needs something to get the adrenaline flowing once again. Stand-up comedy classes seemed like a good idea at the time, but when he is thrown into the deep end, it's sink or swim. Suddenly, the love of his life reappears, a woman who can make things happen for him in comedy. But he wants to be a partner, not a comedian. And he still wants her back.

Ex-solicitor and current stand-up Simon Lipson spills the beans in this edgy, pacey romantic comedy.

To be published Autumn 2012

Lightning Source UK Ltd.
Milton Keynes UK
UKOW030706160312

189070UK00006B/5/P